Winter Seedlings

Julie Roberts Towe

Stitched Wing Publishing

ISBN: 978-0-9908007-0-5 (pbk.)
ISBN: 978-0-9908007-1-2 (ebook)

This book is a work of fiction. All names, characters, places, organizations, businesses and events other than those clearly in the public domain are used fictitiously and are the product of the author's imagination. Any resemblance to actual events, locales, or persons, living or dead, is entirely coincidental.

Stitched Wing Publishing
1719 Angel Parkway, Ste. 400-116
Allen, TX 75002
USA

Cover art and design by Anna Wand

For Charles and Emily

CHAPTER ONE

1990

Her long brown hair falls in ringlets to her waist. The curls bounce and sway as she carries an empty box back to my old bedroom. Allie is wearing a 1950's blue taffeta party dress and matching satin high heels. Only she would wear that crap to break into a trailer and rob the place. Sure, this stuff is technically already mine. But, try telling that to Earl if he shows up while we're taking it.

If I had known she was going to bring me here tonight, I would have never gotten in the car with her. I guess it's my fault for complaining so much about having only one pair of jeans. Or maybe she was tired of the smell I had after wearing them every day.

I wouldn't need to steal my clothes back if Momma had actually planned to take me with her when she left. Instead, she had loaded up all her belongings in the car and had it in reverse before she saw me coming out of the woods. She motioned for me to get in and we took off like we were trying to outrun a tornado.

Momma had packed nothing that belonged to me. Before her impulse to briefly act like a real mother, she had been content to let me stay behind with that asshole. Of course, Momma won't admit to what he did to us because she neglected to stop it. So, according to her, my sister Drew and I are both attention whores. At least Drew got out. Even if she is living in a run down trailer park with her baby boy and no money for diapers, it is better than this place.

I exhale and steadily breathe in to calm myself. The scent of wet cigarettes and deep fryer oil makes my head spin. I might pass out. I steady myself and take a small breath through my mouth and hold it. I force myself to put one foot in front of the other down the narrow hallway. Ten steps and I am at my old bedroom door. I exhale again.

Allie has already removed my posters from the wall and tossed them in the box. Seeing the magazine tear outs of the Sex Pistols and Suicidal Tendencies makes me feel less like an intruder. But the effect doesn't last long.

Allie is going through things on my dresser. She turns around holding out a tube of blood red lipstick. "Look, Jute! I have missed this so much. Here, put it on right now."

"Just put it in the box and let's make this quick," I am too annoyed with her to pretend otherwise.

"Fine," she says, pouting, and tosses it in with the posters.

I glance at the dresser mirror. I look so different since I stood here a few weeks ago. My shaved head is starting to grow hair, mousy brown stubble is all it is. I don't look like the punk I usually am. I look like a first grade boy being treated for lice. I glare at myself for being so ugly, even though being ugly has been my goal for years. I just didn't want to be both ugly and homely at the same time. Maybe I should put on the lipstick.

Allie's box is full. She holds it in her arms to carry it out. Her blue eyes are wide with concern.

"Are you okay?"

"I'm awesome! So glad you kidnapped me and forced me to come back here and steal stuff." I roll my eyes at her in the mirror and turn around.

She smiles her crooked smile. "You're welcome. And don't worry. It's your stuff, you can't steal it."

She walks by me and bumps me with her elbow, nearly

knocking me off balance. I hear her laughing down the hallway.

Now that she is gone, I step fully in front of the mirror. No amount of hair gel could make me look dangerous. My face is full and round. My big mouth is made more repulsive by dry, cracked and peeling lips. I'm disgusting. Even when I had my hair dyed black and spiked in a mohawk, my big lips were still the thing kids joked about. I started wearing red lipstick just to show I don't give a shit. I hope they never stop thinking I'm a freak. I stick my tongue out at myself and try to watch my eyes roll. Stupid.

I lean in closer and look at the small scar on my cheek under my right eye. It looks like a tiny V or a kid's drawing of a bird flying in the distance. I touch it with my finger, imagining I have scared it away. But it doesn't fly off. It stays firmly etched in my pudgy cheek. I'm seventeen and I still look like a middle school kid.

I should get to work. I drop to my knees and open the bottom dresser drawer. My arms scoop everything out in one sweep and toss it all disheveled into the box. I do the same with the next drawer up. I know the top two drawers are empty because they belonged to Drew. But, I open them anyway. Nothing. I pick up the box of clothes and head for the door. I need to get out of here.

Allie is walking up the porch steps as I am coming out. Her breath forms quickly dissipating clouds in the cold January air. The skin on my arms gets prickly with goosebumps. The first week of January is always the coldest.

"The hatch is open, just toss it back there. I'm going to go in and turn off all the lights."

Her blue Camaro is parked in the backyard with its doors open and the hatch up. It looks like an insect ready to take off into the night. A shiver runs through me again and I nearly drop the box. Carefully, I step down the porch steps and walk to the back of the car. I let the box fall in beside the other one before wasting no time getting into the passenger seat. My heart is racing as I stare down the driveway, expecting Earl's truck to drive up it. I try to take deep breaths and reassure myself that he stays at the bar until it closes every Saturday night. But, I feel like I'm suffocating.

Where is Allie? It seems to be taking her forever. She finally steps out the door with a couple of trash bags. She tosses them in the hatch and slams it shut. When she slides into the driver's seat, she looks giddy.

"What was all that?"

She just smiles mischievously and puts the car in reverse. "I have to pick up Shawn. I'm already thirty minutes late."

"You could just let his sorry ass sit at home tonight."

Allie whacks my arm with the back of her hand. "He's a nice guy, Jute! Stop being mean."

We laugh like I was joking. Allie never takes me seriously when I insult Shawn. She just acts like it's an accepted personality flaw of mine; making fun of her boyfriends is what I do. Maybe if she would pick a decent one, I wouldn't dislike them so much. Boys are damn lucky she thinks so badly of herself that she's willing to do stupid things for their approval. I hate them for taking advantage of that.

She drives this sports car like a station wagon. I look at her out of the corner of my eye and shake my head.

Maryville, Tennessee isn't a big town. We get to Shawn's house in no time. He lives in a double wide up on the side of a mountain. He has worked at Pendergrass Auto Repair for three months, but he is already in debt up to his eyeballs. He has Allie pick him up on the weekends because, he claims, he doesn't want to drink and drive. But, he also doesn't want to pay for gas in his new dually truck. He just bought that monstrous thing so it will mask his piss ant stature. I don't say any of this aloud.

Shawn runs out of his house and opens the passenger door. When he sees me sitting there, his expression changes from excitement to apprehension. He knows I'm not a fan.

Even in the dark, I can tell his pimply face is flushed red. He waits for me to climb out of the front seat and into the back. From there, I see Allie lean over the console and wait with her lips puckered. Shawn slides into the seat and immediately leans over and sloppily kisses her for an unbearably long time.

I clear my throat, but all that does is make Allie smile a little and keep kissing him.

"You know, the sooner you take me home, the sooner you two can have your privacy."

Finally, she stops kissing him and puts the car in reverse.

"Lighten up back there," she says, smiling at me in the rearview.

I don't say anything. I just look out the window until we reach my house, which is a tiny old wooden house off Allegheny Loop Road. Momma brilliantly moved us here in a mad dash to get us only six miles away from Earl. But, the rent is cheap, probably because the place should be condemned. All these negative factors might affect her if she actually slept here. I haven't seen her in days.

I'm the last one out of the Camaro because I have to climb out of the backseat. Allie already has the hatch open and Shawn is grabbing the trash bags. I eye him warily as I follow him up the stairs with my box of clothes. He holds the door open and forces a polite smile as I walk by.

The fire has gone out again. The living room is freezing. I turn right and go into my sort-of-bedroom, sort of L-shaped-hallway to nowhere. There is no door, but there is a place for the bed out of view from the living room. As I drop the box beside my pillow, I hear Shawn go into the small bathroom.

In the living room, Allie has the wood stove door open. She is trying to lift a log off the floor without it touching her dress.

"Here, let me do that," I sound exasperated but she is really amusing. I toss the wood on the hot ashes and slam the stove door shut harder than I intended. Behind me I hear the rustling of a trash bag. I stand up and turn around to see Allie pulling my old bed sheet out of a bag. I see my Styx cassette falling out of it. She has stolen my music from Earl. My heart pounds with fear. She lets the sheet fall open on the floor to reveal a pile of cassettes and a few 45's held together with a rubber band.

"Look, it's the Misfits!" She says, holding up a cassette and moving it around like we're playing keep away. She hates the Misfits. Seeing her dance around with it almost makes me laugh, but I feel too sick.

"What's in the other bag?"

"Records," she says, no longer dancing around because I probably look as pale as a ghost.

"Damn it, Allie! Earl paid for some of those. He might have let the clothes thing slide, but he is going to be pissed when he finds all this gone."

"So what if he is? You can't leave all your music there, Jute. These things do belong to you. I mean, I bought you this one," she bends down and picks up The Beatles "Get Back" 45 with "Don't Let Me Down" on the B-side. "Gifts belong to the recipient, not the giver. If he doesn't agree, he can just fuck off."

My laugh escapes this time. Allie rarely says words like 'fuck'. I walk over and hug her, but she stiffens up. I laugh even harder because she is so predictable. She hates to be touched unless she's trying to make a boy love her more.

Finally she brings her arms up and awkwardly pats my back. It's her signal that she is done with it.

Shawn walks out of the bathroom. "Oh, man! Keep it up! Y'all are hot!"

Allie drops her arms and I spin around to look at him.

"Shut up, you fucking dumbass." I want to punch him. Punching him would make me feel so much better. If he wasn't Allie's boyfriend, I would have punched him already. I clench my fists tightly and glare at him. He's looking a little nervous. I have a reputation for unpredictable violence.

"Damn." He says, and puts his hands out to call off the fight. "I was just kidding, Jute. What the hell?"

"Well, you aren't funny. Grow up."

I can see that he is biting his tongue. He puts his hand through his blond hair then shakes his head.

"You ready?" He snaps at Allie.

"I guess," she looks at me like she feels guilty for leaving, or maybe for what Shawn said. She says, "Try not to worry. I'll be here Monday morning to take you to school. I'll be awake early anyway because I have to be at my mom's house in Ohio that afternoon."

I let go of my anger at her boyfriend and tell her goodbye like any other day. From the porch, I watch them walk to her car. She leans in and gets back out before running to me, her high heeled feet moving with ease over the frozen mud.

"I forgot. I wrote something I wanted you to read." She hands me a purple envelope as if it contains the thing I've always wanted.

"Thanks." I smile back at her. I have a million of these.

I watch her car pull away until I can no longer hear the car engine. As soon as I walk inside, I rip open the envelope.

You leaned in and pulled out my heart with your teeth,
Held it in your hand like the baby bird
Whose mother you had swallowed whole.
It pounded like thunder for you.
Sometimes I can still hear it in your chest,
Pounding where yours should be.
Pounding to be set free.

-Allie Vining
January 6, 1990, 9:23 a.m.

CHAPTER TWO

1984

Drew walked into Earl's house carrying her favorite blue rabbit that Momma had made a decade ago. The white velour ears were tattered and brown from my sister's years of chewing them. Drew was thirteen years old and I had just turned twelve. I was not carrying a rabbit and I was embarrassed that Drew was.

I stood outside the trailer and watched her and Momma go inside without me. The day was sweltering hot, even in the shade of all the trees up the mountain slope. I leaned against the front fender of Momma's white Oldsmobile and pushed the eject button on my new Walkman. The Duran Duran cassette made a rattle when I flipped it over. It sounded so high tech. I was on top of the world.

My birthday had been the day before. I had received a Walkman, three cassettes, and Momma had allowed me to get a haircut like Nick Rhodes. I shut the cassette door and pushed play, hearing "The Reflex" start up in the middle of the song. I pushed stop and then rewind.

In the distance, I heard the buzzing of a chainsaw. There were logging roads along the ridge to the north. This was the background noise in the mountains near Maryville, Tennessee. I would have ignored it entirely if it wasn't for the sounds of Drew screaming in the foreground. The combination of chainsaws and screams conjured memories of a movie we watched with Earl. As I pictured meat hooks, the cassette finished rewinding with a whir and the rewind button popped up. I jumped a little. I decided I should go inside and find Drew.

No one was in the living room. I started down the hall toward our room, which was a weird way to think of it because Earl and Momma were just married on Friday at the courthouse. We stayed at our neighbor Trudy's house that night, then we had a party for me on Saturday. This was the first time we would be sleeping in our new house.

Walking past the bathroom, I heard the shower running. I knocked on the door to see if it was Drew.

Momma called out with a laugh, "I'm enjoying a hot shower in my new house, go away!"

I kept walking down the hall. I heard Earl inside my room talking to Drew in a quiet voice, but his tone was anything but calm.

"You need to stop crying. Right now. You are a teenager for Christ's sakes, and you need to act like it. I told you I wasn't going to throw your stupid baby toy away. I was just going to take it from you to prove you don't need it. But, you had to be a brat and hold on until its ear ripped off. I'm trying to help you, Drew. Help you grow up into a good woman. In case you haven't noticed, you have curves now. You ain't no scrawny kid like your sister. That means it's time to stop crying like a baby. Right now."

Through all his talking, I didn't hear Drew cry. I didn't even hear a sniffle. As I stood there outside the door, all I heard was Earl's voice and Drew's silence.

I reached up and knocked gently on the door.

Earl called out, "Hey, Judy, Drew needs a Band-aid. Can you get one?"

"It's not Judy. It's me," I said.

The door flew open and Earl stood there looking down at me with his piercing clear blue eyes. He was a tall, thin man with a long and thin nose full of white hairs. He was 42 years

13

old, but his face had enough wrinkles for a man twice his age. His hair was thick and pure white, brushed back like James Dean's on top but long enough in the back to touch his shirt collar. His lips were naturally thin, but they were even thinner as he clenched his teeth and stared down at me. I felt my teeth clenching, too. Our eyes held each other's briefly, but he quickly moved his eyes to my lips which made me nervous. Usually, people laugh at my lips and say I look like Mick Jagger. Subconsciously, I pulled my bottom lip in and bit it. Earl smirked, moved his gaze down to my shoes and back up.

"I see, it is you, Bones," as if he hadn't known I was there before, like I had just walked in off the street instead of having been driven there by Momma. "I thought you were outside."

His breath smelled like a trash bag full of beer cans, but his cologne was strong and the blend nearly choked me.

"I was, but I came in to play with Drew."

"Drew don't play, Bones. She's too old for that." He paused, waiting for something I couldn't identify. Then he calmly said, "You're in my way."

I backed up against the wall and let him walk by me. When he was headed down the hall, I stepped into the room with Drew. She was on the bottom bunk, lying with her face in my pillow, crying. No wonder I couldn't hear her. Before I could say anything, Earl was back with a Band-aid. He unwrapped it and grabbed her arm. With her face still buried, she pulled her arm away from him and tucked it under the pillow. The blood from her scratch smeared on the pillow case.

"Damn it, Drew!" Earl grabbed her arm and pulled so hard she fell into the floor at his feet. I watched thinking that Drew was too big for him to treat her like this. I had never before thought of her as a little girl. She had always been my big sister. Seeing her yanked around like that was disconcerting.

Earl sat on the bed and wrapped his legs around her to hold her seated on the floor. Somehow he managed to get the

14

Band-aid on while she thrashed around. He released her arm in the same manner he might have thrown a crazed cat. Then he stood up and looked at me looking at him. His eyes were full of rage. The next thing I knew, his hand slapped against my cheek so hard that my whole body twisted around and slammed into our closet door. My eyes burned as I failed to fight back the tears.

"And, you! The next time you touch your sister's rabbit, I will bust your ass." He grabbed my headphones from my head and snapped them in half. "Now you two are even. From now on, both of you need to get along."

He almost laughed, he was so pleased with himself. He put his hand to his lips and pretended to cough to gain his composure. Then he winked at me and left the room. I heard him open the bathroom door where Momma was taking a shower. I heard her squeal and laugh. A few minutes later I heard her moan.

My sister sat on the floor with her knees pulled up and her arms wrapped around her legs. She was looking down, her face buried underneath her long strawberry blond hair which fell all the way to her shoes.

"Drew? Look at me, Drew." My voice shook.

"No, Jute. Just go."

"We need to tell Momma," I said it almost like a question.

"No, Jute. We can't tell Momma."

Drew lifted her face and looked at me. Her big indigo eyes were dry as she glared at me. I could not make sense of what was happening or what she was trying to say to me. What did I do to make her mad at me? I must have looked confused and terrified, because after a minute, her expression got softer. She stood up and pushed her hair away from her face.

"Look, Jute, it's different now. Everything is different. If you want it to be like it was before, you're just going to have to find a quiet place to pretend because it never will be for real. Go to the woods or something. But, you can't ever let him

15

know you want it to be like before."

"I don't want it to be like it was before, with no daddy and Momma sad all the time. I thought she married Earl because he was nice. We need to tell Momma that Earl is the meanest man in the world."

"Momma won't believe you and Earl will make you pay for it."

Drew wrapped her arms around me. She was only a year older, but already a head taller. She got everything good from our real daddy. But he had been in jail for 11 years and would probably die there. I hugged Drew back, but I still wasn't content. I didn't know what she meant by "like it was before". But, I decided to find out before I said anything to Momma about what happened.

We put our things away in the built in drawers in our room. We didn't have a lot and that was good because there wasn't a lot of room. Once our bags were empty, we sat on the bottom bunk so I could paint Drew's toenails. We had three color choices: Peony Pink, Moonlit Mauve, or Amber Kisses. Drew loves pink, but she chose the amber. Amber was my favorite of the three.

"We'll be twins!" I shook up the polish by tapping the bottle against the tanned skin of my thigh. After I had finished painting her toes, I handed her the polish and pulled off my socks to have her do mine. Suddenly, our door flew open. Momma stood there looking down at me. She was mad, I could tell. Her eyes moved from Drew's toes to my socks in the floor and then up to my eyes.

"What do you think you're doing?" She asked me, her mouth tight and her eyes cutting a hole through me.

My voice became very childlike for reasons I couldn't explain, "We're play dress up, Momma. I just painted Drew's-"

"You, little lady, should not be allowed to play anything after what you did. I understand that this is new and you might not like seeing me happy with Earl. But, jealousy is very ugly, Jute. You might think you can make yourself happy by destroying the things other people love, but all you will do is make no one want to be around you. I am so ashamed of you right now, acting this way in front of Earl."

She paused, still staring at me while I stared at the sock fuzz between my toes. Maybe her words would have stopped hurting if I could have understood why she was saying them. I said nothing.

"And you, Drew. I know your sister really hurt you. I know you wanted to get even by breaking her headphones. But, that's not how we're going to be as a family. If Jute ever does anything like this again, come to me. I see that both of you are getting along now, painting nails and being pals. But, Jute doesn't deserve this. You need to put up your makeup and come eat. Earl put burgers on the grill. Jute can sit in here alone and think about her actions."

My eyes met Drew's eyes for just a moment before she stood up to put the polish in her cosmetic box. She walked past Momma and kissed her on the cheek.

Momma looked down at me again. Now that we were alone, I could see that her eyes were filling with tears. She shook her head as if to clear her mind, then looked back to my eyes.

"Why can't you let me have this one thing, Jute?"

She sobbed and covered her mouth with one hand while the other shut the bedroom door, leaving me sitting there in silence.

The smell of the hamburgers on the grill seeped into our open window. Soon after, the sounds of laughter came in with it. I leaned forward and pulled the book The Phantom Tollbooth from the top of our dresser. This would be my fifth time reading it, but it was my only escape.

CHAPTER THREE

1990

It's a cold Sunday morning, no one is going to build another fire if I don't. I glance around at the posters I hung last night and think of Allie. I have a collage of her poems tacked to the wall beside my pillow. She has such a way with words, but mine always come out hurting. I should have been more kind last night. She was just trying to do the right thing.

I get out of bed and slide on my jeans, then pull on my combat boots. On the way to the door, I put on my old Army coat. Taking a deep breath, I open the door. The January air hits me and I hug myself tightly. Sparse flakes of snow fall. It's as if the clouds won't toss the next flake until the first one hits the ground.

I lean back through the doorway and grab my hat from a hook on the wall. It is red plaid with ear flaps and nothing anyone I know would wear, except me. I snap the ear flaps together under my chin.

This yard is just frozen mud. I don't know who lived here in the fall. Judging by the tracks, they must have had big tires, big dogs, and a few dirt bikes. The wood pile is between two trees on the north side of the house. There are only five logs left. I pass by it and head up into the woods to find kindling.

If twigs were money, I'd be rich. My arms are full in no time. When I step out of the woods, I look up and see Momma getting out of the passenger side of a brown GMC Jimmy. She's wearing yellow polyester pants and blue wide collar jacket. There is a short bald man getting out of the driver's side. I've never seen him before. He is grimacing at me and nods a greeting. Momma is waving like I just got off an airplane.

"Well! There's my baby girl!"

Momma opens her arms in my direction like I'm running toward her, but I'm just standing still. The bald man walks to the back of the Jimmy and opens the hatch. I start walking toward them in silence, refusing to shout loud enough for Momma to hear me. The man pulls out a paper grocery bag and a gallon of chocolate milk. Momma just stands beside the Jimmy, teeth glistening in her wide smile, long eyelashes framing her eager eyes. She motions with her hand for me to hurry up.

She looks so skinny. Her cheekbones are the only wide thing about her. It's the Cherokee blood. My sister Drew and I have them, too. No one notices mine because the rest of my face is just as wide. Its roundness never changes, despite being attached to my short skinny body just like Momma's. But, she stays strikingly beautiful no matter how old she gets. Her hair is thick and long, shining in the sunlight. I'm the one that helped her dye it black, the color it was originally. Her roots are showing gray. We can't afford the dye to fix it.

As long as it takes me to walk to her, she never stops smiling. She is like that when people are around. Even when she shouldn't be. She makes it hard to stay mad at her.

"Jute, this is Jerry."

She turns to him and smiles, then looks back at me grinning. She lowers her voice seductively, "We've been sleeping around."

"Momma!" I glare at her. She is trying to be funny but it makes me mad.

"What?" She says, batting her lashes at me and still grinning. "I'm finally free of that asshole. I can do whatever I want."

19

She shrugs and walks past me like she's Marilyn Monroe walking into someone else's run down shack.

"Momma, I don't care what you do or who you do it with. Just keep the details to yourself. Okay?"

I follow her up the porch steps and drop the kindling in the cardboard box by the door. Instead of going inside, I head back to the wood pile and pick up two small logs, leaving the largest for tonight. When I enter the house, Momma is in her bedroom talking to me through the door as if I have been there the whole time.

Ignoring her, I open the wood stove door. The heat is heavenly warmth on my face. I grab the poker and jab at the ashes and burned pieces of wood before throwing on the logs. I hear the snapping and cracking and try to focus on that instead of how angry I am at Momma for being gone so long. I can't keep the door open any longer or the room will fill with smoke. I reluctantly shut it and hear Momma saying, "Jute, are you out there?"

I stand up and take my hat off. Jerry is standing by the couch, rocking on his heels and toes with his back to me. His hands are in his pockets and he's looking at a picture of Jesus. It's the only picture in the room, left here by the previous residents. This must be an awkward moment for Jerry. I don't plan to make it any easier.

Before he has time to gawk at my shaved head, I walk through the kitchen to Momma's room. She is sitting on her bed in her underwear. Her back is to me, bent slightly forward as she puts one leg into her black pants. Her olive skin stretches over her bony spine. Everything about her is not enough. Even the blanket on her bed is threadbare. It wouldn't even keep a dog warm.

A sigh escapes me. "Momma? Momma, what are you doing? We've been here a couple of weeks. You can't run off with the first guy asking if you have change for a dollar."

She doesn't turn around. She looks drained. Her voice lacks all the entertainment qualities it had when Jerry could hear her, "If you had been listening to me a minute ago, you would know he isn't just any guy. I don't know what I would do without him. I have been a prisoner for too long, married to that crazy man. So, don't tell me now that I should still think about that psycho before I make my decisions. I've snagged a nice man this time. He bought us those groceries, you know."

My words come out quiet and empty, "That was nice of Jerry."

Memories of the last week flash through my mind: The day I scraped the mold off the bread and ate it with mustard. I missed the bus Thursday. Missing school meant missing a free lunch. The next day Allie had to pick me up after school so I could make up the Chemistry test. Allie has always made up for Momma's negligence, but Allie graduated early and is moving to Ohio tomorrow. I don't say any of this aloud. Momma doesn't care. If she knew how I felt, she would just use it to hurt me. She didn't even want me here.

I pick up the hair brush and start to brush through the tangles in Momma's hair. I gather it in my hand, turn it in a twist, and pin it. She stares at herself in the mirror. I've always loved to play with Momma's hair. It is bittersweet to do it now. She picks up a small mirror and moves it so she can see the back of her head. She kisses the air and snort laughs.

"Oh, my heavens, who is that wretched old woman?" She giggles before pushing up her nose with her thumb and crossing her eyes.

"Momma, you are beautiful. Shut up." I smile at her reflection, failing again to stay mad at her.

She winks at me.

I tell her, "Now, put on a shirt. And not that red and gold shirt with the clocks all over it. I hate that damn thing."

I leave the room and find Jerry standing at the fridge with the door open. He's pulling a container of cottage cheese out of a grocery bag and putting it in with the other items. There's sliced cheese, bologna, a bag of apples, and a can of peaches. I see bread on the kitchen counter. I pick up the bread box from the kitchen table and carry it to the counter. We can't leave bread out or mice will get in it.

"Got a mouse trap?" I don't look to see if he smiles. It was a bad attempt at humor. I sigh.

Finally, after closing the bread box, I look over at him. He's staring at me, mostly my stubbly hair.

"Is Jute your real name?"

"It wasn't. But, it is now." I don't offer details. I don't tell him that Momma named me Judy after herself. I don't understand why she did that. The name Judy is bad enough without it implying that I am also my mother's replica. I'm nothing like her. When I started kindergarten, I insisted everyone call me Jute. It stuck. We changed it legally when Momma married Earl and he officially adopted us.

"What do you think Judy is doing in there?" I see his eyes land on my tiny scar, then shift around my face trying to find a soft place to land. He gives up and looks away. My face might be full and round, but it isn't a place to find comfort.

"She has trouble making up her mind," I say as though I'm not being mean. "I'll check on her."

Opening the bedroom door, I see her shoving her folded up blanket into the top of her closet. She's wearing the clock shirt. There is a suitcase open on the bed, full of her clothes. Her dresser is cleared except for a bottle of baby lotion.

She turns to me and forces a weak smile. She walks toward me as if she is on a t.v. screen. She is just walking toward the camera.

Her arms wrap around me. The strong smell of lotion snaps me back into reality. She kisses the side of my head where my stubble is growing in. It's a goodbye kiss. Rejection washes over me. Will she ever come back?

Jerry is waiting on the other side of the door.

I take her hands and pull her to sit beside me on her bed. I look at the wall in front of us so I don't have to look at her. If I look at her, she will just do something to make me laugh instead of answering my questions. I keep my voice low so Jerry can't hear us, "Momma, why did you bring me out here if you weren't going to stay? Where have you been the last four days? Does Earl know where we are?"

She sits up taller and puts her hand on her stomach, smoothing out invisible wrinkles in her shirt. Then she sighs and slumps a little.

"You are grown, Jute. My days of taking care of everybody else are over. And where I've been is working at Charlene's Deli. My car broke down and needs a new transmission. I've been staying with Jerry and he has been driving me to work and back. I didn't tell him anything about our situation at first. But, he's been really nice to me. I'm not used to that and I don't want to mess it up."

Momma is crying. Listening to her makes me angry.

I turn to face her so she can see me and hear me despite how quietly I speak. "When you say you didn't tell him anything 'at first', does that mean you told him everything eventually… or does that mean you are still not telling him that you stood by and let Earl molest Drew?"

I watch her eyes and I see her vacate. She isn't seeing me. I know whatever she says next is not because she is my mother. It is because she is Judy. She stays silent long enough that it surprises me when her hand finally comes up and slaps my face.

She speaks quietly through clenched teeth, "I knew I shouldn't have brought him around you, you little jealous bitch! If you weren't so damn ugly, you wouldn't have to work so hard for attention. May God help you, because I am done!"

She stands up so I do, too. Her hands are shaking as she snaps the metal closures on her suitcase. She heaves it up with one hand and walks toward the door. As she passes me, she says, "I do not have secrets, Jute, and neither do you."

She walks out of the bedroom, pushing a loose strand of hair behind her ear.

I stand here, staring at the paneling. I can hear her telling Jerry she is ready to go. Her voice is sweet and cheerful

23

again. I hear them getting farther away, the sound of the front door opening and closing. Car doors shut and an engine starts. The sound of Jerry's Jimmy makes me think about leaving here, but I don't have a car to drive down the back roads and disappear. The thought pops into my head that the name Jerry's Brown Jimmy would be perfect for a punk band. When the laugh escapes me, I realize I have tears in my eyes. I hate all the sadness.

Diversion! I stand up on Momma's bed and start jumping around to the music in my head. I sing "Holidays in the Sun" in my best Johnny Rotten voice. My arms punch the air and I shake my head until all of the pain I feel is forgotten. But, the absence of pain feels unsettling. I need to hurt to forget the dull ache underlying every moment of my life. So, I jump off the bed and slam my shoulder into wall. My head slams forward almost making contact as a jolt of pain screams down my arm and back. I feel alive and instantly I feel dead again. I step back and I slam into the wall even harder, my head misses again. I slide my back down to the floor and curl up with my head between my knees, sobbing. I cry until I can't breathe. I can't breathe. I can't do this anymore. I arch my back and slam the back of my head into the wall behind me. The vibration buzzes in my ears. I lie sideways on the floor completely still, listen to the buzzing, breathe, and close my eyes.

CHAPTER FOUR

1984

That first night we moved in with Earl, after not being allowed to leave my room, I fell asleep early. I wasn't sure if Drew wanted the top bunk or the bottom bunk, but I had fallen asleep on the bottom before I could ask her. When I awoke, I could hear Drew's rhythmic breathing in the bed above me. The small window in our room was still propped open and moonlight flooded over everything. I stood up to see our view for the first time. I was too afraid to do it earlier, afraid they would look up from their hamburgers and see me looking out. I didn't want to give them the satisfaction. But, no one was awake to see me now.

Our bedroom window faced south toward a mountain slope, which curved around to the east and north of us as well. Our yard was nearly entirely bordered by the tree line of the mountain except for a short driveway and a few feet of land touching Turkey Pen Branch Rd. Earl inherited most of the surrounding land from his grandparents, but he only had two acres left after selling most of it off. Whatever he did with the money, there's no sign of it now.

Lightning bugs danced in the yard. What time was it, anyway? I slipped on my shoes and walked to the kitchen to look at the clock. 4:17. I was too awake to go back to bed. I had been in that room for 12 hours.

I could hear Earl and Momma snoring, the clock

ticking, crickets chirping outside, and my stomach growling. Nothing around me felt like home. My brain was disoriented. What would I do if Earl walked in? What if I overheard someone talking about something I don't want to know? What if Momma came in and looked at me like I'm a horrible person?

Taking a deep breath, I mustered the courage to go outside and calm myself. The main door to the porch stood wide open so air could circulate through the screen door. I grabbed the handle and stood motionless, imagining my hand turning it without a sound. I convinced myself that I could do it. Slowly I started to turn it. Little by little, holding my breath, I turned it until it would turn no more. Then I carefully leaned in and slowly pushed the door open toward the porch. The hydraulic arm made a small pop, then another. I stopped pushing and listened. I could still hear Earl snoring, but could not make out Momma's.

I decided that I was too far out now and had to keep going. The door was open just enough to allow me to squeeze through without pushing it more. Once outside, I held enough resistance on the door to keep it from slamming. The door shut with only a gentle click as the handle landed in place.

The steps were the next challenge. I knew the top step creaked, so I held myself steady with the wooden hand rail and stepped over the first and onto the second step down. Then I skipped the last step just to be safe and placed my foot on the tiny gravel of the walkway. My other foot stepped onto the grass and I had made it.

All around me, the mountain sloped higher and the tops of the trees rustled in a breeze too high for me to feel. The moon was incredibly bright, lighting up the yard like the street lamp at our old place in the trailer park. I thought about the times I explored there. The only rule Momma had given was to stay away from the highway. Here, there was less road, more trees, and a lot more land. An overwhelming urge washed over me. I had to hike up the mountain slope. It would get me away for a while.

Noticing there were three cans of soda left on the picnic table from dinner, I walked that way. My stomach growled again, obviously not caring that the sodas had been in the summer heat for hours and were probably lukewarm.

I picked up a can of Shasta Grape and headed toward the southern slope of the mountain. The area had been partially cleared of trees. Earl likely hadn't done it because he didn't own any of the wooded land. Closer to the clearing, I noticed tire tracks leading into the woods toward the east. I'm not sure how I had missed seeing something as big as a logging road, or whatever this was trying to be. Maybe if it wasn't four in the morning and if I wasn't walking around with no flashlight, I would have recognized it.

When I reached the tree line where the road entered into the woods, I popped open my can of soda. It made a loud snap and fizzed. I was pretty sure I was far enough away from the trailer that no one would hear it. But, all the windows were propped open, so I couldn't be sure. I stepped farther into the tree line to better hide from view, then I put the can to my lips and turned it up. The warm liquid was hard to swallow, but once I got it down, the grape flavor lingered and tricked my brain into thinking I was eating something. I drank another swallow and surveyed the path I was on.

The road stopped just beyond the tree line with a pile of dirt blocking anyone from trying to drive any further. I walked up it, hoping it was dry enough not to get my shoes muddy. My feet slid a little as loose dirt gave way. I was glad when I first realized how dry it was, but not so happy when my shoes began to fill with bits of dirt. I jumped down the back side, landing a little harder than I had planned. Some of my grape soda sloshed out on my leg.

"Damn it!" I said under my breath, instantly feeling guilty for saying that word.

I took two more big swallows of the soda. I needed to make sure it wouldn't slosh out again. As I stood there swallowing my drink, my eyes adjusted to the filtered light under the trees. There was a foot path leading up the side of the mountain, diagonally along the slope toward the east. Whatever was up that path had to be so much better than what was behind me. No one was around to stop me from walking up it. I scanned the area for a good sized stick to swat the air in front of me. It was night and I knew spiders were building their webs. I'm not afraid of them in their own space. But, I'm terrified of walking into a web and having one on me.

The stick I found was about three feet long, as thick as a fishing rod, and comically twisted. I pretended it was a sword as I swished it in front of my face, occasionally jabbing at imaginary villains. The path was easy to navigate at first, but when the switchbacks started, so did the rocks. I had to be careful to lift my feet high so I wouldn't trip. I felt myself getting deeper into the woods and farther away from Earl. I was surrounded by nothing but trees and if not for the path, I wouldn't know which direction I needed to walk to get back. I started to worry about time and hope I could make it back before anyone noticed I was gone. Logically, I wanted to turn around. But, this place made me feel so alive and not alone. All I wanted to do was sit down and watch the leaves on the trees blow, lose myself in it.

Just to be dramatic, I spun around like Julie Andrews in the sound of music and sang at the top of my lungs, "These hills are alive with the sound of music!" Then I bent over with laughter. I was sure I was far enough away from the trailer that no one could hear me. That's why, when I heard the dog barking up the trail, I went cold.

Earl didn't have a dog. So, whose dog am I hearing? I froze like a statue, my stick held out like a lightsaber. My ears were straining to make sense of where that dog was and why. The next sound I heard was a man yelling.

"Shut, up, Bonkers! Get back in this house!"

House!? Crap. I was on someone else's property. I still didn't move. I strained to see what was ahead of me and to the left, where the voices were coming from. I kept thinking, "Yes, Bonkers. Go back in the house. Go ahead, Bonkers, do what the man says."

Soon, I stopped thinking that because I heard Bonkers running down the trail. I could hear his tags jingling and his panting just before he came into view. He was a chocolate lab, young, and much friendlier than he sounded. He ran up to me and bumped his side into my leg, circled around and made another pass to bump my other leg. He sat in front of me, looking up at my face and barked a greeting.

"Shhhh!" I practically screamed it, and immediately laughed at my stupidity. Bonkers just sat there staring up at me, wagging his tail. He was licking his lips and yawning with tiny whines, as though it was all he could do not to bark again. I reached down and scratched his head and behind his ears, then knelt to look him in the eyes.

I smiled and whispered, "You are going to give me away! Then we'll both be in trouble. Now, go home!"

Bonkers just shook his head, his ears flapping, and licked my nose.

"Eeww!" I said, a little louder than I meant, and started wiping off my face. I need to work on this "quiet" thing.

"Who is there?" A girl's voice called out. My heart startled and then pounded in my ears. I must not have heard her approach over all the ruckus between Bonkers and me.

I stood up and saw the silhouette of a girl in the moonlight. She looked young, like me, definitely not an adult. I decided not to run, but Bonkers left my side to go to her. I hoped I was right to trust her.

"Jute," I answered, not sure if I was loud enough for her to hear me, and not sure if I wanted to be.

"From school?" Her voice held more excitement than I expected.

"Uhm... I don't know who you are..." I stammered, realizing that trusting a stranger was more appealing than trusting someone from school.

"Allie," she paused, "I was in Ms. Nideffer's class."

She was standing right in front of me now. Her long brown hair looked black in the shadows. A few rays of moonlight made it through the trees to land in jagged shapes across her narrow face. She didn't seem like the Allie from school. This Allie wasn't fancy in a wrinkled, over-sized t-shirt. But when I noticed her purple jelly shoes, I had no doubts it was the same Allie. She was smiling politely while trying to figure out why I was in the woods by her house. I didn't want to tell her and I didn't want to lie.

Breaking the silence, she said, "Are you really here?" and reached out and poked my arm with her finger. She giggled and tilted her head. Her hair had fallen over her cheek. She straightened up and brushed it away with her hand.

"Does your dad know you're out here?" I asked, diverting her attention from me.

"No!" She whispered, sounding alarmed. "I came out here to get Bonkers before Dad gets mad at him. He agreed to let me keep a dog if I take care of it. Our last one disappeared after four straight nights of barking and chewing the furniture. I think Dad took him to the pound. I just can't let that happen to Bonkers. Please, don't tell on me."

"I'm not going to tell on you. Besides, do you think I'm supposed to be walking around in the woods right now?"

Allie squinted at me and waited for me to explain. Her lips were parted a little and I could see her front teeth, which slightly protruded behind her naturally pouty bottom lip. I thought about how my own big mouth looked under the moonlight and soon found myself biting my bottom lip. I wasn't sure whose turn it was to speak.

"So... why ARE you in the woods, Jute?" She asked, cocking her head to the side again.

"I was just exploring." I said it quickly and shrugged, making sure to look at Bonkers so I didn't have to look at her.

"But it's 4:00 in the morning, and you live in a trailer park off of Six Mile Road, that blue trailer with the pinwheels in the yard. That's like… forever away."

Allie was squinting harder at me, her eyebrows pulling together above her long nose.

"We moved today. Momma married Earl Martin on Friday. We live down there," I pointed behind me.

Allie's mouth fell open. I couldn't tell if she was repulsed or excited.

"Oh, wow, Jute! I have been wanting a friend to live near me for forever! Oh, wow! I can't believe it!" She grabbed both my arms and jumped up and down in front of me. Each time she jumped she swung her hair to the opposite side. It was like she was trying to do what happy people do on tv. But, I could tell she was sincerely happy under her fake happy.

"Yes, I guess it's a good thing," I say, unenthusiastically.

Allie stopped jumping but didn't let go of my arms. She looked into my eyes like she could see everything in my brain. She smelled like lilac laundry detergent and mint. It was all I could do not to run away to spare her from the horrible thing that my life had become.

Her voice was so soft and kind. "It will be fine, Jute. Whatever you are worried about, don't. I'm not as bad as people say I am."

She let go of my arms and covered her mouth with her hands and let out a whimper as tears filled her eyes.

"Allie!" I pleaded, and pulled her hands down from her face. "Stop it! I'm not implying you aren't a good friend. I don't even know what people say about you. I'm just worried because Earl doesn't seem so nice."

I try to smile hopefully at her, but thinking about how I just blurted out my opinion of Earl made it hard to smile at all. She looked at my face and let out a relieved sigh and a little laugh.

"Oh, wow! I must seem really self-centered. It's just that I've lost a lot of friends this week. I'm being a cry baby about it."

"I don't mind. I'd rather talk about your problems than mine, anyway. And, speaking of problems, if we both don't get back to our beds soon, I imagine we'll have a lot more."

"Right. Maybe you can walk back up tomorrow?"

"I'm not sure. I'm actually grounded right now."

Allie let out a laugh.

"Shhh!" I put my hand over her mouth. "Now, go home!"

She pulled my hand away and gave it a squeeze.

"Well, you can call me when you aren't grounded. Can you remember my number if I tell it to you?" She was standing with the moonlight in her blue eyes.

"We don't have a phone." I hoped I wasn't standing in any moonlight.

She let go of my hand and jabbed her finger in the air.

"I have an idea! I'm going to tie something on one of these branches tomorrow, maybe a ribbon or something. I'll check every day, and when it's gone, I will know you are ungrounded and came to untie it. We'll meet here at noon the next day. Okay?"

"Brilliant!" I said, barely getting it out of my mouth before Allie hugged me so hard I couldn't breathe. She rocked me from side to side, giggling, then turned and ran up the trail with Bonkers right behind her.

I started to think maybe things would be okay here.

CHAPTER FIVE

1990

I am standing at the base of an old southern red oak tree, my hands raised upward in front of me. The tree is tall and the branches stretch wide. I can not see the top. The leaves are scarlet, so it must be October. A ladder hangs from the lowest branch. I climb it with my bare feet and hands, noticing my fingernails are painted amber. I keep climbing up the branches, looking for footholds. The branches get smaller and smaller. Eventually, I reach the top. I cling to a group of tiny branches. The leaves are like a bouquet of red roses in my hand. When I turn my head to take in the view, I am startled to see a little girl sitting on branches which can not possibly hold her. Her eyes are cornflower blue. She smiles and waves, then her mouth forms an "O". She puts her cupped hands to her mouth as if to whisper a secret. She blows air out in my direction. The wind is strong and cold. I breathe in, but I can't get air. I gasp repeatedly, trying not to pass out. I forget to hold to the branches. I am falling through air which I can not breathe. I can not breathe.

Something is wrong. My eyes spring open, waking me from the dream. Earl's face is only inches from mine. His white hair is wild and dirty. His mouth is clenched tight, his blue eyes are ice cold and locked on mine. His large hand is pressed over my mouth and nose. My hands fly up to pull the hand away. I manage to loosen them enough to pull some air into my lungs, catching the scent of cigarettes and cooking oil. He pulls his hand away from my mouth so he can grab my wrists with both hands. His mouth comes down on mine. I shut my lips and teeth tightly and try to turn away. But, he holds my hands down on either side of my head and I can not move. His tongue is licking my mouth, parting my lips, and getting through to my clenched teeth. His breath smells like beer and vinegar. I grunt and tears begin running down the sides of my face.

He raises his head up and laughs, his breath making me cough and gag. He catches my mouth open and quickly inserts his tongue and pulls it out before I can bite down. I clench my teeth together again and try to shake my head from side to side. He pulls my wrists closer to my face to hold me still and licks my cheeks and my eyelids. His tongue moves over my face in exaggerated swirls as he tries to cover every inch of skin. Then he pulls my wrists away from my face so his head can lean down to my left ear. He whispers, "Where is she?" His words are slurred.

I keep struggling to pull my wrists free and don't answer.

His voice goes from a gentle whisper to a taunt. "Oh, now, Bones. You know someone has to pay for stealing. You might be the ugliest one in the family, but not ugly enough to escape your punishment."

He squeezes my wrists so hard I want to cry out. Then he brings my hands down and shoves them beneath me, holding them together with just one long fingered hand. His other hand reaches into his shirt pocket and pulls out a long slip tie. My eyes widen in panic, knowing I can't let him get that around my wrists. I have so much adrenaline rushing through me that I am nearly blind with it. Desperately, I try to pull my wrists apart to break his grasp, focusing on the weakest part near his thumb. I feel it give way and my right arm is free. I swing it up and claw at his tobacco stained face. As his free hand tries to grab mine, he drops the slip tie.

"Damn, it!" He screams at me. I feel his fist make contact with my mouth. The force of it knocks my head to the side and a sharp stabbing pain on my lips brings more tears to my eyes. Half my face is tingling and throbbing. I taste blood in my mouth and I lick my lip, forgetting to fight. For only a second, I feel too small to do this, but the realization that he is still in my bedroom jolts me into fight mode again. In the time I lost, he has grabbed my free wrist and has both of my hands held under me again. He doesn't make the same mistake of holding them with only one hand.

He shifts around in the bed as he tries to kick the blanket off of me without letting go of my wrists. For the first time, I realize he must have taken his pants off before I woke up. I struggle harder to get free as I feel the cold air rush in when the blankets fall to the floor. I feel naked in only a thin green tank top and panties. I bring my knees up and squeeze my legs together just before he leans his body over to lie on mine. He straddles across my waist.

I throw my head back and plead, "No! No! Please don't do this!" Sobbing escapes my mouth despite every effort to stop it. I am so ashamed to hear myself begging. He sits, still straddling me, with his flaccid penis on my stomach. My sobs have turned into whimpers. I don't look at his face. I close my eyes, turn my head, and wait.

Earl moves his hips to rub his penis around on top of my stomach. "Ah, look at that, Bones. You are so ugly my dick doesn't even know you're a girl. Maybe you need to prove to me you are a girl, or maybe I could just close my eyes and think of your sister." He throws his head back and laughs, momentarily loosening his grip on my wrists. I pull them free and give him a shove backward, then twist my entire body toward the edge of the bed, pulling my legs nearly out from under him. I reach down to the floor with my hands. But, as I am angled there, halfway off the bed with my hands touching the floor, he grabs my hips and presses his fingers hard on my skin. I cry out in pain then push my hands against the mattress

35

to pull free. I let all my weight drop. I feel his fingers start to slip and his fingernails scratch deep into my skin. As I fall, he grabs the waistband of my panties and I crash to the floor without them.

I run toward the front door, opening it with my left hand as my right hand reaches down and grabs my combat boots from the floor. The cold air assaults me, but I embrace it. I run through the frozen mud and enter the woods. My bare feet endure the pain as they slam onto rocks, jagged twigs, and acorns. But, I keep running at full speed up the steep slope of the mountain side. I want my skin to freeze, and all the germs he left on me to die. I want every memory of being touched by him to be destroyed by the numbness of frost bite. I want to feel a new pain so I can forget his pain. I feed this need with every step forward.

There is only a sliver of a moon tonight. I can not make out which direction I am running. I have turned left and right to get around the briar thickets and downed trees. I have pushed my way through dense forest and sprinted through the sparse areas. But now I have reached the logging road at the top of the ridge. I can barely move any more. I drop my boots to the ground beside me and lean forward with my hands on my knees and I vomit.

Thoughts catch up with me and images of Earl flash through my mind. One frightening frame at a time, I see the entire motion picture of his cruelty. A gust of wind jolts me into the present and reminds me of my nakedness. My fear is replaced by shame. I feel dirty and want to wash myself. My skin crawls with the feeling of a thousand unwanted touches. My mind feels him looking at me now, naked. I forget that I am seventeen. I feel so small. I pull my tank top up to rub my cheeks with it, trying to erase the feeling on his touch. The wind now whips in where my shirt is raised. My senses are nearly overloaded. I try to breathe.

"I can breathe," I attempt to reassure myself. "Just breathe."

I inhale deeply through my nose and take in the mineral scent of dead leaves. I stand up and stretch my arms out, moving every muscle to remind my brain that I am unbound. I step my feet into my boots and bend to tie the laces. My fingers are numb from the cold, but they work automatically. I am glad I was able to grab shoes, but the boots do not ease the pain of my feet. The cuts on my soles are still bleeding and dirty.

As much as I don't want to think at all, I must form a plan. My brain rattles off a list of concerns. I don't know what time it is. I am naked except for this tiny top and my boots. It's freezing. My lip and feet are bleeding. Bruising is inevitable. School starts up again in just a few hours. Allie is coming by to take me to school.

My eyes fly wide open. "Oh, no! Allie!" I am speaking into the night. I have to get to her before he does.

With a leap, I jump over the ditch beside the logging road and enter the woods. I begin walking downslope and hope it is in the direction of the house. Visibility isn't great. Maybe that's why I don't recognize the landscape along the route I'm taking. I don't know if this is right, or if I will end up coming out farther down Allegheny Loop Rd. I can certainly find my way from the road, but I'm not really dressed for it. I stop thinking about where I might end up and just focus on getting to the bottom.

In some places, I hold onto tree limbs to keep from sliding down the bank to my right. This slope is too steep to be the way I came up, but it is too late to change course. I try to keep myself from sliding all the way to the valley where the vegetation will be too thick to navigate. I stay on the steep side of the slope, working my way to the edge of the woods.

The sound of leaves crunching under my boots will surely give me away if anyone is trying to find me. The thought of Earl stumbling around in the woods, freezing cold, drunk, trying to find me is actually amusing. I wish he was in front of me now that I am fully awake. I envision myself picking up a large rock and slamming it against his head, hearing his skull crack, and watching him fall and roll all the way to the bottom. But, my mind won't let it rest there. Now I envision him rising up from his death, covered in blood, arms outstretched as he walks with a limp getting closer and closer. I picture his bloody corpse with its hands around my neck, strangling me. With great effort, I try to shut off my mind and just walk.

As soon as I see the tree line, I stop. I close my eyes and concentrate on what my ears can hear. I don't know exactly where I am. Now that I have stopped walking, forest sounds fill my ears. Leaves rustle, tree branches rub against each other in the breeze, squirrels move about overhead. But, then I hear the splintering crash of something breaking apart. It sounds like it's coming from my distant left. I walk slowly forward until I reach the edge of the woods. The road is only six feet away. I recognize it as part of the road north of my house. I am so close, my house is just beyond a vacant lot where a trailer used to sit. The noises I have heard must be Earl. I am considering my next move when I hear a heavier door slam, possibly Earl's truck door.

I run toward the empty lot and am halfway through the open grass area when I hear his engine start. He is revving it a few times to warm it up. I reach the trees behind my house when I hear Earl pop his emergency brake. I still can't see his truck, but I hear him turn it around and once he pulls out onto the road I see his headlights traveling north.

Not knowing how long I had been holding my breath, I exhale.

"He's gone," I whisper, trying to make myself believe it. I have seen his headlights leaving, but I still feel him looking at me. I close my eyes and see the illusion from the woods, see him tumbling down the mountain. I think of his dead body rising up and limping toward me. Terror stabs at my heart, not because I am afraid of a corpse, but because I feel he will always haunt me. I know if I go inside my house, I will still see it in my room, see it in my dreams, and see it in my mirror. I am the damaged one. I'm not going to come out of this alive.

Every single movement I make through the cold toward the front of my house brings more haze. I feel like I am in a movie and someone is pressing pause again and again. They watch me frame by frame, afraid of what will happen. They are so terrified to see the story, they break it apart and take it slow. I am not real.

How long have I been walking these few steps?

In and out of the fog, I realize I am at the corner of the house. I know I can lean forward and look at the driveway and confirm he is gone. My hand is pressed against the wood siding, holding myself up. I exhale, then breathe in and hold my breath again. The smoke from the chimney smells like warmth and makes me think of Allie's house. I want to be inside, for just that second, I think I want to go in. My body moves forward another step and I see an empty driveway.

"He's really gone," I say to the imaginary viewer as I exhale all my breath. I think they will not be so afraid to watch now. They will stop pausing and I can walk inside and sit beside the wood stove. No one is listening. No one is here.

My foot rises and is about to set down on the first porch step when I realize my front door is open. The plank of wood which held the knob is completely broken off the door and laying on the porch. I struggle to focus my eyes on it because my brain keeps pulling me back to my old house where busted things happened weekly. Inside my head is a tornado. I step over the plank and through the door frame. The tornado in my brain becomes eerily silent. I reach for the chain to the overhead light and yank it. I hear the click, but the room stays dark. I can see the bulb is shattered. I yank the chain again to keep the switch off.

My eyes peer over the room in the dark. Everything is gone. What isn't gone has been destroyed. My boxes are gone. My couch has been repeatedly sliced with a knife and food from my refrigerator has been dumped onto it. My cabinet doors are mostly ripped off, a few are still dangling. My kitchen table has been thrown partially through the window. I turn my head to my right and can see my room. Panic rises in me and I know I can't go in there. A trail of bits of paper is left leading out of my bedroom. In the living room, small brown streamers of unwound cassette tape get caught up in the wind that blows through the broken window and door.

A frightening thought comes. I bend to open the wood stove door and the heat hits my face. I feel so frozen that this heat might shatter me. But my fear is validated when I catch a glimpse of melting, twisted plastic and vinyl burning alongside the firewood. He has burned my music. I can barely move to shut the stove door.

I need something to wrap around myself, but there is nothing. I want to crawl into the corner by the stove and curl up on the floor. I imagine myself doing it, but I have no energy to move. I lie down on the floor on my side in front of the stove. Exhaustion is painting all my thoughts into darkness. Jolts of horrific memories crash in randomly like lightning. But the storm fades. I think my eyes are open, but I can not tell.

CHAPTER SIX

1986

"What about this one?"

I tossed a blue fedora across the clothes rack and it bounced off Allie's hands and hit her in the forehead.

"That was a terrible shot," she said, laughing. She carried it to the end of the aisle where she accidentally slammed into the table of Valentine's day decorations. I heard her grunt. She walked around to where I was standing as if she hadn't just bruised herself. She had the hat twirling on her finger and a scowl on her face like she was coming for vengeance. I just laughed at her. She stopped acting tough as she got closer.

"So, are you thinking about buying this for Drew's birthday?"

"No! You know Drew wouldn't wear that hat. You are the only person in Maryville under seventy who still wears hats like that."

Allie slipped the fedora on, cocked it sideways and down over one blue eye. She looked in the mirror and made a kissing face. Then she took it off and handed it back to me.

"Maybe," she said, scanning over the other hats on the wall beside me. She reached up and grabbed a pale brown suede hat, low topped, with a medium brim. A black velvet sash tied in a bow on the front. She slipped it on her head and pulled the floral black lace over her face.

"Wow! This one is great!" She pulled it off and plopped it down on my head. Before I could protest, she pushed me in front of the mirror to my right. I looked at the reflection of the hat, specifically avoiding my face. She pushed her face over beside mine. I looked at her instead. She was looking at my eyes.

"The floral pattern of the black veil brings out the chestnut color in your eyes. I'm buying it for you. I don't care what you say."

She took the brown hat off my head and the blue hat from my hands. She grabbed three other hats from the wall and carried the armload to Maude, the owner and cashier. Maude sat on a stool behind the counter watching TV. She was incredibly tall and much broader at her top than her bottom. Her hair was dyed black and her thin lips were usually painted liberally with bright salmon lipstick. I heard her high pitched raspy voice from where I stood, "Sure, Sweetie. I'll put them right back here until you're ready."

Allie ran back to me, her sandals loudly slapped the linoleum, the neck tie of her yellow blouse blew behind her, and her matching yellow pleated skirt tucked between her legs like culottes. That outfit wasn't meant for running. Her face was lit up like a kid at Christmas. I couldn't stop myself from laughing, maybe a little too much.

"Now, what are you buying for Drew?"

"Maybe a muzzle," I rolled my eyes. Drew and I hadn't been getting along. It was hard to bite my tongue every time Drew acted like she was my mother. She left her chores for me to do, knowing I would be the one to get in trouble if the house wasn't clean. She tried to get me grounded every time she knew I had something to do. She hated the way I dressed, and said she was embarrassed to be seen with me. Supposedly, my ratty black t-shirts made me look poor, which made her look poor. And, at least once a week I searched the house looking for where she hid my combat boots. She had been so furious when I shaved my head on the left side, she refused to speak to me in public for two weeks. It had been an enjoyable two weeks.

Allie didn't like my idea about the muzzle. She slapped my arm, which was common. She had no idea how hard she could slap. I wanted to show her what it felt like. But, I couldn't bring myself to slap a girl in a yellow blouse with a neck ruffle.

"Fine. I'll look through the blue jeans. But, if I find a muzzle, I'm considering it a sign and I'm buying it." I smiled wickedly, squinting my eyes at her. I brushed by her, nudging her out of my way with my elbow. She shoved me with both hands and laughed way too loudly. I caught Maude eying us from the check-out counter.

"Allie, you are so damn mean."

After looking at every pair of jeans, I gave up on the idea. There was only one pair of Levi's in Drew's size, but they had smiley faces drawn all over them in green marker. Plan B was to check out the rack of tops behind me. I looked through it quickly, the clothes hangers making a scraping noise every time I moved one. Halfway down the rack, I pulled back a Burger King t-shirt and my heart stopped when I saw what was behind it: a rich teal velvet blazer, fitted at the waist. It had Drew's name written all over it, not in green marker, but in essence.

"Please don't cost too much," I said, looking sternly at the jacket. I paused, giving it a minute to comply. Then, my hands slid down the sleeves until my right hand snagged the string holding the tag. I lifted it and flipped it over: $3.25.

"Hey, Allie!" I called, not caring if Maude glared at us again.

Allie came around the corner from the dressing room area with a bright green chiffon something draped over her arm. She looked annoyed, mouthed "What?", and glared at me. I blinked a few times, worried that she was really mad at me for elbowing her earlier.

"Are you mad?"

She broke out into a huge laugh. "Right," She rolled her eyes.

"O... K... Are you finished with your Broadway production then? I need to know if I can borrow twenty-five cents to buy this jacket for Drew."

Allie took one look at the jacket and her mouth dropped open. "Wow, Jute! I want it! Drew should be glad it's her birthday or I'd take it home with me. Oh, well."

She picked up the jacket and headed for the check-out. I assumed that meant she was spotting me a quarter. She put the jacket and the flowing green thing down and pointed to the hats behind the counter.

Maude smiled at her, "I'm not about to forget your hats, girl. Never don't you worry about it. My body might be slow, but my mind is still quick."

Her eyes glistened with pride as she glanced from Allie to me, then back to Allie. We both smiled, not knowing what she was waiting for. Maybe we should have told Maude we agreed that she had a mighty brain, even though we had never noticed. As Maude punched keys on the cash register, I decided I would compliment her brain next time I stopped in.

"The total for everything is eleven dollars."

Allie handed her a 20 dollar bill and left her hand out for the change. I laid my three dollars in it. Allie's hand stayed steady, but she jabbed her elbow over at me in jest.

"Thanks for doing this, Allie."

I waited for her to shove the change in her purse. Maude handed me the bags. I carried them toward the door and Allie darted by me to open it. Once we were outside, the warmth of the day ignited me, kick starting hope I had not felt in a while. I couldn't wait until summer when I could get out of the house for the entire day. But, there was a long time to go. It was early February and this heat was unusual, and likely wouldn't last.

We walked up to her dad's blue 1979 Ford Bronco and Allie pounded on the driver's window to wake him. He jerked

44

his head up, his beard staying pressed in an odd shape from resting on his chest. He blinked at us through the window. We were already climbing in on the passenger side before he was finished rubbing the sleep out of his eyes. Hank reminded me of a lumber jack in the face, but he was too short and thin to pull it off entirely. His reddish brown hair was too long for a man his age, and it curled up around the rim of his orange UT cap. I liked Hank because he never paid any attention to me. I could stare at him and make faces for ten minutes and he'd never notice.

The ride back to Allie's house took less than ten minutes. But, somehow, Allie managed to fill it up with thirty minutes worth of chatter about Bobby. She had met him at camp the year before. His family lived in Athens, which was a 45 minute drive from Maryville. It might as well have been Athens, Greece because Allie's dad was too busy to take her that far, and Bobby's family only had one car and three boys old enough to drive it. That's what Allie said, anyway. It made sense, though. If I had a boyfriend in Athens, there would be no way I'd ever see him.

The driveway to Allie's house was gravel, but Hank kept it smooth so we didn't jostle around as he drove to the top and parked outside the garage. The door made a loud creak as it opened and Allie scooted against me, bumping my legs. I slid out before she knocked me out. My nose filled with the lingering wood smoke. I saw very little coming from the chimney and knew Hank was probably going to let it die out because the day was so beautiful.

"Come on!" Allie grabbed my wrist and pulled me into the house and all the way up the steps to her bedroom. She slammed the door behind us and locked it. Her eyes were huge with excitement.

"Let's wrap your present for Drew!" She was excited like we were going to see Billy Idol in concert, not put paper around a three dollar jacket.

"Okay... what is up with you?"

"Well, I wasn't going to say anything in front of Dad, but Bobby might come visit me tonight!" Allie jumped up and down and whispered to me, "Be very quiet about this."

"Allie, he can't just come here without you asking your Dad. And why wouldn't you even tell ME about this?"

"Because," She stopped jumping and grabbed my arms and leaned her face toward mine, "If I say it out loud I will jinx it and he won't come." She let go of me and jumped around the room some more.

"So, why are you telling me now?" I twisted my body to try to look at her but she continued to move around.

"Because I found that green chiffon dress and it made me think of being a princess. You know I am always saying Bobby is my prince. Oh, Jute, you just have to meet him and you'll understand everything. He looks like Elvis, if Elvis was blond, that is. He goes to church all the time and he's so good, Jute. You've read some of his letters, you know how he feels about me. One day we're going to get married and it's going to be amazing!"

Not once had she looked at me while she spoke. When she finished, she had stood staring out the door which led onto a balcony overlooking the woods behind her house. I felt invisible. She only thought of Bobby. I had a feeling he wouldn't come, but maybe I had just hoped he wouldn't.

"Where's your wrapping paper?" I asked.

"Oh!" She ran to her closet and pulled out a roll of paper with balloons on it. "Here," she said, and tossed it like it was on fire. I shook my head at her as she rushed over to her desk to get the tape. Maybe she wanted me to hurry and leave.

We wrapped the present together, sitting on her bed. Allie ripped off pieces of tape for me to use. When the present was wrapped, I wasted no time picking it up and walking toward the door. Allie followed me.

"She's going to love it, Jute. Tell her I said, 'Happy Birthday!'"

"I will." I smiled at her. She held the door open for me.

I stopped as I passed her and turned to look in her eyes.

"So, when will you know?" I whispered.

She looked up at the ceiling and seemed to see something I couldn't, something which made her extremely joyful. She said to the ceiling, "Midnight." Then she dropped her eyes back to mine. "I'll meet him in the woods, if he comes."

I nodded and stepped out the door and into her yard.

"Oh, Jute. I almost forgot. There's something in the mailbox." She winked and shut the door behind me.

I entered the woods and started down the trail toward home. The trail had become well worn from all the trips Allie and I made to and from each other's houses. Soon after we met, Allie had a great idea to put an old mailbox up in the woods. We would write each other letters and put surprises in there for each other. The first thing Allie ever left for me was a Duran Duran article she had clipped from a magazine. The first thing I left for Allie was a bracelet I made with clover flowers.

When I opened the mailbox, I found a small envelope, like the ones intended to be attached to gifts. As always, I opened it right then. Any delay in going home was good. I ripped the envelope open and pulled out a small square card. On the front was a picture of a girl holding a giant heart. Inside, Allie wrote, 'I will love you forever. Your best friend, Allie.'

I slid the card back in the envelope and shoved it into my back pocket. Usually, my heart felt happy when Allie gave me things like that. But, this time Bobby was clouding my thoughts. I headed down the trail.

The smell of hamburgers on the grill reached my nose before I could even see the tree line. That was good news because Earl would be tending the grill and not my business. I hesitated before stepping into the yard. I took a moment to find him and plot a safe path back into the trailer. I didn't see him by the grill, but I saw Drew and Momma at the picnic table. There was a cake in the center and couple of 2-liters of soda. As soon as I stepped into the yard, Drew caught sight of me and started running toward me. Her long strawberry blonde hair swinging from side to side. When she reached me, she grabbed the gift in one hand and put her arm around me with the other.

"Is this for me?"

"No, it's for Earl, stupid." I gave her a playful shove away from me.

"Come here and look what Momma and Earl bought me," she said, pulling me by the hand.

When we reached the table, she bent down and picked up a box from the ground. I looked at Momma and noticed she was looking at the box and smiling, but not looking at me. Drew reached in and pulled out each item one by one: a red lace bra and matching panties, a bottle of red fingernail polish, sparkly necklace and earrings set with fake red gems. Drew smiled at me, obviously very pleased.

"And, last of all…" She said, and reached in again to to pull out a book titled, 'Sex Tips for Women'.

I reached up and grabbed the book from her hands and turned to Momma.

"What the hell is this? She's fifteen, for Christ's sake! What is wrong with you!?"

Momma's face got puckered and angry. Just then, I felt the book being jerked away from me. I turned to see Earl's angry red face so close to me that his nose nearly touched mine.

"We'll have none of this bullshit on your sister's birthday!" He slurred, "I think you need to take that big ugly mouth of yours in the house before I crack it open with my fist."

I saw him lean to his left, as if the book was so heavy it was pulling him over. He was more drunk than normal, and for a moment I considered not saying what was about to come out of my mouth. But, I said it anyway. I got on my tiptoes just to be closer to his face and I let it rip out of me like a volcano.

"You are a fucking pervert, and a sorry ass step-dad! If you touch my sister again, I will slit your fucking throat!"

The feeling of the back of his hand knocking my jaw sideways until it nearly dislocated had been what finally shut me up. I crouched on the ground holding my face and tried to quell the rage bubbling over in my brain. I wanted to kill him. All I could see in my mind was the many times he had walked into our room to tell my sister to get out of bed and come with him. He had thought I was sleeping or didn't care. She would come back a few minutes later and I would listen to her sniffling in her bed. I didn't know who to be mad at most, Earl because he's a sick child molester, Momma because she got us in that mess, or Drew because she was holding up those panties like it was perfectly fine for her parents to buy her lingerie for her fifteenth birthday. That thinking was not soothing my anger. I was still seething when I felt his boot land on my lower back and I flew forward a couple of feet across the ground. The pain was the worst I had ever felt. Later, Momma said he might have kicked my kidney. But, at the time, all I knew was that I hurt too much to get up.

Earl could have walked over and kicked me all he wanted. I wasn't moving. But, instead he went into the house and came back out with my boombox. He threw it like a giant baseball from where he stood on the porch. It landed three feet from my face and shattered into pieces. One of the shards planted into my cheek, just below my eye.

"You little, bitch!" He screamed. "You are about to find out just how bad I am!"

CHAPTER SEVEN

1990

Hands grasp my upper arms. Through the darkness I see Earl's face. He is grinding his teeth and his eyes are bloodshot and angry. Hands that aren't his flip me over. I had been lying on my stomach, but now I am twisted over a lap. Through the darkness, my mother's dark brown eyes look at me. She is singing "All the Pretty Little Horses" and rocking me in her arms. Her hand is on my face, touching my cheek. I see her mouth twist up into a crooked smile that does not belong to Momma. It is Allie. Then she is gone and I can see nothing. But, I still hear her singing to me about Dapples and Grays. Her voice fills up the darkness completely, getting louder, painfully loud.

"Jute!"

My eyes fly open just as Allie's hand lands across my cheek with a smack. She is holding me up on her lap with her right arm while her left is rubbing my cheek where she just smacked it.

"Wake up, dammit!" She is sobbing, which might explain why she doesn't notice that my eyes are already open and I am looking up at her through narrow slits. My face is wet with her tears. I can taste them on my tongue. She finally realizes I am awake.

"Oh, thank God!" She continues to sob, pulling me up and pressing her cheek to mine. Her hair smells like cinnamon

50

apples. I breathe in and try to figure out where I am. There is dim light in the room. This is my living room. It's morning. I can barely feel my fingers and toes. Allie is so warm. I forget wanting to know where I am, wherever it is needs to be forgotten. I close my eyes again.

I hear her whisper, "Jute?" and I know I should answer, but I just want to fade back into the darkness.

She lets me fall onto her lap and I feel her knees slide out from under me. The floor is so cold, but soon something is draped over me. It is already warm and smells like Allie's hair. I feel her hands on my cheeks and her breath is so warm and smells like pancakes. I inhale and feel myself smile. I want to open my eyes. But, I can't remember how.

A vision of my busted door flashes into my brain and I try not to see it. If this is what it means to come out of the darkness, I don't want to ever come out.

Allie is sniffling and I feel her hands move away.

"Please, wake up Jute," Maybe she is screaming. I can't tell. Her voice bounces around in the darkness. I recognize the pleading tone, but can not discern how far away she is. The more I try to listen, the farther away she seems to go. I have to stop her from leaving. I have to say something.

My tongue moves like a stone in my mouth. My lips are painful to open.

"Don't... go." I think I say, but I don't hear the words.

I must have said them aloud because I hear Allie burst into laughter and she is holding my head up to her hair again. I fight with my muscles, urging them to get my arms around her. They ache, but I manage to embrace her. I feel tears pouring out of my eyes and I know I am awake in my house, too awake to find my way back to oblivion. Fear paralyzes me and I don't want to let go of Allie. My brain is frantically trying to come up with a plan, something to tell Allie so she won't know what really happened, something to say to make her think I am in control. She needs to never know how afraid I am. Squeezing the breath out of her is probably not convincing.

51

I pull away and steady myself. It is difficult to sit upright without her support. Allie is facing me, with her legs stretched out behind me. She grabs my shoulders to steady me. I put my head down to avoid making eye contact. I wish I had long hair like hers so I could hide beneath it.

Her left hand touches my chin, pulling my face up to look at her. I have an urge to jerk my head away, but I am too weak to bother. I look into her blue eyes and am relieved to find them not looking back into mine. She is staring at my lip, which reminds me that it must look horrible. Thinking about it just makes it hurt again. Allie's thumb moves down and touches the cut, making me wince.

"Sorry," she whispers, as her eyes dart up to mine. I know she is analyzing me, checking for signs of pain, trying to see my memories replaying on my cornea. I know I should turn my head so she can't see the truth, but I don't. I stare back at her blue eyes because they are soft and kind and I need something to be soft and kind. If I keep them in my sight, the whole world will turn this shade of blue like flying through the summer sky. I will never have to deal with my brokenness. The minutes pile up and I forget that she is reading me like a book. I forget I have a story to hide. I don't even know who I am. My brain is washed out with a tide of blue waves. She blinks her eyes, disrupting the blue, and I am forced out of the clouds and back to this room.

My head must have started to fall back, because she now has my face held firmly between her hands. The pressure helps me feel grounded. I let myself take in all of her face at once. I don't recognize her expression. Her face is puffy and red from crying, but she doesn't look distraught. Not exactly. I feel the corner of my lips go up a little as I realize I am the one trying to read her like a book. I see her sadness and apprehension, but maybe those are mine reflecting. There's something else, though. Joy? It seems out of place here, so I doubt I really see it. I close my eyes.

"I thought I lost you forever, Jute." She says. Her voice

52

is shaky, but not from crying. Maybe I was right and she is apprehensive. I open my eyes and start to smile at her, but feel my cut rip open again. I suck air through my teeth then pull my lip in a little, cracking it more in the process. I taste blood. My face must be a mess, and my lips weren't so great to start with. I think about what I must have looked like to her when she found me on the floor, covered in scratches, and nearly naked. Tears well up in my eyes. I am so ashamed. I desperately want her to stop looking at me. I want to hide, but nowhere in this house feels safe except right here.

Her thumb touches the cut again, this time much more gently.

She looks into my eyes and I hear her whispering, "I am so sorry, Jute. So, so sorry I did this to you."

Before I can say she didn't do anything wrong, I feel her lips gently touch mine. The kiss was so light that my skin barely felt it, but tingling sparks of warmth wash over me. She leans away. I open my eyes and see the blood from my cut is now on her bottom lip. She bites it a little. Her eyes fill with tears as they move from one part of my face to another until the tears spill over onto her cheeks. I reach my hand to her face and touch my finger to the blood on her lip and wipe it away.

"You didn't do anything wrong." I say.

Allie lets go of my face and sobs into her hands. When she speaks, her voice is muffled and she doesn't look at me.

"It's my fault he thinks it was you. I should never have gone into his house and stolen your things back. But Jute, they belong to you! Why is he such a monster? Whatever he did to you, it should have been to me instead. I am so sorry."

I feel my fight instinct returning. The mental image of that prick touching Allie fills me with rage.

"If he ever touches you, I will kill him. Just hearing you say that makes me want to slit his throat." I say, trying to keep my voice calm. We can't keep talking like this. The urge to get up and destroy things is almost uncontrollable. My heart is pounding as my thoughts collide between the feelings I had

53

when Allie held me and the feelings of bloodlust I have now. Neither of these thoughts are acceptable to me, and they certainly aren't thoughts I want Allie to know about.

"I have to get out of here," I say, starting to stand. I feel dizzy and weak, so I stay on my knees until I can acclimate. Allie's coat is draped around me backwards, my hand holding it closed behind me. I feel like I might fall over, but I close my eyes and focus on staying upright.

"Here," She says, standing in front of me with her hands on my shoulders. She is pushing me over and it makes me angry, but I can't really fight her. I fall to a seated position with my legs out to my side. Allie's coat no longer covers me well enough and I feel cold and exposed.

"Just sit there a minute and I'll get a pair of jeans from my suitcase. I'll be right back."

I clearly hear her high heels clomping down the wooden porch steps because the front door is standing wide open. Guilt is ripping at my heart because I know she is supposed to be on her way to Ohio instead of cleaning up my mess. I look around the room and notice how much worse it looks in the light of morning. Beside me on the floor, I see shards of glass from the light bulb. I'm not sure how I have escaped being cut by it, or have I? My body is still so numb. I look at my hands and see my fingertips are pink and splotchy.

Allie walks back in the house with her arms outstretched, holding a pair of purple lace panties in one hand and pink sweatpants in the other.

"I know I said I was going to get jeans, but I thought these would be more comfortable on your skin. I had no idea that bastard was capable of doing this to you."

"He didn't cause those scratches," I say, trying to hold my bleeding lip as still as possible. "I got them from running naked through the woods in the dark... except my lip. So, anyway, do you not have any normal underwear?"

Allie looks at the purple thong panties and then back at me like she doesn't understand why anyone wouldn't like them.

"Just give them to me," I say. When she tosses it down, I quickly roll everything up into a ball so nothing touches the floor. Now that I'm fully aware of the glass around me, I don't plan on cutting myself more.

"Let me help you get your boots off." Allie squats down and unties the laces. Only now do I notice how out of place she looks here. She's wearing a 1960's sage eyelet party dress with sheer lace sleeves. There are spots of blood on the front and the skirt is filthy. My guilt grows, but I am also annoyed that Allie wears stuff like this so early in the morning.

When she pulls off my boot, her mouth falls open and both hands cover it as if holding back a scream. Tingling pain radiates everywhere the boot had been. I look at my toes and see they are splotchy pink and blood is smeared between them. I know the bottoms, which Allie sees but I can not, are covered in scratches and likely filled with dirt and splinters.

"Oh... my... God, Jute!"

Expecting her to pass out any minute, I watch her untie the other boot and pull it off. I suck air through my teeth as the pain comes. At least it doesn't seem to look any worse than the first one. Allie just stays squatted there, looking from one foot to the other with her mouth open.

"You have got to go to the doctor, Jute."

"What I need, Allie, is to get the hell out of Maryville. This is nobody's business but mine."

I didn't mean to snap at her, but the thought of her pitying me fills me with anger.

"Fine," She says, taking her eyes off my feet and looking at my face. I realize it is probably just as splotchy as my the top of my feet. It must have been colder last night than I thought.

Allie puts her hand out, palm up. "Give me back those panties you hate and I'll put them over your feet so you can pull them up."

I throw them at her like I'm throwing a snowball, but

she reaches up and intercepts it before it hits her face. She smiles but I can tell it's forced. She slides the panties over my feet before I can even register the pain of being touched. Once they are within my reach, she turns her head away. I pull them up, but they feel a little big and a lot scratchy. I don't complain. Anything is better than lying naked on a floor covered in broken glass.

"Pants?" I say to get her attention. I toss them at her before she turns to look at me. When she does, the pants hit her in the face. I laugh so hard, feeling my lip crack open. The pain is intense and I immediately stop laughing and pull my lip into my mouth. Tears come to my eyes. Allie looks at me sternly, then concentrates on pulling the legs of the pants over my feet with minimal contact. She carefully stretches the elastic around the hem to go over each foot. Once my feet are in, she pulls the elastic waist up my legs, moving herself around to the side of me. She gives my shoulders a shove so I will lie back on the coat.

"Raise your hips," She snaps. I think she is really mad at me until I see her wink. I don't smile because my lip is still pulled in between my teeth, but I raise my hips as she says. She pulls the sweat pants all the way up and lets the elastic snap back to my waist, hoping for a loud thwap. But, the actual sound was nearly nonexistent because the pants are too big.

Allie stands up and reaches down for my combat boots. I'm hoping she's going to slide them back on my feet, but she walks out with them and comes back with pink heart covered house shoes. I am so happy to see those, but at the same time, I feel guilty because I know my bleeding feet will likely ruin them. She helps me put them on before offering to help me up. I hesitate only briefly, then reach up and put my hands in hers. She pulls and I am surprised at how strong she is.

Finally standing, I immediately feel the room spinning. Allie wraps one of my arms around her shoulders and hugs her other arm around my waist. My head feels full of swirling wind and my feet feel like they are stepping on needles. But, we make it to Allie's blue Camaro where the engine is running, the heat is on, and the passenger door is open and waiting. I slide into heaven, adjust the seat back a little, and close my eyes. "I Wanna Have Some Fun" by Samantha Fox is coming through the speakers. Why does she listen to this junk? But, somehow it doesn't ruin the peace I feel inside, knowing that soon I will be far away from here.

By the end of the song, the car shakes as Allie opens the trunk and closes it. I open my eyes and look over as she opens the driver's side door and slides in, tossing a yellow blanket at me. I recognize it as the one from her bed at her Dad's house. She has worn this thing out. I unfold it so that it covers me from my chin to my feet. She looks at me and smiles, but her eyes prove that her mind is somewhere else. The sun comes in through the T-tops and I know I must look a thousand times worse out here than I did in the house. But she doesn't seem to notice.

CHAPTER EIGHT

1986

The snow fell through the night and by Monday morning it was piled higher than my snow boots. It was unlike any April I had seen before. The pine branches were so weighted down with snow they touched the ground. All around me, as far as I could see, everything was still. Nothing moved except an occasional clump of snow falling loose from a tree or a rooftop. I didn't want to ruin the beauty by walking through it, but I knew that being up in those woods would mean becoming a part of it. Nothing could have kept me out of those woods. I set out toward Allie's house.

My boots crunched into the snow with every step. Once I had entered the woods, the beauty around me brought tears to my eyes. I felt I had entered a magical world on another planet. This one was pure and good. I created a story, imagined I had entered it after being called by the inhabitants to save their queen. It had been so easy to get lost in my fantasy. In no time, my hands were jutting up to my forehead and out in a salute. I introduced myself to the trees and declared myself their savior. I reached down and picked up a good sized stick and pretended it was my magical staff. I was excited for Allie to join me.

When I had nearly reached our secret hideout, which was actually a small clearing in the middle of a circle of cedar trees, I saw footprints in the snow coming from the direction of

Allie's house.

In a regal voice I said, "Who has entered the Castle of Jutallia?"

Allie called out from within the circle, "It is I, Princess Allie!"

Just then, a snowball flew between the branches and narrowly missed my head. After it, Allie came darting out and wrapped both arms around me, knocking us both over into the snow. She laughed more than I did, but I tried my best not to laugh at all. I pushed her off of me and onto her back in the snow. I leaned over her, "Oh, it is you. I thought it was Bonkers jumping up on me again. You are so much like your dog."

She gave me a crooked smile and pushed me off so she could get up. We both patted the snow off our clothes. I was in a lot worse shape than Allie because she was wearing purple snow pants and the snow slid right off. I was wearing jeans and three sweaters. Everywhere that wasn't wet was caked with snow. The magic was gone, I started to feel the cold.

"Let's go to your house and warm up," I said.

"No, way, Jute! I just got out here. We should go for a walk and see if anyone else is out down the street."

That thought had seemed more appealing than sitting in Allie's warm house by the fireplace. Lately, she and I had spent a lot of time walking every square inch of a two mile radius around her house. All we needed to do was cross a hill here or there and find ourselves near other kids from our school. Any reason to get out of the house was good on a normal day. But, on a cold day like this, it took thoughts of James Alford to make me want to hike over a hilltop in the snow. I just needed to convince Allie to head in that direction without telling her why.

"Well, Kathy was sick on Friday, so we probably shouldn't go to her house," I said. "Maybe we could walk that way. It would be easier." I pointed down her driveway.

She looked at me suspiciously. "You mean, in the

direction of the place we ran into those boys last week and played basketball in their driveway? James Alford and Travis Keen, those two?"

"Well, basketball in the snow sounds fun."

Allie seemed to ponder this for a while, staring at the clouds in the hazy gray sky. Her eyes followed a couple of sparrows. I began to think she wasn't going to respond at all. But, she finally gave a quick shrug and said, "Ok."

I'm sure our boots together made twice as much crunching in the snow as my pair alone, but I didn't notice it. Allie talked nearly the entire way to James Alford's house. I tried to listen to every word, but it sounded exactly like what she had said yesterday and the day before that. Actually, she hadn't talked about anything except Bobby Inman in months.

According to Allie, Bobby was so cute and handsome and hot. He worshiped the ground she walked on. He called her Princess and Angel. He was going to marry her, and they would lose their virginity together on their wedding night. He was so romantic and she loved kissing him and touching his blond hair. No one had ever loved her so much and no one could ever love her more. Bobby was her Prince Charming. Blah, blah, blah, and on and on.

She stayed lost in her monologue, talking about how close they had come to having sex, how they had already done everything short of actual intercourse. She gave every little detail of those encounters as if it shouldn't bother me at all to hear it. I was relieved when we finally stepped onto James's driveway. Suddenly, she just stopped talking. I gave her a quick look to make sure she wasn't mad at me for not really listening. She didn't seem to notice. Her eyes were looking up the driveway, which was short and steep, ending in a flat area where the basketball goal was attached above the garage. There were tire tracks leading down it and onto the road and beyond our sight.

She leaned in and whispered, "Do you think he's home?"

I wasn't sure why we were whispering, but I kept it up, "I don't know, maybe we should knock."

I turned my head to look at her and was surprised to see her nervousness. Allie could be so paradoxical. One minute she would act like a princess and the next she would be terrified to knock on a door. She didn't say why she was nervous, but I knew she thought all the kids hated her. It wasn't true at all. But, she believed it and that made Bobby Inman even more special.

My arm wrapped around her and pulled her with me up to James's house and pushed the doorbell. I heard the bing-bong inside and I looked over to give her a reassuring smile. I tried not to let on that I had a crush on James. I was still looking at her when the door flew open. I turned to see James standing there in red sweat pants and no shirt. Allie and I both just blinked at him and said nothing. He didn't seem able to speak either.

Finally Allie said, "We were taking a walk in the snow and thought we would see if you wanted to play."

She didn't sound as nervous as I felt. I could barely hear her over my heart beating in my ears. All I could think about was how stupid I had been to suggest going there.

"Sure," he said, stepping aside and swinging his arm toward his living room to invite us in. His older brother, Alex, was on the couch playing Super Mario Bros. That game was awesome. I had wanted it for a long time, but we couldn't afford a Nintendo. I had played it at Kathy's house a couple of times, but not enough to be good at it. Trying not to interrupt Alex, I walked over to the couch and stood quietly off to the side. It was really entertaining to watch his elbows jerk this way and that as he moved the controller. When Kathy and I had played, we hadn't been nearly so animated. Maybe Alex's way was better because he was farther along in the game than we had gotten.

Finally Alex looked up at me as if he knew I was there. He picked up the other control and tossed it in my direction. I watched it land on the couch cushion near me, but I didn't let it sit there long. I snatched it up and sat down where it had landed. I heard Allie and James laugh behind me and I assumed they must be laughing at me and my eagerness to play. But, I heard them laugh now and then while I played the game, so it must be something they were talking about. I tried to focus on what they were saying, but every time I did, I would die in the game. Every time I died in the game, Alex reached over and gave me a punch in the arm. By the third time, I started punching him back. We laughed about it, but I knew we were both punching to cause pain.

Time got lost. The snow was lost. The day was lost. I don't know how long I played that game. When Alex stood up and asked me if I wanted some 7up, I finally remembered where I was. I nodded my head and looked around for a clock. It was already late afternoon and we hadn't had a single snowball fight, unless I counted the one Allie threw at me earlier. I owed her.

"Where's Allie?" I asked Alex when he came back with a tall glass of clear lemon-lime goodness.

He shrugged and sat back down where he had been sitting for hours. He didn't look at me when he said, "She's probably fucking James."

Alex's lips touched the top of his glass before he tipped it up to take a drink. I watched him take two more swigs while the noise in my head swirled to a stop. It must have been confusing to Alex because he looked back at me and said, "What about you? Do you wanna fuck, too?"

I nearly dropped my glass.

"No!" I shouted at him. I felt my face burning and knew he could tell how embarrassed he had made me. I wanted to reach over and punch his arm again, this time hard enough to make him cry. But the thought of touching him at all was terrifying. "We need to go home," I said, as if my parents were waiting in the driveway. But, we both knew they weren't.

I got up and walked down a hallway. All the doors

were closed and I didn't know which was James's room, so I listened. I heard Alex start another game in the living room and knew I wouldn't hear anything over it. So, I started to open every door. First I came to a bathroom on my right, then an office on my left, then on to the next door which was on my left. I turned the knob and flung it open expecting to see a little boy's bedroom. Instead, I saw the master bedroom. Allie was lying on the big bed with her pants off. James was naked on top of her.

I pulled the door shut so quickly that it slammed much harder than I intended. It sounded like an angry slam, but anger wasn't how I felt at that moment. I was confused, overwhelmed, jealous, and scared. I barely had time to register these feelings before I was knocking on the door and steadying my voice to say, "Allie, we need to go now."

Only a few minutes passed before the door swung open again. James had opened it. He smiled at me, beaming, as though he had just scored the winning basket. Then he quickly pushed past me on his way to the bathroom. I stepped into the bedroom to see Allie was dressed, sitting on the bed looking up at me. I could tell she felt all of the things I was, except maybe the jealous part. The sight of her worried expression erased any jealous I had. I wanted to know what happened, but most of all I wanted to get her out of there. I reached out my hand and took hers, pulled her up and we left without saying goodbye. She didn't even put on her coat until we were on the road toward home.

What a difference it had been, the walk home versus the walk to James's house. The snow had started to melt a little and was very slushy under our boots. I tried to stay focused on the sound and wait for Allie to talk. We were almost to her driveway when I gave up waiting.

"So, did you do it?"

Allie didn't look at me and I could barely hear her when she said, "I told him no."

"So, you didn't do it?" I asked, reaching out to touch

63

her arm and stop her from walking. She gently pulled her arm away and looked at the trees beside the road.

"I don't know," she said. "I mean, I told him to stop." She paused, deep in thought, before continuing, "But, he kept going, so I don't know if I'm a virgin anymore. Maybe it doesn't count because he didn't finish, you know, and I didn't bleed. I finally pushed him hard and he got off me, but he had been inside me, and..." Allie still wasn't looking at me, but I could tell she was crying. I reached up to pull her face around to look at me, but she pushed my hand away. I watched her shiver, not a cold shiver, but the kind of shiver I get when Earl is too close to me. I felt like a car had slammed into me. How could I have let this happen to her? How can she ever forgive me? Tears filled my eyes and spilled over onto my cheeks. Neither of us could speak now. It was all I could do not to sob.

Finally, she turned to look at me. When she saw I was crying, she shook her head gently.

"Stop it," she said, and motioned with her hand for me to follow her up the hill. But, she continued to wipe her tears away, so I didn't know why she had said for me to stop.

"I should have knocked sooner," I offered, knowing nothing I said would have made things be the way they were before.

"Jute," she turned to look at me, "Do you think James likes me? Why would he do that if he didn't want to be my boyfriend?"

"I-I don't know..." I replied, confused by her question. "A lot of people like you, Allie. You just never see it."

I watched her face as she reflected on what I had said. The range of emotions I saw in her eyes was innumerable. Predominately, I saw self-loathing. I wanted to put my arms around her, but she had made it clear how uncomfortable that made her. I felt helpless standing there, watching her look right through me. She could only see the things that might come and nothing that already was.

CHAPTER NINE

1990

Allie backs her Camaro up in the yard and heads out onto Allegheny Loop Rd. I reach down to lay the seat back as flat as I can get it. The last thing I want is for someone to recognize me as we drive through Maryville. Allie is singing under her breath to a Samantha Fox song. Thankfully, I don't know the words. I close my eyes and tell myself not to think about what has happened to me. I need to think only good thoughts. Instantly all of my senses remember Allie leaning in close to me and a warmth rushes over me. It's like it is happening now.

Panic soon follows as I try to push the thoughts out of my mind. My arms cross under the blanket and my fingernails scratch at my elbows, trying to make pain to override the tingling. Before I know it, my fingernails break the skin and now my body is feeling every cut and bruise.

I keep my eyes closed and think about the time Allie and I performed in the eighth grade talent show. We lip synced to "Wild Boys" by Duran Duran. I dressed like Simon Le Bon in fake leather pants and Allie dressed like a dystopian woman with big paper wings. She danced around me, smashing post-apocalyptic props. The best part of that was making her costume. We had ripped up bed sheets and wrapped them around her in every imaginable way until we got it just right. After I sewed it together, we took it outside and threw it in the dirt and stomped all over it. I still can't believe I talked her into that, but I'm glad I did.

I turn my head to look at her, but can't see much with my seat laid back all the way. I want to ask if she remembers that show, but at the same time I don't want to talk at all. The distance between us feels so heavy and impregnable.

I have no idea where she is taking me. She has no idea what I've been through. Neither of us ask. Yet, here we are stuck together unless she decides to throw me out. I don't know why this makes me chuckle.

"What's so funny?" She says, and reaches up to adjust the rear view mirror so she can see me.

"You might need that to drive, maybe?"

"Well, it's hard to see you all the way in the back seat," she smirks. "By the way, I'm taking you to Shawn's house so we can clean you up. He's at work, so don't worry. We should get through Maryville without anyone seeing you and calling the truancy police."

"I can make it to your mom's house. I'll be fine."

"Actually, right now you look like a train wreck. You should be glad I'm not driving you to the hospital. If I had any brains, we'd be headed there now."

"Right, you are such a ditz." I roll my eyes. She graduated half a year early, of course she has brains.

Her eyes are full of pity when she looks at me in the rear view mirror. I wish she would look at the road instead. I worry she will drive off the road and into a tree. I'm already anxious enough.

"Damn it!" I sit the seat up and push the rear view mirror back into a position that looks right. Allie adjusts it a little more.

I look at her and realize I'm not the only one looking a little worse for wear and tear. If she looks this filthy from trying to wake me up, I really don't want to see myself in the sunlight.

"You look like you fell off the back of a hay wagon," I say, trying to tease. But, I feel so guilty. "I'm sorry about your dress."

Her mouth tightens a little and she shrugs. I've seen her do that so many times and it usually ends with tears pouring out over her cheeks. But thankfully, she keeps her eyes on the road. Her hand reaches over and squeezes my hand, then she lets her hand rest in mine. Every bit of heat left in me rushes to that connection. I feel like I'm spinning, which makes it impossible to concentrate. I pull my hand free and casually wipe my hands on the blanket, then tuck them under it. I pull the blanket up to my chin again and sit there like a big yellow potato sack. I should put the seat down again, but I don't.

"Are you cold?" She asks, adjusting the heat. "It's supposed to snow later. Most of it should land north of here. Hopefully we can get out of here before it starts."

The road Shawn lives on is riddled with switchbacks and blind curves. This road has never bothered me before, but my head is already dizzy. By the time she pulls up his gravel driveway, my fingers are squeezing the arm rest. All I can think of is keeping my head still.

She gets out and runs over and opens my door, reaches down to help lift my legs out. Her arms wrap around me and she pulls me up to a stand. Sharp pains stab at my soles. We walk quickly to the front door. Ally shoves a key in the lock and two seconds later we are walking in the living room.

Shawn's double wide is amazing. Everything inside is so modern compared to Earl's trailer. This one smells like eucalyptus and a hint of motor oil.

The walls are covered with Home Interiors decor. Shawn's mom sells it. Everywhere I look there are fake flowers, candle holders, and potpourri jars. The bathroom wallpaper is covered with delicate swirls of pearly white, baby blue, and pink, like dancing brush strokes. The tub is the biggest one I've ever seen. The sound of the water rushing into it fills me with anticipation.

Allie leans over the tub to get the water just right while I sit on the toilet lid and wait. When the tub is filled, she says,

"I'm leaving while you bathe. I have to get some things to bandage you up. I won't be gone long."

She can tell I don't like the idea, but she leaves anyway. I hear her car backing over the gravels outside as I get undressed.

The water is almost too warm. I add a little more cold to it, worrying about my pink fingers and toes. They are no longer tingling and the feeling has mostly returned. I slip into the water quickly and raise my feet back up to rest on the edge of the tub. The pain of submerging them is intense, but slowly I work at it until they are under. The water turns gray and opaque with dirt. It looks like one bath may not be enough. I gently go over my body with a washcloth, then let the water go down the drain.

It hurts to stand on my feet, but I do it any way. I turn on the shower so I can rinse the dirty water off of me. I finally start to feel clean. I let the water run over my body until all the hot water runs out. The ice cold water hurts in a way that distracts me from my other pain. I stand in it as long as I can.

Giving in, I turn off the faucet and step out onto a towel. I don't want my feet to bleed on the rug. I dry off before spreading two more towels on the floor. I lie down, hoping I will be able to fall asleep and forget what I have been through. The heater is whirring above me and I feel safe. I drift in and out of nightmares, never sleeping long enough to die in them.

I am startled awake by the sound of the front door shutting. I stand and flip the heater off. My tongue is prepared to call out to Allie. But I recognize Shawn's voice. Is he with Allie or alone? I should call out to him and let him know I'm here. But, before I can speak, I hear the sound of a woman laughing. It's not Allie.

What a piece of shit.

But, what can I do when I'm naked and trespassing in his house? He could easily take this towel I'm wrapped in and throw me out. As bad as I hate to do it, I grab my pile of dirty clothes and put them on again. My mind avoids thinking about the smell of wood smoke which saturates them.

The sound of Shawn's voice drifts clearly into the bathroom from the kitchen.

"Would you like a drink?"

The woman giggles. "I wanna see your bedroom."

By the sound of their movements, I know they are kissing. The thought of it causes a pang of guilt because Allie is going to be inconsolable when she sees them. As much as I want Shawn to be revealed as the lowlife he is, the truth will crush her. She believes Shawn is safe because he is not what most women go after. Allie chooses pathetic boys in hopes they will never see her flaws. She is blinded by the magnifying glass she keeps on herself. She completely misses the blatant narcissism of the jerks she dates. Allie is about to learn, again, that ugly boys break hearts, too.

I don't have shoes, and I know I'm going to track blood across his carpet, but I step out of the bathroom anyway. My heart is racing, but I am careful to stay quiet. I reach the end of the hall where I see Shawn at the kitchen table. His back is to me. He is naked except for his pants around his ankles. His back is covered with acne and his hair is greasy. The girl's legs are around him as she lies back on the table. I can't see her face, but I hear her sighs getting louder with each thrust of Shawn's hips.

I fight the urge to stab him in his tiny heart. I don't move for fear I will be unable to control myself if I start to lash out. I have so much anger and pain inside of me. I want to make him pay for it all, even the parts that don't belong to him. But, I may truly kill him.

The sound of wheels on gravel hits my ears before it hits Shawn's. He is grunting and thrusting harder, slamming the table into the wall beside it. He groans as his body shakes. The woman screams in ecstasy. Shawn leans his body on top of hers and they giggle and kiss.

My fists are clenched so hard that my fingernails are digging into my flesh.

Shawn starts to reach for his pants as Allie pushes the door open. She walks into the kitchen just in time to see what I can't from my angle, the face of the naked woman on the table.

Everything Allie was carrying falls out of her hands and is now scattered on the floor.

The woman sees her and quickly sits up to get dressed, spying me as well. She looks older than us, maybe thirty. Her face is red and angry. She keeps her eyes down while she pulls on her dress and buttons it up.

Allie stands there with her mouth open, shaking her head slowly in disbelief.

"What the hell are you two doing here?" Shawn screams at Allie and only barely looks at me. As much as I want to punch him, there is no doubt that now is the time to run. The rage in me is so fierce that I can barely control it.

I dart past Shawn and stoop to gather up the bags Allie had dropped. Standing up, I grab her wrist and try to pull her to the door. She won't budge.

"Come on!" I demand, "Let it go, Allie. You are finally seeing the real Shawn Reynolds. You don't deserve this jackass, and I'm so pissed that I'm about to kill him."

But she stays still, just looking at him in disbelief. It's as if I am not even there.

The woman starts screaming at Shawn, "You said you broke up with her! You lied to me, you bastard!" She is looking up from the kitchen chair where she sits, struggling to buckle the straps on her high heel shoe.

Shawn ignores her just like Allie is ignoring me. His face is redder than ever as he makes his way over to her. His eyes are full of rage. This is what I expected, but I'm not sure what Allie was hoping for by waiting. He reaches down and grabs her keys, twisting them free from her clenched fist and causing her to gasp in pain. He quickly removes his house key and slams the key ring back into her hand. Allie's face is drowning in tears, and she begins to sob uncontrollably. Her arms go up as if to embrace him. I can not understand this at all. He knocks her arms to the side, away from him. Allie turns away, wailing with emotional pain.

I can't take it. I draw back and punch him below his left eye. I follow quickly with my left fist to his ear. He stumbles only a little. I know he's going to punch me back any minute. I grab Allie around the waist and drag her toward the door. She seems to snap out of her shocked state, pulls free from me and runs ahead. Outside, snow is falling heavily from a dark gray sky. It is beautiful and menacing. We have so far to go.

By the time I reach her car, Allie has already started it and has put it in reverse. I jump in quickly and she slams the gas pedal down before I can grab my seatbelt. The wheels kick up rocks and my head slams forward, nearly hitting the dash. Allie, puts the Camaro in drive and we speed dangerously down Shawn's driveway.

When we finally reach asphalt, the car seems eerily silent. Many minutes pass before she says, "Sorry," a delayed apology for nearly knocking me out on the dash.

"I'm okay." I say, trying to keep my voice steady. The adrenaline still has me shaking all over.

CHAPTER TEN

We head south on Highway 411 in silence. I don't ask why we aren't driving toward Knoxville. I don't talk about Shawn. I don't ask how she feels. I want to ask. I want to reach over and touch her shoulder to comfort her. I want to hold her hand the way she did mine just hours ago. But, I am not Allie. She is not me. Every time I have tried to help her, I hurt her instead.

The snow is still coming down heavily, accumulating on the grass and trees. It reminds me of the snowy day Allie lost her virginity with James. Bobby lived too far away to find out about it, but everyone at our school knew. Boys came out of the woodwork to flirt with her. Allie was suddenly the girl boys wanted and for the first time she believed she was pretty.

She had asked me if James had sex with her because he liked her. I didn't have an answer for her at the time. But, the answer was no. None of those boys know anything about Allie Vining. Watching them touch her in the hallway and the classroom made me so angry. I finally tried to talk to her about it. But, it sounded like I was jealous.

We had our biggest argument that June. But, it only took three days until she came to my house. She wanted to talk to me privately. On the walk to the woods, she told me she was afraid Bobby would find out about James. She said he had told her that if she didn't bleed when they finally had sex that there would be trouble. Allie knew she wouldn't bleed. She didn't even bleed when she had sex with James. It never occurred to her that Bobby was a dumbass and not worth her tears. All she could think about was how she was damaged now.

A few days later I followed Bobby's screaming into the woods. I got close enough to see them. Allie was begging him to believe she had told James to stop but he wouldn't. Bobby called her a whore and a slut. I had watched him pull her dress open in a rage and yank her bra up over her breasts. He bent his head and bit her repeatedly. She had sobbed and winced but didn't tell him to stop.

I had looked around for a large stick to bash his brains in, but part of me was terrified she would hate me. I was so conflicted that I couldn't move. I hoped she would push him away and it would finally be over between them. But, she didn't. She just stood there sobbing and pulling down her bra while Bobby unzipped his pants. He had seemed calm until he grabbed her and pinned her face down on the ground. He had thrown her skirt up around her waist and jerked her panties to the side. Bobby entered her so violently I thought she would most certainly rip. But, Allie had gone silent. As he continued thrusting into her, she began to sigh with pleasure. She encouraged him to keep going. Her voice was shaky and awkward. I knew she was faking because she sounded like my sister when she was with Earl.

I had ran, blinded by tears. I had failed to stop her from being raped again. But even now, Allie won't call it rape. She believes Bobby did what he did because she really is trash, ruined because she is no longer a virgin and can never be desired for anything but sex.

When I punched Shawn this morning, I finally felt some relief from my guilt. But, thinking about all this now brings tears to my eyes again. I feel useless in this passenger seat, broken down. This morning Allie tried to drive me to my safety and ended up in so much of her own pain. I'm a coward for not reaching over to her. I don't even turn my head to look at her.

"You deserve so much better, Allie."

She sniffs and I know she is crying. I wish I hadn't brought it up again. I reluctantly turn to look at her. She is wringing the steering wheel with both hands and trying to focus on the road through her tears.

"I'm sorry all this happened. You wouldn't have been there if it wasn't for me."

"I would have found out sooner or later." She sighs and shakes her head. "Jute, do you ever just get sick of yourself?"

"No. Especially not because of a stupid boy. The only thing you should be sick of is letting them treat you like shit."

"What's that supposed to mean?"

"It means you don't expect anyone to like you for more than sex, and as long as you keep thinking that, no one will treat you right." As soon as I say it, as truthful as it feels to me, I know it will hit Allie's ears as an insult.

Her mouth tightens, but she says nothing. Finally I give up and look back to my window.

She turns on the radio and I realize just how long we've driven in silence. As she turns up the volume, I hear "Rio" by Duran Duran and nearly laugh out loud. I look over and see Allie wink at me.

"I called the radio station and requested it just for you," She says sweetly, batting her eye lashes.

"Right. Because you have an invisible car phone connected to your thought waves. Hey, can you call in and request John Lennon's 'Mind Games' next?"

"Even better, I'll sing it!" She turns the radio off and begins crooning and squealing out the lyrics.

"Stop! Oh, God, Allie, what the hell?"

"Come on Jute, sing it with me…"

And I do, loudly, trying to drown out whatever she is doing, which isn't singing. Eventually she gets quiet and I finish the the rest of the song.

"That was amazing. Sing it again."

"No. Not until you tell me where we are going."

"I haven't figured that out yet. But when I do, I'll have

them announce it to you on the radio."

This time she gives me a full smile and I know we have officially forgotten that the world is falling apart.

"I'm starving," Allie declares. Now that she has brought it up, my stomach growls. I turn on the radio.

We pass over the Tennessee/Georgia line and pull into a gas station. Normally, I would pump the gas for her, but I'm not wearing shoes. She walks into the gas station, still wearing the dirty sage green party dress. She and I both look like a bad horror movie. At least she isn't beat up.

She comes back carrying a brown bag and two bottles of Fanta Grape soda. She opens the door and tosses the bag in the driver's seat and leans in to hand me the sodas. While she pumps gas, I sit in the car smelling the delicious scent of country sausage. My stomach rolls with hunger. I try to remember the last time I ate anything. It was the cottage cheese Jerry had bought yesterday. That seems like a lifetime ago.

As Allie gets into the car, she picks up the brown bag so she won't sit on it. She tosses the bag into my lap and slides into her seat. She slips off her high heels before she even shuts her door. Small flakes of snow are falling outside, but nothing like it had been in Maryville.

We pull back onto Highway 411. She turns the radio down so I can hear her. "Can you hand me one of those sausage biscuits? The lady in there says she makes them at home before she comes to work. They were buy one get one free because it's almost noon. I got two for each of us. You don't have to eat them both now if you don't feel like it. But, at least try to eat a few bites."

She always tells me things aren't expensive so I won't feel bad about taking it. It doesn't work. I hand her one and try not to act too eager as I get one for myself. Allie puts in a mixed tape of her favorite songs and we eat without talking until we finish.

"I have an idea! Let's go all the way to the ocean!"

"What?" My jaw drops.

"Well, we can't go north because of the snow storm, so let's go to Myrtle Beach. It will give us time to come up with a plan."

"A plan for what? Did we just rob a bank? Besides, you already have a plan. You are going to work for your mom in Ohio. There is your plan. And we really don't need to talk about my situation."

"Then we'll make it our plan not to talk about plans. We'll just go to see the ocean and to forget Tennessee for a while." She squeezes my hand, but quickly lets go to put it back on the steering wheel. I settle back into the passenger seat and look at her from the corner of my eye. She is smiling and her eyes are full of joy. I don't know what she has to be joyful about, but I'm glad to see it. I close my eyes as Allie turns up the radio a little to drown out the road noise.

CHAPTER ELEVEN

The key chain is a Kelly green diamond slab of plastic. There is a big white number 627 on one side. It was the only thing I was allowed to carry, and we are lucky to have it. Hurricane Hugo really tore up the town last September. We managed to find an ocean front hotel still open. Allie said the room was surprisingly inexpensive because there aren't many tourists this time of year. Maybe that is true, or maybe she doesn't want me to feel ashamed that I can't help her pay for it. She is outside gathering some things from her car. She insisted I take the key and go on to the room.

I am in the elevator now, wearing my combat boots again. Every inch of my soles throbs in pain. I close my eyes and try to suppress it, knowing I'll be in the room soon. The elevator dings and the door opens. I start to exit but realize this isn't my floor.

A guy steps on the elevator and pushes the six, which is already lit up from when I pushed it. He is tall and thin, but I can't discern if he is a teenager or an adult. His dark brown hair is long and curly and he's wearing a Guns-n-Roses t-shirt, which isn't exactly a grown-up style. Maybe he's a musician or just likes dressing like one.

He leans his back against the wall opposite me and stares unflinchingly into my eyes. His face is too pretty for a boy. His thick eyebrows draw my gaze to his deep set eyes, which are nearly the identical shade of blue as Allie's. He seems naturally dangerous and I feel a bit envious.

I've never been the kind of person to divert my eyes from strangers when they stare. Usually, staring back at them makes them look away. Usually, however, I don't look like I've been attacked by a bear. Still, I refuse to come across as weak, so I lock my eyes onto his.

"What happened to you?" His voice is unexpectedly deep. His expression is one of curiosity, not judgment. The question makes me wish I could disappear. I try not to show it.

"Nothing that's going to happen twice." I keep my voice calm and indifferent.

The elevator dings and the doors open. I wait, wanting him to get out first. But he sweeps his hand out in a gesture for me to go. I don't, so the doors begin to close. He reaches out and stops them with his hand. He looks back at me confused but unrelenting.

"This is your stop?"

"Yeah."

I hesitate only a minute more before I give in and begin to walk past him. He steps out behind me. I clench my teeth and try to focus on walking as if I'm not in pain. I hear his steps getting closer and I start to panic. I brace myself for the worst.

"Hey!" he calls out, jogging a few steps to catch up. He puts his hand on my shoulder to stop me and leans over to look at my face. "Are you okay? I mean, if you need somebody wiped off the face of the Earth, I know some people who might know some people." Not only is he not smiling, but he is looking at me like he means it. I guess that is what makes it so funny and I have to laugh.

"Sure, have your people call my people," I say, annoyed. He smiles, but his eyes are still worried. This guy is extremely weird.

"I'm Tracy." He puts his hand out.

"What kind of name is Tracy?"

"It's my name and my Dad's name. I'm Tracy Duren the third, actually. And you don't have to tell me your name, but I'd like to know it."

He puts his outstretched hand down when he realizes I'm not going to shake it. I regret that I didn't.

"My name is Jute Martin."

"What kind of name is Jute?" he mimics me.

"Strangely similar to your story, I was named after my mom. But, I hated it. I insisted she call me Jute instead. She had it changed legally five years ago."

"See, I knew you were interesting. I haven't seen many interesting people around here lately. You should come watch me play open mic tonight. It's just downstairs in the lounge. Ten o'clock."

"Is that why you followed me up here?"

"Uh, no. I wasn't following you. I have a room on this floor. My dad owns the hotel and I live here until I come up with an escape plan," he pauses, smiling nervously, "I used to live with my mom before she was remarried, but her new husband thinks I'm a creep and won't let me stay there."

"Lucky you," I sound sarcastic, but I mean it. Creepy is something I work hard to be.

"Are your parents here?" He looks around as if they are going to pop into this empty hallway from some other universe. I wonder how old he thinks I am. He could very likely believe I'm twelve. That would mean his level of creepiness exceeds my comfort zone.

As if on cue, the elevator dings. Allie steps into the hallway carrying her suitcase in one hand while her arms struggles to hold onto a very familiar box. I can't believe what I'm seeing. That's the box she stole from Earl's house. Only, he stole it back. So, how does she have it? Rage lights up my face. With all my might, I try to calm myself and wait for an explanation.

Tracy is looking from me to her. Allie walks toward us, smiling weakly as if she knows what I'm thinking. She barely even looks at Tracy, keeping her eyes locked on mine. It is so hard to be angry with her, but I am.

She sets her suitcase down at my feet so she can hold the box with two hands. It's the one filled with my worn out clothes. Allie smiles at me like she is giving me a present. She looks dirty and poor, with my blood still on the shoulder of her dress. I just can not be angry, but my apprehension is nearly overwhelming.

"You made a friend," she says almost like a question, looking at Tracy and then back to me.

Tracy seems a little uneasy. I almost feel sorry for him, but at the same time I think he's lucky to be on the outside of this looking in.

"I don't know, Allie, I think you might be scaring him off." I playfully push Tracy off balance. He catches his footing and finally stops gawking at Allie.

"Well, I'll go, then. Is this our room?" She points to the door behind me.

"No, our room is that way. I just walked this way to throw this guy off my trail."

"Great job, Jute," She teases, "I send you up here ahead of me so you can be off your feet. But, instead you decide to take a walk up and down the hallway."

"But, what if he had plans to kill me?"

"No one is going to kill you because I've taken care of all that." Her eyes lock onto mine long enough for me to see there is something behind what she just said. But, she seamlessly moves on. "I'm going to the room now since you aren't going to introduce him to me."

She takes the key chain out of my hand and looks at the number. She picks up her suitcase and turns to head down the hall behind her.

I call out, "His name is Tracy!"

She doesn't turn around, "Nice to meet you, Tracy. I'm Allie, the normal one!"

I watch her the entire way, knowing I should follow her. But, I want her to worry that I won't. I also don't want Tracy to see my limping again. Maybe if I stand here long enough he will go away. After a few seconds of not hearing any footsteps, I take a deep breath and turn to look at him. He is painfully attractive, which is not the issue I wanted to address. I can't even remember what I was going to say.

"So..." he begins, then stops and looks at me as if I already have the rest of the words.

"So...?"

"Don't you need to be in bed?" He asks, looking in the direction of our room.

He waits for me to answer, but after a few minutes of silence he gives up. He bends down, picks me up over his shoulder and starts walking down the hall. Fifteen minutes ago, this would have gotten him punched. But now it just makes me feel weak, which makes me angry for an entirely different reason. I squirm around in protest, but I don't truthfully want him to put me down.

When we get to room 627, he lets me down in front of him and knocks on the door.

Allie calls out, "I'm changing, wait just a second."

I can't hear anything except Tracy breathing, standing so close to me that I can feel his chest rising and falling against my back. I wish he didn't seem like such a nice guy. I don't need the guilt when he realizes I'm not what he thinks I am.

Allie opens the door. She is wearing a silky floral robe pulled tight around her. I'm sure she thinks this is appropriate to wear around strange men, but it isn't.

"I thought you were getting dressed." I walk past her into the room and hear Tracy walk in behind me. Why won't he go away?

"I'm fine, Jute. Mind your own clothes." It's the same dialog we've had a hundred times. I often complain because I think Allie dresses too sexy. In response, she tells me to mind my own business. I should listen to her, because I can't seem to reason with her.

I sit down on the bed and start unlacing my boots. Allie walks over and helps pull them off. I wince and suck air

81

through my clenched teeth. I think some of the cuts pulled open again. Allie lifts each of my feet and looks closely at different areas on the soles.

"You're going to need to wash them again, Jute. You have more dirt in the wounds, probably from Shawn's driveway and wearing your boots again. I'll go run a bath, okay?"

She doesn't wait for an answer. She runs to the bathroom to start the water. Why is she running now? It has been twelve hours since she found me on the floor of my house. She walks out of the bathroom as the tub continues to fill and heads over to her suitcase. It is laying open on the bed beside Tracy. She chooses the dress on top, which is a pink and orange color block shift dress from the 60's.

"Tracy, can you go watch that and turn it off when it gets high enough?"

He nods and walks in that direction.

"Don't let it get too hot!"

When he is in the bathroom, Allie turns away from me and lets her robe fall off into the floor.

"I have to go find a magnifying glass so I can get your splinters out. Maybe there will be one in the gift shop. If not, I'll need to find a nearby store. Will you be okay here with him? I can ask him to get the hell out of here if you want."

Her last sentence is muffled as she pulls the dress on over her head. Once it's on, she walks over to the bed and sits down with her back to me. She holds up her hair in a heaping pile of ringlets. I zip her dress, amazed at how quickly she can go from looking poor to glamorous.

"He's fine," I say, watching her slip on her high heels. I hope he's fine.

"Well, if he isn't, just punch him like you did Shawn," she smiles into the mirror over the dresser. After applying a thick layer of rosy pink lipstick and rubbing her lips together, she turns and walks over to me again. She leans down and puts her lips to my forehead, making an obnoxious kissing sound.

Her hair falls over my face and it smells like wood smoke from my house and a little like sweat.

"You need a bath, Allie." I give her a gentle push on her shoulders to get her away from me.

"Shut up." Her voice is playfully indifferent. She waves over her shoulder as she walks out the door.

CHAPTER TWELVE

I close my eyes and try to slow my heartbeat. I hear the tub faucet being turned off, the sound of the running water comes to a stop. Tracy steps back into the room and looks around, probably for Allie. When he realizes she has left, he looks at me nervously.

"Do you need help getting in there?" he asks. He starts walking toward me as if he already knows the answer. I hate feeling pitied.

"I'm fine," I say, and begin to slide my feet to the edge of the bed.

Tracy quickly leans down and grabs my ankles to stop me. His eyes linger on the soles of my feet and I watch as he studies them. I can't read his thoughts, but I realize I have been holding my breath as I try.

"They're not too bad," he says, looking up at me, but not letting go of my ankles.

He sits beside me on the bed. I know he can do anything he wants to me and I couldn't stop him. Surprisingly, this thought does not make me nervous. I can't explain why, but it has something to do with how perfect he looks. His hair, his eyes, his skin, his body, his kindness, his wit, everything I have seen so far has been so perfect. No one like him would be interested in me that way. He seems curious about my story, which is admittedly odd. But, sexually, I'm sure I fall way off his radar. He is staring at me as if he's waiting for me to say something, but nothing comes to mind.

"Okay," he says, standing back up, "Let's go."

He bends down and scoops me up, groaning like he can barely carry my weight. I know from past experience that he is faking the struggle. He pretends to stumble in the bathroom and sits me down on the sink cabinet as if saving me from falling out of his arms. He laughs at his comedic act and it's contagious.

There is a mirror behind me, but I am avoiding it. I want off the counter, but I don't really want my bare feet on the bathroom floor.

"Can you throw another towel down, so I don't have to stand on the floor?" I ask him, sounding more demanding than I intended.

"Anything for you," He sounds sincere, but I know it's sarcasm. He tosses down a white towel. "Is there anything else I can help you with? Maybe getting you out of those deplorable clothes?" He raises one eyebrow and smiles at me, but he does not seem to be flirting. I must be stupid, but I let him pull my tank top over my head. I realize a bit too late that I am not wearing a bra and I fight the urge to cross my arms over my breasts. I tell myself they are too small to be of any interest to him.

I watch his eyes as he looks at my naked skin, not lingering in any one place, but glancing at all the scratches on my arms and the cuts on my chest from the broken glass. I know this is the story he wants to know about. His eyes are hungry for answers. But, I don't feel like thinking about it. I just focus on what he is doing right now and try to let that override any thoughts about last night.

Tracy puts his hands on the waistband of the sweat pants I have been wearing. I raise myself up so he can slide them over my hips. He pulls them down slowly, as if the information is too much and may overwhelm him. My legs are covered in scratches, many more than are on my feet, but not as deep. There are welts from where limbs slapped my legs and scratches from thorns. The florescent light in the room seems to magnify the contrast between what is injured and what is not. I look down and see that I am still wearing Allie's purple lace panties. They are certainly the only visually pleasant thing about me. I keep staring down at them, but my eyes go out of focus. I am avoiding looking at Tracy's eyes again. But, I do see his right hand touch the waistband of his pants, his fingers dip behind it and down into his pants. A panic rises in me, but subsides when I see him pull out a rolled up plastic bag.

"This should help," he says, not looking into my eyes. His head stays down as he unrolls the bag of pot and sits it on the counter. His face is focused as he opens it to roll a joint. I stare at him, his perfect skin and hair making me feel incredibly flawed in contrast.

In the past, I have smoked pot a few times at parties. It has never affected me much. Allie becomes so uptight when she's around it. Every time she would see me smoking pot, she would get a look of disappointment on her face. After not feeling much effect, I gave up on it. I started getting drunk instead, which Allie didn't like any better. But, at least I was less aware of her opinion when I was drunk than when I was failing to get high. I feel guilty for thinking this way about her now, knowing how hard she tries to help me. But, I don't feel guilty enough to turn down the joint.

Tracy lights it and takes a hit. The smell is sickeningly sweet, earthy, and familiar. He passes the joint to me and I take a small hit and hold it in briefly, watching him lean in toward my face, his eyes on my lips. I exhale and he breathes deeply, inhaling the smoke. He takes the joint from my hand and puts it to his lips, so close to mine now. I watch the tip smolder as he sucks air through the joint. My mouth opens slightly, waiting for him to breathe out the smoke so I can breathe it in. He leans forward, his lips covering mine, and gently pushes the smoke into my mouth. I breathe in the warmth, feeling the room spin. I am afraid to move.

He stands up straight and hands the joint to me. I reach for it slowly, trying to be very still so he won't see me shaking.

His voice is so deep, "You need to get in the bath before your water gets cold. Besides, I have a show to get ready for."

I exhale the smoke in his direction and say, "It isn't a show. It's open mic."

"I'm the only one who ever shows up," he says, taking the joint from my hand and tapping it out on the sink. "Last week I played for three hours. I'd call that a show, wouldn't you?"

He puts his hands on my hips and starts to pull down my panties. I raise my hips to let him slide them off. He is so careful not to hurt my wounds.

"Then maybe I'll show up, too. I can sing," I say. I hear myself giggling. I am not a giggler, not even on pot… normally.

Tracy moves beside me, very close, and puts one arm around my shoulders and reaches his other arm under my knees. He lifts me up and turns to lower me into the bath.

"You realize I am 17, not 12, right?" I ask. Laughter pours out of me, despite the voice in my head telling me I sound ridiculous.

He is laughing, too. "Well, you should realize I really am 12 and you are a very bad influence."

"You, sir, are a horrible liar." I can't stop giggling. I think I liked pot better when it had no effect. I try to stop laughing, but trying to stop laughing is oddly hilarious. I finally get serious again when Tracy pulls off his shirt. I have to catch my breath.

"You are so beautiful," I say. I reach up to put my hand over his heart because I know I can hear it pounding in my ears.

He takes my hand away, kisses the palm, and puts it back into the water. I am immersed in the sound of his beating heart filling up the entire room. Maybe it isn't his heart, maybe it is mine. Maybe it is both. I feel him start to wash my feet. He is holding my right foot and gently going over it with a washcloth. Every move he makes echoes, sound waves rippling in my ears. He looks as focused as a hawk as he stares at the sole of my foot. I'm pretty sure he doesn't even know I'm attached to that foot. I let him go over it again and again with the washcloth. I enjoy the sound it makes.

Eventually I say, "I actually have two of those."

I expect my words will startle him out of his daze. But, he doesn't change his expression at all. He just lets my foot down into the water. He adds soap to the washcloth and picks up my left one. A sharp pain shoots through my body when he touches the ball of my foot under my big toe. I suck in air every time he passes over it. The sounds from my lips echo and add to the symphony of sounds in the room.

His eyes are on mine now. I think he is trying to see if he is hurting me. I think about how I feel. I am weightless and thirsty. All this water in the tub but I can't drink it. I stop watching Tracy wash me and close my eyes.

Time doesn't exist again until Allie opens the bathroom door. My eyes fly open to see Tracy sitting on the sink counter, his shirt still off, smoking the rest of the joint. I quickly glance at Allie and I immediately know what is going to come out of her mouth. Here we go.

"What are you doing?" She screams at Tracy.

"Smoking weed," he says, exhaling away from her, but not diverting his eyes.

"Are you trying to get us kicked out of here? What if someone smells that and reports it to the front desk? What if we get arrested? Are you crazy?" Allie's face is bright red and she keeps screaming. I should point out that right now she looks like the crazy one. I try to keep my laugh on the inside.

"My dad owns the hotel." Tracy's voice is so deep and soothing. I'm interested to see how long Allie maintains her rage.

Her mouth opens to speak, but stops. She just stands there with it open for a while, processing what he just said. Finally, I see her relax a little. She looks down at me in the tub. I realize my water is freezing. I don't know how long I've been in here. I should get out, but I don't think my arms and legs will work. I feel like they are so far away from me.

"Come on." She yanks a towel off the towel bar and holds it open so I can step out in privacy. I don't think it's necessary at this point. A laugh escapes me before I can stop it.

"I got this," Tracy says as he reaches down and picks me up out of the tub the same way he put me in. I am dripping tub water all over the bathroom, into the hotel room, and all over the bed where he plops me down in the same place I started. He falls into bed beside me, then props up on his elbow. He is staring at my face, all over my face. I want him to stop.

"Can you hold the magnifying glass while I get her splinters out?"

Allie saves the day again. Tracy can't stare at my face if he's staring at my feet. He slides to the foot of the bed and kneels down beside Allie. I feel her touching my feet. Certain things she does causes me to cry out, but I quickly fall back into weightlessness. I feel my body stretching out over the whole state of South Carolina.

"Okay," I hear her say, "I think that will do it for now."

The room comes into focus and I look down at Allie. She is looking at me in a way I haven't seen her look at me before. Maybe it's the pot. Or maybe it's that I'm naked, which suddenly bothers me. I feel my brain screaming that this is awkward, logically, but I can't seem to decide what to do about it. I reach my hands up to cover my face, suppressing a giggle at how much this solution fails.

I feel Tracy touching my legs. His fingers draw short, gentle lines. I guess he is following my scratches. I hear him ask Allie what happened. Off in some far away part of my body, this makes me angry. He should ask me, not her. I pull my hands away from my face to see Allie gently shaking her head at him. She isn't going to say. She always does the right thing. Sometimes I doubt her, but she comes through every time. No one in the world loves me except Allie. She is all I have, but so much more than I deserve.

"I love you," I say to her, my voice echoing around the room. She doesn't respond, not even her eyes. Maybe I didn't actually say it.

"I need to go," Tracy says. "I'll have the kitchen send up some drinks and a pizza. I hope you two can make it to the show."

"It's not a -" I stop because I realize I'm still not actually saying anything.

"Jute can't walk, Tracy," Allie is being a bit snide. I wish she wouldn't.

"There are wheelchairs downstairs. I'll send one up. You can wheel her down."

"Wheel me down!" This time I'm sure I spoke because they both laugh.

"Fine, send it up. If I can get her to act human I'll bring her down."

CHAPTER THIRTEEN

The pizza is the fourth of July in my mouth. I am on my third slice and have downed half a two-liter of soda. Allie is staring at me, looking worried. It annoys me, which means I must not be as high as I was.

"Are you ready to get dressed?" She asks.

She has taken a shower and put on a 60's mini-dress with baby blue and white swirls of paisley all over it. I've been staring at it while I eat. I am still naked, wrapped in a towel. I don't want to be, but I am afraid to wear my clothes because I have to get them out of that box.

"Are you ready to tell me how you got my clothes back from Earl?" I sound like I'm mocking her. I wish I didn't sound so mean.

"I drove up and took them out of his truck."

"That was so stupid!" I feel like I'm swimming toward anger, but can't get there. We should not have this conversation right now.

"Guess what else?" Her eyebrow is raised and she is smiling an evil crooked smile. "The door to his trailer was left wide open. He was passed out on the couch with something in his hand."

"What was it?" I don't know if I want her to answer. Just imagining this actually happening is making me nauseous.

Allie reaches into the box and pulls out my panties, the ones Earl pulled off of me.

"We can't let him keep these, can we?" She is laughing

with pride and vengeance. A tornado of emotions rips at my mind and I can't stop the tears running down my face. I am terrified for her, envious of her strength, grateful, and in awe. But, I can't find any words at all.

She sits beside me and hugs me close to her. "Stop crying, it was nothing. Now, let's get ready and do something fun,"

She reaches down into the box, then holds up my Misfits t-shirt. It's the one she hates, but she is smiling now. I guess she's trying to make up for screaming about the pot and for upsetting me now.

"That shirt isn't worth what you risked to get it," I say.

"I know, but just put it on and try to enjoy it. I'd hate to think you smoked pot just to give me mean looks all night. By the way, I bought you some underwear while I was out," she walks over to her shopping bags and tosses one at me.

"Please tell me they aren't itchy purple lace," I say, looking warily at her sparkling blue eyes. I brace myself for the sight of something audacious. When I open the bag, I'm pleasantly surprised. I pull out a cheetah print bra and matching panties. I love it, and I never thought I'd feel that way about underwear. I don't say any of this aloud because it makes me feel ashamed. I just rip off the tags and put them on.

"Go look in the mirror," she says.

I feel reluctant, but obligated. I walk in front of the floor length mirror and slowly force my eyes to look at my reflection. Instead of me, for a brief second, I see the corpse from the woods. I turn away, but I still see it in my mind. I have to reach out for the wall to steady myself. My heart is racing. I feel that thing here. It's still staring at me with meat hanging off it. I will never get away from it. My hand is over my mouth as I try not to scream.

I feel Allie's arms go around me. She is hugging me from behind to help hold me up. Or, maybe it isn't really her? My heart is racing. My head is spinning. I try to pull the arms off of me. Hands are pulling me around to face it. I don't want to look, but when I do, I see only Allie. It's really her. I touch her hair. I am still sobbing. She takes my hands and pulls me. I hear her talking, I can't make out the words through my sobs. She makes me sit on the bed beside her. I feel her holding me so tight, I let myself sink into it. I can barely breathe, but I don't want to breathe. I hold my breath and let her rock me back and forth. The whirring in my ears begins to quiet. I recognize that Allie is humming something. I focus on the sound and the motion of her rocking me. Finally, I make out that she is humming All the Pretty Little Horses. I laugh, but it comes out sounding much like a sob. I pull away from her and try to wipe off my face with my already soaked hands.

Allie stands up to get a tissue. Then sits beside me while I wipe off my face. I try to laugh all this off as nothing. I don't want her to know how crazy I have become.

"I guess I scare myself," I say.

She puts a hand on each of my shoulders and turns me to look at her. I don't want to. I try hard not to. But, eventually I meet her eyes and feel like I am sucked into them. I have never seen them look so deep. I'm spinning again. I tell myself to keep it under control. Her fingers squeeze my shoulders and I feel it all the way to my finger tips. I want to say something but can't get to what it is.

"Jute, you are the most beautiful thing I've ever seen. Why don't you see it? You try so hard to make people reject you, which takes immense strength day after day. People see your fearlessness and want to be part of it. But, a few of us see past that. We see you as you were born to be and we love you despite everything you do to try to bury it. Just stop trying to destroy it. Please!" Her eyes are filling with tears, only making them more mesmerizing.

"Your eyes are... incredible," I think I say. I can't be sure.

"So are yours," I think she says. I can't be sure.

Her hands move to hold my face between them. I see her blink tears away and lean into me. Blue light fills the room and her lips are on mine. She is kissing me and I am letting her. Every touch is a thousand touches. I am lost in them all. But then she has pulled away her hands, her lips, her eyes. I still feel them, but I see she isn't touching me.

"I wish you weren't high," she says, sniffing a little, "Are you ready to go watch the show?"

"It's not a show," I say and smile, "And if you didn't notice, I'm still in my underwear."

She hands me my shirt and I pull it over my head. It smells like my childhood. I start to feel sick. Allie is helping me get my feet into my jeans without unraveling the bandages. I focus on getting them on and push the past out of my mind. I stand up and Allie pulls my pants up over my hips and starts to button them when I stop her.

"I can do it, Allie. I'm not completely helpless," I catch a hurt look flash across her face, "But, thank you," I add. I reach out and hug her, giving her a tight squeeze which forces air out of her lungs. I think it's funny, but I try not to giggle anymore. She steps back away from me.

"Do you want to push that yourself, too?" She is pointing at the wheelchair.

"No way! You have to push it!"

"What if I push it down the stairs?"

"Then everyone will say how fearlessly I lived my life."

Allie glares at me. I think she believes I'm too high to be aware of what is happening or remember anything she has said. Of course she would think that, considering her lack of firsthand knowledge about smoking pot.

"Shut up and sit down," she says, stepping behind the wheelchair.

I do as she says, raising my bandaged feet up to the footrests.

"Do you want to wear your boots?"

"If they'll fit," I say.

Allie loosens the laces all the way to the bottom, then slides them on easily. Before we leave the room, I stand up to

94

test them out. My feet still hurt a little, but nothing like how they felt when we first arrived.

"You are a witch," I say and smile, "a good witch."

"We'll see if you're still saying that from the bottom of the stairs," she quips and pushes the wheelchair to the door without me in it. She struggles to hold the door open and get the wheelchair through at the same time. I help by holding the door for her. Once we are in the hall, I sit down and prepare to be plunged to my death.

"Hey! Wait!" The sound of Tracy's voice bounces around the the hall. I hear him running and soon he is in front of us. "I'm glad you are going to make it. Better late than never." He must have noticed our confusion at seeing him up here at 11:00. He added, "I just came up to change my shirt, I spilled my drink."

"Oh," I say, "Well, I still won't be making it to your show… I mean, open mic. Allie is going to throw me down the stairs, but you can come to my funeral. Maybe someone will let you sing for me there," I say with a straight face.

"Good for you," he says to Allie and pats her on the shoulder. He walks over to the door to the stairs and holds it open.

"Asshole," I say, not amused.

He and Allie are nearly on the floor laughing. Even in the elevator, they take turns giggling. I am over it. When the doors open, Tracy pats me on my head, and I feel his hand linger there. His fingers are making swirls through my short stubbly hair as Allie pushes me toward the lounge.

"I'm sorry, Jute," he says. "You should have known we were joking."

"I'll forgive you after you sing with me."

"Really?" he asks, cautiously hiding his excitement behind doubt. I don't respond immediately, letting him wonder.

Only three of the tables in the lounge have customers and there are two men sitting at the bar. I couldn't be happier.

Tracy takes over pushing the wheelchair. He parks me at a table in front of the stage. There is a karaoke machine and a couple of guitars on stands.

"What should we sing?"

"Something by the Beatles. Maybe, 'Don't Let Me Down' if you know it," I say.

"Of course I know it! Let's do it!"

Allie asks if I want her to push the wheelchair on stage. I insist on standing at the microphone. Tracy picks up a guitar and does a brief sound check. A couple of people turn their heads with interest. Maybe it would be easier to do this with a full house. Then maybe at least one of them would want to hear us.

Allie sits at the table right in front of the stage. I keep my eyes on the swirling paisley pattern on her dress, but when Tracy starts playing his guitar the music pulls me away. He plays through the first verse to warm up. When he moves to the mic, he looks to me for a signal that I am ready to start. I smile at him and nod. He cycles into the beginning again and our voices sing out the first line in unison.

Tracy and I smile at each other, instantly realizing I am singing John Lennon and he is singing Paul McCartney. He knows every word and intonation just like I do. I don't need to glance at him for cues, I know he's going to nail it. I just focus on looking at Allie as she stands up and moves her hips to the music. The song is perfect for her because she really does love me unlike anyone else.

Singing with Tracy has me feeling so alive and wrapped up in joy. When the song ends, I realize my lip has cracked open again. I don't care. Allie runs up on stage and wraps her arms around both of us. Somewhere in the room, a few hands clap.

"Go sit down!" He is laughing. When she lets go of him, he starts to play "Gimme Shelter" by the Rolling Stones.

"You know this one, too, right?"

I stay on stage to sing backup. His voice is deep and

smooth with a perfect amount of grittiness. The emotion he invests is intense and I feel it inside me. He must have done this many times before.

A few more people have taken seats at the tables closer to us. Allie carries a chair onto the stage for me to sit in. I guess she doesn't want me to destroy all her efforts to heal my feet.

Just before the song ends, a waitress brings drinks for our table. Allie screams song requests between sips of her vanilla cream soda. She is our one adoring fan. But soon, people are calling out requests from the bar. At first the suggestions are for popular classics, but as the night goes on we are challenged with more obscure titles. Some of them I have never heard of, but Tracy never fails to please. On the rare occasion he doesn't know every word of a song, he knows enough to play the tune and add some quirky made up lyrics as filler. The few people in the audience seem to enjoy it.

I can't remember when Allie and I have laughed so much. Before we know it, the lights are turning on and the lounge is closing. It is two o'clock in the morning and I feel like I haven't slept in years. But, my heart is full and happy.

"Do you want to come up with us?" Allie asks Tracy. Her face is blushed pink from dancing. Her eyes are shining.

"Absolutely."

He puts his electric guitar in the stand and picks up his acoustic one. He flips it around on the strap to rest on his back before grabbing the handles of the wheelchair. I sit down as Allie slides her arm through his. With a playful jerk, he starts pushing me toward the elevator.

"You sounded amazing!" Allie says to Tracy. I can tell by the sound of her voice that she is flirting. The elevator doors close. Our reflection is in the mirrored walls. It is a strange tension that fills the tiny room. I can't wait to get out of it.

CHAPTER FOURTEEN

"Let me out right here."

Tracy stops the wheelchair just outside our hotel room door. I stand up, feeling my feet protest. All I want to do is lie down and sleep.

"I'm going to leave this in the hall."

He picks me up. I am cradled in his arms and he whirls me around a couple of times. Allie is already in the room, holding the door open for us. He runs to the bed and drops me a little too enthusiastically. My reflexes take over as if I'm falling to concrete, my elbows jut out to catch myself. When I land, my head falls backwards.

"Oops!" he says, then he slides his acoustic guitar off his back and leans it against the wall by the dresser. He turns around with a mischievous look and jumps toward me. I brace myself to have the wind knocked out of my lungs. He lands with his stomach across mine, but he puts his hands out to take most of the impact. He turns to grin at me and I slap the seat of his jeans and tell him to get off.

"Not until you tell me who is this Jute Martin, really?"

Allie chimes in, "Great idea! What do you think, Jute? Should we play Truth or Dare?"

"Not really. But, if it will get Tracy off me, let's do it."

Tracy pushes himself up to sit beside me on the bed. Allie is rummaging around in her suitcase which sits on the other bed. I keep my eyes on her because I don't want to look at Tracy. I'm afraid of what he will see in my eyes, as if what happened to me is playing on a screen there. I don't know what will happen when he gets the answers he wants. But, he has yet to have a predictable reaction to anything.

"Okay, we'll do this with a twist," Allie announces. "We'll put Truth questions in this hat and Dares in this purse,"

She sets them on the bed at my feet and opens up her notebook. She rips out three blank pages. I've never seen her rip her notebooks before. Allie has always obsessed over keeping them whole and filling them from front to back with poetry. She dates each entry including the time it was completed. She doesn't even skip pages, much less rip them out. Now she is holding the removed pages and ripping them into strips.

"We each get ten strips of paper. Write five questions and five dares. I'll pull out one question at a time. We each have to choose to answer it, or draw from the purse and take the dare."

Allie is excited enough for both of us. I have always hated this game. I refuse to lie, but my secrets are too bad to ever tell. As a kid, I would always suggest we take turns reading a book aloud instead. I wish I had a book right now.

I am the last to finish writing my questions. Tracy lies beside me and peeks as I write the last dare, so I write, "Kiss my ass." I fold it up and hand the strips to Allie. She puts them in their appropriate fashion accessory. Grinning like it's her birthday, she swirls her hand around in the hat to mix the papers.

"Okay, find a comfy spot to get started."

I am already in one and not moving. Tracy sits up and pats the pillow for Allie to sit beside my head. Then he moves to stretch out at the foot of the bed. He's propped on his elbow like he's posing to be a calendar boy. His blues eyes are staring at mine. Boys this pretty make me nervous. He puts a hand on top of my bandaged right foot and pets it absentmindedly as if it's a cat.

Allie clears her throat, "First question: How old are

99

you? This has to be yours Tracy. And to answer, I'm 18." She holds her head up high and smiles like that means something.

"17," I say.

"18" Tracy says, winking at me.

Allie shrugs and reaches in the hat again.

"This one was mine," she shakes her hands in excitement, "How old were you when you had sex for the first time? And my answer is 14."

I can't believe she asked that, or that she answered like she's bragging. This is when it hits me. She is doing that thing I hate. She is pretending to be what she thinks will make a guy like her. I try to push the anger back out of my mind, but it stays. I just try to hide it.

"I was 13," says Tracy.

His answer would be more shocking if it wasn't the same answer I would give if I answered truthfully. But, not even Allie knows that story. I decide not to answer and reach out for the purse. Allie jerks it away from me and squints her eyes in objection. She can't understand why I don't want to answer such an easy question. Maybe she's hoping to see that I am joking, but I'm not. I lean over her as far as I can reach and grab the purse out of her hand. I pull out a strip of paper, unfold it to see Allie's handwriting.

"It says: Take off your shirt. I suppose this was intended for Tracy?" I ask, raising an eyebrow at her. I hand her the purse and pull my Misfits t-shirt over my head. They have already seen me naked, but wearing the cheetah print bra makes me feel self-conscious. Or, maybe I feel that way because I'm not high this time.

"Nice," Tracy gives me a thumbs up.

"Whatever," Allie barks. She's mad because she thinks I'm not playing fair. She reaches in and draws out our third question.

"This is Jute's-"

"Would you stop saying who wrote it?" I snap at her. As soon as the words are out, I know I've hurt her feelings.

Every time I get annoyed with her for real, she cries. But now she's trying to fight it because she's in her impress-a-boy mode. She starts reading it again with attitude.

"This one is from a mysterious contributor: What would you do if you could go back in time?"

Tracy answers first, "I would go to Egypt and find out if aliens really built the pyramids."

He doesn't look like he's joking. It's not a bad answer.

Allie says, "I would go back and kill Hitler."

"No you wouldn't!" This time, even I recognize how rude I am being, but I keep going, "You, Allie Vining, would not kill a dying insect. And even if you did go back in time and kill Hitler, it might change too much and end up causing you not to have been born."

I look away before I roll my eyes. I'm not proud of myself right now, but I feel frustrated. I wish Allie would just be herself for a change.

"Then what would you do, Jute?"

"I would go back to April of 1986 and I would never leave your side." I don't look at either of them. A feeling of exhaustion washes over me and I roll over so I don't have to look at them.

"What happened in April of 1986?" Tracy asks.

"A snowstorm," I mumble. There is a picture of sea gulls on the wall. We are at the beach and I have yet to touch the sand.

"I lost my virginity." She leaves out the details. I hear her hand in the hat again. I guess I'm not the only one not wanting to talk about the past.

"Next question," she says flatly, "and I won't say whose handwriting it's in: What is your biggest secret?"

Silence.

I have no intentions of answering this one, but I'll wait to draw another dare. While the other two decide whether or not to answer, I wonder to myself about who submitted the question. Maybe I shouldn't have made Allie stop saying. I

101

don't think she wrote it unless she planned to lie about her answer. Allie has been known to bend the truth in front of boys.

Tracy interrupts my thoughts when his hand finds my foot again, his fingers make swirls around my ankle. He begins to speak low like he is going to sing, but he doesn't.

"I'm gay. When I lost my virginity, it was with my step-dad's son from a previous marriage. He was seventeen." He pauses and takes a breath, "I think girls are beautiful and I've had sex with a few, but I've known I was gay since I was ten."

My back is to him. I can't see the look on his face. I can't see how Allie is reacting. But, I don't have any emotional response at all. It hasn't occurred to me that he is gay, but I'm not surprised. The only thing I feel is sorry that it has to be his biggest secret.

Allie's protest interrupts my thoughts. "But, what about you and Jute?"

I close my eyes in embarrassment, but Allie can't see me doing it.

"What about us?" we say in unison, only Tracy's voice is curious and mine is defensive.

"I thought you two had sex?" She is trying to make sense of the word gay.

Tracy pauses, and I think he is waiting for me to speak. When he realizes I'm not going to, he says, "I think I'm a little bit in love with her. But, I'm definitely gay."

I'm tempted to turn around just to see Allie's face. But, I don't. What Tracy is saying makes sense to me. I think back to everything that has happened between us. It all fits perfectly with his words. I want to move close to him and wrap my arms around him, but I don't want him to misconstrue it as pity.

"Give me the purse," I hold up my hand and feel Allie plop it forcefully onto my palm.

"Aren't you going to answer anything?"

My hand pulls out a strip of paper. I open it quickly,

102

but I feel like shoving it back in the purse when I read it. Now I know why Tracy moved and had Allie sit on the pillow.

"Well, what does it say?" Allie wants to know. "Are you regretting not answering the question?" She probably thinks it says to lick the toilet or something.

I turn over on my back and sit up, giving Tracy an evil glare.

"It says, kiss the person on your left. And, if you want to know, Tracy wrote it."

I watch Allie stop laughing. The room seems so bright, like a surgical area. I don't even know if I can look at her. I really want to laugh this off. I could pretend to be mad at Tracy for putting me in this situation. I could pretend to be so mad that I am not going to play the game anymore. That is exactly what I would have done in this situation two days ago. But, we aren't the same people now.

Maybe Allie will laugh it off so I don't have to. Her hand is in a fist and her fingers are against her lips. Her eyes are huge, maybe apologetic, but intoxicating. I shouldn't look at her, this isn't helping. But, I can't really stop. I remember her kissing me before we went to the lounge. I still don't know why she did it. I think she was trying to make me stop crying. This is different. Everything is different. I move closer to her so that I can keep my voice low.

"It's okay, right?"

I reach up and pull her hand away from her mouth, holding on to her wrist. Her eyes are locked on mine as I lean in and touch my lips to hers. She kisses me back, and I feel paralyzed. Her tongue enters my parted lips. She tastes like sweet mint and smells like vanilla. I focus on the taste, the feel of her lips, my hand sliding up her arm and into her hair. I focus on these details because the energy around her is so intense. I am afraid I'll get lost in it. If I fall into this, I see no hope of ever getting out.

It feels like minutes, but the kiss only lasts a few seconds before I pull away from her. I take my hand from her hair and touch her lips with my thumb. They are still wet from the kiss. Her eyes are still wide, hungry. I see it coming, that she is going to kiss me again. I don't want her to. I can't do this.

I slide down into the bed, turning away from them again. As I do, I reach up to turn the lamp light off.

"I don't want to play anymore," I say.

I feel drained and overwhelmed. I just want to sleep. I close my eyes and listen to Allie get out of bed and walk to the bathroom. I hear unzipping and the sound of clothes being removed. I feel Tracy slide into bed behind me and pull me close to him. His arms are tight around me and his naked skin is warm on my back. He kisses my shoulder and puts his cheek against my hair.

He whispers, "You need to tell her."

I turn toward him and his arm slides down across my stomach. I look into his eyes in the dim moonlight. They are as blue as Allie's, but calm.

"Tell her what?" I am careful to keep my voice low.

"That you love her... like that."

"I do love her, but not... like that."

"Yes you do, exactly like that." He kisses my cheek, close to my ear. "Jute, you are so beautiful inside and out. She feels it. I know she does. I don't know if I will ever find someone to share what you have with Allie. But, it would be a dream come true if I did. You can't just ignore this. People can love you. I do. She does. Denying it isn't fair to her."

"Well, love does not equal sex."

"You mean, sex does not equal love. That is true, but this isn't about sex. It's about what you do when you have found the one person that means everything to you. What is the answer, Jute? What is true love and how do you express it?"

"Now you sound like Allie. She thinks no one will love her unless she gives them orgasms in fifty different positions."

"No, you are just trying not to hear me. Allie believes that because all the proof she has supports it. You could have

104

changed her way of seeing herself a long time ago. Just tell her the truth about how you feel."

"She doesn't want that from me. I've tried to tell her that she is too good to put up with abuse, but she accuses me of just being jealous. How could you possibly know anything about us when we only met you today?"

My face is hot with anger. Allie's suffering is not my fault. I'm not the one who raped her and beat her up every weekend. How can he blame me? But, deep inside I do feel guilty. I turn my back to him again, but I don't pull away. I won't admit he is right, but concede that I know he is trying to do something good. I just want him to stop it.

Allie walks back in the room. I can see her in the moonlight through the curtain. She is wearing her slip.

"Scoot over," she says, sliding into bed beside me.

Tracy and I both move back to make room for her. She lies on the edge with her back to me. The space between us seems infinite. Maybe she is angry with me, but then why isn't she in the other bed? But, if she isn't angry, why is she so far away? I feel paralyzed with confusion. Tracy reaches over to her. He puts his hand on her hip and I feel him tug at her to move closer.

"We won't bite," he says, as if he is half asleep. I know he is pretending. Allie moves closer to me. I lift my arm to make room for her and place it around her waist. I pull her close, the way Tracy is holding me. I want her to feel warm and loved.

"Tell her," Tracy's mouth is speaking directly into my ear, yet his voice is barely audible. I shake my head, I can't.

CHAPTER FIFTEEN

I hear the hotel curtains slide open with a scraping sound and sunlight floods the room. I don't want to open my eyes. I pull the blanket over my head and stretch out beneath it. I am alone in the bed. Someone is in the shower, I hear the water through the open bathroom door. What time is it?

"Wake up, wake up!"

Allie pulls the blankets completely off the bed. I squint and groan at her.

"It's almost noon, Jute! You have to wake up. We only have one more night here and we haven't seen the beach yet."

She sounds way too energetic. I rub my eyes with both hands, then squint as I look at her. She is wearing jeans and a purple Myrtle Beach t-shirt. It's weird to see her in normal clothes.

"You are an impostor. What did you do with Allie?" I grumble. I need coffee.

"I got you a shirt just like it! Yours is black." She holds my new shirt out and shakes it at me.

"You need to stop buying stuff for me. You know that makes me feel like shit," I am being rude. I need coffee. Help.

I sit up and swing my legs off the edge of the bed. My feet hit the floor and I don't feel stabs of pain. This is good. But, my head is pounding. I drop my face into the palms of my hands.

"I need coffee," I mumble.

"Sorry, I would get you some, but I don't want to make

you feel like shit." Allie is teasing, and I'm relieved I haven't hurt her feelings with my gruffness.

"I'm used to it. Please, get me coffee."

I hear her pick up the phone and order breakfast for three, including coffee. I don't really feel like eating anything, I just want caffeine. She hangs up the phone and dives onto the bed behind me. If she doesn't stop acting so happy, I might have to slap her.

"Okay, enough! What is going on with you?"

"I don't know," she shrugs, "But, do you think Tracy is really gay? I mean, he slept with his hand on my hip last night and I could barely sleep for feeling tingly all over. He is so hot."

"Well, I don't think he would say it if it wasn't true. It's not the kind of thing people usually make up."

"That's why it's so weird. Maybe he just said it as a trick, you know, to get our guard down so he could get in bed with us. I mean, he did try to get us to kiss in front of him. Maybe he is turned on by us kissing. Do you think he wants to have sex with both of us at the same time? That would explain it, I think." She sighs and flops over on her back, staring at the ceiling.

"He was sleeping against me last night, Allie. I assure you he was not turned on or I would have felt it."

"Maybe that's because nothing was happening. Maybe if he was between us he would have been turned on. Do you think we should try that?" She sits up and leans close to me. She lowers her voice to a whisper, "I mean, you think he's cute, too, right? Maybe we could try an experiment tonight and see if we can turn him on."

"You can't be serious, Allie! He said he has had sex with girls. I'm sure it is possible to turn him on. But, I don't understand why you want to. He's a great guy. He's our friend. I don't want to experiment with him like a lab rat."

"How are we going to hurt him by having sex with him? Jute, you need to learn to say yes every now and then."

"Maybe you need to say no every now and then."

Her face turns red and she glares at me. I regret what I said. I know Allie's past, and I know it isn't her fault that she has a messed up view of relationships. I don't want to hurt her, but I am hurt, too. She looked right through me last night. After I took a chance and kissed her, she still feels nothing except a need to prove something to Tracy.

My hurt turns to anger at Allie and bleeds into anger at Tracy. He thinks he knows us, but he doesn't. Maybe he knows me. At least, his assumptions about me have been right so far. But, he doesn't know Allie at all. I want to tell him just how bad his plan failed, but I can't without revealing Allie's not-so-admirable plan. I don't want him to think badly of her. I need to think carefully before I say anything at all.

The shower turns off and I hear Tracy vigorously drying himself off with a towel.

"We'll talk about this later, Allie. Just don't try anything until we've discussed it, okay?"

"Great!" She says happily, obviously misunderstanding what I said. "Do you think we should be kissing when he comes back in the room?"

"Seriously? Are you not hearing me? No! We are not doing this!"

I am standing up, still in my jeans and my bra from last night. I am pointing my finger in Allie's face when Tracy steps into the room. He is naked, with his towel draped over his shoulders. His blue eyes dart from me to Allie and back again. I am distracted by his body, which is pale for a boy living by the ocean, but he does have tan lines. His shoulders are broad and his muscles well defined. He doesn't seem self-conscious at all. However, his timing is horrible.

"Go away and put some clothes on!" I yell at him.

"Jute! You are screwing it up!" Allie yells at me.

"I'm not screwing anything, Allie. Take notes on how it's done!"

She is angry and screaming at me through tears, "That's

108

because no one ever asks you to, Jute! You act like a freak and try to scare them off. Is that what you want me to do? Shave my head and punch every boy brave enough to make a move? You realize that's not normal, right?"

She continues to scream similar things to the back of my head while I sit on the bed and slide on my boots. I leave the Myrtle Beach shirt on the bed and grab a white t shirt out of the box. Once I have it on, I realize it's my Rolling Stones t-shirt with the big lips logo. I almost never wear this in public. Someone bought it for me as a joke at a flea market because of my lips. It's threadbare and old and I can see my bra through it. But, I don't even care right now. I just want out of here. I grab the key from the dresser and hear Allie asking where I am going. I don't answer, I just walk out the door and toward the elevator.

My feet feel okay except the area on my left foot just below my big toe. I try not to put weight on it.

I ride the elevator to the lobby. There is a man at the front desk. He looks up and smiles, raising his hand to wave. Maybe he waves at everyone. Maybe he is Tracy's dad. The shape of his face and the color of his hair is similar to Tracy. His eyes are blue, but darker. I try to return the smile just in case. I wave back, but quickly look away and head for the door.

The temperature outside is much colder than I expected. The sun through the hotel window was a liar. I cross my arms to try to keep warm. A long string of profanity escapes my mouth, much too low for anyone to hear. But, soon my voice is rising until I finally punch the stop sign as I exit the hotel parking lot. I don't think I can walk much farther without re-injuring my foot.

There is a bench on the sidewalk up ahead. Just as I reach it, someone in the surf shop behind it clicks the locks open. Judging from the sign in the window, noon has arrived. A blond man with a crew cut looks through the panes and waves at me. This is the friendliest place I've ever been. Unfortunately, I find all the niceties annoying.

The bench has enough room for me to put my left foot out beside me. I want to take my boot off and see what damage I've done, but I also dread it. I can either do it now or do it in front of Allie later. Her voice echos in my head, saying *I told you so*. I undo the laces and pull the boot off quickly. The bandages have stuck to the bottom of my boot and they pull against the wound as the boot comes off. I unwrap all the bandages, not thinking about how I will get back to the hotel without them. I turn so I can place my left foot over my right knee to see it better. The sole of my left foot is generally good, better than I imagined. But, the ball of my foot has a large gash in the center of what must have been a blister. Seeing it makes the throbbing pain even more intense. Tears well up, not because of the pain I feel but the pain I cause. I am such a burden on everyone.

An elderly couple jog past me with a young black Labrador on a leash. The dog pulls on the leash to get closer to me, sniffing the air. The man tugs it away and looks at me with equal parts pity and disgust. I smile at the backs of their heads as they jog away, trying not to be the scary freak Allie just accused me of being. Maybe this town really isn't so friendly.

The door to the surf shop opens and a bell above it jingles. The man from the shop is standing beside me. I don't look up. I already know he's going to ask me to leave.

"Just let me put my boot back on and I'll go."

"Go where? It doesn't look like you should be walking anywhere." He's not from around here. He sounds like a guy I know from Iowa. Why is he working in a surf shop in South Carolina? "I'm not running you off. I just came out to see if you need help."

"I need help alright, but I doubt I can get it from you."

I still don't look up, I just start wrapping the dirty bandage back around my foot and try not to wince. I hear the door open with a jingle and close again. I sigh, glad he's gone. But, a couple of minutes pass and he walks out again. I ignore it and keep fighting with the dirty bandage. Every way I try to

110

wrap it, it is painful and too chunky to fit in my boot.

A suntanned hand shoves a roll of clean white gauze in front of my face. It smells like coconut, or the guy holding it smells like coconut. I look up at his steel blue eyes staring down at me. They are spaced a bit close together above a small turned up nose. I'm sure he was an adorable baby, but not so much now. He makes no attempt to look cool or impress me. He doesn't even bother to close his mouth, but leaves it open a little to breathe through it.

"Thanks." I give him a weak smile. I reach up to take the gauze from his hand, but he drops to his knees in front of me and starts pulling off my old bandages like he's doing first aid on a battle field. In the time it takes me to blink a few times, he has wrapped my foot again without nearly as much pain as when I tried. He looks up and I see how proud he is. I can tell he wants me to be impressed and I am. I guess it isn't every day he gets to show off this particular skill. "Wow, nice work!" I say, and mean it.

"My name is Luke." He puts his hand out and I give it a firm and appreciative shake.

"My name is Jute."

"I thought so. There aren't too many girls from Tennessee stumbling around with a bandaged foot."

I try not to look panicked that he knows who I am.

"Don't worry. I talked to Tracy on the phone before open mic. He told me about you and your friend."

I would like to tell Luke that Tracy also told me about him, but he hadn't. It was an awkward moment, one I don't want to stay in any longer than necessary. I carefully stand up before saying, "Speaking of Allie. I need to get back there and apologize. It was nice to meet you. Maybe we'll see you around later."

He is quiet, watching me try not to limp as I walk past him. Then I hear the bell jingle again. But, I hear footsteps approaching and soon he is by my side.

"I locked up the shop so I can help you. It's not like

111

anyone is going to come by, unless it's the owner. Let's hope that doesn't happen. He already gives me hell." Luke bends down and picks me up. He is much more broad than Tracy, and taller. I don't usually notice these things about the people around me, but the people around me aren't usually picking me up.

Luke walks quickly, as if we are being timed. We reach the hotel doors and he is still not out of breath from the effort. As he carries me through the lobby, I notice the man behind the front desk is gawking, looking a bit panicked. Luke passes right by him to the elevator. He hits the up arrow with the hand at my back.

When the doors open, Luke carries me in and pushes the number six button repeatedly until the doors close.

He smiles and for once doesn't look defensive. Maybe I should worry about bringing a stranger up uninvited, but I want to see the look on Allie's face when we walk in. She'll probably suggest we all have sex. I roll my eyes.

Despite all the jokes about it in my mind, thinking about our argument makes a lump rise in my throat. The heartache hurts worse than my left foot and I don't think Luke's magic bandages will fix it. Allie and I need to talk privately. There's so much I need to say to her.

CHAPTER SIXTEEN

I pull the key from the pocket of my jeans. Luke bends a little so I can reach down and slide it in the door knob. I tighten my grip around his muscular shoulders and turn the knob. With a mischievous grin on my face, I push the door open. Luke steps into the room with me and kicks the door closed behind him. Suddenly, his hold on me loosens and I am falling to the floor. I manage to get my right leg and arm out to catch myself, but crumple into a pile of limbs at his feet.

"What the hell?" I say into the carpet my face is planted into, but I hear Luke saying the exact same words at the exact same time. I turn to look up at him and see he is staring at something in the room. His face is red and his teeth are clenched. I panic, thinking there must be a dead body in here. I scramble to my feet and turn to see Tracy and Allie lying on the bed. Tracy is propped up on one elbow and is sliding his arm away from Ally's stomach. He is wearing only his briefs, which is better than finding him still naked. Allie is wearing her jeans, but her shirt and bra are off. She has a pillow thrown over her breasts.

This scene strikes me as odd, but nothing to cry about. I turn to look at Luke again to make sure my eyes weren't playing tricks on me. He is definitely crying.

"Luke, what are you doing here?" It's Tracy's voice. Before I can turn to look, Tracy has already crossed the room and has his arms wrapped around Luke like he's a long lost brother. Luke doesn't hug Tracy, he just stands there in tears.

Tracy speaks over Luke's shoulder, "You shouldn't be here. Did my dad see you? You have to go before he calls the police."

Luke is looking up to the ceiling, blinking away tear after tear. Finally, he pushes Tracy away from him. His words come out slow and pained, "Is that why you want me to leave?" He points to Allie. "After everything I have been through for you, and you can't even wait until we can see each other? I thought I meant something to you."

Tracy is shaking his head at Luke's words, but lets him finish before he speaks, "It's not what it looks like, Luke. You know I love you. Allie is just a friend of mine... a friend of Jute's. Nothing happened and nothing ever would have happened, even if you didn't walk in carrying Jute." At this he gives Luke a smile, "And that was a little weird, too, you have to admit."

Luke smiles, the first time I've seen him smile wide enough to see his teeth. They are brilliantly white and perfectly straight. He reaches out and pulls Tracy to him, holding him like his life depends on it. I don't know how Tracy can breathe.

I look back to the bed and see that Allie is sitting on the edge facing away from me. She finishes fastening her bra and reaches over for her purple t shirt. She puts it on and pulls her long hair up out of it, the brown spirals bounce when she lets them drop. She stands up and turns, startled that I am so close to her. I grab the hem of my Rolling Stones shirt and pull it off over my head. She is looking at me with confusion, which makes me laugh. That confuses her even more. I bend down to the floor and pick up the black Myrtle Beach t-shirt and slide it on over my head. I put my hands out, "Ta-da!" and turn like a super model.

She relaxes and gives me two thumbs up.

I nudge my head toward the embracing boys and say in a low voice, "What do you know, Allie Vining can be wrong sometimes." I wink at her.

"About that," she says, but before she can say anything else there is a loud knock at the door. I key rattles in the door before it flies open.

The man from the front desk and a security guard walk into the room. The man's face is red and he is shaking with rage. He walks up to Tracy and begins to scream at him, spit flying out of his mouth along with his words. "I told you if he ever shows his face here again I would have him arrested, didn't I?"

His finger jabs at Tracy's naked chest. "You are both vile and disgusting animals! You are an embarrassment and you are dirtying up my hotel! I will not have it! If this man would just stay away from you, maybe you'd take interest in these pretty girls. I put that girl on the same floor as you for a reason!"

He throws his hand out in Allie's direction. "But, you refuse to be normal. I can not put up with it any more. Get your things and get out. And you," He jabs his finger at Luke, "you filthy fag, I called Mr. Smithington about you. I hope he fires you, you pervert. Now, I suggest you stay away from my son or I'll have you arrested!"

Luke's face is white. I start to doubt his ability to move at all. I give a desperate look to Allie and see she is already throwing our things into her suitcase. I gather up our toiletries and toss them into my box of clothes. I pick it up and walk over to Luke.

My hand finds his and I give it a firm squeeze while looking Tracy's dad in the eyes, "Don't talk about my boyfriend like that. You are a dirty minded old man."

I pull Luke's hand toward the door and he lets me lead him. For a moment, I wasn't sure if he would snap out of it. I push the down arrow and wait for the doors to open. When they do, Allie runs up to us with her arms full. The three of us step onto the elevator and the doors close us in.

"Thanks," Luke's voice is distant and sad. "Where is Tracy?" He is looking at Allie now.

"He had to go to his room to get his things. I told him I would wait for him in the parking lot."

"I can't stay in the parking lot or Mr. Duren will call the police. I appreciate what you just did back there, but I can't wait with you."

The elevator doors open into the lobby. Luke picks me up again and follows Allie to her car. She opens the passenger door for me.

"Nice car," he comments as he lets me down. He looks off into the distance around us. I catch myself doing the same. It is so beautiful here. The waves are crashing just out of sight. I want to run off, too, and never look back. But, I don't want Luke to run. I understand that the thing that will save him isn't out beyond the palm trees. The thing that will save him is on the sixth floor, gathering up his things and will be here soon.

"Get in the backseat," I say to him. "No one will see you. I'll even scoot my seat up to give you extra leg room." It was a weak attempt to make him smile and it failed. But, he did look at me and nod. I pulled the seat forward and watched him climb in awkwardly.

Allie leaves the hatch open for Tracy's things and she walks around to where I am standing, watching Luke squirm around to find a comfortable way to fit his legs and feet behind my seat.

"Hmmm," she says, "You don't think you should ask me before inviting strange men into my car?"

"As soon as I met him, I knew he'd find his way to the back seat of your car. I just didn't imagine it would be like this."

Allie punches my arm and it actually hurt. I wince before I remember to act tough. She puts her arms around me and hugs me. "I am the luckiest girl in the world to have a friend like you, Jute. Don't ever stop being my friend, no matter what happens. Let's always fix it and make it right."

We hear footsteps running, getting closer. We step around the car and see Tracy coming toward us with all the speed he can muster. He is carrying a duffel bag and a guitar case. I have never seen such anguish as what I see on his face

116

now. His eyes are swollen from crying and tears are still pouring out of him. He is running so fast that he nearly crashes into the back of Allie's car.

Tracy's arms move in unison to toss in all his belongings. He pats them down so the hatch will close. Allie reaches up and closes it while I grab his hand and pull him to the side of the car. I desperately want to hug him, but I see his dad running out of the hotel doors. We have to get Tracy out of here. I pull him to the open passenger door where he catches sight of Luke and freezes. Allie starts the engine. I give Tracy a push, causing him to fall forward on top of Luke. He pulls his legs in with Luke's help and I push my seat back so I can get in. As I pull the door closed, Allie pushes the gas pedal hard. The tires squeal and spin, then launch us out toward the road.

Allie and I are silent, listening helplessly as Tracy sobs. It would be too easy to turn and tell him all the reasons he shouldn't care what his dad thinks. I have never cared about mine, the real one in jail or the fake one who molested us. But, I think of Allie's dad and how much he loves her. If a man like Hank ever turned his back on his child, I just can't fathom the pain it would cause. For a moment, I feel fortunate not to know that kind of parental love. I never need to worry about losing it. Maybe that's why I am free to be the scary freak I have become, and why I have assumed that the worst thing that can happen when you love someone is that they won't love you back. Obviously, that is not the worst thing that can happen.

"Do you need to get anything from your place, Luke?" Allie looks up at him in her rear view mirror.

"We can't go there. I violated a restraining order by going to the hotel. I'm sure Tracy's dad called the police."

"I'm so sorry," Tracy is wiping his eyes, but it's pointless. He is leaning far away from Luke, trying to squeeze into the smallest possible position. Luke has his hand on Tracy's knee, but his body is rigid. I turn in my seat to look into his eyes and see they are also filled with tears. He turns his head away from me. It must be hard to adjust to looking into someone's eyes and not seeing condemnation.

I unbuckle my seat belt and crawl between the seats to the back. Tracy and Luke both move away from each other to make room for me. Tracy can't move much farther. I still don't have enough room to sit on the seat, so I sit on Luke's lap. I wrap my arms around his neck and hug him tightly. I feel his head relax against my shoulder as his breathing becomes uneven. I let him cry. Tracy is looking at me, his tears have stopped. I reach out one arm to him and he puts his hand in mine.

Luke pushes me away a little, just to give himself room to breathe. He has stopped crying and is clearing his throat, "That was bad," He says mostly to himself.

"Me suffocating you, or our escape from oppression?" I smile at him, but he doesn't smile back. Obviously, he doesn't want to talk about it. Surely he can't be like this all the time. If he is, what does Tracy see in him?

Tracy has his hands over his face, rubbing his eyes. "I'm sorry I have dragged all of you into this. Dad is probably reporting us all to the police for robbery or some other made up charge."

"He has already had me charged with assault," Luke adds, looking into Tracy's eyes. "He was slapping Tracy across the face and calling him a fag. I couldn't stop myself from punching him. Tracy and I ran off, but his dad called the police and filed a complaint. He said I just walked up and punched him for no reason." Luke shakes his head, "That's when he had the restraining order issued. Tracy was underage back then. But, his old man didn't want to press charges because the police might question the bruises on Tracy's face. It was pretty messed up."

"So, Tracy's dad locked him away like Cinderella?" I ask, watching Tracy smile because it does seem funny. But, the pain in his eyes lingers. "It's no wonder you are so pale."

Allie chimes in, "All the more reason to find public beach access and get our toes in the sand... except you, Jute.

No sand anywhere near those feet. Luke is going to carry you over his shoulder the entire time."

We have been on the road for about thirty minutes, so it seems safe enough when Allie pulls into a parking area just north of North Myrtle Beach. We file out of the car and try not to think about the cold January wind hitting us. The waves crash loudly just over the dunes. Tracy takes off running up the wooden steps leading over to the beach, Allie is so close behind him that she may pass him by. It's amazing how well she runs when she's not wearing high heels. Luke bends down and picks me up, cradling me in his arms. He keeps his eyes focused ahead.

"My hero!" I say sweetly, trying to make him laugh. It doesn't work.

"All I do is make people miserable," he says flatly, still not looking at me. "I should have never left Rio."

"You are from Rio?"

"Rio, Wisconsin."

CHAPTER SEVENTEEN

The steps lead up to a wooden pathway over the dunes. When we get to the top, we see Tracy and Allie pulling off their shoes. I shiver at the idea of getting in that water with this cold wind blowing. Luke lets me down on the wooden pathway, but keeps his arm around me for support. We both stare out over the vast ocean. I feel small, lost, and cold.

Luke's hand is rubbing my upper arm, trying to keep me warm. To be so sullen, he is still very thoughtful. I wish I knew what I could say to cheer him up. But, I struggle with my own pessimistic thoughts. My life is falling apart. Allie is going to Ohio and I need to go back to school. I can't go back to my house, so I might as well be homeless. I wonder if Momma has come back to see the destruction Earl left behind. I wonder if she is concerned that I'm not there. Does she think Earl might have murdered me in the night? She may be relieved to think I am dead and all our secrets are safe.

And what about Earl? Is he looking for revenge now that Allie has gone and stolen my things again? I feel my throat clench tight. I don't want Allie hurt.

"I'm going to go talk to Tracy. Do you want to sit here and wait for me?"

"Sure, I'll be fine."

I sit on the top step which leads down to the beach. Luke pulls off his shoes and walks barefoot out toward Tracy and Allie. He holds his back straight with his broad shoulders pulled back, like he is marching into war.

Tracy and Allie stand facing each other with their heads down, each holding on to the elbows of the other. They look like they are praying, but they are actually watching their toes wiggle away down under the wet sand. Something makes Tracy look up, maybe he catches sight of Luke walking in his direction. Tracy lets go of Allie and runs toward Luke, tackling him. He is barely strong enough to topple him over. I'm not entirely convinced that Luke didn't fall down intentionally so Tracy wouldn't feel weak. After falling, Luke throws Tracy off of him, face down in the sand. He holds Tracy's arm behind his back, just like a big brother would wrestle a younger one. They are both laughing, especially Luke. It transforms him and suddenly I can see him as Tracy does.

Allie is walking in my direction. By the time I notice, she is already at the bottom step of the walkway. Her long hair is being whipped around in the wind, falling in front of her smiling face, then blowing back away. She puts a hand up to hold it down and looks at me with her blue eyes overflowing with joy. Her purple t shirt has sand sticking to it on the shoulder. Her jeans are wet all the way up to the knees. Any normal person would be freezing. I smile at her, so glad she isn't normal.

"You are out of your mind! How can you get in that cold water?"

"I had to do it while I could. We won't be here much longer." She sits beside me and I watch her eyes drift out over the ocean, taking it all in. The sunlight on her skin magnifies her glow. She is so beautiful. I hope she doesn't look at me. I certainly don't want the sun magnifying my flaws. But she finally does turn her head in my direction. She seems surprised to catch me looking so intently at her, but I don't look away.

She laughs, "Do I have seaweed on my face or something?"

"Yes. Right there," I say, and slap the palm of my hand against her forehead. She grabs my wrist and tries to pretend she's mad.

"You jerk!" She says, shoving me back onto the walkway. She climbs on top of me and straddles my waist. My wrists are held above my head. She is looking down at me with her hair whipping around in the wind. Her mouth is pulled dramatically tight in fake anger. I want to laugh because I know she is trying to be funny. But, fear keeps me frozen. My body wants to move but can't. I close my eyes to try to calm myself. Feeling my heart race, I focus on slowing it. But the darkness behind my eyelids fills with images of Earl. I see him glaring down at me in my bedroom. I don't want to see this right now. I try to force the images away as tears push past my eyelids. Allie's hair is touching my face. I feel her leaning toward me, the space between us growing smaller and smaller. I know it is Allie, but my body remembers Earl. I open my mouth to beg her to stop, but as I do, her mouth opens, too. She is kissing me, but I am lost in a forest fire. The sound of the ocean wind becomes a hurricane, whirling destruction around inside my head, uprooting trees and shattering windows. I won't get out alive. I won't get out. Get out.

My eyes fly open when I realize I am sitting up against the railing. Allie is on her side, across the walkway. I must have thrown her off of me. She quickly sits up and covers her face with her hands. She leans her shoulder against the railing opposite me. She is crying. Because of me, she is doubting every amazing thing she is. I did this and I hate myself. She and I can not dance around this any longer. I move to sit beside her, my legs stretched out behind her so I can lean over and look her in the eyes. I did not intend to be shelter from the wind, but I'm pleased that it's helping.

"Stop crying, Allie. Whatever you think happened just now, you are wrong,"

Her hands come down, but she doesn't look up at me,

"You think I'm a whore."

My brain tries to make sense of what she just said, tries to understand why she would believe I would think that about her. Then I remember how many times Bobby called her that

122

and worse. I feel hurt that she thinks I'm capable of being like Bobby. However, I did just throw her off of me because she kissed me. What else would she think? This is no time to take her self-loathing personally.

"I have never thought of you as a whore. Never. I remember you as that little girl in a frilly yellow dress and the most beautiful blue eyes I've ever seen." She looks up at me, listening. "I think of you as a girl who would do anything to be loved. You work so hard to do everything exactly right, over and over again, in hopes that someone will truly love you. You would allow yourself to be tied to the train tracks if it would prove you are worthy of love. That is not what whores do, Allie. No one deserves to be loved more than you."

Her hand touches my cheek and she smiles, "Why can't boys be like you, Jute?"

"Sometimes I don't feel so different from them," I pause, second guessing what I want to say next. But, I can't let these secrets keep us apart. "I have hurt you so much. I'm the reason you were with James that night."

Allie opens her mouth to protest, but I put my fingertips to her lips.

"Wait. Listen. What you don't know is that I was also there when Bobby raped you the first time."

I see confusion in her eyes, but I understand it. The word rape doesn't match her memory of things. I reach down and hold her hand.

"That night, I was in the woods hiding from Earl, waiting for him to pass out so I could go back home. I heard everything Bobby said to you." I look up to the sky and take a deep breath. I exhale and force myself to look into her eyes and continue. "Then I saw him rape you. I wanted to run out and knock him off of you. I cried listening to you beg him to keep going because it's what my sister would say so Earl wouldn't hit her. I will never let anyone hurt you like that again."

She isn't crying at all. She looks relieved. "It's not your fault. I believed he was my Prince and I was his Princess. You

123

couldn't have stopped it no matter what. I allowed that. I'm to blame."

"Bobby is to blame. You did not deserve any of it."

"Did I deserve to have you throw me into the hand railing because I kissed you?"

"Allie, about that..." She sits up a little straighter and puts her hands in her lap nervously and listens. "I can't imagine my life without you in it. The only love I've ever felt has been from you, certainly not my family. I don't want anything to ruin what we have." Allie puts her arms around me to hug me. I let her for a moment, but I need to look at her to continue. I pull her arms off of me and hold her hands in her lap. Her eyes look so innocent, yet worried. "I'm not finished. I'm trying to tell you that I really love you, Allie."

"I love you, too, Jute!" she says, tears in her eyes.

"Allie... I don't mean like best friends forever. I mean, I am in love with you bigger than Earth. I feel for you like John loves Yoko. I just want you near me. I'm not telling you this because my expectations have changed. I'm telling you the truth now because I don't want you to kiss me."

Allie stiffens a little, confusion in her eyes. She is so quick to feel rejected. "What do you mean you don't want me to kiss you?"

The wind whips her hair into her face and I push it away, holding it back so I can look into her eyes, "If we kiss, I know I will fall into you and never get out. It's hard enough now, just looking in your eyes and knowing that I can't always do this. One day you will find someone to settle down with, someone who deserves you, and I won't be able to do what I'm doing right now. I don't want to become more than friends with you just to find out you can't love me the same way."

Tears are sliding down her face to the corner of her mouth. She takes a deep breath and licks the tears from her lips.

"I don't want to lose you," I say, trying to give her a reassuring smile. I have admitted to lying for years about my feelings for her. I have abandoned my armor and I try to prepare myself for rejection. She could so easily shatter me into a thousand pieces.

"So, the only reason you don't want me to kiss you is because you love me and want to kiss me?" Her eyebrow is raised and she looks at me like I have really lost my mind.

A laugh escapes me before I have time to consider how truly sad our reality is.

"Not exactly," I clear my throat and can't believe I'm going to tell her the truth, "I didn't do it on purpose. I thought you were Earl. I'm sorry." I hug her so I don't have to see the look on her face when she realizes I need professional help.

She speaks over my shoulder, "You don't have to worry about him, Jute. He is never going to hurt you again." She hugs me tighter. "And you aren't the only one that hasn't been entirely truthful. But, let's try to look ahead and heal from all this."

Tracy's voice invades our moment, "I am so damn cold! Are you girls ready to get out of here?"

"To go where?" Allie asks, standing up and dusting herself off.

Luke offers me his hand to help pull me up. He is actually smiling and it changes the look of his face entirely.

"Wow, Luke. If I didn't know better, I'd say you are in love." I wink at him just before he reaches down and picks me up.

We are almost to the parking lot when Tracy says, "I think we should get some breakfast since we left before room service came. Besides, we need to make a plan. That is, if you two are interested in helping us."

"I don't know," Allie looks over her shoulder and gives him an evil smile, "The only thing we're good at is finding more trouble."

He puts his arm around her and kisses her cheek, "We'll take our chances."

CHAPTER EIGHTEEN

The Golden Griddle Pancake House smells like Sunday morning at Allie's house. Her dad always made the best pancakes. I scan the menu looking for peanut butter pancakes, but no luck. I decide to order blueberry pancakes, and sit my menu on the round table. Allie is sitting across from me, Tracy on my left, and Luke on my right. I watch them look at their menus as if the only worry on their mind is whether to add bacon or sausage.

When our food comes, my hunger kicks in. All I want to do is eat, but I force myself to focus on the discussion at the table.

"About this plan," Allie starts, "I need to take Jute back to Tennessee. She has school."

The guys look at each other a little uneasily. I don't know if it's the realization that I am technically still a minor or if it's the thought of being openly gay in east Tennessee. Luke is tapping his fork on the tablecloth. I reach out and put my hand over his.

"Allie, I don't think I can go back to Tennessee. What about Earl? What about my house?"

"Earl isn't going to bother you, Jute. Maybe Tracy and Luke will help us get your house repaired. Everything is going to be perfect from now on. I will have to go to Ohio, but I will drive to see you on the weekends when I can."

"Have you lost your mind? I can not possibly go back!"

Luke and Tracy are wide eyed and I can tell Luke is a

126

little embarrassed by the scene I am causing. He squeezes my hand, though, and tries to look supportive. He might not know the details of my distress, but he understands the emotion.

"Look, we'll drive back and you'll see. You don't need to be afraid anymore." She is serious. I can't believe she is serious.

I speak through clenched teeth so I won't get too loud, "How the Hell are you so sure it's safe? Earl is probably searching everywhere for us. And, does anyone even know where we are? Have you talked to your family?"

Allie's mouth tightens into a straight line and then she exhales. "I called Dad last night. And, you don't have to worry because Earl is dead."

My mouth forms the word *how*, but the word doesn't come out.

Allie stands up, gives me a nervous glance, and then walks outside to the pay phone. Tracy heads to the checkout to pay. Luke and I are alone and the silence is awkward.

"Who is Earl?" Luke's voice is soft but blunt. It's understandable that he would want to know what he and Tracy are getting into. But now even I don't know what we're getting into.

"Earl is my step-dad," I answer.

"Oh, so he did this to you and destroyed your house?"

"Yes, something like that..."

"Is your mom alive?"

"Something like that," I repeat, looking up to give him a brief smile. His eyes are focused on mine. He knows I'm not telling the entire truth. I just hope he can read my mind so I won't have to tell the rest of this aloud.

Luke's chair scrapes across the wooden floor as he stands up. He is looking toward the door, so I follow his gaze and see Tracy leaving. I guess it's time to go. Luke picks me up and carries me out the door. The waitress smiles sweetly at us. She winks at Luke and pats his arm.

"You all have a nice day, now. Come back and see us."

127

Tracy is climbing into the backseat of the Camaro and Allie is already starting the car. Once Luke and I are in, I pull the door closed and look at Allie expecting to be told the whole story. But, she looks pale and nervous. I am too terrified to ask questions.

The road goes on forever in front and behind us. No one has been able to figure out what to say to each other. The wheels on the interstate lull us with gentle clunking as they roll over sections of pavement. Allie hasn't turned on the radio. From the corner of my eye, I have looked at her many times. She is always staring ahead, her hands squeezing the steering wheel so hard that her knuckles are white. She seems to get more and more determined with every mile marker we pass. I just don't know what she is determined to do.

The tension and fear in the front of the car is almost palpable. I imagine it is the same in the backseat. It is like we are all waiting for Allie to tell us the plan she has been mulling over in her mind. No one wants to interrupt her thoughts.

Slowly, I turn my head to look at Luke and Tracy. I expect they will look at me questioningly and all I will be able to do is shrug. But, they don't even see me look at them. They are kissing, Tracy's hand on Luke's face and Luke's hand on Tracy's knee. They look so at ease, I have to wonder how long they've been at it. Their stealth is impressive, but I guess they had to learn that quickly with a dad like Tracy's around.

I decide not to disturb them and turn back toward the front. I catch Allie looking at me out of the corner of her eye. Her face is a bit more relaxed, so I bravely ask, "Are you okay?"

"Sure," she shrugs. "Are you?"

"I try not to think about how I am, now or any other time."

Allie takes my hand in hers. I let her this time, and give her a gentle squeeze.

"You are going to be just fine, Jute. I won't let anything bad happen to you."

"You keep saying that like you have something up your sleeve. I hope you aren't trying to be my knight in shining armor."

"That's a weird visual considering how afraid I am of horses, but okay," she says before looking over at me for what feels like too long.

"Watch the road!" I yell at her, then look back at the boys with apologetic eyes. But, they don't seem disturbed.

"You know, I was a perfect driver until you started freaking out all the time. Would you just trust me and let me drive?"

She turns the radio on and Bruce Springsteen's voice fills the car. "Dancing in the Dark" is nearly over, but Tracy immediately joins in singing the lyrics. Luke adds his voice to the chorus, their harmony gives me chills. I turn to see their over-the-top dramatic Bruce interpretation, their arms jutting about in bad dance moves. They hold nothing back with their amazing voices. Allie is watching them in her rear view mirror. I fight my panic about her eyes not being on the road.

I let myself join in the singing just as the song ends and fades into Blondie's "Heart of Glass".

"This one's yours, Jute!" Tracy calls out. So, I unbuckle my seatbelt and turn as much as I can to face them and try to be equally entertaining. I try to make my eyes wide and seductive, plump my lips out, and try to look bored the way Blondie does. I move my shoulders up and down with the music and sway a little. They howl with laughter.

I can actually sing this song pretty well, so eventually they stop laughing to listen. Tracy sings along with the chorus. Luke watches him sing like he is ice cream that needs eaten before it melts. It's funny, but I don't dare laugh. I know I've looked at Allie that way more times than I want to admit.

When the song is over, Luke kisses Tracy again.

Allie is smiling, glancing up at the action in the backseat.

"I saw that coming."

"Yes, me, too."

"So, do you want to talk?" She asks this like I'm the one who has been sitting in my seat squeezing off the blood flow to my fingers and gritting my teeth in silence.

Cautiously I respond, "Whenever you're ready."

"I've been ready."

"That's just crazy, Allie. You've been sitting over there grinding your teeth down to the gums and squeezing the wheel so hard that your knuckles are white. You obviously were NOT ready to talk."

She looks at me out of the corner of her eye, then back to the road. I keep my eyes on her and watch her do everything I just accused her of.

"I just don't want you to be hurt. Ever. If I could, I would take us all to Ohio. But, you have to finish school. If you don't, I will never forgive myself. I mean, you were always the smartest kid in class, always reading and coming up with amazing ideas. You should have graduated early instead of me. And I'm the one who should be struggling to get a passing grade."

"I'll pass." I assure her. Allie always makes a big deal out of things she shouldn't and completely ignores things she should worry about. "But, I don't know if I can still live in that house. The owner might not even rent it out to Momma after seeing what Earl did to it. So, I'm not going to worry about school until I know if I have somewhere to live. And Luke and Tracy..." I cock my head toward the backseat and don't say anything else. I know Allie is aware that this is no longer just about us.

"Dad said Judy has to pay for the damage because she signed the lease. What he didn't say, and excuse me if I cross a line by saying it myself, is that we all know your mom will never pay him. She'll just default. But, if we get back, we can talk to the owner about fixing everything ourselves. I already asked Dad to contact him and let him know that's what we planned to do.

"Was your Dad mad at us?"

"Mad is an understatement. Earl's trailer burned down and Dad thought we might have been in it."

Allie's face is staring far off up ahead of us. I watch her holding her breath. Something about her worries me.

I don't know what expression I have on my face when she finally looks at me from the corner of her eye. But, she registers my expression and gives me a single nod. Maybe she is admitting her involvement in what happened at Earl's trailer, which I can not even wrap my mind around, but it's better if we don't talk about it now.

"What about my mom? Was she worried?"

"You know how she is, Jute." Allie puts her hand on my shoulder and rubs my back. "Let it go."

She sits up and arches her back to stretch her muscles, raising her shoulders then dropping them again. She has been driving a long time.

"Do you want me to drive a while?"

"I'm fine. I just need to get us home and get all the bad stuff behind us."

We don't speak for a while, differently than before. This time, I know we are both trying to figure out what we should expect when we get back. There isn't any certainty to grasp onto, except that Hank is upset, Momma probably wishes I was dead, and Earl really is dead. I think about all these things and how much my life has changed so much in such a tiny fragment of time. Whether it has changed for the better, I can not say.

I listen to an occasional snore coming from the back, growing louder than the sound of the radio. Every time I look behind me, I see Tracy's head in a different position, but always asleep and always with his mouth open. Luke is usually staring out the window, but sometimes I catch him looking at Tracy. I hope they decide to stay with me for a while. There will be nothing there to keep them from leaving.

CHAPTER NINETEEN

The Savannah River welcomes us into Georgia. Sun lights up the hills, but my eyes strain to see all the way to the horizon. I look all around for a glimpse of the Tennessee mountains, but we are nowhere near them. I am eager to be back in the woods, held close between two mountain slopes. There are so many bad things that have happened there, but it's the only place that feels like home. As long as I think about the ash trees, the pin oaks, the white pines, I can imagine myself at peace. I avoid any memories of being indoors, though.

By the time we reach Atlanta, we have been in the car for over five hours. Allie gets through the heavy traffic and takes an exit into Cartersville.

"I think I'm going to piss all over myself," Tracy says from the back. We all laugh in agreement. We've pushed our bodies' limits.

"Everybody try to hold their pee just a minute more," Allie looks a little anxious. "I'm pulling in to that restaurant up ahead. We'll grab a bite to eat and kill two birds with one stone."

As soon as Allie shifts into park, I open my door and get out. I pull the seat forward to let Luke and Tracy file out. They head inside the restaurant without so much as a nod. Luke forgets to carry me, but I'm glad. I've been off my feet for hours. Surely I can make it across a parking lot. Besides, he can't exactly carry me to the toilet.

I start walking toward the doors when Allie catches up to me. She lifts my arm over her shoulders for support. Her other arm is around my waist. It feels like it has been forever ago that she and I were this close.

"I'm okay, you know. I can make it in."

"I know." She says, but doesn't let go.

By the time we get to the restroom doors, the guys have already gone in and are now back out.

"That was quick," Allie and I say in unison.

"You two are just slow," Tracy winks at Allie.

"I'm sorry I ran off and left you back there," Luke seems worried about it.

"I'm fine. Allie is doing a fantastic job, unnecessarily, but very remarkable none the less."

Tracy taps Luke's chest with the back of his hand, "We'll go get a table and order everyone's drinks. Same as breakfast?"

We both nod.

This is a buffet style restaurant, so I'm sure he and Tracy will start eating before we ever get to the table.

Allie turns the door knob to the bathroom but it is locked. A lady on the other side calls out, "Just a minute!"

She finally comes out holding a little girl's hand. They have matching brown hair in the exact same bobbed hair style. The little girl looks up at Allie's arms around me, holding me up like I've broken my leg. She checks my face for signs of pain, but I just smile at her. She smiles back at me over her shoulder as her mom pulls her toward the dining area.

Allie pushes the door open and we go in together. She lets go of me and darts into the only stall. I call out, "I see how I rank."

I lock the door and lean against it as I wait.

"I'm sorry, but I had to go. I'll hurry."

She does, flushing and hopping out of the stall before her pants are even pulled up.

"Ok, go!"

I laugh, which makes me only need to pee worse. She looks like she's running a sack race, but she doesn't know why I'm laughing. If I took the time to look at her, I would probably see a hurt expression on her face. But, my bladder doesn't care.

The hand dryer kicks on as I am pulling my jeans back up. I step out of the stall. Allie has the dryer turned to blow on her face and is humming into it. She doesn't do weird things like this around anyone else but me.

I walk over to the sink and watch her in the mirror as I wash my hands. She looks over and catches me staring at her. The air dryer whips her hair up on one side, making her look more punk than any of my friends back home. Her face is so serious. The contrast is hilarious and beautiful.

"What?" She demands, walking behind me and resting her head on my shoulder.

We look at each other in the mirror. I try not to look at myself at all. I keep my eyes on hers. The last thing I want to do is look at myself and see that horror again. Just thinking I might is causing panic to rise up inside me. I feel insane. But, Allie's face is calm and happy. The fluorescent lights brighten her blue eyes. I think how pointless it was to drive to the ocean when I could have just stayed in Tennessee and looked into this blue instead.

Her eyes do not stay on mine. They are looking at all of my face and everywhere she can see reflected of me in the mirror. I begin to feel self-conscious, worrying about what she is seeing, but I don't dare focus on my reflection.

"You are so beautiful, Jute." She is whispering this, but it feels like a punch inside my head. "Look at yourself," her eyes close and I am forced out of their safety. She turns her head and kisses me behind my ear, kissing me again on my neck, whispering in between, "Your big brown eyes and delicious mouth. I have imagined myself kissing your lips since the night I met you in the woods."

The whirring in my head is deafening, only letting in

the soft sound of her voice. I forget where I am, I only see what she is saying. I see her mouth kissing my neck, I see my brown eyes, and I look at my mouth, trying to make my eyes believe what my ears are hearing. I try, but I only see my usual big ugly mouth, something that isn't good enough to be dreamed about by someone like Allie.

Her hands touch the skin at my waist under my t-shirt. She stops kissing my neck to pull the shirt over my head. She drapes the shirt across the stall and puts her hands on my back, sliding them around to my stomach.

"Tell me you see what I see, Jute," she says.

I can't see it. All I see is a flashback to the beach when I asked her not to do this. It is so cruel and painful. I close my eyes and remember how she looked with the wind blowing her hair and the tears in her eyes.

"Open your eyes. You have to do this. Now." Her voice is still a whisper, but much more demanding. I don't want to open them, but I do.

I keep my eyes fixed on her eyes until she steps directly behind me and I can not see her. I can only see her hands on my stomach as they move up to my bra. I feel her kissing the back of my neck where I can not see her. My skin is burning everywhere there is contact. The contact with her, with my jeans, even down to my feet, it is all on fire. Inside of me, a thousands tiny hands are punching away at my heart to halt this pleasure. I hurt to feel this good. I will die if I fall from this height. I am terrified. I am paralyzed.

I close my eyes again and feel her hands undo my bra. I let her take it, feeling the cold air rush in as she moves to hang it over the stall. When her warmth returns, she pulls me around to face her.

"Open your eyes, Jute!" She is not whispering now. I open my eyes and I am looking directly into her eyes.

"If you won't see yourself in the mirror, then see yourself in my eyes. Don't get lost. Stay right here in my eyes and watch me seeing you like this."

She kisses my top lip, then my bottom lip, then both. Her hands are on my hips and she is pushing me until my back hits the stall. It is cold and chills cover my flesh and make my nipples so hard they hurt. Her hands move up to my breasts and I hear her catch her breath.

"Your body is amazing," she sighs into my mouth as she continues to explore my tongue with hers. I want to close my eyes and drift into this euphoria, but I don't want to disappoint her. I keep my eyes open and on hers.

She stops kissing me and smiles her crooked smile, never letting her eyes leave mine. "Watch me," she says, then lets her gaze drop from my eyes. She kisses my chin, down the center of my neck, and drops lower toward my breasts. I watch her eyes follow the circular movements of her hands as she lightly runs her fingers all over my skin. I watch her smile between quick kisses to every curve of my body. I watch her eyes close in pleasure when her mouth covers my nipple. I see my skin against hers and I never want to stop looking.

I reach down and pull her up so I can kiss her, really kiss her. I grab her upper arms and pull her around so that her back is now against the stall. I put my lips to the soft skin on her neck and breathe in the lilac scent of the shampoo from the hotel. Her skin tastes salty sweet. I hear her sigh as her body relaxes, held up by mine pressing against hers.

My arms wrap around her waist and my hands grab the fabric of her purple t shirt. I pull to untuck it. Her body stiffens and her hands grab mine. I hear her saying, "wait," but I am swimming in desire and can't make sense of it. She holds my hands tightly in hers. "Wait, Jute. Stop." Her words are gentle yet pleading. I stop kissing her and look in her eyes to try to understand what is happening.

Just then, someone knocks on the bathroom door. "Is anyone in there?" a raspy man's voice calls out.

We hear keys in the lock. I manage to get my shirt on before the door flies open and a trashcan on wheels is shoved into the room with us. A middle aged man with a shaggy beard looks startled when he sees us. I have no doubt that Allie and I both look a bit disheveled and wild eyed. We push past him without an introduction. I wad up my bra and hand it to Allie. She shoves it into her purse as we reach our table.

We take our seats across from Luke and Tracy. They have two empty plates stacked at the edge of the table and a plate of dessert in front of them. The ice in our glasses of soda has melted and left a thick layer of water on top. Tracy and Luke look at us and simultaneously start to snicker.

"Shut up," Allie tries to sound offended, but she is smiling. She slams her purse down at her seat and storms off to the buffet in an impressive imitation of an angry girl.

CHAPTER TWENTY

The sun set about the time we crossed the Tennessee state line. Tracy started singing "Rocky Top" in a bad Southern accent. I don't know which was more entertaining, Tracy pretending to be a hillbilly or Luke looking at him with both repulsion and concern. I joined in singing with him because I secretly like country music, too. I also secretly like the reaction it causes in Luke. It reminded me of the looks I give Allie sometimes when she plays really shallow pop songs.

We're making our way toward Madisonville, Tennessee right now. Everyone is quiet and staring wide-eyed out the window at the piles of snow along the road. It must have really come down here after we left. There are patches of snow still on the road and Allie is driving much slower. There probably wasn't any school today, so at least that's one day I won't have to make up.

"Maybe we should pull off and stop at a hotel." Tracy is nervously tapping his knee with his fingertips and looking out all our windows.

Luke laughs, "You'd think you've never seen snow before!"

"Fine, let the guy from Wisconsin make fun of the Southerns driving in the snow. You know, Allie isn't used to driving in the snow, so if you want to laugh, you might be laughing yourself all the way into a ditch."

Allie protests, "Hey! What is it with you people thinking I can't drive? I've gotten you this far, haven't I?"

I look at her and see her smile, but in her eyes I can see how exhausting this has all been.

"Maybe we should stop and rest for the night," I say, forgetting that I don't have any money for a hotel.

"I vote we stop, too," says Luke. "Not because I think the roads are bad, but because there's nothing we can do to make Jute's house livable at this hour. We won't even be able to talk to Allie's dad about it until the morning. I'll pay, just find us a hotel."

Tracy's eyes are still darting all around the snow covered landscape when he calls out, "There's a Motor Inn!"

Allie jerks the steering wheel so we don't miss the turn and the Camaro slides a little on a patch of ice before catching on the dry part of the pavement. I want to look at Luke's expression right now, but I'm afraid to take my eyes off the road. I don't know what good it will do since I'm not driving, but the adrenaline keeps me focused on every bump and jostle.

The Motor Inn is familiar to me, being just a thirty minute drive from Maryville. My friends come here sometimes after partying in the mountains. It's a warm, dry place to crash. No one could ever get away with being loud and belligerent here, which is why only my more mellow friends came. Not everyone in the punk crowd was actually punk-like. It's a small town area, so our crowd attracted anyone who didn't fit in to "normal". Allie, for example, is far from punk. But, she is also far from normal.

The parking lot is crowded for a Tuesday night, but I'm sure the weather is to blame. Allie parks and lets the boys out on her side. I haven't had to stand up for a while, but I'm sure I could have let them out on my side just fine. I will be glad when all this pitying is over. Allie gets back in the car and we sit in silence watching the guys go into the hotel office together.

"It's going to be weird sleeping in a room with Tracy and Luke," Allie says, mostly to herself.

I look at her and try not to seem as confused as I am. It just seems like a weird thing to be troubled by with so much other things going on at the moment. She finally looks over at me and raises her eyebrows as if she has been waiting for me to say something.

I look out my window and quietly mumble, "That's very un-Allie-like of you to say." But, she managed to hear me anyway.

"Well, it's just going to be tense, is all. I don't care that they are gay, if that's what you think I was implying," She sounds defensive, but I don't look at her to see her expression.

In no time, Tracy comes out carrying two keys. Luke follows him, looking down at his wallet while he tucks in his change and a receipt.

"I guess it won't be weird for you now," I say, thinking more about going to sleep than trying to figure out what she means by tension.

We get out of the car and I walk on my own to the back so Allie doesn't need to carry everything. There is no need in taking the entire box of my clothes, so I pull a t-shirt off the top and a pair of black jeans from the bottom. I don't have any underwear in the box. Maybe Allie will give me some of hers, but I won't ask.

Tracy hands me one of the hotel keys and winks. He looks happy and exhausted. There must be so much he and Luke need to discuss. I hope we made the right choice by asking them to come with us here, but they made the choice as well. For all of us, choices are very limited.

We walk up a flight of stairs outside the hotel to reach the balcony of the second floor. Our rooms are side by side just around the corner. Tracy gets their door open first and they disappear into their room. I hear Allie's impatient fidgeting while I try to get the key turned the right way in the lock. My hands are shaking and I try to hide it with my body, but Allie isn't looking anyway. Her eyes are staring down the length of the balcony away from me. I glance in that direction to see what is so interesting, but it's only more doors like ours and the gray concrete walkway.

The door swings open into a room barely warmer than the outside air. I walk over to the heater by the window, pull back the heavy maroon curtains, and pop open the flap covering the controls on the unit. I hear Allie opening her suitcase on the bed behind me. By the time I have turned up the thermostat, she is already in the bathroom. She must be taking a shower because I hear the water turn on.

There are two double beds in our room. Both are covered in a country blue bedspread with giant whirling maroon tulips all over it. I sit down on the one by the window, the one Allie's suitcase isn't on. I trace the pattern of the arcing tulips with my fingers as I try to relax. Nothing about any of this feels right. Maybe it's being in Tennessee again. Maybe it's how useless I feel. Maybe it's because Allie hasn't said a word about what happened in the restaurant.

I lie down and think back to our drive. She was unusually quiet after we left Cartersville. But, we were all unusually quiet. The day has been full of uncertainty and pain. Thinking about that moment when I kissed her and nearly lost myself, it seems out of place with everything else that is happening. I can understand if she regrets it, but I fight back anger at her for doing it when I asked her not to. It seems that Allie believes her power to seduce trumps my power to refuse to be seduced. To me, this isn't a game. My feelings are intense and deep, and for so long my life has depended on protecting them.

The water turns off and I barely hear it because my eyelids are so heavy and I am falling asleep. But, I sit up when Allie comes into the room. She is wearing her Victorian cotton gown. She has been wearing this every time we've spent the night together for years. It is the opposite of sexy, reminding me of an Amish girl.

"Your turn," she says, giving me a tired smile.

She has already pulled her suitcase off the other bed and pulled back the covers before I even get to the shower. She is either really tired, or avoiding sleeping with me.

Resentment is making my face hot, and I find my hand turning the faucets to a hotter setting as well. I pull off my clothes while mumbling under my breath. I repeat all the things I told her at the ocean. She is treating me like I did something wrong to her and I have done nothing at all. But, maybe this is just how it is with her screwed up past. She thinks any sexual thought she has makes her a slut, whether or not the person she is having them with views her that way or not.

I unwrap my bandages and am pleased that they haven't stuck to my wounds. I step in the shower and feel the water burning my flesh. I let it, despite the tears in my eyes. I also let my brain finally remember Allie's hands on me. The pain inside of me burns hotter than the water hitting my skin. It isn't her fault she has a warped view of herself. But, no matter how innocent she is, it doesn't stop the pain this tension is causing. She and I need to talk and I am not going to go to sleep until we do.

Feeling truly clean and clear headed for the first time in days, I step out of the shower and dry my hair in a frenzy of towel. I don't have enough hair to warrant all the motion over my head, but I like the way the sound of the towel over my ears muffles everything else. I like the movement of my arms, finally out of that cramped car. I pull the towel away from my head and swipe it across the mirror to clear the condensation. My hair is long enough on top to finally lie down, but I don't look at it long before the mirror fogs up. I throw on the t-shirt I plan to wear tomorrow. It's long enough to come to my thighs, so I leave off my pants. I'm uncomfortable not having underwear, but have more important things to discuss with Allie.

I walk into the bedroom area and see her sleeping with her back to me. She has turned off the light beside her bed, but not the light to the other bed. I think she was hoping to avoid talking to me.

I sit on the bed next to her and gently move her wet hair

away from her face. The room still has a chill, but the heater is working hard to get it warm. I feel like waking her up to talk to me, but it seems wrong.

This must be how she used to feel when she spent the night with me and I fell asleep. There were many times when we were younger that she would come to my house to watch Friday Night Videos. She would say, "I'm not coming over unless you promise not to fall asleep before the show is over." She hated being in my house when everyone was asleep except her. But, I never could stay awake. I'd open my eyes at two o'clock in the morning, the tv would be showing static, and Allie would be gone. She had walked home through the woods in her nightgown. My parents would get up the next day and accuse me of being mean to her. I stayed mad at her for a few hours the next day, but nothing more. It never stopped me from asking her over again, and it never stopped her from demanding the same conditions and ultimately agreeing to come.

What would I do if I lost her?

Waking her up just isn't an option, so I climb into the other bed and turn off the light. The heater finally kicks off, leaving the room warm and silent. But, the sounds from outside the room bleed in through the walls. I hear shuffling and movement in the boys room. They must still be awake. I'm sure they are enjoying this time alone together. I smile, forcing myself to be happy for them and not feel sorry for myself.

I close my eyes tightly and put the other pillow over my head to block any sound. When the heater kicks on again, I finally find enough peace to drift off to sleep.

CHAPTER TWENTY-ONE

The bark is flaky and hot, warming my arms wrapped tight around the trunk. I don't know how I got here, but I don't want to fall. The sun must have warmed this tree, but darkness has settled and I can't even see the sky. I am surrounded by branches stretching wide above me and below me. My feet push against the trunk, inching me higher to a branch big enough to hold my weight. Pieces of bark fall off and fall far below me. White Oak. This is a white oak tree. Usually, I feel a secret pride when I identify a tree by its winter bark. But, nothing like that comes now. That reliable voice of contradiction in my head is eerily absent.

My hand lets go to grab the branch, the muscles in my arm pull me up as my other hand lets go of the trunk. My feet kick off the trunk, pieces of bark scatter. I swing up and one leg makes it over the branch. I inch my foot across, pulling my body up until I am lying face down, hugging the branch and trying to make the forest stop spinning. I have knocked more bark loose. The acrid smell burns my nose. I carefully sit up, my arms embracing the wide trunk beside me. When I feel balanced and safe, I close my eyes and exhale weakly, then inhale deeply. The air is dry and hurts my nostrils.

The nagging pain of a scratch on my knee comes to my attention. The skin tingles and itches as the blood begins to dry. As the itch turns into a throbbing pain shooting out along the skin of my leg, I remove a hand from the trunk and scratch it. My knee rises up to meet my hand. The pain intensifies. I feel myself fall backwards off the branch. I open my mouth to scream, but my voice sounds like a screeching bird, an injured raven.

I tumble out into nothing, spinning over and over with only visions of the dark starry sky coming into view with every rotation. Stars, then nothing, then stars again. My body feels nothing except the wind as I spin over and over. I don't want it to end. I know I will die when I land. But, I don't think about that. I only think about the wind and the stars.

A river catches me, moving swiftly. I swim toward the surface, frantic for oxygen. My human arms are stretched out in front of me and I see only the muscles and no skin. I break through to the surface and gasp deeply for air before the rapids pull me under. My arms continue to fight to keep my head above water, skinless with rotten meat hanging by tendons. I touch my face and feel my skull. I am already dead. That thought repeats over and over as I let myself go under. I try to drown. But, I do not die. The river sweeps me downstream for miles and miles, thrashing me against rocks and entangling me in fallen logs, but I still don't die. I tumble in the rapids, the water burning my lungs.

CHAPTER TWENTY-TWO

I sit up, gasping, I believe. But, my mouth is rigid and closed. I am in bed. The heater is whirring. My heart is racing. My hands go to my face and feel soft, smooth skin. I throw the blankets aside and walk toward the mirrors near the bathroom. I don't get far before the horrific reflection comes into view. I turn and run from the hotel room, the cold winter air blowing against my legs and up and through my shirt. I remember how nearly naked I am. One of my hands holds my t shirt down while the other beats on the boys' door.

"It's me," I am trying not to scream, but my voice is barely under my control.

The door swings open and Tracy's calm and beautiful face comes into view. How can he not panic at the sight of me? But, his eyes stay gentle as his hand reaches out and pulls me into the room. All the lights are on, a sci-fi movie is on the tv. Aliens. Luke is missing. I hear the shower. I don't know when I stopped holding my breath, but I am breathing now. I smell pizza and marijuana.

"You look like you need this." Tracy is handing me a joint. It is now that I see his naked chest, his skin blushed red in splotches from recent embraces.

I nod, taking the joint and inhaling deeply. Maybe too deeply. I don't want to give it back to him.

Tracy takes my hand and leads me to the only bed in the room. It is a king sized bed, which I have never seen. The bedspread is like the one in our room, only it is sage green with country blue tulips. He holds it up and climbs under, then pats his hand on the sheet beside him. I slide in, sitting up so I can smoke the joint.

I don't feel like talking and Tracy doesn't force me. He hugs his arm across my thighs, resting his head on my hip. Finally, I pass the joint back to him, but he shakes his head to refuse it. I lick my fingers and tap the end to put it out. I do it a couple of times to be sure, then lean over to the nightstand. It is so far away that I have to stretch my body to reach it. Tracy's head falls off my hip. When I turn back around, I see he is propped up on one elbow looking at me and smiling.

"How was it?" He asks.

"Why? Is it different than what we smoked last time?"

"Not the pot! I'm talking about Allie."

It takes a minute before I realize what he is asking. I try to act nonchalant.

"She fell asleep. I had a bad dream, but I didn't want to wake her." I am intentionally vague because I don't feel like talking about it. I try to focus on the tv, but regret it when I see the alien bite off a man's arm. Blood squirts out of it as he wobbles around before he falls through a window. This is not what I want to watch while getting high.

Luke steps out of the bathroom and looks into the mirror. He has a towel wrapped around his waist and a giant United States Marine Corps tattoo on his back. I'm surprised, not because he was a marine, but because he hasn't mentioned it. The muscles of his back and arms are very well defined. No wonder he could carry me around so effortlessly. I see why Tracy finds him attractive, despite his close set eyes and turned up nose. Actually, who am I to say that close set eyes and turned up noses aren't what he loves most?

Maybe I am watching Luke for too long, but he is better to look at than the horror on the tv. Tracy is pushing his face into my hip again, half asleep. His hand is on my thigh, which didn't mean anything when we were sleeping with Allie. But, having Luke in the room while he has his body so close to mine makes me nervous. I slide down under the blankets so Tracy's hand can rest on my stomach instead. He hugs me close and rests his face against the top of my head.

"You still awake?" Luke calls from around the partition.

"Yes," Tracy calls back, stretching his arms above his head to try to wake up. "Jute came in. She's in bed with me." He says it like it is a perfectly normal thing to say to your boyfriend. I hope he's right. I can't see Luke now that I'm lying down in bed, so I wait for him to come into the room.

Luke walks by the tv and picks up the remote, pointing it toward the screen. The time flashes in the top corner: 11:37. That seems too early. The picture on the tv goes to black and the room gets silent.

Luke sits down on the bed beside me, leaning back against the headboard. He is still wrapped in the towel. He and I share this burden of not having clean clothes to wear, but my situation would be worse if not for Allie's stupidity. Even if I don't take into account my box of stolen clothes, I'm still better off because I might be able to fit into Allie's clothes. Luke could never wear Tracy's.

"So, did you wear Allie out and decide to come see if Tracy had anything left for you?" His mouth is smiling, but his eyes aren't.

I feel Tracy's muscles stiffen. He sits up and props his knee up and rests his arm on it. Every time he moves, it's a snapshot from a magazine. It is exhausting to be around. "She's a friend, Luke. It's not like that."

Luke raises up the blankets and looks down at my half-naked body close to his boyfriend. "I see," he says, smirking.

I think I should go. I start to sit up when Luke slides down under the blankets and pulls me close to him. My high is kicking in and the embrace feels warm. My brain is trying not to panic. I don't get the same peaceful vibe from Luke that I get from Tracy, but there is a peaceful vibe artificially running through my veins right now.

Luke takes his hands from my hips and just lies beside

me, propped up on his elbow. He lowers his voice and tries to sound relaxed, "You didn't answer my question. Did you and Allie have a good time?"

"We didn't have sex, if that's what you are implying," I know he is trying to upset me, but I am floating inside my skin and find it easy to ignore his intentions.

"Why not? A lesbian like you and a beautiful girl like her... I don't understand women, not even ones like you, Jute."

Tracy's hand had gone back to my stomach at some point. I didn't notice when, but I do notice now that he lifts it away and reaches out to Luke's. "Cool it," he says evenly.

"I'm not a lesbian," I say. I am serious, but I giggle a little at hearing myself.

Luke laughs so hard he has to sit up and catch his breath. "You. Not a lesbian? The girl who looks like a boy and is in love with a girl says she isn't gay." He laughs more before and then his eyes grow serious, "So, is that why you came to our room? Because Tracy likes boys and you think you're close enough to pass?"

I instinctively start to sit up to punch him. My high makes me feel like too much momentum will launch me into the ceiling. Tracy's arm holds me back and I don't even have it in me to fight that.

"She's been through a lot, Luke. Try to lay off."

My brain studies the wetness on my eyelashes as if from afar. Why are there tears? How long will they stay? Are they not falling down my cheeks because my eyelashes have grown? If my eyelashes grow longer, will I look like a girl? I think of all these things, but not a single thought about how to explain who I am to Luke. I know I don't owe him an explanation, but my mind eventually shifts from analyzing my tears to analyzing my womanhood. I am mad at Luke because he instigated this.

"The point you are missing, Luke," I say, "is that I don't want to have sex. Not with Tracy. Not with Allie. Not with you. Not with anyone. I have told Allie this, too. I don't

149

know why it's so hard to comprehend."

Luke lies on his back and looks at the ceiling thoughtfully.

"But, you love her like that, I can tell. You can't get mad at me for seeing how you dress and cut your hair, looking at how you act around Allie, and assuming you are a lesbian."

I put my arm across his chest, hoping it is a reassuring gesture which will help him take my words seriously.

"I love Allie because she's Allie. If she was a boy, but everything else was the same, I would feel the same way."

Tracy's voice is soft in my ear, "And what way is that?"

My throat tightens, unsure if I should let out the truth to these people I barely know. But, the words do find their way out, "Like if she kissed me I would fall into her and never find my way out. Like she is the answer to every question I have ever asked. But, I have nothing to offer her. How I feel about her is selfish. She would do anything for me, but that doesn't mean it's right to let her."

Tracy snuggles up behind me and puts his arm over Luke, on top of mine. He rubs the length of my arm with his warm hand. I focus on the feeling on my skin until I am lost in the sensation. He whispers in my ear, "Allie loves you, too, Jute. I see it in her eyes."

The mention of her eyes gives me the sensation of being pulled up out of the bed and carried off toward her. I feel warm and light. I try to push the thought away.

"I can't do this," I say, thinking of everything that has happened with Allie today. I can't stay in this bed, listening to advice from people who barely know us. I push myself to sit up and begin to roll out of bed over Luke. He seems startled at first, as if he believes I'm making a move on him. When my feet hit the floor I stand and pull my t-shirt down as far as I can..

"Don't worry, Luke, I wasn't going to molest you," I roll my eyes at him. "I'll see you two tomorrow." I head for the door and walk out to the icy air.

CHAPTER TWENTY-THREE

The door was left unlocked. I didn't think about locking it when I left. I didn't think about Allie at all. I take the door knob in my hand and horrible images flash through my mind. Guilt rises up as if I have caused her death, but maybe she is sleeping soundly and unharmed. I push the door open and see her sitting on the edge of her bed, crying into her hands. I didn't think I could hate myself more, but I do right now. Whatever has happened, happened because of me.

I shut the door behind me and turn to lock it. I pause briefly, stalling, staring at the brush strokes left when someone painted it beige. They remind me of saplings in winter, long vertical lines. I want to get lost in them, dreading what I have to face when I turn around. I touch the door and suddenly all the trees are just paint strokes again.

Taking a deep breath, I turn to face her. Allie is no longer sitting up, but fallen over on her side on the bed. Her feet are still on the floor, her hands still over her face. She is still crying.

I walk to her, but my body feels as light as air. The sound of my feet walking across the carpet is indistinguishable from the beat of my heart. I can't tell where my body separates from the room.

I climb onto the bed behind her and tentatively rest my hand on her arm. Her skin is soft and warm. My hand must feel like ice to her. I should move it away, but when I try, it doesn't go anywhere. I give up, let it stay, and lower my head to the pillow behind her.

"Are you okay?" My voice is weak and shaky.

"No." She says sadly.

There isn't a lot to go on. I try to think of what might have happened, but my brain offers me ridiculous suggestions like maybe someone came in and stole her shoes, maybe she is really hungry because I am really hungry, maybe an alien bit her arm. I mentally swat at these crazy suggestions like flies in my brain. Minutes seem like hours before I realize I will never be able to guess.

"Did someone hurt you?" My voice reminds me of a game show contestant. I don't mean to sound this way.

Allie had been wiping her eyes, but she stops to yell at me, "Who would hurt me, Jute? Let's see... maybe someone who says they love me but leaves me in the middle of the night. Just say it, you don't want to be around me anymore."

"You were sleeping!" I protest too loudly.

Allie surprises me with laughter, turning to face me with tears still covering her puffy red eyes. "I guess it serves me right after all those times I left you in the middle of the night."

Her eyes are filling the room up with blue. I roll onto my back beside her so I don't have to look into them.

"Well, I never liked it when you left. My parents gave me hell the next morning, accusing me of being mean to you. But I don't remember crying until my eyes were puffy and red. Where did you think I had gone?" Talking up to the ceiling was so much easier.

"I knew where you had gone. You went over to smoke pot with Tracy. And don't lie. I smell it on you." Her words are very matter-of-fact. I don't look at her face, but I see the words swirling up on the ceiling. Knew. Had Gone. Smoke.

"I had a bad dream," I offer as explanation. I would rather talk about the nightmare of meat hanging from bones than to fight with her because I smoked half a joint.

"And you couldn't wake me up to talk to me about it

instead?"

"I could have done a lot of things. I could have walked outside and leaped off the balcony. I could have stripped naked and run downstairs screaming, I could have called the office and asked them to send up some meat hooks." I could keep going, but I stop when Allie's hand whaps my stomach much harder than if she were kidding around.

"So, is that how I rank?" She pouts.

"Just under meat hooks? Do you honestly think so, Allie? Try not to be an asshole to yourself. You don't deserve it."

"What do I deserve, then?" She is baiting me. I try to pull myself back into my body so I can focus on answering her just right.

"You deserve a brain which will refuse to believe the lies people have told you. You are too easy to love not to have someone do it the right way." No, I don't think that was enough.

"Then why won't you?" Her arms cross.

"I do. You just think it doesn't mean anything unless we have sex. But, I understand why you think that way. You've been brainwashed by depraved boyfriends." All the words are coming out before I have time to check them. Once they leave, I feel like someone else said them. The words 'depraved boyfriends' play over in my mind.

Allie sits up and spins around to look down at me. Her knee is bent and touching my ribs, her other leg is draped off the edge of the bed.

"It's true then. You think all I care about is sex. What makes you any different than everyone else who calls me a slut? Oh, I know... the difference is that you have no interest in touching me. So, not only am I a slut to you, but I'm also repulsive."

How could she warp what I said into this ridiculous accusation?

I don't look at her, "I have never thought you were a

153

slut or repulsive. I just think you think sex fixes things. You look at me and you see a broken girl and you want to fix me. So, it's natural for you to want to do that with sex. But, it's not your fault you are like that, Allie."

She is silent too long. I finally give in and stop watching the swirls on the ceiling. I turn to look at her face, which is red and angry and hurt. I don't understand at all what is happening. But, I know I don't want to argue right now.

"I'm sorry, Allie. Please don't be mad. Can't we just be friends like we used to be?"

She still doesn't speak for far too long. I look back at her to see her face is no longer red and her eyes aren't glaring at me. They are soft and blue and sad. I hate it so much when she is sad. I move my hand from under the pillow to pat her knee. The sound makes tiny echoes in my head. I close my eyes to listen to them, feeling so heavy. I think maybe she forgives me.

Allie grabs my hand like it's a bird about to fly away. She holds it to keep it from tapping. I now have nothing to distract me from the sound of her voice. She speaks so quietly, "Is the real reason you told me not to kiss you because you don't think you are good enough?"

She waits for me to answer, but I don't.

"Ah," she says, "Or maybe you aren't attracted to me in the same way. I'm kind of ruined."

My eyes open, searching her face and hoping she is joking. She looks away when she sees I am looking at her.

I give her fingers a gentle squeeze. "It's just this, Allie. I don't want to have sex at all, with anyone."

She looks at me again and I try to focus on her dark brown hair draped across her shoulders and over the front of her white cotton gown. I just don't want to look in her eyes.

"Because of Earl?"

I nod, keeping my eyes on her hair. I am ashamed at how deceptive I have become. Everything I do is to hide from Earl or hide from the pain inside of me. I am too much of a coward to even know who I am.

"He's gone." She pauses to let it sink in. "You can't live your life in fear of him. Let someone love you."

Tears have come to my eyes and I try to blink them away, "It isn't just him, now. It's me. I look in the mirror and I don't see me. I see a dead person. My brain is cracked. I have nightmares that I am a walking corpse. I am so fucked up and it scares me. How could I possibly love you like you need to be loved?"

She lets go of my hand and starts to unbutton her nightgown. The tiny pearl buttons are hard to maneuver through the button holes. I feel myself wanting to get lost in the movements of her fingers. But, I don't.

"What are you doing?"

"I am showing you that you aren't the only one with scars."

Images flash in my mind. Halloween of 1988. I had followed Bobby's voice through the woods. He had been screaming insults at her. I found them in our secret place. I peered through the branches to see him sitting on her naked body, holding her down on the dry leaves. He wasn't screaming when I got there. His voice was quiet and seething. He had said something about love, but nothing about his voice or actions looked like love. It had hurt to watch. I had walked away to wait at home for her to find me before the party. When she did, there was fake blood on her Marilyn Monroe costume. I told her it looked awesome.

A chill runs through me now because all those thoughts I had pushed away are back. I look up at her eyes and she is looking deep into mine, unflinching.

I sit up to face her. "Stop."

"No," Her fingers drop to the fourth button. I look at her hands, but that seems even more dangerous than looking into her eyes. So, I look back into her determined stare. Nothing about this feels right, but I don't know how to stop her. I wish she would just tell me what is going on. I feel desperate, helpless, frantic to stop her.

I lean into her and put my lips on hers. The painful thoughts of wounds and scars and damaged girls were overwhelming. Kissing her is a coward's escape, I know. Earlier today, it was the bravest thing I had ever done. But, right now it is just an escape from even more frightening things.

Her lips taste salty from tears. I hope that mine do not taste like pot. I don't want to turn her off. But, does this mean that I am trying to turn her on? It's too much to think about. I just try to be gentle and kind and everything she has never had. This is nothing like our time in the restroom. She is not trying to prove anything. She lets me kiss her, holding back all of the desire I felt from her earlier.

I take her hands in mine, forcing her to stop unbuttoning her gown. She already has it undone to her stomach. Whatever she wanted to show me, it is within my reach. A magical thought comes to mind. The thought makes me warm and extraordinary and I know it is the right thing to do. I know it is right for Allie. It may destroy me in the end, but this moment is not about me.

My hands let go of hers and move slowly up her arms, squeezing her gently every time my tongue enters her mouth. I try to kiss her the way she kissed me earlier, mimicking it exactly. I fight to keep only Allie's kisses in my mind, the gentle yet urgent touch of her lips. I had been so afraid to get lost in her kisses. But, now I am afraid of what will happen if I don't.

I push her to lie back on the bed. She looks up at me, her beautiful narrow face smiles. Her pouty bottom lip is wet from my kisses. Her eyes are wide and full of desire. I don't see a trace of pity, but maybe a hint of apprehension. Whatever she is afraid of, I need her to know it won't change how I feel about her.

I pull my t shirt off over my head. Before I have my arms out, Allie already has her hands on me. She is touching every rib, every small curve of my flesh as if it is far more

156

interesting than I perceive it. Looking at her looking at me, I can't deny that she likes what she is seeing and touching. I can barely look at her without tears coming to my eyes. No one has ever looked at me this way.

Leaning down, I kiss her mouth again. I kiss her cheek, toward her ear, and down to her neck. I feel her fighting the urge to wrap herself around me. Her hands rise up to touch me and fall away sharply as if she is forcing them down. She is letting me do whatever I am ready to do, careful not to push me. I smile against the skin of her neck, feeling her pulse racing. She hasn't figured out that I am in this all the way. She doesn't know that I have finally figured out a way to make up for all the bad things I let happen to her.

I let her believe it for a little while longer. I take my time kissing her neck, finding all the places which cause her back to arch. Her sighs are soft, cracking now and then as her eyes fill with tears. I test her patience, and she holds off pulling me to her for longer than I would have guessed. When she does finally break, and pulls me close, I pull away to sit up. I look down at her flushed, wet cheeks and smile at her. I want her to see there is no pity in my eyes, either.

Rising up onto my knees, I move to straddle her. Her hands move up my thighs to my hips and on to my breasts. I am nearly distracted from my mission. I sigh, but push her arms away. Now her eyes are full of curiosity. My hands find the next button of her gown while my eyes stay fixed on hers. As I undo it, I see panic on her face.

I stop unbuttoning to let my hands slide under the light cotton fabric to her breasts. Our eyes are locked, hers are frightened like an animal. As my fingers gently swirl around on her skin, I feel the scars I anticipated. She feels that I am touching them, tracing them with my fingertips. The tears in her eyes are different now. She has to come through this.

"You are not ruined. You are beautiful." I say to her, watching her blink away her tears only to have more come to the brim. I pull my hands out of her night gown and hold her face. I lean down and kiss her until I feel her tension leave.

Sitting back to look into her eyes, I continue, "I was there when Bobby cut you. I just wanted to believe you when you said it was fake blood. I'm sorry I let you down."

Tears pour out of her. She fights back the sobs. I have no words to stop it.

"I love you, Allie," I say, hoping she hears me. "You have always been the thing I love most in the world, now more than ever. Nothing that has happened to you in the past will change how I feel about you now."

My hands pull open her nightgown and I wait for her eyes to look into mine. I want her to see me look at her, but she keeps her head turned away. I kiss her neck and make my way down to her breasts. If she will not look at me, she will have to feel me. My tongue seeks out every line and jagged angle of scar. I have to fight to stay focused on the damaged skin because I am distracted by her nipples standing hard against my touch. Finally, I raise my head to see that she is looking down at me, completely consumed by pleasure.

I slide off of her and sit beside her with one foot on the floor. I move my fingertips across her breasts and let her watch me as I take in all of it at once. My mind processes the brutality her scars imply. Bobby had tried to write the word "slut" across her chest. The 's' and 'l' much more successful than the 'u' and 't'. Possibly he started to regain some sanity by the time he got to the end. I try to imagine what it must have been like for her to go through, and the shame she has felt since then.

"I have never seen anything more beautiful than you."

I reach for the hem of her nightgown. She sits up to allow me to pull it over her head. I straddle her again before pulling it off her arms. I toss it into the floor, but before I can lower my body back to hers, she has her mouth around my left nipple. Her teeth gently pull at it and I think I might explode. I shudder and she laughs before moving her mouth to kiss the right one.

Hours pass. My exhaustion is replaced by adrenaline.

There is no part of her my tongue has not touched. I have called her name a hundred times. I have never believed that sex equals love. But, if this is not love, I am okay to settle for less.

Wednesday, January 10, 1990
6:38 p.m.

Dear Jute,

I miss you terribly and I just got here! I thought about you all the way to Ohio. Thoughts of you kept me awake while I drove. I am exhausted. I am not even kidding that I could sleep for an entire week. But, Mom had me up at 6 o'clock this morning. She wanted to give me the tour of the Felicity Grocery before anyone else got there. You should see how tiny it is! It's cute, but I can't say that to Mom. She takes it so seriously.

Mom wants me to hang Valentine's decorations tomorrow, but I don't know if the snowmen are ready to come down yet. Brrrr, it's cold here today. But, I'll try to do what Mom wants and not complain. Maybe we'll learn to let the past go. I'm trying.

I appreciate that she is letting me stay with her when my classes start at University of Cincinnati. You know, working at my mom's grocery store is not exactly what I want to do my entire life, but it will give me some money to pay tuition fees. I am so nervous about all of this.

I'm also rambling on about a lot of boring stuff. I'm sorry. I just wanted you to know that I love you more than anything. You make me feel good about myself.

I'll see you in ten days. Write to me so I know you haven't forgotten me.

Love,
Allie

CHAPTER TWENTY-FOUR

Hank is standing in the living room waiting on Luke to get out of the shower. He shifts his weight nervously. I can't help staring. Hank is never fidgety.

"Are these boys okay here, Jute?" His eyes were full or concern, either for my safety and for his own possible overstep into my business.

"They don't bother me, Hank."

I hand him a cup of coffee and he looks at it hesitantly.

"I really didn't want to stay this long. That boy needs to get up earlier if he wants to keep his job. The guys will be on the truck, ready to head to the work site and waiting on us."

He takes the cup anyway and takes a big sip.

"How are you holding up with this fire and Earl passing on?"

I think about Allie and wonder if he knows she was there that day. I forget to answer his question.

Hank offers, "Earl was a bad person. But, we still mourn for bad people sometimes. When my Daddy died, I was still believing he'd stop drinking one day. I never thought he'd die a drunk. I mourn him, but I hate the bastard for not being worth the pain I get when I think about him."

"Well, I'm glad Earl's dead."

An image flashes in my mind of the scorched earth which used to be my home. There was nothing left of him except a few bone fragments, but it doesn't matter. No one wants to give him a funeral. Momma has not been to see me since she took off with Jerry. Drew refuses to acknowledge he ever existed. The only person to say his name to me is Hank.

Luke walks out of the bathroom wearing a pair of secondhand jeans and a work shirt. Hank got him a job with the city and has been nice enough to drive him to work every day until he can afford a car. It's Friday, and he has been excited to get his first paycheck today.

Hank hands me his coffee cup and touches his cap, "If you see my youngin' before I see her, tell her I'm cooking dinner on Sunday. Y'all come up."

"I will. You two be careful."

I close the door and watch until they leave. I finally allow myself to feel the rush of anticipation wash over me. Allie will be here tonight. I am blushing and laughing at myself. Thankfully, I did not act this way in front of Hank.

The bus will be here in thirty minutes. I skip into my room like a little girl and grab the black Myrtle Beach t-shirt from the top of my clothes stack. I want to get dressed quickly so I'll have time to talk to Tracy before I leave. As if he read my mind, I feel his hands grab my waist as I slide the t-shirt over my head. He takes the hem and helps pulls it down.

"Where did you come from?"

I turn around and see the sleepiness in his eyes. His head is probably still full of dreams.

"I waited for Hank to leave before I came out. I don't trust myself around Luke in public." He smiles dreamily.

"Allie comes home today!"

"I know! I bet she won't recognize this place after all the work we've put into repairs."

I kiss his cheek and step away so I can look him in his eyes. "Thanks. I don't know what I would do without you and Luke."

His gaze lingers on my eyes. Maybe he is really looking right through me. I wonder what he is thinking about.

"I have to go." I say, patting his cheek with my hand and watching him come out of his trance. "I'll see you after while, crocodile."

The day is spent staring at the clock. Every class is long and tedious. When I finally climb the steps onto the bus, my heart races and my hands shake. I don't know what I will do to pass the time when I get home. Allie will not leave Ohio until after work, maybe she is leaving now. I usually don't mind being the last stop on the bus route, but today I just want to be home.

When the bus pulls up in front of my house, I see the blue Camaro in my driveway. The brakes squeal to a stop and I stand up and run toward the front of the bus. Skeet, the bus driver, opens the doors and I jump over the steps and straight out the door.

Allie is already standing by the roadside. Skeet hasn't even closed the doors before her arms embrace me. I bury my face in her hair and breath in the scent of an unfamiliar perfume. It is both floral and earthy and makes my body weak. I don't break the moment with words. I hold her, motionless, feeling every connection between us.

Finally, she lets go and grabs my hand. We walk toward the house together.

"Did I surprise you? I took the day off so I could come early. I couldn't stand being away for another minute! But Mom would only let me if I agreed to be back Sunday night in time for church."

We rush into the house out of the cold. The wood stove fills the room with warmth and I start peeling off my coat. The smell of hamburgers frying fills the air. My stomach growls, but I am in no hurry for dinner. I hang up my coat by the door and turn back to Allie.

She looks so much older than she did two weeks ago. Her eyes search my face as I search hers. The blue of her eyes is set off by the blue silk flower she has pinned in her hair. Her knee length pencil skirt is red, the same color as her high heeled shoes. Her frilly blouse is delicate, white, and sheer. She has a camisole underneath, but it isn't enough to hide the lines

163

of her breasts. I feel suddenly small in front of her. She could pull me in and devour me into nothing. But the thoughts of that excite me more than they scare me.

"Tracy is cooking," she says as if it isn't what she wants to say, "Do you want to eat?"

I don't want to eat, but I feel mute. My brain is overwhelmed at the sight of her. She cocks her head sideways, curious about my silence. She reaches out her hand and takes mine, the jolt of pleasure is so intense that it hurts. She leads me into my bedroom and I follow her like a dog at her heels.

She sits on my bed and pulls me to sit beside her. I can't look at her. I need to kiss her or die. I hear her voice, speaking with so much calm. Where does it come from? I have none of it inside of me.

"What are we going to do with this?" She asks.

I still don't turn my head to look at her, but I know what she is asking. I just don't know what the answer is. I have nothing to lose and if I did, I would give it all up to have her. But, she has a life outside of this. So, she is the only one of us able to decide what comes next.

She sighs when she realizes I am not answering. "Mom would never allow us to be together. She hates gay people. You should hear what she says about her neighbors, two women living together. It's awful. She just can not ever know."

Allie is wringing her hands. I can see them in my peripheral vision, but I don't look into her eyes. I don't have to see them to know she is worrying about being seen as flawed. It is her Achilles' heel. I reach over and put my hand over hers.

"Don't let what she thinks of you ruin your happiness," I brave a glance at her. The light coming through the plastic covered window is just enough to make her blue eyes turn the color of an autumn sky. There is a second part to what I was saying. There is the part where I tell her she is beautiful no matter what. But, I don't say it.

I exhale the breath I didn't know I was holding and try to push away the sound of my heart pounding in my ears. I lick

164

my lips nervously. What is wrong with me?

Her lipstick is red. I haven't seen her wear red lipstick since she stole mine and put it on as a joke. Now she is here in my bed, inches away, with lips the color of cherry candy. I hate myself that these thoughts are reeking havoc when I should be reassuring her, not craving her. Damn it.

I lean in and kiss her, the desire is too strong to be held back by my self-loathing. I don't want to see her wringing her hands with worry. I want to see her sighing with pleasure. She deserves it every day of her life. Soon I feel her anxiety fade away as her fingers slide over my short hair and pull me closer. Finally, she is completely here, completely in demand of what she wants, completely unashamed of her desire.

We stay in bed, warm under the blanket, long after every impulse has been acted upon. We talk about the past two weeks as if our need to share our lives is just as desirable as sharing our bodies. Hearing her laugh at my recounting of school mishaps fills me with joy. When she tells me about working at the grocery and her mother's strict rules, I feel desperate to make it better for her.

In the middle of our discussion about why Allie's parents had divorced, Tracy walks in the room. He stands beside the bed where the headboard would be if I had one. He looks down at our naked bodies, the blanket only up to our waist. I realize Allie isn't hiding her scars, but I remember that she was naked in the hotel with him. I feel a tinge of jealousy, but also hope that she will no longer feel shame.

"Are you two ever coming out of here?"

"What's the hurry?"

"Well, for one thing, Hank should have been here with Luke thirty minutes ago."

Allie's eyes grow wide as she slides out of the bed and grabs her clothes. She runs into the bathroom and I hear the sink turn on.

Tracy sits on the edge of the bed beside me. I smile up at him, knowing he can relate to how complete I am with Allie here.

He laughs loudly, infectiously, and I laugh, too. I'm not even sure if we are laughing for the same reasons.

Allie steps into the room again. She is wearing only her skirt.

"I dropped my camisole."

She bends to pick it up from the floor beside the bed. I see the lines of her body and immediately stop laughing. I sit up on my knees and reach my hand out to touch her. "I think you are a witch," I tease as she catches her breath.

Just then, the outside door opens. Allie leans away from me so hard that she falls over. I slide off the bed to help her up just as Hank turns his head and sees us. The smile on his face drops into a straight line as he turns and quickly walks back outside. We throw on our clothes, terrified but giggling.

"Oh no, Jute! What do you think he thinks we were doing?"

I lean in and kiss her. She puts her hand to the back of my head and pulls me to kiss her harder.

Tracy clears his throat. We laugh as we finish getting dressed. We walk into the living room just before a knock lands on the door. Tracy opens it and Hank reenters. He smiles at me and touches the bill of his cap.

"Sorry I barged in like that."

Then he turns and opens his arms to Allie. She hugs him and he picks her up off her feet. I see his face is lit up with joy.

"My baby's home!" he calls out to the ceiling and spins her in a circle like she is three years old. Allie laughs. I am so happy for them, happy that Allie is here, happy that he is not upset with her. But, I also feel a pang of sadness seeing them share something I never will know.

Wednesday, February 7, 1990
10:57 p.m.

Dear Jute,

Mom read my notebooks and your letters while I was at work. We are in so much trouble, and I am sorry because it is all my fault for leaving it out. I tried to tell her it wasn't what she thought, but she would not even let me explain. She just said that if I want to stay with her while I go to college, I am not allowed to come to Tennessee until I "repent and am made whole."
I could just leave, but I have nowhere to go except to Tennessee. I want to, because I miss you. But, if I can just stay here a little longer, I can save enough money for a place of my own and I won't have to drop out of school.
I am so sorry, Jute. But, you can not write me here. I will write to you when she isn't around, but please don't reply. I need her to forget about us. I have agreed to go to six weeks of counseling at her church. Maybe it will calm her down. But, in the meantime, please don't forget about me. I will think of you every minute until I see you again.

Love you always,
Allie

CHAPTER TWENTY-FIVE

I stand up and pass rows of empty seats on my way toward the school bus doors. I am the last stop, so Skeet is always happy to see me leave. He's a scrawny little man with tobacco juice stains in his beard. His face is deceptively friendly because his temper has a short fuse. Luckily, I've never been on the receiving end of his tirades. I can't blame him for screaming at the kids I ride to school with. A lot them deserve more than the cussing streak he lays on them.

Skeet opens the doors before I get to them. He turns with a smile, "It's spring break, girl. You go on enjoy it, now."

"I will enjoy being away from these brats."

"Well, they's not all so bad, now."

"You're too good for them, Skeet."

I step off onto my driveway and give him a wave over my shoulder. The bus doors squeak closed behind me and I hear the bus revving up to speed, then easing up as it approaches the curve just beyond my house. I don't know why he revs it up like that just to have to slow it back down. I guess he's feeling excited about the days off ahead.

The sound of a guitar playing Beast of Burden reaches my ears before I can see Tracy sitting on a turned over bucket on the porch. He has been outside on the porch a lot, lately. Right now he's waiting on Luke to get home from work. Some days, he sits there for hours. He looks up and smiles at me, nodding his head to keep rhythm. I start to sing the lyrics loud enough for him to hear me. Tracy joins in at the chorus, his

168

voice tinged with sadness.

His singing voice is so deep and full of emotion. I have seen him sing a sad song so passionately that he sings himself right to tears. Since he has been living here, I have noticed my own singing voice becoming more intense. I let myself express emotions I could have never even pretended a few months ago. Maybe it's easier now that Earl is dead in the ground. Maybe it's easier because I love someone. I survived the plunge into the blue of her eyes and I reemerged more alive than ever. But, my heart aches to be near her.

"You are a damn rock star!" I call up to him as I walk up the steps onto the porch. I tell him this all the time. His response is equally predictable.

"But I'll never be as badass as you!"

He sits his guitar down and leans it against the house, then stands up to hug me.

"How was school, youngin'?" His fake Southern drawl makes me laugh every time I hear it.

"Out for spring break, finally! What about you, how was your day?"

"Well, let's see," He cocks his head and puts his finger to his chin, "I washed the dishes. I made the beds, including yours. I soaked in the tub for about an hour. And... yeah, it was thrilling."

I gently squeeze his arm and wink at him, "You're such a good wife."

Usually, he responds with "I'm not the wife, I'm the whore." But today he just turns away from me and goes back to his guitar. Seeing him try to sit back on the upside down bucket makes me think we really need a lawn chair. He balances the guitar across his knee and keeps his eyes on it as he tunes it. His long curly hair falls forward to hide most of his face. When he starts to play, I recognize the Dwight Yoakam song my sister played all the time. Tracy doesn't sing at all, just plays parts of it and goes right into a Steve Earle song. I drop my backpack down on the porch and take a seat on the top step

169

just to listen to him. I find myself singing along in my head to a few of the snippets, but I'm worried. Whatever is going on with him, I don't want to interrupt it by throwing my voice into it.

Thirty minutes go by, he has gone through pieces and parts of country songs from the last three decades. I've noticed Tracy plays more and more country music since moving here, usually when it's just the two of us. I imagine he probably plays it when I'm not around, too. But I don't ever hear him play it around Luke.

The songs seem to bounce off the hills of this hollow. Looking out over my yard, everything has changed so much. Grass is growing where before there was only mud with tire tracks. At some point, someone must have planted irises along the far south edge of the yard. They are standing tall and should bloom soon. I am excited to see what color they will be. In the woods, there are redbud trees flowering purple. I am filled with an urge to walk up the hill and touch the branches, put my hand against the bark of the trees, look for the shoots of wildflowers like trillium, bloodroot, rue anemone; so many possibilities up on that hillside.

I don't notice the sound of tires coming up the driveway until Tracy has already stopped playing. Luke is home early. I watch his little silver Chevette pull up so close to the porch that I think he might drive right through me. I stand up and stumble back onto the porch, wide-eyed. I can see his laughing face through the windshield.

"Asshole!" I scream at him. He can't hear me over his turned up radio, but he can read my lips.

Luke steps out of his car, still laughing, "What's the matter, Jute? You're stumbling all over the place."

He runs up the steps past me and wraps his arms around Tracy, swinging his upper body back and forth like a rag doll. Luke normally avoids acting like he and Tracy are a couple when he is outside, even here on the porch. When my friends come over, they avoid each other entirely. My friends assume they don't really like each other because they both like me. That always takes me by surprise because who would think two hot guys would be interested in someone like me?

Luke lets Tracy go and holds his face in his hands, kisses him quickly on the mouth, then takes his hand and pulls him into the house. I don't follow them, but I have an uneasy feeling that something is going on that I should know about. Tracy has been very quiet and Luke acts like he won the lottery. For half a minute, I consider going inside and demanding the truth. But, I'm too proud to act like they owe me anything, even an explanation. And, besides, I can hear sounds coming out of the house that have nothing to do with serious discussions.

I step off the bottom porch step and head out across the yard. My mind is taken off of the boys when I see the irises at the edge of the yard. One of them has a bud ready to bloom. It looks like it will be yellow. It makes me think of Allie. It reminds me of how long it has been since I have seen her. It was winter then.

Walking farther into the woods, I am surrounded by the sounds of birds calling to each other. I make it nearly all the way to the logging road before I see the outcrop of rocks. In front of them are a plethora of trout lilies. Their deep green and splotchy leaves are held up toward the sky while their blooms bow their heads. The white petals are like tiny hats over their pointy yellow faces. I walk over and pick one, taking a seat on the rocks to pull it apart in exploration. The silky feeling of the petals between my fingers reminds me of Allie's skin. A warmth washes over me. Will everything good and beautiful always make me think of her? And what things make her think of me? I can't guess a single good thing that might.

I hop down from the rocks and carefully dig up three of the flowers to take back to the house. Maybe they will grow if I plant them in the woods closer to the house where Allie can see them without hiking way up the hill. This is no place for pink high heels. I think of the times we played in the woods when we were kids. She wore a pair of white leather slip on loafers almost every day. Leaves would get in them and she'd have to stop and shake them clean, wobbling as she stood on one foot at a time.

When I reach the yard, I hear the mail carrier coming up the road in her old rusty Nova. She is running a little late today, but I'm glad to see her pulling up to my mailbox and stopping. I head in that direction, watching her lean out the window to pull open the lid. Before driving away, she looks up and waves at me. The sound of her engine rises again as she heads around the curve. I reach the mailbox and hear the squeal of her worn break pads as she slows for the next box in the distance. I pull hard to open the mailbox, grumbling under my breath because she always closes it too tightly. Finally, it pops open and I see a pink envelope.

Wednesday, 21 March 1990
1:17 p.m.

Dear Jute

    Dad came to visit me a couple of days ago. He mentioned you and the boys. I know I have not been writing as often. There have been some exciting things going on!
    I started volunteering with the church. We prepare a meal every week for the homeless and poor in our community. They do it every Wednesday and I've been helping for the last two weeks. So many of our customers from the grocery store come through the line to be served the free meal. It is heartbreaking to realize how much they are struggling. The children have such sad little faces. They seemed so ashamed to have to be there. It shouldn't be like that, Jute. So, I had the idea to help some of these families grow food in their own yards. I talked it over with the youth minister from the church, Jim Billings (the kids call him Jim-Bill, but he hates it). Anyway, Jim said he thinks it would be a good project for the kids in the church. But, if we want to do this, we have to get everything ready before planting season.
    It feels so good to do something nice for people! I've never felt so alive. I feel like I've been reborn and given a second chance to be a good person. I just want you to know, because I think of you often and hope that you are finding your way to happiness as well.
    Tell Tracy and Luke I said, "Hello."

    Love,
    Allie

CHAPTER TWENTY-SIX

I put the letter to my nose and inhale, smelling nothing of Allie. There is a hint of cigarette smoke and dust. I fold it up and slide it back into the envelope, pick up the wilting trout lilies off the mailbox lid, and walk back toward the house. I can hear Tracy's deep voice muffling out through the drafty walls of the house, but I no longer care what they're talking about. I put Allie's letter under a rock on the porch so I can plant the wildflowers before they are too stressed to live.

The tree line surrounding the yard is slightly elevated from the yard itself. I walk along the edge, looking up into the woods for a large rock. I hope to see a habitat similar to their old one. I find a small rock toward the back of the yard, just a few steps into the woods. It will have to do. I dig the holes with my fingers, the soil feels right. I drop the little roots into the ground, then push the dirt carefully around them. Their stems sag, the little hatted heads touching the forest floor.

I've probably done this for nothing. They will bloom and go to seed before Allie ever sees them.

There is a water spigot on this side of the house, but no cup outside to carry the water. I need to go inside. I am reluctant because I don't want to interrupt them, and more truthfully because I don't want to tell them that Allie made no mention of seeing me. I walk slowly, looking around the yard as if every new blade of grass is noteworthy. Eventually, I get to the porch. I feel like turning back around and heading back into the woods. I don't.

I give Allie's letter a tug to slide it out from under the rock as I make my way up the steps. The rock rolls away and clatters a few times against the boards. I decide to knock on the door. Luke opens it, looking annoyed, "You know this is your house, right?"

"I just didn't want to interrupt any gross boy kissing," I never pass up an opportunity to tease them.

"No worries there," Luke's voice is full of sarcasm. He looks over at Tracy as if waiting for him to respond. Tracy is sitting on a kitchen chair by the wood stove. That chair has been there for weeks, and most of the time Tracy is in it with his guitar. Right now, Tracy seems naked without it, staring at his shoes.

"I see," I don't know what to say. I just want to leave and come back when they make up.

I head for the kitchen for a plastic cup. As I reach into the cabinet, I hear Tracy getting up from his chair. He walks by me and says nothing on his way to the back bedroom. He shuts the door a bit too hard causing the picture over the kitchen table to fall. It happens frequently. Fortunately, decoupaged wood can't be easily broken.

"Sorry," he says from behind the closed door.

"I'm pretty sure you broke it this time. You owe me two dollars!" I think I'm funny, but he probably isn't in the mood for it. Considering how I'm left in the dark about what's going on, I shouldn't care how he feels.

With a cup full of water, I head back outside where the birds are still singing for a mate. I don't imagine it would benefit them to sound like humans, bickering from the highest branch. The image of fighting birds tumbling out of the sky fills my mind. I'm already pouring the water over the lilies when I see they have raised up their heads a little just from being returned to the soil. Good for them. But, too bad they don't need anything else because I need an excuse not to go back inside. Mediating isn't something I do well.

A loud thud comes from the house, followed by the

175

sound of a couple of bulls crashing into things. Bulls are the first thing I imagine, but as I listen, I am reminded of the sounds of Earl's drunken rages. I shiver. This could be bad.

I'm already half way to the door when I hear Luke screaming, "You can't do this one thing for me? After I have given up everything for you? I was discharged from the Marines because of you! I was disowned by my family! I worked in a fucking surf shop just to be near you! I kept your secret from your family while my own family refused to even speak to me! And here we sit in this Hell Hole of a town with some fucked up kid! I'm working my ass off digging ditches for sewer lines while you two strum your fucking guitar and yodel to each other. I'm sick of it!" Luke's voice gets quiet and steady. I can barely make out his words. "I have tried to be here for you, but I'm tired of wondering if you would do any of this for me. I'm leaving in the morning, with or without you."

I realize my mouth is open in shock. I stand motionless in the yard, blindsided by Luke's words. Generally, I stay out of people's business. Maybe I've been wrong not to ask a few personal questions since they arrived. I have assumed this whole time that they were both happy with the arrangement, that they could stay here together until they had enough money to go elsewhere. Hank had gotten him a great job and Luke was already making more money than most construction workers in the area, certainly more than he could have made at the surf shop. The rent on this house is half what it had cost Luke for his one bedroom apartment in South Carolina, plus there was no need to explain their relationship to the renters. Luke had saved up enough money to buy a decent used car with two pay checks. I thought it was all good. I am so confused. I focus on trying to make sense of why he doesn't like it here. I focus on anything that will keep my mind off what Luke said about me personally.

My brain is still reeling when Luke opens the front door so hard it flies back and knocks Tracy's bucket over. He jogs down the steps and is in his car like he's off to an emergency.

Surely he sees me in his peripheral vision, but he doesn't turn his head. Even when he looks around to make sure he can back up safely, he does not acknowledge that I'm standing there. I watch him turn his car around and drive off, heading north toward town, or possibly toward the highway out of here.

I take a deep breath and put my hand to my forehead. It's time for the hard part.

The door is still standing wide open, so I see Tracy sitting on the couch before I even step foot inside. He's holding his guitar and gently plucking the strings and making random pings of sound. His face is turned down, looking at what his hands are doing as if he is too numb to know by feel. The thought of interrupting him to inquire about anything at all seems awkward and rude. Who am I to help him, when it seems I have done so much to hurt him? I just stand on the porch and stare at him for a long time. My legs start to get restless and I shift my weight. I consider walking over to get the bucket and take a seat out here.

Tracy doesn't look up, "It's your house, you can come in if you want to, Jute."

"I wasn't sure if you wanted me around right now."

"Doesn't matter." He strums a chord now instead of plucking randomly at the strings. "Get in here before I feel like shit for making you stand out there."

I step inside and pull the door closed, but I don't go any further. I just watch him melt over his guitar. I could see his face better from the porch. Now I see mostly the top of his head, dark brown curls jiggling ever so slightly when he moves. Without seeing his face, it's hard to imagine a sad person under all that happy hair. Maybe if I knew the whole story, I wouldn't think such stupid things. I so badly want to pretend everything is fine, but I know he's hurting.

"You know, I never thought you'd be this girl."

I don't know why this is suddenly about me again. I don't even know what he means.

He plucks a string. "When I met you, you looked like

177

you had been in a cat fight. You were full of quick wit and defiance. I never thought I'd see the day when you'd stand in your own living room and be afraid to move. I guess I have a way of ruining people."

Anger makes my face heat up, "So, you think I'm ruined now, do you? You think my scars got too heavy and now I'm tired of fighting? Well, don't be so sure about that!" I feel like I should be saying this to Luke, but he isn't here.

Tracy finally looks up at me and I can tell from his expression that he's high. "Don't be stupid. I'm sorry you had to hear what Luke said."

"You can't apologize for someone else's words. But just so you won't feel confused about which I am, the cat fight girl or the fucked up kid, I'd like to point out a few things. I've always been afraid. Never in my life have I not been afraid. Afraid of being beaten, afraid of being torn apart with cruel words, afraid that I'll never be loved, afraid of hurting people I care about, and very afraid of spiders." I want to smile, but I can't. "Right now I'm afraid I've messed things up with you and Luke..."

He sighs and puts his guitar down, leaning it against the wall. He pulls out a nearly empty bag of pot from his front pocket.

"Want to share my last joint? It will be a while before I can afford more." He leans forward to get the rolling papers from his back pocket.

"Is that why Luke is upset? Because he wants you to stop smoking pot?"

"Nope."

I wait, hoping Tracy will elaborate without me pressing him. He doesn't.

Finally, I say, "Okay."

He is sitting in the center of the couch. I sit on the end to his left, sideways so I can face him, my legs crossed in front of me. My jeans are too tight for this to be comfortable, but I have to look at him or I can't figure out what is going on. We

178

smoke in silence until he takes the last hit. It has been a while since I have smoked with him. I find myself wishing Allie would walk in and catch us. I used to hate it when she would look down on me for getting high or drunk, but now I just wish she was looking at me any way at all.

My senses start to mesh and weave in and out of each other, I'm not going to think about Allie right now. I'm just going to enjoy this feeling.

Tracy gets up and walks into the bathroom. He creates a breeze of scent like sweat and lemon dish liquid. I want to giggle, but I don't. I just close my eyes and try to contain all the thoughts racing through my mind about birds and bread boxes and hanging up Allie's clothes when she visits and green grass and the taste of envelope glue and red lips and...

I want to go back outside so badly. I want to be high while lying in the grass, or the leaves under the trees, or sitting on rocks. I slide my body around so my feet touch the floor. I can't stay in here another minute. I head toward the door and have my hand on the knob when Tracy comes back into the room.

"Where are you going?" He sounds alarmed.

"For a walk in the woods. Want to come see some trout lilies?"

CHAPTER TWENTY-SEVEN

Tracy's blue eyes look at me now. The color is the same shade as Allie's, but his blue fades toward the edge at the thin indigo rim of his iris. Allie's is more uniform to the edge, with a few flecks of pale blue shooting out from her pupil. Maybe I am staring too hard, thinking too much. Time is hard to assess. What I do know is that I'm supposed to be making him feel better, not obsessing about all things Allie.

"Okay, let's go see the fish flowers." Tracy says, then takes a deep breath and lets it out. "You lead the way, and don't bring me back with splinters and holes in my feet."

I slap his arm with the back of my hand. "You are such an insensitive ass."

"So I hear."

He leans in front of me to push the door open. As he brushes by me, he takes my hand and we head out together. I decide to take him up toward the ridge. If we take a different route I might find wildflowers I didn't see earlier.

"Those are redbud trees," I point out the purple splotches of color along the hillside in front of us. "Let's head toward that one and maybe we'll find some trillium."

Surprisingly, Tracy is full of questions about every green thing poking out of the ground. He probably won't remember what I tell him about the difference between Christmas ferns and Long Beech ferns. But he must be enjoying the distraction of listening to me talk about plant and tree identification.

The outcrop of rocks is just ahead. We pick up the pace. When we reach it, I'm out of breath but so happy to be in this spot. I climb up on the flat rocks and lie down to look at the tops of the trees above me. My body feels every notch and knob of the rock so precisely that I feel like I am part of it. Some areas have been warmed by a ray of sun through the trees, other areas are cool to the touch. I could lie here forever, only I am so incredibly thirsty and wish I had thought to grab a few apples.

Tracy climbs up beside me and sits down at my head with his feet hanging off toward the lilies.

"They are incredibly beautiful. Thanks for bringing me up here."

"I just found them an hour ago. I brought some to plant near the house for Allie. I didn't think she'd want to ruin her high heels getting up here."

"You did all that since you got home from school? Wow." He sounds like he means it. But, when he's high he says wow about a lot of things that aren't really wow-worthy.

"So, why is Luke mad at us?"

"Us?" he asks, leaning over to look down at me and blocking my view of the tree tops.

I reach up and push him away.

"Well," he says, "First, he isn't mad at us. He's mad at me because I don't want to move to Texas with him. A guy he works with got a job on an oil rig. Luke asked him to try to get him on, too. Well, it all worked out and he got the job. But, he never bothered to tell me any of that before he accepted the offer."

I arch my neck so I can see Tracy's face better. He is chewing the inside of his lips thoughtfully. His eyes seem to be looking around the woods, but I know he's probably replaying their conversation inside his head.

"Try not to worry. Allie is in Ohio but we're still doing okay."

"Really? Then why didn't she come by when she met

181

Hank in Knoxville last weekend?"

I open my mouth to contradict him, but nothing comes out. I don't think Tracy would lie.

"I'm sorry, Jute. It's none of my business. I'm sure everything will be fine between the two of you. But, what you have with Allie is not what I have with Luke. It didn't start out being about love and friendship. I don't think it ever will be. I mean, I care about him and he obviously cares about me. But, I'm just a thing he has been trying to possess for years." He pauses and sniffs, then laughs a little. "I was fifteen when I got involved with him. It caused a lot of shit to hit the fan, mostly for him. But, despite what he said, my family didn't take it lightly. There was never a time I saw Luke that my dad didn't somehow find out about it and give me hell."

I sit up beside him. He is leaning forward with his hands gripping his knees, rocking slightly forward and back. I put my arm around him and pull him down to lie in my lap. He stays on his side, looking out at the trees. I hold his hand in mine while he talks.

"When I ran out of the hotel toward Allie's car, I thought I was getting away from all of it. My dad. Luke. The whispers behind my back. My friends never came around except a few guys who wanted to have sex in secret. I wanted to leave it all." He takes a deep breath and sighs. "But, there he was in the backseat. I thought maybe we could make it, you know. Maybe it was love, like what I saw in your eyes when you look at Allie. Maybe all I had to do was leave and things would be different. But, they aren't. Luke wants a pet, not a boyfriend."

The tears are gone from his eyes and I watch his face transform with determination. He turns his head to look up at me and I smile down at him. It's ridiculous how gorgeous his face is. How has it not yet ruined his personality?

"Besides," he sits up and turns to face me. Leaning across me, he seems to search my eyes. "I want to move to Nashville and try to get a record deal. I think we should go

182

together after you graduate."

"What?" There is shock in my voice. "I think you're just high."

"I'm serious! I love listening to you sing. Your voice is like butter. Not just butter, but cinnamon and sugar butter. You have a better shot at it than I do."

"What about Allie?"

"It's the same distance for her to drive to Nashville as it is for her to drive here. Besides, she's starting college this summer. Are you going to move up there and live in her dorm room?"

"What makes you so sure I'm not going to go to Cincinnati University as well?" I can't believe I said that. My eyes look away from him because I'm ashamed of what a joke it is that I would ever be accepted there, or could ever afford it if I was.

He puts a hand on my cheek and pulls me to look at him again.

"Whatever you want to do, you should go for it. But, in the meantime, we need to pay the bills. Maybe we can get some gigs in town on the weekends."

"You're full of crazy ideas, Tracy Duren, rock star." I wink at him, before getting caught up in the changing blue of his eyes. The color has shifted with the sun lowering beyond the western ridge.

"Does that mean you'll do it?"

"Play gigs or move to Nashville?"

"Both, of course!"

"I'll say yes to trying to get gigs because we're two broke-ass delinquents. But, I'm not making any promises about Nashville."

His huge smile makes his eyes squint nearly closed. He brings his other hand up to my face to give me a gleeful squeeze. I feel his fingertips pushing a little too hard behind my ears. I wince just as he plants a quick kiss right on my mouth.

"You are too cool for school!" He jumps off the rock and

puts his hand out for mine.

"Cheesy, much?" I take his hand and slide off the rock. Dusting off the seat of my pants, I take one more look at the trout lilies. Their heads bob around in a breeze. "We better get back before the sun disappears. Otherwise you might actually get a few scratches on your supermodel skin."

CHAPTER TWENTY-EIGHT

Along our way to the house, I pick up a few decent sized twigs for kindling. We've had to build a fire every night despite spring arriving just a few days ago. My arms are full by the time we reach the yard. I drop the wood in a box on the porch and kick off my boots to leave them outside.

"Tracy, take your shoes off out here. Traipsing through the woods in the spring can sometimes get you covered in chigger bites. We probably should rinse off, too, just in case."

A look of horror takes over Tracy's face as he starts pulling off his shoes, followed by his shirt and pants. I laugh, but he's too frantic to respond. I have never seen such a frightened expression on anyone before. My lingering buzz only intensifies my laughter. I think I am going to wet myself. Tracy darts into the house and heads for the bathroom. I am still bent over laughing, but I call after him, "Wait, I need to get in there first. I'm going to pee all over myself!"

"Serves you right," he says from somewhere in the house.

I head to the bathroom and find the door closed. I knock, but only hear the water from the shower in response.

"Come on!" I scream through the door. "I need in there for just a second. Your water probably isn't even hot yet!"

"I'm in the shower already, slow poke," he calls back. I turn the knob and walk in anyway. Tracy isn't in the shower. He's standing beside the shower in his underwear, leaning in to check the water temperature. On his back are three red welts which are turning to bruises. They are all about the same size, elongated like he was hit with something. He turns his head and is startled when he sees me standing there. He turns to face me so I can't see the bruises, but I do see another one at his waist below his ribs.

My eyes are wide as I process this. I can't just stand here and stare at him like he's grotesque. I look up at his eyes and I recognize the shame in them instantly.

"Did Luke do this?" I keep my voice steady.

He keeps his eyes on mine, too. But he is not able to keep his voice calm, "I don't want you involved in this. I'll deal with it, alright?"

"Who was dealing with it while you were being beaten by a guy twice your size?"

I reach out to touch the bruise below his ribs. He doesn't move away, but he doesn't look at me.

"He's not twice my size. And sometimes I deserve it. Just forget about it, okay?"

"He may not be twice your size, but he is much stronger," I try to give him a smile just because I think he needs one. "We'll talk about letting this go, or not, after you've washed off your chiggers. Now, get in the shower or get out of the bathroom. I need to pee and I don't need an audience."

His shoulders relax a little and he bites his lip to hold back a smile, "Considering it's your fault I'm potentially covered in microscopic bugs, I should tickle you instead."

I glare at him, giving him a well practiced threatening look. He quickly steps over into the shower before I can actually hurt him. The curtain slides shut and I hear the water hitting his body.

"Do you usually take a shower in your underwear?"

He doesn't say anything. But as I sit on the toilet, his wet underwear lands on my lap. He must have thrown it over the curtain rod. I see him peeking out at me, laughing.

"You were right about deserving a beating!" I am not even joking.

"Sometimes beatings are good, just not when your boyfriend is secretly pissed off."

I stand up and flush the toilet causing his water to get suddenly very hot. He lets loose a string of profanity that is music to my vengeful ears. I laugh at him while I wash my hands, "I think we're even now."

"Oh, hell no!" He says, opening the curtain and stepping out of the shower. He picks me up and before I can fight him off, he tosses me in the tub where the shower water is now ice cold. He climbs in to push my head under the stream. "We have to get your chiggers off, Jute!"

I'm able to reach out with my hand and turn the water back to warm. Tracy takes his hand off my forehead so I can take a breath without inhaling the water running down my face. I want to punch him, but he's bruised enough. I just stand up under the shower head to warm back up.

Tracy leans against the back of the shower and watches me, amused.

"What?" I give him a mean look, but I'm not really mad.

I try to peel off my wet clothes. I feel like they have soaked up fifty pounds of water. My pants are already too tight, so I fight to get them to my knees. Then I sit down and raise one foot at a time for Tracy to pull. Finally he tugs hard enough to pull them free. He stands there, holding my pants by the ankles.

"Do you need help removing anything else?"

Suddenly someone pulls the shower curtain back. We are startled to see that Luke is back.

He stares into Tracy's eyes. He doesn't look at me at all. Even when I stand up to get the water out of my face, he doesn't turn his head. I quickly rinse off and get out, leaving the shower running. Tracy and Luke are still not talking, just looking at each other as if both are waiting for the other to apologize. No one says anything while I dry off with a towel. Only when I open the door does Luke speak.

187

"I brought pizza," Luke's voice cracks a little from being silent so long. He clears his throat. "I also stopped at the grocery store and bought a cake. I won't be here for your birthday."

Tracy clears his throat, too. "I-I just need to rinse off. I'll be right out and we can talk."

"Yeah," Luke looks down at his shoes.

I walk out and into my bedroom to get dressed. I want to give them privacy, but after seeing Tracy's bruises, I don't trust him. I also don't know if I trust myself to be around Luke and not punch him. I would just stay in my room if I wasn't so hungry. I grab a clean pair of jeans and take a folded t-shirt from the top of the stack. It happens to be the Sex Pistols. I welcome the bombardment of punk songs filling my head, taking my mind off things which are none of my business. I sit on my bed and hum.

I hear the bathroom door open, but the shower is still running. Luke steps around the corner in my bedroom and looks at me like he's being sent to death row. I have never seen him look so miserable.

"Tracy said he told you I plan to leave."

I nod, not knowing what to say.

"I want to give you the money for the next two months in rent. I don't want you to give it to Tracy because he can be a little irresponsible."

Tears are in Luke's eyes. He pulls a wad of folded bills from his pocket and holds it out for me. I take the money, looking at it with confusion.

He makes a great effort to keep his voice steady. "Obviously, Tracy and I are never going to be a couple. We tried. I appreciate you and Allie for all you have done to give us a chance to make this work." He takes a breath, like he has planned this speech but struggles to get the words out, "We always thought, well, I always thought our problems had to do with the people around us. So, earlier today I found myself trying to blame you. I am sorry."

188

My mind is filled with images of Tracy's back. I just look at him as expressionless as I can.

"And..." He takes a deep breath and then lets it out, "I also want to sign the car over to you. I know it looks like a piece of shit, but it should get you two wherever you need to go. I'm signing it to you because you are less likely to run off and leave him than he is to run off and leave you. He needs someone, even if he denies it. Just, don't let him get hurt, alright?"

I am stunned. Why does Luke think I can keep Tracy from being hurt when I couldn't even keep Luke from hurting him? And who am I protecting him from now? I don't know what to say. I want to be snide, but I let it go. He's right that I won't be leaving Tracy anytime soon. I can't refuse his request.

"Okay," I nod.

Luke gives me a weak smile and walks out of my room. I get up and put the money in an old peanut can on my dresser. I'm putting the lid back on when Tracy comes out of the bathroom. He has a towel wrapped around him. He sees me and smiles like nothing strange is happening, turns and heads out toward his room.

I wait a few minutes before leaving my room. Tracy and I reach the kitchen at the same time. He's dressed in pajama pants with reindeer and trees all over them. He isn't wearing a shirt. I suspect he is intentionally exposing his bruises. He takes a seat at the table, leaving the middle seat for me. Luke has placed plates at each setting, a slice of pizza already on them. The cake is in the center of the table. It has light blue icing with black music notes drifting around the top. "Happy Birthday Tracy" is written in dark blue.

I hesitate to sit down. I had hoped to take the food to my room and let them be alone. But, evidently Luke has other plans. Hoping to make this quick, I gently slide out my chair to sit down. Luke hops up from his seat and says, "I almost forgot. I have beer in the fridge."

He brings us each a bottle, cracking them open as he sits

them on the table. Tracy turns his up immediately. I am more interested in the pizza. I eat it and stare at the table.

No one speaks. By the time everyone is on their third slice, I can't stand it anymore. "So, let's cut this cake so you guys can chat without me crashing your party."

I open the lid to the cake and push in the candles. Luke had bought a big blue number one and a huge green nine to make nineteen.

"Shall we sing?" I ask.

"Oh, wait! I'm going to grab my guitar."

As Tracy walks out of the room, I call out, "So you can serenade yourself? How narcissistic!"

"That's me," he responds as he walks back in holding his guitar by the neck like a chicken he caught for supper. He is being so weird, but I can understand why. He slides the strap around his neck and starts to play random tunes while I struggle to light the candle wicks. Finally, I succeed and Tracy works his way around to play the Happy Birthday song. I make sure to sing it with an exaggerated Southern drawl. Luke is singing loudly as well, so much so that I can't even hear Tracy singing. We are atrocious. We laugh as Tracy blows out his candles.

"What did you wish for?" I ask, slicing into the cake and plopping the first piece down on Tracy's plate. He turns up his second beer and takes a long drink, then begins playing the Beatles song "Can't Buy Me Love". I glance at Luke as I slice a piece of cake for him. His teeth or clenched, but his eyes aren't angry. He looks at Tracy playing the song but his mind seems far away. When I put the cake on Luke's plate, he startles like he forgot where he was.

"Thanks," he smiles weakly then pokes his fork in his slice, pulling off a big bite.

Enough of this. I put a piece of cake on my plate and take it back to my room. I place the beer on my dresser and sit on my bed. The cake is sweet, the icing a bit gritty with sugar. I finish it quickly so I can go to bed and crash.

April 3, 1990
7:22 a.m.

Dear Jute,

I heard Luke got a job in Texas. I hope Tracy is handling it okay. He is such a sweet guy. He deserves to be happy. I'm sure it is difficult for him living in Maryville. Maybe he should move out west where people accept his lifestyle. Tennessee isn't an easy place to be gay. Even here in Ohio, I can't really talk about Tracy and Luke, not even to Jim. He believes homosexuality is a sin. We have been talking a lot about what the Bible says about it.

You know, when I was very little, Mom took me to church. But, Dad never cared for it. Sometimes I wish Dad had taken me more often. There is so much I am in the dark about. I'm trying to catch up by asking Jim a lot of questions. I think it would be good for me to have a better understanding of that kind of love. I haven't exactly had the best track record.

I hope you are well. I know you are probably mad at me because we aren't together. But, it is really for the best that I am not tempted. I do love you and hope you are well.

Love,
Allie

CHAPTER TWENTY-NINE

I have a term paper due in six days. But, all I can think about is Allie's letter. I have had it for a week, but I still can't get the words "for the best that I am not tempted" out of my mind. I can't write to her. I can't talk to her. I just need to see her, to look in her eyes, and find out how she feels.

When she left in January, she kissed me goodbye and it felt like foreplay. She never showed any sign that she would not be back into my arms before now. I don't think either of us could imagine we would have been apart this long. It seems she gets more distant with every letter she writes. I feel powerless to bring her closer.

Term paper. Think about my term paper. How did WWI affect civil liberties? That is what I need to focus on. I have two more hours here at the library before Tracy picks me up. He's downtown at the bar talking to Macky about allowing us to play tonight. We had a decent response when we played the two open mic nights. I haven't mentioned anything to Tracy about the money Luke gave us. We are going to need more money than Tracy thinks if we end up moving to Nashville. It's best to not let him know the extra money exists.

Absentmindedly, my hand copies down page after page of notes from the reference books which I can't check out. I have a stack of five other books that I can bring home with me and read through later. Between reading off the lines to copy, my mind drifts to flashbacks of my time with Allie. I don't think much about when we were kids any more. I have let most of those years die along with Earl. I don't think about him. I think about Allie's apple shampoo. I think about her crooked smile. I think about her in a fashion show of hats. Does she still wear them in Ohio? I think about how her skin feels soft like the inside of a rose petal and tastes salty sweet.

I feel myself blushing and force myself to focus on my writing. I've been writing through the line and it looks like all my words have been crossed out. I skip a line and start again, jotting down the last paragraph I need from the reference book.

A hand taps my shoulder and I turn, knowing it is Tracy sneaking up on me. It isn't. It's Melinda Isbell, a girl from my history class. Her hair is very long, blond, and curly. It is sprayed stiff to stand up three inches above her bangs before falling to frame her face with ringlets. Her eyes are green and her lips are pearly pink. She's the kind of perfect I hate. She is smiling sweetly, so I smile as politely as I can manage.

"Are you finished with this one?" She points to one of the books I had planned to check out.

"Actually, I am going to check it out."

"Oh. But, you haven't yet?"

That is such a stupid question. I glare at her. "I already told you that I haven't."

"Good," she says, picking up the book.

She is walking between tall bookshelves toward the check out with it. I stand up and run after her, grabbing the book from her hand. She turns, a sneer on her face. She glances over every feature of my face and body, sizing me up. She is probably calculating whether or not to fight for the book.

I speak very quietly through clenched teeth so only she can hear me, "We have three days left. Just go put a hold on it and you can check it out after I bring it back tomorrow. Try not to be such a bitch."

I turn and start to walk back to my table. She grabs my arm and pulls me around so I face her. Her voice is low. She is relaxed and smiling.

"You know what I heard, Jutey?" I wait for it, knowing she's going to insult me. She continues, "I think you would do anything for a pretty girl."

Her grip on my arm tightens as she leans down and kisses me hard, her tongue invading my mouth like a hand in a pocket. She's searching me like she is sure I have something hidden there. Her lipstick tastes like it's been in a drawer since 1967. I fight a gag reflex and grab her shoulders to push her away. She has a defiant expression on her face.

"Well, that sucked," she says snidely.

I take one hand off her shoulder and quickly connect a punch to her jaw bone. She stumbles back and falls into the floor just as a librarian walks around the corner.

"What in heaven's name is going on here?" She rushes over and helps Melinda to her feet.

"She stole my book," Melinda sobs and her voice is high pitched, making her sound like a tiny little girl. "I had it first and she grabbed it from me and hit me."

The librarian's face sours and puckers. She takes two steps toward me, but comes no closer than necessary to grab the book from my arm. Melinda is behind her, angrily staring at me with her hand on her cheek. She puckers her lips and makes a silent kiss in my direction.

"Gross," I mouth the word to Melinda, but the librarian sees it. What she doesn't see behind her is Melinda's middle finger go up in response.

The librarian jabs her finger inches from my face, "You, young lady, need to leave this instant. I will not tolerate bullies like you any longer. Your kind come in here dressed up like Halloween, stealing and destroying the books, writing on the bathroom walls, and you think there will never be consequences. If you are not out of my library in five minutes, I will call the police and have you arrested."

Melinda is no longer looking at me. She is pretending to look at the books on the shelves behind her.

I look back at the librarian. Her name tag is pinned to

her gray hand-knitted sweater. She is shaking and afraid. I feel sorry for her. I am angry at Melinda for upsetting her. Kids like to treat me like shit, but this is different.

"I am sorry you feel this way, Mrs. Gralton." I am sincere, but I know she doesn't think I am.

I walk to the table and gather my notes, knowing I do not have enough sources to complete my paper. I'll need to go to school early tomorrow and use the library there. I bet all the relevant books have been checked out. Why else would Melinda be so desperate to get these? A sigh escapes me as I shove my jacket down into my backpack. I close my eyes and think of Allie because it feels good. I imagine her face, the way she looks at me when people say mean things to us. She often winks like we are the only ones with the secret treasure. I throw my backpack strap up on my shoulder and turn around, bumping right into Tracy's chest.

"Ready already?" He seems shocked, and possibly disappointed.

"Nope," I say, pushing past him. "I've been kicked out."

Tracy walks quickly to catch up to me. "How did that happen?"

I appreciate his non-accusatory tone. I push the library doors open and feel a warm spring breeze hit me in the face. The smell of hamburgers from a downtown restaurant makes my stomach growl. "This girl named Melinda walked up and kissed me, then I punched her, then she said I stole her book, which was actually my book. Who do you think they believed?"

His hand grabs my arm to keep me from walking ahead, "Did you say a girl kissed you?" He looks at me like this is a major news event.

"It was a joke, stupid. She said she heard I would do anything for a pretty girl, but I don't believe it. She just thinks I dress like this because I'm a lesbian."

"Well, aren't you?"

"No!" I scream at him, forgetting we are downtown at lunchtime and there are people everywhere.

Tracy shakes his head at me like I'm too young to understand whatever his brilliant adult mind has decided about me. If this continues, I might punch him, too.

"Are you hungry?" He must have heard my stomach over the traffic.

"A little," which is an understatement, "Have you talked to Macky yet?"

"No, he was gone to lunch. I thought I'd see if you wanted to grab a bite before I have to go back. I guess now you can come with me and we'll talk to him together."

"Let's go to Rudy's and get a hamburger. They have a special this week. Buy two burgers, get a free large order of onion rings. We can split them." My stomach growls again.

"That's within the budget!" He is mocking me.

We cross the street to Rudy's. Tracy goes in to order while I sit outside at one of the cast iron tables and chairs near the sidewalk. He reemerges with a number 16 sign for our table. Instead of sitting across from me, he sits beside me and pulls his chair close.

"Are you going to tell me a secret?" I tease.

"Yes," he leans in to my ear and says, "I am jealous."

I am confused. I try to think of any boy he has mentioned since Luke left. Macky? Ick. Macky is misogynistic and predictably unbathed, not Tracy's type. There is one guy that comes to our shows alone. He wears a fedora and a camel-color Members Only jacket. I think his name is Terry or something like that. He always talks to Tracy about music, but I haven't noticed any energy between them.

Tracy seems amused by my confusion. He makes no offer to clarify his statement. He grins when the food arrives and is already grabbing an onion ring off the plate before the waiter even sits our hamburgers down. He's not the only one distracted by the food. We say nothing else to each other until our plates are empty and our sodas are drained.

"Now wasn't that better than sitting in a stupid library?"

"Libraries aren't stupid, but yes. That was so delicious. Are you ready to go talk to Macky?"

He stands up and puts his bent arm down for me to take. "Let's," he says gentlemanly.

My words come out in a British accent, "If you are trying to make me feel better by treating me like a lady, know that I am indifferent to your manipulations."

Tracy exaggerates a frown.

We walk arm in arm for the four blocks to Green Light Willy's. The place won't open for another three hours or so. Tracy knocks on the door and we stand there waiting. The minutes pass and I'm thinking this is a waste of time. I look at him with concern on my face, but he just crosses his eyes and sticks his tongue out at me. Just then the doors swing open and there stands Macky with his exuberantly greasy hair and storm cloud eyes. He looks down at me and seems to contemplate kicking me away like a stray dog so he and Tracy can talk business. I guess he decides it's okay if the little girl stays. But, he never even looks at me again.

"I thought about it, kid. I got one early slot tonight between seven o'clock and nine. Take it or leave it. But, if they like you, you can come back next week and take a later spot. One of my regular bands will be out of town."

Tracy is smiling and nodding, but Macky puts his hand out like a sideways chop through the air, "But, now I'm going to tell you straight up. This ain't open mic night. These people that come here on Friday like it rowdy, like it country, and like it loud. I don't know how they're going to take to... her." He flops his hand in my direction because he can't even be bothered to point a finger.

Tracy doesn't miss a beat. He gets into Paul McCartney mode and belts out the first line of "I Saw Her Standing There" about a girl being seventeen. Macky shakes his head watching Tracy twist his hips. A few people stop and stare at

197

what looks like a romantic serenade. He gets all the way to the chorus before Macky cuts him off with coughs and a grunt or two.

"You kids get on outta here. I'll see you tonight. Don't be late." He slams the door shut and locks it.

The car is parked a couple of blocks away. Tracy is still singing that song as we walk. Heads turn. Some people smile, others scowl. I don't care what they think. Most people assume the worst about me, that's how it has always been. But they get it wrong.

I start singing along with him and forget about everyone else. When we finish the Beatles song, Tracy stops walking and wraps his arms around me. I hug him back, a little confused.

"You make me feel so free and alive," he says with his mouth pressed sideways to the top of my head. The words come out muffled and sound like a cartoon voice.

I laugh and push him away, "Well you aren't free. You're stuck here, just like I am." I wink at him and take his hand to lead him toward the car. He slumps his shoulders like a scolded kid and shuffles his feet behind me. This gets even more stares.

We finally make it to the car. Maryville will have to wait until tonight to get any more entertainment out of us.

CHAPTER THIRTY

Our set ended at nine o'clock, despite a lot of drunken applause for it to go on. We deviated a bit from Macky's suggestion to keep it rowdy, loud, and country. Tracy has always impressed me with his ability to predict what an audience wants. He keeps his eyes moving around the room, assessing the moods and desires of the crowd. It really paid off tonight in tips when he nailed it with a perfectly timed slow dance, and later when he sang Girls Just Want to Have Fun by Cyndi Lauper. At first, some of the guys booed. But when the shy group of girls in the back moved to the dance floor, the guys changed their minds.

We're on our way home now, driving empty roads after midnight. I still have work to do on my report, but I don't see how I can do anything tonight. I'll have to get up early and drive into Knoxville. Maybe I can have some peace at that library where no one knows me. Maybe I can put on a pink dress and shiny white mary jane shoes so no one accuses me of being a book thief. I snort laugh at the images in my head, forgetting that I haven't said any of this aloud and Tracy has no idea why I'm laughing. He looks over at me like I've lost my mind. His eyes look tired, and maybe a little drunk from the free and illegal beer we were offered by the audience. He drank both his and mine. I snicker at him and let him think all my laughter is at him.

When I pull up to the house, I see a box on the porch right under the overhead light. I nudge Tracy to wake up.

"Are you expecting a gift?"

Maybe this has something to do with his birthday two weeks ago. Or maybe it's a clue to his secret jealousy. Maybe he has a secret admirer. Maybe his admirer is married or has a girlfriend or something.

"Tracy! Wake up!"

He doesn't look at me. He just opens the car door and tries not to fall out of it. I decide to move the box before he stumbles over it in his drunken stupor. It's the size of a large shoe box, but heavier than shoes. The wrapping paper has Easter bunnies all over it. Tracy slinks past me and heads toward the bathroom while I read the tag. It says: To the Very Naughty Boy.

"Have you been a naughty boy?" I yell through the bathroom door.

"Hell, yes!" Tracy's words are slurred.

"With who?"

"I'll be naughty with whoever you want." I hear small things falling out of the medicine cabinet and crashing onto the floor, probably my toothbrush and many other things I don't want there. Tracy's voice is full of frustration. "Damn it! Where's my vanilla pudding?"

I set the box down on my bed and go back to retrieve Tracy from the bathroom. He obviously believes he is in the kitchen. I push open the door and see him leaning against the sink counter with his knuckles white from holding on so tight.

"Room spinning?" I ask.

He nods.

"Did you pee?" I feel like I'm talking to a five year old.

"What?"

"In the toilet. Did you pee? If not, do it now because I don't want you peeing in the fridge later. I'm shutting the door. You pee. Now."

I shut the door and wait until I hear the toilet flush before I open it again. I turn the water on in the sink and take each of his hands in mine and help lather soap on them. I can't

200

decide if I am more annoyed or amused. He isn't even trying to help. He's just staring at me, probably trying to remember who I am.

"Come on, I'll get your pudding," I say, taking his clean hands and leading him toward the kitchen. I push him down into a chair, turn and get his pudding from the fridge. "Here. Can you manage this, or do I need to feed it to you?"

"Feed it to me," he snickers.

"I'll feed you the pudding if you tell me who is sending you presents and who is making you jealous."

"You are sending me presents and you are making me jealous."

"Okay, focus." I pull the lid off the pudding cup and dip the spoon in. "The answer is not Jute. So, fess up!"

Tracy reaches for the spoon. He puts the bite in his mouth then reaches up with his other hand to take the cup. He just sits there and eats bite after bite, saying nothing.

"Fine, if you won't answer me, I'm going to go open it and see for myself."

I get the box from my bed and bring it to the kitchen table. Tracy ignores it. I pull the tag off and put it up to his face, "It says: To the Naughty Boy. That is you, is it not?"

"It could be you," he says, eating his last bite. He looks serious.

"It's not for me! Look, I'll prove it..."

I start pulling off the bunny paper, ripping through pictures of colorful eggs, making a point to toss some paper at Tracy in the process. The box is in fact a shoe box, men's Timberland boots, size 12. I point to the label and raise an eyebrow at Tracy. He shrugs, indifferent to the box, but very amused at me. I glare at him as I run my finger under the lid to break the tape. I pull the lid off, still looking at Tracy as if I have finally proved him wrong. He leans over and looks into the box at the same time I do.

Books. World War I books from the library. This is so confusing.

"These are the books I was going to check out, did you get these?"

Tracy's head goes back and he laughs hard, stomping his foot on the floor and slapping his leg. He is laughing at me. I fight the urge to punch him.

"Jute, you are so stupid!"

Now I really want to punch him. I feel my face grow hot with anger. Is he playing a trick on me? Rage is making me shake.

Tracy reaches into the box and pulls out a tube of lipstick. Pearly pink lipstick. My jaw drops and I realize this is not a joke. Not Tracy's joke, anyway. I am numb with disbelief. Why would Melinda bring me these and how does she even know where I live?

"She's probably going to say I stole them."

"Maybe you should read the card." He hands me a blue envelope.

"I don't want to read it. It's probably full of insults. She already called me a 'naughty boy' on the tag. Here," I hand the card back to him. "Read it if you want to, but I refuse!"

"Alright," he doesn't hesitate. He rips the flap open and pulls out a piece of pale blue paper with lacy cut outs around the edge. He unfolds it and clears his throat. I almost grab the paper away from him, but I don't. He starts to read, "Dear brown eyes, I'm finished with these. Your turn. I hope this means peace. If not, you can draw bloody goat heads all over the pages and the librarian will blame me. Love, Mel. P.S. You taste like caramel ice cream."

I expect Tracy to laugh at me, but he doesn't look up. He folds the paper and focuses intently on getting his hands to cooperate as he slips it back into the envelope.

"I'm sorry I yelled at you," I offer.

"I don't care if you yell at me." He is staring at the box, but then raises his eyes to look at me, "I care that you let her kiss you when you obviously dislike her. But you never kiss the people you do like."

Tracy stands up and puts his hands on my face, pulling me to look up at him. His fingers are pressing firmly behind my ears in a way that has become so familiar to me.

"I just have to know…" he says. He closes his eyes and lowers his lips to mine. I am stunned, my mind racing with so many thoughts that I can barely focus on the movements of his lips and tongue. I feel like a robot that someone is trying to program to understand 'kiss'. I feel as if pieces of me are splitting apart in different directions, bickering about the significance or insignificance of every touch and every thought. We are friends, he is the most beautiful boy I've ever seen, he could never like me, he prefers boys, he likes me, we love each other, I love Allie, he is so gentle, he is being so rude, and on and on.

He has stopped kissing me and is staring at me before I realize it. I open my eyes as if out of a dream. I still don't know what to express with my eyes, or with my words. I look back and forth between his eyes, his blue eyes the color of Allie's. Allie. Where is she? I feel the tears start. I've held them back for weeks, not wanting to tell him that I think she has left me forever. I don't want to have these thoughts, much less speak them out loud. I just want to wake up one morning and have her here again. I turn away from Tracy so he can't see me crying.

"I'm tired. I think I'm going to bed," I say. I walk out of the room, but feel like I'm running.

I never imagined I would think of my bed as the safest place in this house. Usually, I don't sleep in here. I slept on the couch a lot when Luke was here. After he left, I found myself falling asleep with Tracy. It was never a big deal. Even before he opened up about being gay, I never felt uncomfortable being close to him. I'm not sure if things will be that carefree again. Maybe if I understand why he kissed me, I could let it go. But, I can't ask him now. I can't trust his words tonight when he is drunk. Earlier, I thought I could interrogate him while he had his guard down and find out his secrets, but now I don't know if I really want to know. I tell myself that maybe he wasn't revealing secrets at all. Maybe he is just doing stupid things and tomorrow he will be just as shocked as I am now.

I close my eyes and listen for Tracy to go to bed. I decide that once he is asleep, I will move to the couch. I can't stay in this bed.

CHAPTER THIRTY-ONE

Oxygen. I try to fill my lungs, but I can not raise my chest. I hear someone else breathing, why can't I? I attempt to raise my arms to push the weight off of me, but I am paralyzed. I try to arch my back, but can not move. Am I buried alive? Something touches my hand, fingers, curling around mine. Warm, wet, and sticky with blood. I know it's back. I know what this is. I open my eyes and see absolute darkness.

A raspy whisper is breathed sensually into my ear, "I will devour you."

I feel the weight on me turn to liquid, thick and warm like blood, washing over me. I still can not move. I must breathe soon or I will die. Maybe I am already dead. I struggle to pull air into my lungs as the flesh of my face starts to melt and slide away. Thick blood clogs my throat, gagging me. I can not heave to vomit it away.

Flashes of light dance before me. I know it's only the effects of oxygen loss to my neurons. I watch them intently, giving up my fight for air. I let go of all hope of being saved. The lights are so beautiful, colors of bright white and blue swirling and flashing. Fading.

My body becomes weightless, lifted up into cool air. I gasp, shocked to feel air in my lungs. I exhale and inhale again. I am alive.

"Jute?" Tracy's voice is full of sleep. I feel his body behind me, curved against mine. His hand is warm on my ribs.

"Have you slept enough?"

I can't help but let out a small laugh. "You are waking me up to ask me if I slept enough?"

"I'll let you go back to sleep if you want," he sounds barely awake himself, his head still on the pillow and his breath hitting the back of my head. "I was just worried about you."

Suddenly I remember last night and wonder how I got into his bed. What else happened while I was asleep? As soon as this question enters my mind, I feel ashamed for thinking it. "Why are you worried? You were the one drunk last night."

"I know. I'm sorry that happened. I shouldn't have kissed you and I won't do it again. Just try not to be afraid of me."

I turn to look at him, "I'm not afraid of you. That's crazy. Why would you think that?"

"Because you are generally afraid of sex and I kissed you last night. I woke up at two o'clock in the morning and realized you weren't here." He licks his lips nervously. "I went to find you and I'm pretty sure you were having a seizure or something. You were twitching and gasping for air. I carried you in here and you seemed fine after that. I just feel so stupid for kissing you. But, please don't think you can't trust me. I am not going to do anything to hurt you."

I remember dreaming about being covered in blood. I shake the memory from my mind.

"Well, first of all, I'm not afraid of sex. Secondly, I am not afraid of you. The only stupid thing that happened last night was you trying to find pudding in the medicine cabinet."

His smile makes his eyes squint, "Right, that was pretty stupid. But, you are lying about not being afraid of sex. Other than Allie, when was the last time?"

I bite my lip, then let the words come out as if they don't hurt. "When I was thirteen and I walked in on my step-dad raping my sister." I cringe, feeling too vulnerable. I turn away from him because I don't want to see the pity on his face.

"What about kissing? Surely you have kissed boys."

I am so grateful that he moved on seamlessly and didn't force me to talk about my step-dad. "Yes, a few boys have kissed me."

"But, have you kissed them?" His hand taps my ribs absentmindedly when he speaks.

"No." I laugh, "I have a reputation for punching boys who kiss me. It tends to keep strange hands off me."

"So, that proves my point. You are afraid of sex. And I had this crazy idea about helping you get over that," I hear him laugh behind me and I turn to see him looking up at the ceiling. He covers his face with his hands and rubs his eyes as if trying to clear away his thoughts. "It was really stupid. But, I thought if I was gentle enough and patient enough, and if I let you tell me to stop a hundred times and every single time I would stop when you wanted me to, I thought that would be enough to fix the broken part of you."

His words circulate in my mind. I know he is right. I know there is something broken inside me. It isn't normal to punch people when they kiss me, especially when some of them are people I like. Last night when Tracy kissed me, I didn't feel afraid at all. It wasn't all sparks and tingles like kissing Allie. But, I certainly didn't punch him. What he is saying makes sense. But, there's a problem.

"But I'm in a relationship with Allie and you are gay."

He seems to choose his words carefully. "I am gay, and most likely so are you. But, this isn't about that kind of relationship. Speaking of Allie, when does she plan to visit?"

The question hurts my heart.

"I don't know. She is involved with a church in Ohio, setting up vegetable gardens for the poor. She hasn't had a lot of time for anything else. Plus, her mom read my letters to her. She hates me."

Tracy puts his arms around me and pulls me close to him, my back against his stomach. He bends to rests his head on my head, which I find annoying. I can't decide if he's trying to be annoying, so I stay quiet and hope he moves soon.

"She'll make her way back to you," he says, hugging me so tightly I can't breathe, then he quickly relaxes. He doesn't move his head off of mine.

I pull free from him and get out of bed. The clock on the dresser says it is six o'clock and I have to catch the bus in an hour.

"I'm going to make coffee. Do you want some, or are you going back to sleep?"

"I'll get up. I'm going to drive into Knoxville today and try to make some contacts for gigs. If this doesn't pan out soon, we may need to rob a train."

"You are hilarious, in a sad kind of way. Jokes aside, you don't think Macky will give us a weekend slot? They loved you last night, especially that girl in the white leather jacket with the fringe." I wink at him. "She had some mighty big boobs."

He makes a gagging sound, "Not my thing. But, I'll look the other way if you want to go after it."

"I'm not a lesbian," I am so tired of repeating myself. I think every time I say it, he just gets more determined to mess with me.

While the coffee maker works its magic, I go to my room to get dressed. I frown at the low stack of clean clothes. Tracy does laundry once a week while I am at school, but he has fallen a little behind. I'll have to help out after school. But in the meantime, I have no clean pants. I can either wear a dirty pair or put on the maxi skirt Allie left here. It's golden yellow and comes with a thick black belt. I don't hate it on her, but it's not exactly my style. But, it will have to be for today.

I slide it up over my hips and button the large front buttons. The length of the skirt is a bit too long, but wearing my boots with it should keep it off the floor. The belt is pretty cool, at least. I put on my only-wear-it-when-I-have-nothing-else Rolling Stones t-shirt with the lips. I tuck it in so the belt of the skirt is visible. I look in the mirror and prepare myself for the jokes and comments about my lips. I lean in closer and put on dark red lipstick. Fuck them all. I don't care.

After pulling on my combat boots and lacing them up, I go back to the kitchen with jut enough time to drink a few sips of coffee. Tracy already has mine poured in a cup. I pick it up and inhale the steam. The clock shows I have five minutes before Skeet's normal drive-by time. Tracy is watching me eye the clock.

"If you want to take a few minutes to enjoy that, I can drive you to school."

Now that is a plan I like. "That would be great! Wow," I smile at him and sit down at the table, "you saved the day."

"I can't believe you are wearing a skirt."

"I'm sure no one will notice."

"Melinda will notice." Tracy blows me a kiss.

"Shut up, asshole." I pretend to be mad, but I'm not convincing.

CHAPTER THIRTY-TWO

Thump, thump, thump, thump…

Someone is kicking my seat. I look up from my book at all the rows of bus seats in front of me. I knew I should have sat in the very back instead of one up from it. I bite my tongue and look back down. I've lost my place in the book.

Thump, thump, thump, thump…

I don't even take the time to look up before yelling, "If you don't stop kicking my seat, I'm going to shove your shoe up your ass!"

No response. I am so angry that I don't even remember what I was reading. It's not like I was enjoying this detailed account of daily life during World War I. My day has been filled with taunts and laughter about my clothes from people assuming I am their friend. I most certainly am not anyone's friend, especially at this moment, on this bus, when I hate everyone.

Thump, thump, thump, thump…

"Damn it!"

I stand up and turn around, ready to break a nose. Melinda is actually lying down on the seat behind me with her feet propped up in the seat across the aisle.

"What the hell are you doing?" I try to lower my voice so the people in the front of the bus will lose interest and stop staring at me. I don't expect this conversation to be something I want overheard.

"I'm riding the bus to my grandpa's house. You know,

the blue one just around the bend from you?"

"I don't care where you get off, I just want you to stop hitting the back of my seat."

She sits up and her hair looks the same as it did when she was lying down, all splayed out from being teased and sprayed stiff. She probably uses an entire bottle of hair spray every morning.

"But, I thought you might like to sit with me."

I don't want to sit with her, but I also don't want to draw attention to myself trying to talk to her over the back of the seat. I grab my things and get up to go back there. She looks surprised, and scoots over to make room.

"You know," I say in an angry whisper, "You have a very messed up way of communicating. It isn't normal to repeatedly hit a seat when you want to talk to someone. And it isn't normal to walk up and kiss people because you want a library book." I glance around to see if anyone heard me.

Melinda keeps a smile on her face, not put off in the least.

"I see you got the box," she says, pointing to the book in my hands.

I sigh with exasperation, "Yes. I got the box. I don't know what you were trying to prove, but at least it saved me a trip to Knoxville library."

"That's good." She is smiling like it's her birthday.

"Are you this happy all the time, or is your mom off buying you a case of Aqua Net?" I miss Allie. Sarcasm is something we are good at together. It just feels lonely with Melinda. I don't show it, though. I smile like I really care about hair spray.

"Don't be a jerk. I know you aren't really as bad as you pretend, even if you did punch me. I'm sorry about all that. I'm not as bad as I seem, either. Try to understand. I know it will be hard for you to see the good in anyone except Allie."

"It's not that, Melinda. You don't seem to be bad, you just try too hard to seem good. Every day you sit with the preppy girls eating salads and giggling about crushes on football players. You wear pink jeans, for god's sake! How is that 'seeming' to be bad?"

Her face goes a little stiff and I see how hard she is fighting to keep the smile on her face. I almost feel guilty, but not enough to apologize. She licks her lips and looks like she's about to say something, but then turns her head to look out the window. I decide I don't care and open my book again. I just stare at it, though, not reading anything. The silence between us is way too loud in my head.

She finally turns back to me. I look up at her and see that she has been crying. She says, "I envy you. There is nothing anyone could say about you that would matter to you. Do you know how lucky you are? Even if I wanted to, I could never be that carefree. You act like it's my choice to be like this. But, my parents would never let me dress like you. And they certainly wouldn't let me shave my head, or wear dark red lipstick." She pauses briefly, then shakes her finger at me. "And what do you think would happen if I came to school wearing combat boots?" She wipes tears from her cheeks with both hands. To me, it sounds like a princess crying over a pea under her mattress. Who cares about those snobs she hangs around? I stare at her like she's an alien from some other universe.

"Well," I finally answer, "If you came to school wearing combat boots, I guess you would have stronger leg muscles because they are damn heavy."

She sniffs and laughs, nodding her head while she wipes her eyes again.

"See, you just don't care what people say and that means people can't hurt you. I envy that."

I stop smiling because she has this part so wrong. "People have hurt me my entire life, Melinda. They do it every day. The only difference between you and me is that I don't expect it to be any other way. Being a freak doesn't give you a free pass into bliss. It just makes people hurt you from farther away."

Melinda blinks at me like she actually came out of her own misery to consider mine. I try to control the anger at her for pulling this vulnerable truth out of me. It was really hard today to ignore everyone's insults, but to end it by divulging to Melinda that I actually do have feelings is just the last straw. It's all I can do not to get up and sit somewhere else. But, I don't want to have people turn around and stare. Only fifteen minutes until I am home. I pick up my book and start reading on a random page.

"I don't think you are a freak," her words catch me off guard because I thought we were finished talking. My house is only five miles away. I'll get off the bus and then she will be the new last stop. I keep my eyes on the page while she continues. "No one knows this, not even my best friend Jennifer. No one. But, I want you to know it. I like girls. I have always felt like I'm really a boy. I just needed someone to talk to about it and I thought you would understand. I just dress really girly to hide it because I think I'll die if anyone finds out. I admire you so much for being open about being a lesbian. I wish I could be open about it like you."

I can't explain just how upset her words have made me, or why. The bus turns the last curve before my house. I gather my things in my arms and stand up. I don't even look at her when I say, "You are wrong. I am not gay. But, good luck with that."

She is sniffling behind me as I walk up the aisle. By the time I get to the front of the bus, I hear her sobbing in the back. My heart is bursting with guilt. I'm a jerk. She should run up here and shove me out the door into the ditch. I would deserve it.

Skeet stops the bus. He looks at me disappointedly, then glances in his rear view mirror at Melinda's sobbing. "What's going on there?" He nudges his head in her direction.

"She'll be fine." I say as he moves the lever to open the doors.

I step off the bus and walk over to the mailbox. I am

213

filled with dread. Usually, opening the mailbox leads to disappointment. I decide it's just one more bad thing to deal with and I might as well get it over with. I pull open the lid, see only shadows against gray metal, and close it quickly. Part of my brain is relieved that I don't have to spend a minute more hoping I'll get a letter today. Another part of my brain counters with hope that the mail carrier is late.

I sigh and look up at the house to see if Tracy is home. The car is gone, but Hank's truck is parked in my driveway. As I make my way around his truck, I see him sitting on my porch steps. He's wearing an orange Stihl cap and his hair is curling up around the edges. There are more gray hairs than I remember. He stands up when he sees me, a big smile across his face.

"Hey, girl! How you been doin'?" He walks over and hugs me and I hug him back. He smells like Allie's house when we were kids, but I guess he should.

"I'm good," I say, noticing my voice is more high pitched then normal. I always feel like a kid around him. "I just can't wait for school to be over."

"You see your momma lately?"

I look at him like he should know better than to ask that, "Not since January. She's a busy woman, Hank."

He shakes his head, "I talked to her a few weeks ago about wanting to buy Earl's land. She said that it didn't belong to her. I didn't want to cause any trouble. I didn't know they were divorced before he, uhm... before he passed away."

His head is bowed low, but his eyes look up at me to see if I am upset. I am not. "So, she said I needed to talk to you and Drew about it because you two are his children."

"I'm not his child." A shiver goes through me and I suddenly feel very dirty. I want to go inside and take a shower and wash away everything I feel right now.

"I know, Jute," Hank's voice is low and gentle as if trying to convince a mad dog not to bite. "I'm so sorry. I wouldn't have even come here, but I thought your momma might not tell you. If it just sits over there and no one pays the taxes, it could be auctioned off. I don't want that for you girls. I will pay you a fair price if you'll let me buy it."

I wish his words didn't feel so suffocating. I've never met a dad more meek and kind than Hank. How sick I feel has nothing to do with him. I try to take a couple of steady breaths so that I can speak without the anger in my voice.

"Whatever Drew wants to do is fine. I think you should have it. I will never live on it. Just see what she says."

Hank nods, "Alright, girl. I'll go on over to Drew's. Sorry to bother you."

"You aren't bothering me, Hank," I finally exhale and feel myself loosen up. "You come here any time. I certainly never hesitated to come to your place and make myself at home."

"Well, you can still come to my place any time you want. It makes nary a difference if Allie is here or not. Just come on over and I'll cook you supper." He puts his hand out for me to shake, which he has done a hundred times since I was a kid. I put my hand in his and feel his calluses exactly where I anticipate them. "Speakin' of that ol' gal, have you heard from my daughter? Man, she was out of here like a bolt of lightning and she just ain't looking back." Pride gleams in his eyes.

"She's got the entire state of Ohio fighting for her attention," I say as if it doesn't hurt. "You raised a beautiful, smart, hard working girl. You should be proud of everything she's doing up there."

"Yes, well..." he looks down a little. "I worry about her. She's all I got. But, I am certainly proud of her."

Hank gives my hand a final shake and then salutes me as he walks toward his truck. I wave and watch him pull his truck onto the road.

I stand in the yard, listening to his engine noise disappear around the bend. I strain to hear it as long as I can, as if it isn't just Hank driving away, but Allie as well. When I can no longer pretend to still hear it, my mind turns to Melinda. I am filled with guilt for how I treated her. I know I need to make it right. I walk down the driveway toward the road, then turn in the direction of the blue house with all the hens in the yard.

CHAPTER THIRTY-THREE

There's an old Walker Coonhound stretched out in front of the door. His muzzle is peppered with white hair. His eyes blink at me but he does not raise his head. He must be mostly blind from the cataracts. I am standing only six feet away from him, but I am not sure I won't startle him.

I clear my throat, but he still doesn't raise his head.

"Good boy," I say quietly in a high pitched voice. I hold my hand out, hoping he'll get up and sniff me. He just blinks and moves his head to rest on his outstretched front legs. "I'm coming up the stairs now, please don't bite me..." I am on the second step when I hear Melinda's voice behind me.

"He's not going to bite you, stupid."

I turn around and say, "One can never be too careful." I smile like she's suppose to find it funny. She doesn't seem to. She just crosses her arms and stares at me like she's waiting for me to say whatever I came to say. I guess I might as well get on with it.

"I came to apologize for being completely subhuman on the bus." I look down at my feet and then back to her. "I know what you said wasn't easy."

"Shhh!" Her eyes dart around the yard and at the windows of her grandpa's house. "Can we take a walk and talk about this?"

Without waiting for me to answer, she walks up on the porch and taps on the window of the screen door. She calls out, "Pap-pap, I'm going for a walk to my friend's house. Did you hear me?"

A scratchy deep voice calls from within the house, "Okay, darlin'. If you walk in the road, you watch real good for cars now. Don't let Rufus follow you, he can't see to get home."

"Okay. I'll be back before dark. I love you!"

I can tell she really does love him and I hate how jealous I am that she has family to feel that way about. She runs back to me with a little too much excitement in her eyes.

"Where to now?" She asks like the walk was my idea.

"I don't know, you are the one that suggested it."

"Right. Okay, then how about we walk back to your house." She goes up on her toes like it's all she can do not to jump up and down.

"If you can try not to be weird about it, then fine."

I walk past her to the road and she follows behind me. We don't say anything at all until I can see my driveway, and my mailbox. My heart aches, knowing I will check it again and it will be empty again. Mumbling under my breath, I tell myself not to even look inside. Just walk on by. Don't set myself up for the pain. I sound like a hell of a coach. But, I'm also being too loud.

"Don't look at what?" she says from behind me as she takes a few quick steps to get beside me.

"Nothing," I say, but it's obvious to her when I walk over and pull the mailbox lid open. Nothing. I don't even bother worrying about what Melinda thinks. I just slam the lid shut and head toward the house.

"It's so cool you get to live on your own."

"I don't really live on my own. I have a roommate."

"Oh, I know about Tracy. But, he isn't your parent or anything. I mean, no one tells you what to do."

I glance over at her and envy her naivete. "I also don't have anyone to pay the bills, buy food, or take off the trash."

"Really?" She looks stunned. "I thought your mom was giving you money."

"Why the hell are you and your friends talking about

whether or not my mom is paying my damn bills?" I know I might be overreacting, but this conversation is hitting all my nerves.

"Whoa! Calm down. It's not like you didn't know my friends are shallow, self-righteous, thumb suckers incapable of wiping their asses without parental inspection." She smiles and nods at me like that proved something.

"Did that feel good?"

"Absolutely," She nods again. I can't help but smile back at her.

"Alrighty, then. Ready for me to cut your hair?"

Her eyes pop open wide like I just asked if she would stand still and let me shoot a fly off her nose. I laugh so hard I have to sit down on the porch steps to compose myself.

"Are you serious?" She is leaning toward me, squinting hard with skepticism. I laugh even more.

Taking deep breaths, I finally stop giggling. She's still wide-eyed and blinking at me. I clear my throat and say, "I'm only as serious as you want me to be. I do cut my own hair and I can do yours if you want. But, something tells me you aren't really a boy hiding under your pretty blond hair. So, why don't you tell me why you are really interested in talking to me?"

Melinda sits beside me. She smells like pork chops, but she didn't on the bus. I imagine her Grandpa had supper waiting on her. My stomach makes a quiet growl and I hope she didn't hear it. I stare out over the yard and wait to hear what she has to say.

"I wasn't lying to you. But, I've spent a lot of years lying to myself. Things were going really well, I mean obviously. I hang out with the popular crowd. But, then I went to a party and I was making out with this guy. Travis Garrett. You know him right?"

I nod.

"Well, we were kissing and I really like kissing." She nudges me with her elbow. "Anyway, we were kissing and he asked if I wanted to go outside behind the house, which is what we usually do when we are going to smoke. Is that what you all do when you want to get high?"

She looks at me with interest. I shake my head, "My friends get high wherever they want. But, my friends are split into two groups. One that gets fucking wasted. And the other just likes to hang out and listen to music, talk about movies and books and drink a little beer. But, no, none of them go behind the house unless the bathroom is occupied and they need to pee." I resist the urge to roll my eyes. Her friends are stupid.

"Oh, cool. Well, it's a thing with us, so I just went around back with Travis and he starts taking off his clothes. I was like 'hold on', but he stripped completely naked. He took my hand and put it on his dick and it was the most disgusting thing I've ever touched. Nasty."

She shakes her head and I can't help but laugh. I think about all the times I've seen Tracy naked and how I have never thought of him as nasty. But, at the same time, I agree with Melinda. The first time I saw a penis was my step-dad's. I reacted just like she is describing. Thinking about it now makes my stomach tighten and I feel a little sick. I stop laughing.

"So you think you are gay because Travis has a gross penis?" I wink at her.

"No!" She screams at me. After a deep breath, she says, "I think I'm gay because when I was little girl I always pretended to be the prince so Jennifer could be the princess. We used to really kiss like in the movie. I liked it so much. But then her mother caught us and said we couldn't play that way any more. It was devastating. I have never imagined having sex with boys. I don't even like boys. I like girls. All the time. I wish I was a boy so no one would question that. Like now, since that thing with Travis, boys have been calling me a lesbian. I don't think they really think I am one. I think they are just trying to manipulate me. But, I don't know what I will do if they realize that I really am."

I put my arm around her and hope she knows I am doing it as a friend, "I guess you need to decide if you want to grow up and find your princess and kiss happily ever after, or if you want to spend your life touching gross penises."

"Very funny, Jute. It's not that simple."

"Why not? We graduate in seven weeks. You'll go off to college and never see most of those kids again." I squeeze her arm a little and feel like I am being the mother I never had.

"But my parents..." she sighs and puts her hands on my face, "Oh, God. I hate this, but you are so right. I knew you would say this. I guess I wanted to talk to you because I needed someone to say it. You are the only gay person I know, but I am really glad you turned out to be nicer than you act." She gives me a smile and I try hard not to get defensive about being called gay again. She hugs me and my face is buried in a giant cloud of hair.

"Let's cut it," She says.

"How do you want it?" I feel excited. I have a lot of friends who are willing to take risks and do insane things. Most of my friends know they are oddballs and they don't care. But, I have never had a chance to help someone come out like this. I think of Tracy and Luke, even myself and Allie, and how hard it is to find someone to see you as you really are. Melinda may not understand exactly who I am. But, I can help validate the person she is underneath all this fluff.

"Well," she taps a finger to her lips, "Not anything as radical as yours, Jute. Maybe something more Sheena Easton, with a little curl left on the top." She raises an eyebrow at me as if to ask if I can do it.

"Just sit right there." I stand up and dust off my skirt. "I'll be right back with the scissors."

When I walk back out, I take a moment to look at all her blond hair spiraling down her back to her waist. It is absolutely amazing. What I am about to do will likely make many people upset, not just at Melinda, but also at me. But, I believe she wants it done, and I believe she wants at least one person who will accept her decision. I have her sit on Tracy's bucket. I stand behind her and gather up her hair in my hand

and use one of Tracy's rubber bands to put it in a ponytail.

"Last call." I say and wait.

"I can't wait!" She says, "Ready, set, go!"

I cut her pony tail off and place the heaping amount of hair into a paper grocery bag. I put it to the side so no other pieces of hair fall into it. She could probably sell it for a small fortune or donate it. Cutting the rest feels less radical. I ask a lot of questions to make sure I know exactly how she wants it to look. I move around in front of her to see if I have everything even. She has a few spiral curls falling forward to her right eyebrow, but the back is cut like a boy's haircut. I am in awe at how it has transformed her face. I look at her and see her eyes and lips much more prominently. It is a stunning transformation. I can't imagine anyone not loving it.

"Go look," I say, taking her arm and urging her to her feet. She dusts the hair off her lap as best she can. "There's a mirror in the bathroom. Go in the house, turn right, then left."

I get the broom and start sweeping the hair off the porch when Tracy drives up. I keep sweeping and don't look up. I hear the car door slam and soon after he steps on the porch step. He must have skipped a few, because the next foot lands on the porch. His arms wrap around me and he is squeezing me tight, rocking me back and forth, laughing like a crazy person.

"What the hell?" I push him off of me.

"We got a gig in Knoxville tonight! TO-NIGHT!" He runs off the porch and around the car and back on the porch like a dog let off a chain. I can't help but laugh at him. But he freezes when he sees Melinda in the doorway. I don't blame him, she is breathtaking.

"Can I go, too?" She asks, her eyes lit up. She's on her toes again, bouncing with excitement.

Tracy looks from her to me and back again a few times.

"Let me guess, you are Melinda?" Tracy puts his hand out to her.

She nods excitedly, "And you are Tracy, the mystery

guy," Melinda puts her hand in his.

"No, I'm just a stray dog Jute took in," He winks at me and I slap his arm because I want him to stop talking to her. "She beats me with newspapers when I have accidents on the carpet."

Melinda laughs, but her eyes stay on me. "I'm sorry I'm laughing, Jute. But, he's funny. I see why you keep him around." She puts a hand up to touch her hair, "By the way, I love my hair. Thank you so much!"

She walks over to me and hugs me close to her, which makes me uncomfortable. I put my hands on her hips to push her away, but a spark of electricity goes through me. It scares me and I shove her away harder than I intended. We both seem to want to pretend none of that happened, and I am relieved. She really needs to go home now.

"So," says Tracy, "We need to load up the car and hit the road. We can busk on the street downtown for an hour and still have time for the gig if we leave right now." And then he does it. He turns to Melinda and says, "Are you coming?"

CHAPTER THIRTY-FOUR

One o'clock in the afternoon, I am the only one awake. Tracy barely moved when I rolled out of his arms a few minutes ago. Melinda is sleeping in my room, better she than I.

I pour coffee into a blue mug covered in painted white snowflakes and look out the kitchen window. A few dogwood blooms are showing on the hillside. There should be many more in the coming days. Easter Sunday is tomorrow. I tell myself this is the reason Allie won't visit me today. I try to believe it and think nothing of the other weeks that I have held out hope and been disappointed. But, the sun is bright and the day is beautiful. There must be something fun to do. Maybe Melinda would like to go to thrift stores. The thought of taking a preppy girl to buy second-hand vintage clothes makes me laugh.

The coffee is hot and so pleasurably painful to drink, burning my lips a little. I think about last night while I wait for the caffeine to kick in. We made more money than we ever have. Surprisingly, most of it came from busking on the street. I don't know if people stopped to listen because we harmonized so well, or if it was to watch Melinda dance. She must have spent a lot of time studying sexy ways a girl can move. She had it down to an art. I think she had fun. If we had stayed on the street, she probably wouldn't have run into trouble. But because she danced on stage with us at the bar, a lot of men bought her drinks. By the time we got home, Tracy had to carry her inside. At least he stayed sober this time.

The empty mug clinks against the bottom of the sink, as I set it down to run a little water into it. I can't wait to get in the shower and wash the cigarette smell off of me. It reminds me of living with Earl, which is the last thing I want on my mind. Quietly, I walk into the bathroom and shut the door.

Turning the water on in the bathtub is really loud, and so is pulling the tab to turn the shower on. I have probably interrupted some dreams in this house, but they need to get up anyway. While I wash off, I hum. Then I sing. Then I sing loudly and hope they can hear me. I laugh imagining them grumbling and wishing I would shut up.

After I turn off the shower, I open up the bathroom door to let the steam out. I smell bacon cooking in the kitchen and assume Tracy is awake. I hear the spatula scraping a skillet and visualize the swirly beginnings of scrambled eggs. I dry myself quickly and wrap the towel around me. We still haven't done laundry, so I think I'll go to Tracy's room and borrow a clean pair of pajama pants and a t-shirt.

Before going to the other side of the house, I check on Melinda. She is still in my bed with the blanket over her head. I watch her for a minute to make sure I see her chest rise and fall. I remember watching Earl when he would pass out drunk. I would stare at him to see if he was breathing. I would hope that if I stared at him long enough, his chest would stop rising and falling. I hoped he would just die. Maybe the years of having those bad thoughts is what makes me check on Melinda now. I hope my wishes for Earl won't backfire and one day someone I care about will meet the fate I wished for him. My thoughts are not always rational.

"Are you out, Jute?" Tracy is calling to me. I'm worried he'll wake up Melinda, so I rush out of the room so I can tell him to shut up without yelling. I take two steps into the living room and freeze.

Allie is sitting on the couch. She stands up when she seems me, smiling weakly and holding her hands out as if to say *I am finally here*. I almost can't believe it is true.

She is wearing navy blue slacks like my mom wears and a white oxford shirt. I look down at her feet and she is wearing navy blue flats. Her hair is braided and wrapped up in a bun on top of her head.

"Who the hell are you?" I say, knowing she will laugh because she thinks she looks ridiculous, too.

But, she doesn't laugh. She just puts her hands to her thighs and nervously wipes sweat off them.

"Jute, I need to talk to you. In private. Can we sit outside?"

She looks like something terrible has happened. My mind races to try to figure out what is going on with her and I forget I am wearing only a towel. I turn to walk outside but stop when Allie clears her throat. "You might want to put on some clothes first."

"Right." I point my finger in the air as if the idea were my own. I smile nervously. "Be right back."

Tracy's clean clothes are just as scarce as mine. I grab pajama pants from a drawer. They are orange and brown plaid, and seriously ugly. I grab a plain white undershirt to wear with them. In less than two minutes, I walk out onto the porch and find Allie already sitting on the top porch step. She has taken a dry towel from the bathroom to sit on so she doesn't get her pants dirty. When I shut the door behind her, she turns to look at me.

"So you are wearing each other's clothes, now?" Her eyes light up like they always do when she teases me.

"Laundry crisis," I explain, sitting down beside her. My body aches to touch her skin. But, I don't want her to think that is all I care about. I don't look at her so maybe she won't see it.

"I need to talk to you." I feel her turn to look at me and my heart pounds. "It's about what happened before I moved. You know, I've always tried to be a good person. But, so many times I do things because they seem right when they are actually wrong. I have been discussing this with Jim and he has been reading passages from the Bible to me. He has really helped me understand what it means to be good in the eyes of God. Jute, what we did was wrong. We both need to ask for forgiveness."

I hear her words, but I can't understand them. It isn't that I don't know what she is saying. I just refuse to believe she is saying it. My heart doesn't get the message. It still aches to touch her, wants desperately for her to kiss me like she loves me. Her words turn around in my head in someone else's voice. It can't possibly be Allie saying this. Finally, I look at her. She is staring down at her shoes. I keep my eyes on her face when I speak.

"So, Jim told you that loving me is bad?"

"No, Jute. The Bible told me that having sex with you is bad. I will always love you. And because I love you, I want to ask you to forgive me for leading you astray. And..."

She looks into my eyes now. Electricity runs through me and I don't know if I can breathe with her so close. "I need to confess something in order to be forgiven," her voice is nearly a whisper. "I have confessed it to God, but I must confess it to you."

She leans in close so I can hear her, the words barely audible.

"Please forgive me for what I am about to tell you and for not being honest with you before. You know I was very upset when I found you on the floor, covered in scratches and freezing. I decided to take you to Shawn's house so I could go to Earl's trailer and get your things back. When I got there, I saw a box of your clothes in the back of his truck. I put them in my car, but, I wanted to confront him. He didn't answer when I knocked so I let myself in."

My heart is racing with adrenaline. But, I still don't understand how any of this needs to be confessed. I already knew she did these things.

Allie bites her lips nervously and looks down away from my eyes. "I let myself in and I saw Earl passed out on the couch. He was sitting up with a lit cigarette hanging from his lips. There was a glass of vodka in one hand and your panties in his other hand. Seeing him holding your underwear made me so angry." Allie is crying now. "I pulled them out of this hand. He didn't wake up, but his other hand twitched and the vodka glass tipped over. It spilled all down his pants and on the couch. I wanted him to pay, Jute. I didn't plan to kill him. But, God forgive me, I took the cigarette from his lips and dropped it onto his lap. His clothes caught on fire and I did nothing to put it out. It wasn't an accident. I killed him because I wanted him to die."

She covers her face and sobs. "I don't know if God will ever forgive me for what I have done. I am a horrible person. Please don't think I don't love you. I love you so much and I want us both to be saved."

I wrap my arms around her. I can't forgive her for something I don't think needs forgiveness. Of course, she thinks she is in the wrong. But all of this is my fault. She is only guilty of trying to protect me. No one has ever loved me as much as she does. Yet, now she thinks this love is evil because a man said so. Unfortunately, Allie has always been predictable in this way. She completely loses herself in trying to win approval of men. I thought it would be different now, that we were connected more profoundly. But, Allie has allowed Jim to make her feel undeserving of happiness. Now, she will jump through the hoops he sets up for her.

"You are so incredibly good, Allie. What you did probably saved my life. I can't forgive you for doing something I wish I could have done years ago."

Her hands are pressed to her face as she leans into my shoulder. I squeeze her tighter. The more I think about what is happening, the angrier I become. "Besides, who the fuck is Jim to say it's a sin for you to love me like this?"

She pushes herself out of my arms and inches away. She looks at me indignantly. "He is a youth minister at an Assembly of God!" She is actually shouting at me. "Who do you think you are to believe you can do whatever you please?

228

You aren't God, Jute, and you don't get to make the rules. Please, repent with me right now. We can not continue to have feelings for each other in that way!" She sounds so desperate, the way she used to get when I would imply that Bobby wasn't such a good guy.

The door to the house flies open and Melinda is standing there in Tracy's undershirt which barely covers her panties. Her breasts fill out the shirt, stretching the fabric until there is little left to the imagination. She smiles at Allie, but it isn't sincere. "Well, I guess this means Jute is free to date other people?"

Allie looks at me as if I have been possessed by a demon. I look at her much the same way, but I don't blame supernatural forces. I know the truth, which is that Allie is not being Allie. She's being Jim's minion.

CHAPTER THIRTY-FIVE

I don't know why Allie did it. Melinda was the one upsetting her. Yet, I am the one that Allie slapped across the cheek. Now, her eyes are wide, as if she is shocked at what she just did. She stands and runs to her car. Before I can catch up with her, she is already in the driver's seat. I try to hold the door so she can't close it.

"Wait!" I plead, clutching the top of the door tightly in my grip.

But she doesn't even try to pull it closed as she starts the car. I think I can walk around to climb on top of her so she won't leave without me. But, before the plan is fully formed, she pops the car in reverse and hits the gas. The car door is ripped out of my hands. I fall forward in the new grass which is just making its way up after years of being driven over. I hear her stop, finally shut her door, then rev the engine as her car pulls onto the road.

I stay face down where I fell, thinking maybe I am in the same place where Allie's feet once walked. I imagine her navy blue flats pushing down the same blades of grass that I press my face against now. Tears run from my eyes, but I don't make a sound. I don't want to get up. I don't want to move for fear I will physically break apart.

I don't open my eyes when I feel Melinda's body lying in the grass beside me. I feel her arm touch my back. The sun has warmed my shirt and her hand presses the heat against my skin. I think of many hateful things to say to her, but I can't say them. In my mind, I am blaming her for making Allie leave. But, in my heart, I know Allie was already gone weeks ago.

Melinda's voice is almost too soft and sweet, "I feel so sorry for her, Jute. I wish I could make it easier for you."

"So far, I think you just made it worse." I open my eyes to glare at her, but I can't. Her new look is shocking in a way that takes my breath away, even though I should expect it because I helped create it. The short boyish cut is in sharp contrast with her soft china doll lips, small and plump in the center. I can't imagine her lips on a boy. Even if she changes everything about herself, her face is strikingly feminine and beautiful. It is everything mine is not.

She just stares at me with her pale green eyes lit up in the afternoon sun. I can't remember whose turn it is to speak, but I can't think of anything to say. My mind wanders between her face and thoughts of a future without Allie. I don't know how to live without her. I imagine myself dying so many different ways. What a relief it would be just to put a gun to my head. But, those green eyes stay locked on mine and I don't move. I stay in the grass and let her hand move in circles on my back. I want to run into the house and beat my head against the walls. But, I stay under the sun and watch Melinda's nostrils flare slightly when she breathes.

Her mouth opens to speak then pauses. I see the edges of her bright white teeth. She closes her mouth again, a bit firmly, then says in a whisper, "If I kiss you now, will you punch me?"

"I might." I say, my voice flat and without conviction. The thought of her kissing me is so much better than the thoughts of killing my brain to disable the pain inside of me.

"Hmmm," She says, "I don't want to make things worse. Maybe I am being very selfish by wanting to touch you."

Her hand slides to the hem of my shirt and moves under it, her fingers trace the skin up my spine before resting between my shoulder blades. There, she makes gentle swirls. I close my eyes and focus on her touch, hoping it will drown out my suicidal wishes.

Her voice is still like honey, but deeper, "You can tell me to stop if this isn't helping."

She sits up and the sunlight is briefly shaded from my eyes. I feel her straddle me, her thighs against my pelvis. Her hands pull the hem of my shirt up in the back. She pulls again at the sides to raise my shirt over my breasts. The grass against my skin is like a thousand fingers as it settles back into place under my weight. I try not to think about what she is planning to do. I try not to think about her at all. I think about the grass and the sun, the slight breeze and the birds singing. I try to get lost from myself. But, eventually, Melinda pulls at my shoulder, urging me to turn over.

I twist my shoulders around and then Melinda rises up enough to allow the rest of me to roll over. I open my eyes and see her naked breasts. The breeze is cool on my flesh while the sun heats it. The mosaic of warmth and chill causes my skin to become taut, my nipples are painfully hard. It is comforting when her hands cover them. The heat of her palms rushes through me. She is leaning slightly forward, her skin is blushed pink. I stare at her breasts. They are as perfect as the rest of her, pale pink nipples the same color as her china doll smile.

"Is this good?" She asks sincerely. The word 'good' repeats in my head again and again until I hear it in Allie's voice instead. My heart feels like it might crumble beneath the crushing pain. I know tears have come to my eyes, but I try to think about the grass and the sky and find my way back to being lost. I can't answer her.

She leans down and kisses my lips, our skin touching in so many places that I can't distinguish hers from mine. She is gentle and cautious, as if I am feral. This kiss is nothing like the one from the library. Remembering the kiss from the library gives me a jolt of pleasure, making my skin tingle. I realize I have not punched her. I am not afraid of this. Something has changed inside of me.

"Stop," I say.

She sits up and takes her hands off my breasts. Her eyes are full of desire, but she is smiling as she slides off of me and sits cross-legged in the grass. She reaches out and pulls my shirt down to cover me, biting her lip in restraint.

"Thank you," I say, still motionless in the grass. I smile up at her, "I know I'm hard to deal with."

I reach up and brush the back of my fingers against her nipples, watching her mouth fall open as she catches her breath. I prop myself up on one elbow and lean in toward her, taking one of her nipples into my mouth. I gently bite it and pull with my teeth the way Allie did to mine. I feel the past collide with now and I can barely keep sane. I want Allie so badly and feel guilty for trying to have those feelings with Melinda.

Suddenly Melinda's hand pushes hard against my shoulder and I fall back away from her. I see her arms pull forward to cover her breasts just as I hear an old man screaming, "What're you doin', yougin'?"

I sit up and turn to see Melinda's grandpa coming up the driveway with his hound by his side. By the time I get to my feet, Melinda is already inside the house. The old man is shaking as he walks. I can't tell if it's old age or anger. He stares at my house, pretending like I don't exist.

The door opens and Melinda comes outside wearing her clothes from yesterday. She jogs down the steps in a happy way, but I can see the fear in her eyes. She walks up to her grandpa and takes his arm. "I didn't know what time it was. I'm sorry, Pap-pap."

"Your Momma's been waiting at my house for forty-five minutes. You're damn lucky she ain't come up here and seen you naked with that boy."

"Jute is a girl, Pap-Pap. And I don't care what Momma sees."

She winks at me and pulls the old man around to walk down the driveway. I can't make out the words he is saying to

233

her, but I pick up on his pleading tone. Maybe he is begging her not to be gay. Maybe he is pleading with her not to tell her mother. I watch them until they step out of sight around the tall hedges onto the road.

I can't believe what just happened. Only now do I realize that my hands are shaking just as badly as Melinda's had been. I don't think I have been so on fire since my last night with Allie. My legs are weak as I make my way up the porch steps. I push open the door and see Tracy on the couch with his guitar. He looks up at me, his blue eyes full of both concern and amusement.

I must be giving him a puzzled look. He says, "Yes, I saw everything." He pauses to let it sink in before saying, "I cooked breakfast. It's probably ice cold by now."

"But I'm on fire," I say, moving toward him through a cloud of warring emotions. I pick up his guitar and lean it against the wall. I climb onto his lap, facing him. I hold his face between my hands as I press my lips against his. I don't know what I am doing, I just want to quench this desire. My tongue searches his mouth as if the answer is somewhere inside him. It isn't enough. I want his skin against mine. I pull at his shirt to get it over his head. He pulls at mine. My hands slide to his nipples as his hands slide to my hips and pull me down against him. His body is so hard beneath me. I move my hips the way I remember moving them against Allie. The electricity through our clothes is so intense that I explode into orgasm, crying out and feeling tears come to my eyes. But, it isn't enough.

Tracy lifts me up as I am still straddling him, and turns so that I am lying on the couch. He pulls off the rest of my clothes. I watch him stand to remove his pants. I have seen him naked so many times before. I have slept with him and never once felt him hard against me. But, today is different. Today I don't just see a beautiful long-haired gay boy. I see the only boy who can prove that my demons are dead. Today I feel unafraid, but am I truly? Can I let myself feel this and not flashback to when I was a little girl? The usual horrific images flash through my mind and I realize that my desire is not lessened by them. I push them away easily. Maybe I will not be able to go through with this, but I need to try.

"I don't want to hurt you, Jute," his voice is raspy and breathless. He gets on his knees between mine. He moves his hands up my ribs and over my small breasts. For the first time, I feel beautiful because of my boyish looks, not despite them. His eyes are locked on mine. "Tell me what you want."

I wrap my legs around him and pull him close. He kisses me while his hand reaches down to guide himself into me. I push against him, wanting everything. The more he thrusts into me, the more I want this feeling to never end. There are no flashbacks, no shame, only exhilaration masking the nagging ache for Allie's touch. I think about the night we met Tracy, when she suggested we have sex with him together. I feel him move inside me now and imagine it isn't his hands on my nipples, but Allie's. I wrap my legs tighter around him as I feel another orgasm building inside me. His body begins to shake. He tries to pull away, but I cling tightly.

"No," he moans into my ear before I feel him erupt inside me. I meet his intensity with my own explosion of electric tremors. His body falls onto mine as he pants into my ear, "What... are we... doing?"

CHAPTER THIRTY-SIX

The bathtub is full of unbearably hot water and Tracy. I've been sitting on the toilet lid for ten minutes, waiting for the temperature to drop enough to tolerate. Tracy will be a shriveled prune before I even get in with him. His head is leaned back and his eyes are closed. I glance over the length of his body through the clear water, his skin has turned pink from the heat.

"Did Luke like his water scalding hot, too?" I ask.

"If it wasn't scalding hot before he got in, it sure was hot as hell afterward," he grins, but doesn't open his eyes. "What about you and Allie? Did you take baths together when you were younger?"

Since this afternoon, it seems the floodgates to our thoughts have opened. No question seems too personal to ask. Tracy has answered all my questions about why he prefers men and how he likes to be touched. I tried to do them all, but some were not possible. I loved watching Tracy's face contort with pleasure when I got things right. He asked me a lot about Allie, too. He was already more knowledgeable about a woman's body than I was about a man's. But, he tried to recreate the feeling of Allie's touch specifically. We spent hours trying to increase our proficiency and perfect our skills. We wanted to give what the other longed to have.

I answer, "We took a bath at her house once when we were 13. It was just a whim. We missed being little. It wasn't sexual at all. I needed it not to be."

I dip my toe in the water and decide it has cooled enough. Tracy pulls his knees up so that I can sit down between his legs. I lean back against his chest, my head resting just below his shoulder. He picks up a washcloth and covers it with soap. The almond scent is divine. I breathe in deeply and exhale, feeling more relaxed than I ever have.

"Sit up," he says, his deep voice like warm melted chocolate. He holds my arm with one hand and washes my back with the other. I hug my knees and remember how intently he washed my wounded feet at the hotel. He is making giant swirls over my back and humming. When he starts singing "Little Red Corvette" sounding just like Prince. I giggle and join in. He sings every word so perfectly that I glance back to make sure Prince isn't behind me.

"How do you know all these songs?"

Still in a Prince voice, he sings the lyric about being too fast. Then he switches to his real voice to add, "I had a lot of records in South Carolina."

I turn to face him. He makes room for me to wrap my legs around his back. "Well, you are amazing. I'm going to quiz you. Sing Judas Priest."

His voice goes high and shrill as he belts out the chorus of "Riding on the Wind".

I laugh, "Holy crap, Tracy. That was dead on. Let's see… I have to think of a hard one. What about Echo and the Bunnymen?"

Tracy's starts singing the song "Lips Like Sugar", his voice low and longing. He hits the chorus with perfect pitch, so loudly that it's like he's on a stage. Listening to him fills me with joy.

"Okay, so what can't you sing?"

"Well, I can't get my James Brown to sound like James Brown."

"What about your Tracy Duren? I've watched you writing your own songs. When can I hear those?"

His eyes are full of pleasure from singing. "Maybe

sometime you can help me write," he says, leaning forward and kissing my bottom lip, then my top lip. He sits back and smiles at me. "But for now, I think it's your turn to wash me."

He hands me the washcloth. "Anything for the rock star." I bat my eyelashes at him. I slide the washcloth over his skin, now less pink as the water begins to cool. He sighs and I watch his muscles relax.

"You make me miss having a boyfriend," he says.

"I thought you were already missing having a boyfriend."

"Not really. Where there's pleasure, there is usually pain. I needed to take a break from the pain part. But, thinking about the pleasure side makes me reconsider. It might be worth it. The only problem is, trying to find a boyfriend around here might get a guy killed ."

We hear a knock on the outside door that startles us both. "I know you are in there, let me in!" Three more pounding knocks land on the door.

"That's Melinda." I say to Tracy as if he might know why she is here. He shrugs to indicate he has no idea.

I yell loud enough for her to hear me, causing Tracy to cover his ears, "You know where the key is, dumbass. Use it!" I giggle and wink at Tracy.

I hear the key in the door knob and then the door pushes open. "Where are you?"

"In the bathroom, you can come in."

Tracy's eyes widen and he pulls the washcloth from my hands to lay it across his lap. He has always been so comfortable around me and Allie that I never questioned whether or not he would be comfortable around Melinda. I can't fault him. This time yesterday, I would have been covering myself up as well.

Melinda pushes the bathroom door open and freezes at the sight of us together in the tub. She points at me and opens her mouth to speak, but the words seem lost in her mind. Finally, she says, "You...?"

"We...?" I try to fill in for her, "are taking a bath."

She walks closer and kneels beside the tub. Her face is red and splotchy from crying. There is a welt beside her left eye.

She asks, "Does this mean you aren't gay?"

Tracy and I both laugh, thinking about how much effort we have invested in trying to be what the other one wants. "Relax," I say, taking her hand in mine and dripping water on the floor in the process. "I'm still in love with a girl and Tracy is desperate for a boyfriend. So, you're in good company. Now, tell me what the hell happened to your face."

Melinda touches her welt, "I told my parents I was gay."

Anger rises in me, "And they beat you? Because beating you is more righteous than allowing you to date girls?"

"You should see the rest of me where I fell down the stairs after Mom slapped me. But, it's okay," she says with determination in her eyes. "I don't need their permission. I put most of my stuff in my car and left. Can I stay here with you until school is out? I'm going to try to get a job, but in the meantime, I will pay you by doing all the laundry and dishes." She blinks back tears. "If you don't let me stay, I have nowhere to go. Even Pap-pap won't let me stay with him."

"Fuck them," Tracy says, reaching out and taking her other hand. "I spent years trying to be straight so my Dad wouldn't treat me like a disappointment. It doesn't work, Mel. I've never been happier than I am here where I don't have to hide who I am. I've also never been more poor or hungry, but I'm happier. You did the right thing."

She looks at me and then at him, obviously confused by how gay we sound but how straight we look together in the bathtub. She shakes her head, "I'm going to get my stuff out of the car. I guess I'll put it in Jute's room since you two are... something... together."

Tracy grins at her, "You can sleep with us if you want. Just keep your boobs away from me." He winks at her.

"You two are out of your minds." She gets up and walks out of the bathroom.

"We should help her," I say, standing up and grabbing a towel from the rack. I dry off quickly and realize I still have no clean clothes. I walk out of the bathroom with the towel wrapped around me. I hear Tracy open the plug allowing the water to drain. The clock on the wall says it is 7:00.

Melinda walks in with a pink suitcase covered with images of teddy bears. She stops when she sees me standing in the living room with only a towel around me.

"Uhm, do you want to borrow some clothes?" She points to her suitcase.

I cringe at the thought of what is in there, but I nod anyway. I follow her to her room, thankful that I don't need to call it mine anymore. She digs through her suitcase to find regular blue jeans and a light blue t-shirt. Then she tosses a pair of panties on the bed. They are baby blue with pink and yellow clouds. I think about Allie's itchy purple lace panties and wish I had them back.

"I have a plan," Melinda says, her eyes sparkling. She takes the blue t-shirt and helps me put it on just to rush things alone. Then she takes the panties and kneels down for me to step in.

"I can dress myself you know."

She stands back up and tosses the underwear into my outstretched hand. She is smirking at me.

I clear my throat and try not to feel awkward, "So, what is this plan?"

"We are going to drive to Ohio tomorrow and you are going to get Allie back." Her smile is wide. I stare at the curve of her top lip as it narrows to nothing near the corners of her mouth. In the center, her lips stay plump and soft. Seeing her happy is infectious. I smile, too. But, my heart is pounding with uncertainty.

"And you say Tracy and I are out of our minds? I think you fit in here better than you want to admit."

240

"I'm being serious, Jute. Despite whatever you have going on with Tracy, I know Allie is your true love. You only get one of those. And, because I was eavesdropping, I also know why she feels so in need of redemption. She was willing to lose everything for you. Aren't you willing to do that to save her from screwing up her life?"

"It always backfires, Mel. You have no idea..."

"I know all I need to know. You and Allie should be together. We're going. Period."

I sigh and shake my head at her. "Fine, we'll go. But, it's Easter Sunday tomorrow. Whatever plan you have, it's going to have to happen around a lot of other people."

"You are right. We shouldn't wait. We should go now. We'll get there while it's still nighttime. No one will see you pecking on her window. You can do your magic without anyone else knowing."

"My magic?" I raise and eyebrow at her.

"You know..." She leans forward and kisses me hard, this time moving her hands under my shirt against the skin of my back. My knees feel weak and I fight not to give into it. She pulls back from me and seems amused at the expression on my face.

She calls out over my shoulder, "Tracy, pack an overnight bag! We're leaving right now for Ohio!"

CHAPTER THIRTY-SEVEN

Allie's mother's house sits behind the grocery store in the middle of town. It is a small white farm house with a chain link fence around it. We pulled into the grocery store parking lot at a little after one o'clock. We have been sitting here staring at the house for ten minutes. Tracy is asleep in the back seat of Melinda's Oldsmobile. I am trying to guess which room belongs to Allie. All the lights are off and I can't even discern where the kitchen would be.

Melinda leans over her steering wheel and whispers, "Maybe it's the room at the top, see that window where an attic should be?"

I don't know why she is whispering, but I do it, too. "It might just be an attic. Why would you choose the hardest window to get to?" I glance sideways at her, annoyed.

"I am not choosing it. If she is up there, then she chose it. You can bitch at her for it later." She shoves my arm and giggles.

"Stop it." I sigh, exasperated. "We shouldn't have come."

"Are you seriously giving up after coming all this way?"

"I gave up before we even got in the car."

"Oh, no. You are not doing this."

Melinda opens her car door and gets out. She is walking toward the house. I panic, open my door, and call out to her in a loud whisper, "Stop! You are going to get us arrested!"

She doesn't turn around, just waves her hand behind her like she's trying to shew me away. She has unlatched the gate and is walking into the yard when I catch up with her. We step into the yard and stop, looking up at the attic window like we are two angel statues in a cemetery looking up to heaven. There is no way to get up there.

Melinda walks over to the walkway and picks up a small gravel. I watch her throw it toward the window, my heart pounding. It hits the window with a tink. Melinda has impressive aim. We wait, but nothing happens. She chooses another rock and throws again. It makes a louder noise against the glass, then falls onto the roof. It reminds me of squirrels. Even if Allie heard it, I'm not sure she would come to the window to see what it was. Still, I keep my eyes glued to the window, hoping I am wrong.

Finally, I turn toward Melinda, prepared to say it's time to go. Instead, I see her standing on the porch with the handle to the screen door in her hand. She is pulling it open and I hear the spring squeak and pop as it stretches.

"Melinda, no!" I cringe at the sound of my loud voice.

The porch light flickers on and my heart stops. We are going to get shot, I know it. But, I feel paralyzed as I watch Melinda stand there and wait for someone to come to the door. Finally, the door unlocks and a short woman in curlers wearing a fuzzy blue bathrobe emerges from behind it. She looks at Melinda and then at me.

"Jute Martin?" She sounds confused. Then a realization hits her and she says, "Oh, my Lord! Have you come for salvation? Praise Jesus! My Allie said she was going to talk to you and set you straight. God is doing amazing work through her."

Allie's mom is crying.

"Ms. Vining, is Allie home?" My voice is shaking like I have seen a ghost, but I can't do anything about it.

"No, honey," she says as if I should have known she wasn't. "She is at the church preparing for sunrise service.

243

Tomorrow is Easter. Don't you know about Easter?" Her eyes squint at me and she shakes her head.

"Actually," Melinda says, "today is Easter. It's after one in the morning. Don't you know about clocks?" She rolls her eyes at Mrs. Vining. I would slap Melinda, but she is too far away.

"Well," Ms. Vining raises her head high and speaks defensively, "I do know about clocks. I know it's time for sleeping, not knocking on other people's doors. Now, if you will excuse me, I need to get a few more hours in. If you want to find Allie, you'll have to go to church. You might actually learn something while you're there."

Ms. Vining is shutting the door behind her when Melinda grabs it to hold it open a minute longer.

"Which church?"

"Go down toward the river and follow it west. You can't miss it. I'll pray you find it and that it does you some good." She pulls the door loose from Melinda's grip and slams it shut. I hear it lock and glance at Melinda's face. She is smiling and hopping on her toes with excitement. She runs toward me with her hand up for a high five. I don't move. I'm still stunned by this whole endeavor. She puts her hand down and wraps her arms around me instead, hugging me tightly and rocking me back and forth.

"Let's go get your girl!"

"How?" I push her off of me and hold her arms in my grip to make her focus on me. "She is probably with Jim. This is not good, Mel. Not good at all!"

"I'll take care of Jim. You just focus on getting alone with Allie."

"Seriously? If this plan fails and Allie ends up hating me, I will never forgive you. Ever."

The drive takes less than fifteen minutes. It isn't enough time. I don't know if fifteen hours would be enough time. Melinda is convinced that all I need to do is give Allie a true love's kiss and she will immediately give up everything she has

244

built here. I know Allie better. I can't hope for so much. I only want her not to hate me or herself for what we had together, even if we can never be more than friends again.

There is only one car in the church parking lot. It is Allie's blue Camaro. Seeing it makes my heart skip a beat. Melinda parks beside it and turns off the engine. She leans over and slaps the seat of Tracy's pants, "Wake up, we're here!"

He jumps up and looks around trying to figure out where 'here' is. I laugh at him, "Were you dreaming about your own comfy bed in Tennessee?"

He rubs his eyes, "I don't have my own comfy bed. It's always invaded by lesbian women."

"Don't be an ass." I am teasing, but there is a hint of warning in my voice. "We're at the church. Allie is inside, probably with Jim. She's helping get the church ready for sunrise services."

"Okay..." he says, not sure why any of this is significant.

Melinda speaks up, "Here's the plan. We are going to go in and say that we are here because I want to repent. I'm going to try to get Jim to take me off into another room to counsel me. While he is there, you tell Allie to come outside with you for a minute. Once she is outside, you give her a refresher on why you love her so much. Sound good?"

"But, what do I do?" Tracy asks.

"You just sit up here in the driver's seat in case there's trouble. Awake." Melinda glares at him.

I don't like hearing her mention the possibility of trouble, but everything else she says sounds like a decent plan. I take a deep breath and exhale.

"Okay. Let's go." I say.

We walk up the front steps and try the doors. They are locked.

"Maybe we should try the side door." I suggest.

We walk around behind the church. Most of the lights are off, which is strange. How can she decorate in the dark? I don't have a good feeling about this. Maybe Allie isn't even here. Maybe she parked her car here and went somewhere else with Jim.

We have walked nearly all the way around the church before we spy a light coming from an underground window well. We stop in our tracks and look at each other before we make our way to it. She is holding my hand as we slowly get on our knees to look inside.

The room is an office. I see Allie inside, lying naked on top of a desk. I drop to my knees to get see the entire room. Melinda kneels beside me. She takes my hand in hers and squeezes it. This is not what we planned to find.

A short man in a gray suit is pacing around the desk with a book held open in his left hand. I assume it is a Bible. He is reading from it with a lot of hand motions. His face is full of passion, flushed red and sweating. I can hear his voice, but I can't make out his words. He wipes his receding hairline with his handkerchief.

Allie lies still, a white piece of folded cloth laid over her face so she can not see him. It is the only thing covering her. The scars on her breasts are exposed and I feel guilty for having Melinda here to see them. I remember tracing the lines with my fingers and tongue. I want to reach out to her and make her understand that she is already perfect. But, before I can move toward the door, Jim does something that makes me freeze.

He closes his Bible and sets it on the desk beside Allie's head. She can not know it, but I can make out his erection through his pants. I watch him look at her body and touch her hair, soothing her. I don't know what he is saying, but I see her nod her head.

He unfolds the cloth over her eyes so that it can be laid over her scars. She still can not see him as he walks around the table, his fingers tracing along her skin as he moves. He speaks to her and she nods again.

Jim begins to undress and my heart is shattering. I

flashback to seeing her with Bobby in the woods. I did nothing to stop him. I can't let this happen again. But, I am terrified.

"We have to stop this," Melinda says to me. She is crying.

I point at the door and she nods. We quietly stand up and walk over to turn the door knob. We open it with barely a sound. Standing in the hall, I hear what Jim is saying. He is repeating, "See now that I, *even* I, *am* he, and *there is* no god with me: I kill, and I make alive; I wound, and I heal: neither *is there any* that can deliver out of my hand."

His voice is increasingly raspy, nearly out of breath, but he utters this verse over and over as if casting a spell. I hear Allie cry out and I can not stop myself. I push open the door to the office and see Jim on top of her. He nearly falls off the desk when he sees us. But, Allie doesn't move except for her lungs pulling in air.

I walk up to her and pull the cloth from her eyes. She opens them, startled by the brightness. But, when she sees me, she covers her mouth in shock. She shakes her head at me as if all she needs to do is deny that I am here and I will vanish into the night.

"No. No. No. Jute, no!" She gets off the desk and grabs a choir robe to wrap around herself. I don't see her clothes. Did he make her wear that? I am angry at her for allowing this to happen. My heart is breaking apart and all she can say to me is 'no'.

I grab her arm and hold her to look at me, "Is this love?" I point at Jim, crouching behind the desk while he tries to dress himself. "You are breaking my heart for this lying fraud? A liar to you and a liar to his entire congregation, this entire town? This is worth destroying what we have?"

"We have nothing!" She spits the words out like a feral animal and jerks her arm away from me. "You have ruined my chance for healing! Tonight is the only night it would work! It's a full moon on Easter Sunday! And you have tainted this sacred place with your evil! Do not touch me. The Bible says,

247

'Be ye not unequally yoked together with unbelievers: for what fellowship hath righteousness with unrighteousness? and what communion hath light with darkness?' Please take your darkness away from me. If you love me like you claim to love me, stay away from me!"

Jim stands up, fully dressed. He is ridiculously holding a crucifix at arm's length in my direction. He is speaking in tongues and holding his empty hand up toward the ceiling. Rage boils over inside me. I walk up to him and punch him square in the nose. I watch him stumble as blood spurts over his lip. The sight of his blood pouring over his clothes causes me to loose sight of him. One minute he is there, stooped over and holding his nose. The next minute he is the corpse from my nightmares.

My peripheral vision blacks out, leaving nothing in my sight except Jim's face as he rises up to look at me. His eyes are nearly black, or maybe these are not his real eyes.

"You are a Jezebel!" he screams at me, raising both hands into the air. Blood is still running from his nose. He spits it to clear it from his mouth before screaming, "You will leave my wife to be healed by her husband!"

"Wife?" Melinda shouts from somewhere outside of my vision.

Jim looks away from me, but I keep my eyes fixed on him. "We have planned our wedding for June. She will be an honest and good woman, unlike you filthy, vile animals."

"Is that true?"

Melinda's voice is followed by Allie's, "Yes." The word is so quiet. But, when she says it, Jim looks at me with his lips curled upward in a sneer. Everything goes black.

I am on top of him, straddling him on the floor, punching his face. Right. Left. Right. Left. Right. Left. Right.

Blackness.

Hands are pulling my arms. I can not swing. The corpse is under me, sticky blood on my hands. Screams.

Blackness.

Hands on my arms.

Allie's face in front of me. Her hair disheveled. Her eyes full of fear. I have to tell her not to be afraid. I open my mouth just before her fist lands against my jaw. My teeth slice into my lip as my head whips back.

The blackness pulls me into silence. I feel hands on me. I am being carried. Someone is running with me. The backseat. Then nothing.

CHAPTER THIRTY-EIGHT

I pull the blankets close to me. I am so cold. It is the third Sunday in May and I have been sleeping alone for two weeks. But, I have never missed Tracy as much as I do now. I want his warm body next to mine. I shiver and pull the extra pillow against my back, hoping it will help. A sick feeling churns inside my stomach and my throat feels tight. Great, this cold seems to never end. I hope it passes before the finals next week.

I roll over and look at the clock. 7:15. Melinda has probably already left for work at the pharmacy. That means I am in charge of all the laundry today, which I do not feel like doing. I don't even feel like rolling back over. I stay twisted in an awkward position and close my eyes.

Just like every morning, I think about Allie. I have stopped thinking about where she is now. I only think about her the way she was before. I imagine her in front of me, smiling her crooked smile, her narrow fingers reaching out and sliding under my shirt. I imagine these things so often that my daydreams are like familiar memories, as if in some other universe they are real. I can still remember how she tastes and the smell of lilac soap. Thinking about it now, my body feels warm and happy.

For another hour, I stay in bed and dream. But, I need to get up and make coffee and start packing to move. Tracy is already in Nashville, living in a little house we leased in the northern part of town. I will move after graduation next

Saturday. Melinda hasn't decided if she will stay for a while and keep working at the pharmacy, or if she will move with us. At first she was excited to get out of Maryville. But last week she met a girl from Knoxville and has obsessed about her since. It's strange how quickly people change their minds.

I sigh, then groan and dramatically toss the pillow against the wall. I feel so sick. I need coffee. I need medication. I need to vomit.

Somehow I manage to get dressed and eat a piece of toast, but I can't keep it down. I feel guilty for not washing Mel's clothes while she is working to pay rent. But, I just can't do it. I go back to bed with a trashcan nearby. I try to sleep, but all I do is toss and turn with dreams about Allie.

The nausea subsides a little by late morning. I decide to try to get up again, sitting up in the bed and turning so that my feet are on the floor. I hear the front door open and keys jingling before they hit the kitchen counter. Melinda must be home. I don't want to open my mouth to speak because I might vomit again. I hear her walk into the room behind me, but I don't turn to look at her.

"Still sick?" She asks, walking around to sit beside me. Her hand makes circles on my back. My throat gets tight. I barely have time to lean over to the trashcan before I vomit again. "I'll take that as a 'yes'."

She hands me a tissue and pushes me to lie down. She pulls the blankets up over me and crawls into bed behind me. She holds me the way Tracy does. Her body doesn't fit as well, but she is warm and it feels nice.

"Why are you home?" I ask. "I thought you were scheduled to work until four."

"I am. But, I started my period."

I laugh, but stop myself because I don't want to vomit again. "You can't work because you are on your period?"

Melinda slaps my arm. "That would be stupid, Jute. Of course I can work while I'm on my period. It's just that it reminded me of something."

251

She pauses like I'm suppose to know what it is, but I don't know. I just lie there and wait until she decides to elaborate.

"You know, I've lived here for five weeks. This is the second time I have had a period while I've lived here."

She waits and I get annoyed. "This conversation is getting weird. You do realize that, right?"

"It's only weird because you are an idiot, Jute. I'm only mentioning my periods so you will think about yours. As in, you haven't had one. Most women keep track of things like that, why don't you?"

My heart stops. The panic is so intense that I think I'm going to pass out. I sit upright and look at her, my eyes wide in disbelief. Melinda is grinning at me. I don't know if I want to punch her or take shelter in her arms. I shake my head in denial. She nods, raising her eyebrows in confirmation.

"I brought you a pregnancy test from the pharmacy. I will wait for you to take it before I go back. Or, if you'd rather, I can let you have your privacy. It's up to you. The test is in a bag on the kitchen table."

My head is light and dizzy. Melinda's hand reaches out and touches my arm. Her voice is sweet, like she is speaking to a child. "Come on." She slides off the bed and takes my hand to pull me to a stand. "There's no point in worrying about something you haven't confirmed yet. Go take the test before you freak out for no reason."

In the bathroom, she unwraps the package and tells me exactly how to take the test. She leaves it on the bathroom counter before closing the door behind her. I stare at the little plastic thing, knowing she is right. There is no point in reacting until I know.

I reread the instructions twice before I take the test. I stay seated on the toilet and place the used test on the counter beside me. The instructions say to wait three minutes, but I don't need to. Less than a minute has passed when I see the plus sign appear in the results window. I am pregnant.

My mind is blank. I don't know how I feel, or even what I should feel. My hands are shaking as I pull up my pajama pants. Nausea washes over me again but I try hard to fight it. My muscles ache from vomiting so much. I take steady breaths and it helps.

I hear Melinda's delicate knock at the door.

"Are you okay?" She calls through the door.

"Yeah." My throat is so tight that my voice cracks.

"Can I come in?" She asks, her excitement contrasting harshly with how I feel.

"Yeah." I sit down on the bathroom floor with my back against the side of the cold tub.

Melinda walks in and looks at the test before she looks at me. I watch her like she is a character in a movie, because nothing about this moment feels real. She is jumping up and down and squealing like a little girl. She puts her hands on my cheeks. She is so pretty when she is happy. I try to give her a weak smile, but it feels empty.

"This is incredible, Jute! I can't believe it!" She takes her hands from my cheeks and puts them on my stomach, which is as flat as it has ever been. "You are going to have Tracy's baby and you only had sex that one day. It must be fate, Jute. I am so happy for you."

"What the hell are you saying?" I am screaming at her, but it feels like someone on tv, someone else's voice. "How are you happy about this? I can't be a mother. Only horrible things happen to me, this isn't a fairytale. There is no happily ever after for me to give!" I am sobbing and screaming and just want to disappear, "I am a freak! My heart is full of hate and resentment! I can't love this thing! Everything I love gets broken!"

I push her away from me. I run toward the back bedroom and out the back door. I make it to the yard before I fall on my knees and vomit again in the grass. There are so many tears in my eyes that I can't see anything. My mind is racing to find a way for me to die. A cliff to jump from or a bridge? Where can I get a gun? I know I am not sane, but sanity does not seem attainable. I can not see anything good in front of me. It has been hard enough living with my own pain. I can never allow it to ruin the life of someone else.

Melinda is beside me. She pulls my shoulder up so that I will look at her, but I pull away. "Come on, Jute. I'm running you a warm bath. It will make you feel better. Just give yourself some time."

"I don't want to take a bath," but I stand up because I don't want to keep staring at my vomit in the grass. She takes my hand and I walk with her back into the house. I try to take deep breaths to calm myself. I am so tired of hurting.

Melinda undresses me and I get in the water. It's a bit too hot but I welcome the burn. I lean back and watch her remove her shirt and fold it on the counter. She kneels down to bathe me. Everyone keeps doing this, as if I am a child.

"Why do people think I need to be washed all the time?" I say. But, she continues lathering up a washcloth. It is dripping with tiny soap bubbles when she finally places it on my shoulder and swipes it across my collar bone. The lather is like a layer of sponge, soft against my skin. She squeezes the washcloth and causes a stream of bubbles to fall from it, landing over my heart and covering my chest. I look down at my legs and see the scars left there. I feel ashamed that I have pretended to be beautiful when I am not. I am damaged and can only hurt and disappoint anyone stupid enough to love me.

Melinda's voice comes steady, "I know I don't have to do this, we all know it isn't necessary. We just like it when your defenses are down and we get to see the real you. It doesn't happen often."

She gives me a reassuring smile and drops the washcloth into the water. Suds lift out over the surface and make a faint sound like television static as they pop. Melinda's hand slides between my legs. I catch my breath and have a fleeting thought to stop her. But, her fingers already swirl with precision. I give in. She leans to whisper in my ear, "You didn't have to share your home with outcasts, you don't have to see beauty where others are repulsed, you don't have to stand up for what is right. But, you have done all of those things for us. You don't have to open yourself to love, especially when you know it will hurt." She pauses to watch her hand move under the water. Her voice is low and soft, "We are not the children our parents said we are. You never were that child. He was a liar. You are beautiful and he hated you because your heart never wavered."

She pulls her hand out of the water too soon. My eyes dart up to hers in protest and confusion. Why did she stop?

"You don't need to hear this from me, Jute. You already know it. Everything you need to love yourself is within you already." She takes my hand and slides it along my stomach and into the void she had left against my skin. My fingers pick up the rhythm she had set before. "You know you are beautiful and powerful and dangerous when you need to be. Stop hiding from it and own it."

When her hand moves up and brushes my nipple, I explode and time explodes with me. Waves of energy crash through my body. Behind my closed eyes, I see the universe. Nothing but darkness and pinpricks of light in all directions, I am swallowed up inside of it. I feel the stars move, opening space for something new in the distance heading toward me. I feel its warmth already.

CHAPTER THIRTY-NINE

Five days haven't been long enough. Tonight, Tracy will come in. Tomorrow afternoon, I will graduate. Tomorrow night, I will leave this house forever. These are things I know. What I don't know is what to do about my pregnancy, how to tell Tracy, *if* I should tell Tracy. Forget *if*. I must.

I set my spoon down in my half-eaten bowl of macaroni and cheese. I sigh and lift another spoonful to my mouth. The taste of it is repulsive, but I force myself to take another bite and fight to keep it down.

"You are not making this easy for me," I say, touching my pelvic area. I feel overwhelmed with ignorance. How will I ever be a mom to this thing?

I think about how my mother treated me and my sister. My throat tightens. I have to place my palms flat on the table and put all my effort into not vomiting. No, I can not think about her. There is no way I will ever be like her. For my own well being, I need to think of something else.

Hank. I think about him, how he loves Allie the way a parent should. I remember, when I first met Allie, thinking I would like to marry a man like Hank. I thought he was a saint, but now I know he has his faults. They just pale in comparison to the faults of my own family. I still respect him, but I certainly don't want to marry someone like him. Do I need to?

I created a system when I was still a kid, a way to keep mean people away from me. I may not be able to give a child a perfect life, but I feel confident that I would never let anyone hurt it the way Drew was hurt. Or the way Allie was hurt. I won't be like Hank and turn a blind eye.

These thoughts feel foreign, yet natural. I have always been a mother to myself, even if I have not looked the part. This is nothing new, yet it comes from a frightening place I have tried to never go: love.

I finish the entire bowl of macaroni and cheese, exhausted from thinking and feeling. I walk to the living room and plop down on the couch, kick off my shoes, and curl up for a nap. I stare at the wood stove in front of me, cold from lack of use. The days have been so warm. Even now, a gentle breeze blows in through the screen door but it isn't enough to cool me. I hear the occasional whistle of air as it pushes harder through the cracks of the door frame, but no birds chirping outside. It wouldn't be hard to imagine that I am the only person left alive on Earth, a thought which used to comfort me. But, now it tugs at me with fear. It is one thing to be alone and away from the pain. It is another to be alone and away from joy. Whatever I was once running from is gone, leaving me a whole new mountain of trouble to climb.

Falling in and out of sleep, I dream many different things. I dream I am lying on my back in a field of corn, the sound of a combine harvesting in the distance. I dream I am standing naked in a dressing room with no idea how I got in there or where my clothes have gone. I dream I am looking in hollow trees for honey like a bear, but in every hole I find a different dead animal covered in maggots. It is during this last dream, as I turn away from a rotting mallard duck and see my emaciated bear cub crying behind me, that the screen door slams and I sit up with a jolt.

Tracy leaps on top of me and knocks me back down. He is hugging me and laughing. He is heavy. I try to push him off of me. "Get off! You scared the crap out of me!"

He rolls off into the floor beside me. "Sorry. I'm just excited. I have news!"

I finally get a good look at him. His face is covered with

stubble, neatly trimmed and precise. I reach out and touch it, finding it surprisingly soft. "Damn, if that doesn't get you a boyfriend, there's no hope for you."

I hear a cough and turn to see a towering Black man standing in the doorway. He nods at me and raises an eyebrow at Tracy. I look back to Tracy and see he is a bit flustered. "Oh, uhm, Jute, this is Dawson. He's going to help us move."

"Is that it?" Dawson's voice is so deep it rattles my insides like a purr. "I think there might be a little more to it."

I stand up, determined to hide my nausea. Dawson steps forward with his hand stretched out. I forget to move, staring at the curves of his muscular arms all the way up until they disappear in the sleeve of his blue t-shirt. His shoulders are twice as broad as Tracy's, magnified by the contrast of his narrow waist. I hear Tracy clear his throat and I realize I haven't taken Dawson's hand yet. I reach out and put my hand in his, surprised to find his handshake is warm and gentle.

"My name is actually Ulysses, but don't call me that." His smile is wide and sincere, revealing perfect white teeth to complete his heart throb appearance. He lets go of my hand and I am embarrassed by how much I am sweating.

"Damn," escapes my lips before I can stop it. I look at Tracy and see he is blushing. "How much more to it is there, Tracy?"

"Almost more than I can handle," he says, looking uncomfortably around the room. Dawson laughs loudly and it is so smooth and rich that I could almost eat it. I just want to sit back on the couch, listen to him talk, and forget about everything else. But, I can't.

"Well, it's nice to meet you Dawson. Thanks for helping us out here, and I apologize in advance for staring at your muscles... both now and in the future. Feel free to pick up large objects with your shirt off any time the urge hits you."

He laughs again, making me want to tease him more. "I have heard a lot about you, Jute. But, I didn't expect you to be this funny. Tracy tells me you have a powerful right fist."

When the smile drops from my face, he says, "Relax. Tracy has told me what is going on with you and I'm not judging you. If you knew what I have been through, you wouldn't doubt I'm telling the truth. But, I got through it. I have a great job with the Nashville Police Department, my own place to live, and now I have an amazing relationship." He looks at Tracy and winks before looking back at me. "Hang in there, girl."

He reaches out and wraps his strong arms around me and squeezes me a little too tightly before letting me go. "You are a tiny thing." He laughs, "I can't even imagine you breaking that guy's fingers, but I don't plan to test you."

"I had a little help from Jesus," I say, referring to the crucifix that was still in Jim's hand when I stomped on it. I don't remember doing it, but that is what Melinda and Tracy both said happened.

Dawson tips his head to the side and looks at me curiously. He nods and says, "Jesus knows the good guys outside the city gates and the bad guys in the church. I just wish your lady could see it, too."

The image of Allie punching me rushes into my mind before I can stop it. My throat tightens and I know it's coming. I don't excuse myself because if I open my mouth I might vomit on Dawson's shoes. I just turn and run to the bathroom, not taking the time to close the door. It sounds awful and I am so embarrassed, but I can't stop myself.

Tracy runs into the bathroom, shuts the door, and drops to his knees nearby. He puts his hand on my back as I try to regain my composure. His voice is full of concern. "Are you sick?"

"No." I manage to say. I keep my voice low. I don't know how to tell him. I reach for the towel he has pulled from the rack and wipe my face. I look at him, focus on the blue of his eyes. I'm tired of worrying about how to do this the right way. I just say it. "I am pregnant."

He blinks a few times, but doesn't move otherwise. He just stares at me for what feels like eternity. I give up waiting for a response and stand up. I flush the toilet and move around him to wash my hands.

By the time I am reaching under the sink for a fresh towel, Tracy is standing up beside me. I don't really want to look at him again, but I do. He has tears running down his cheeks and into his new stubbly beard. I don't know if he is happy or sad. He puts his hand over his mouth for a moment and then wraps his arms around me. I hug him, feeling that I am helping him stay upright. He is crying with his cheek pressed to the side of my head.

Finally, he composes himself and leans away from me to ask, "How do you feel about this?"

"I've only known since Sunday, so I haven't had a lot of time to process it. But, I've come to terms with the idea. I mean, I think I could be a good mom."

A smile stretches across his face and he hugs me again. His mouth is close to my ear when he says softly, "I used to be so afraid of accepting that I was gay because I thought it would mean I would never have a family. I know I sound crazy, but I am so happy."

My body relaxes into him now. We stand there holding each other, tears streaming down our faces. Finally, the crying starts to feel ridiculous. We begin laughing.

"I thought you would be upset."

"No! I mean, I certainly wouldn't have asked you to have my child. But, I can't think of any other woman I love more." He gives me a quick wink and kisses my forehead. "I won't let you down."

"What about Dawson?"

Tracy shakes his head, "Don't worry about it. He knows everything else, things that would embarrass you to know he knows. I've told him all about us and my life before I met you. But, he hasn't flinched so far. Besides, he has a three year old daughter named Iris. He'll understand. And if he doesn't, then I'll know I was wrong about him."

"Do you think we should wait to tell him? I mean, I

should probably see a doctor and make sure everything is fine."

"It makes sense if you want to keep it a secret for a while, but I can't keep this from Dawson. He'll see right through me."

Tracy opens the door and yanks me by the hand. We find Dawson standing in the front yard by his truck. When he hears us, he spins around with a nervous look on his face.

"Do we need to take you to Urgent Care?"

I am too nervous to laugh, even though I think it's funny. Tracy lets go of my hand and runs to Dawson, wrapping his arms around him. Dawson pats his back and looks at me with confusion. I can't look at him. I glance away awkwardly.

Tracy is still embracing Dawson when I hear him say, "Jute is pregnant! I'm going to be a dad!"

Dawson leans his head back and laughs up to the sky, then picks Tracy up off his feet and whirls him around like he is weightless. He puts Tracy down and walks over to me, his arms open wide. His smile is so joyful that I can't help but smile back at him. He hugs me, more gently this time. Tracy walks behind me and wraps his arms around the both of us. All the layers of protection I have hidden under crumble at our feet. To make room for the joy I hope will come, I let my fears fly away in the wind.

CHAPTER FORTY

Heat lightning dances in the night sky above the distant trees. I've been staring at it for a while, beneath the glare of the floodlights. If I look back to the stage in the center of the football field, my eyes will be full of light and blind to the flashes in the distance. Principal Hamilton is calling the T surnames now, this should be over soon.

Songs buzz in my mind to pass the time. I try to remember all the lyrics to that Toto song about rain in Africa. I imagine myself in Tanzania, so far from here, watching the lightning over the savanna instead of the ash and oak trees. When Mr. Hamilton calls Kimberly Vale, I look up out of habit. Allie's name is always called after Kimberly's. I know she isn't here, but they will call her name anyway.

"Allie Vining" The principal says, then waits. He has forgotten she graduated in December and opted out of the ceremony.

A hand reaches over and takes mine. I know without looking that it belongs to Casey Matthews, a boy from my AP English class. I think of all the days I've sat beside him, worked on assignments together, and yet I have never told him a single thing about my life. I don't know how he knows that I miss her terribly. He gives my hand a light squeeze and lets go. I look down at my hands in my lap. There was a time when I would have punched Casey without even looking to see who he was. I would still be that person if it wasn't for Allie and all of Tracy's patience.

What if I had never had them in my life? I shudder to think about it, but I think about it anyway. I think of Melinda's mom slapping her face just because she is attracted to girls. I think about Tracy's family rejecting him. I think about the troubled kids I've known through high school, some of their families make mine seem like a basket of purring kittens. Tomorrow, I will be on my way to Nashville. The other misfits will still be here in Maryville. Their fathers will still get drunk and kick them with steel toe boots. Their mothers will still send them to bed without food as punishment. They may get jobs and move on, but some of them believe they have no value. They take pills and cut themselves, wanting to die. Who am I to be free of that fate? I have called them friends, but I have done nothing to help them.

A thought enters my mind, a tiny half-thought, which causes my heart to skip a beat. I think that I am not finished fighting abuse. I don't know exactly how. I don't even know where to begin. But, the thought fills me with energy. I look back to the stage just as Mr. Hamilton finishes a short speech about beginning the next phase of our lives with dignity and hard work.

"Now you may move your tassels to the left. Congratulations, Class of 1990!"

The band begins to play the school anthem and I join my classmates as we all throw our caps into the air. There are happy tears in my eyes which I can not fully explain. I just know that things will be different, that now this life belongs to me alone. If I fail, it will be my own failure. If I succeed, it will be my own success, in whatever way I define that. At this moment, everything is new.

I look over at Casey. He is talking with a couple of friends. He towers above them. He must be over six feet tall. But his little boy face and blond wavy hair make him look too young to be graduating high school. I step closer and take his hand, pulling him around to look at me. I let go before it starts to feel awkward.

"Thanks," I say just loud enough for him to hear. I don't want to take up his time, I just want him to know that I appreciate the gesture. I wave and start to walk off, but he grabs my hand again.

"Hey, it was nothing." He starts to walk and lets go of my hand once we are walking in the same pace. "I just know how close you two were and I figured you were missing her."

I look at him curiously, "That was quite astute of you." The words sound more guarded than I intended.

He grimaces, "Honestly, I've missed her, too. I just noticed you two together all the time because I stared at her a lot, trying to get the nerve to talk to her." His lips form an embarrassed smile. "We had Spanish class together. She used to touch the back of my neck with her pencil eraser and pass me random notes. One of them said, 'If werewolves had umbrellas, they could block the moonlight well, they might be decent fellas, without hair and fangs and tail.'" He looks at me as if I can explain it.

"You should have talked to her. You would have been better for her than Shawn, that asshole."

Casey laughs, "I wasn't worried about Shawn. I was worried about you." He pauses, but I don't know how to respond. He continues, "Right before Christmas break, she gave me a note with her telephone number. It said, "Make a circular motion." I could never figure out if she meant dialing the phone or..." His voice trails off and he blushes.

I feel my throat get tight at the thought of touching her. My body tingles in remembrance, but it is too much. The last thing I want to do is vomit. I try to be very still and quiet and hope it passes.

"Are you okay?" Casey is leaning down so his gray eyes are level with mine. I really don't want to look at him. Jealousy is eating at my heart.

"Hey there young lady!" a man's voice is behind me. Arms wrap around me and I smell Hank's sweaty sawdust scent. He lets go and steps around so I can see him. He nods his head to Casey while touching the brim of his cap. Then he looks down at me, "I brought you a graduation gift."

He grins and holds out an envelope. My heart leaps in anticipation. Could this be a letter from Allie? I rip it open and find a check inside. The amount is more than any of my family makes in a year. Maybe some people wouldn't think it was a lot, but it is mind blowing to me. I look up, confused.

"It's your part of the money for the land. Drew signed all the paperwork yesterday. The land is mine and the money was split between you and your sister. I went by your house earlier and dropped off a box of Allie's things she asked me to give you. But, I thought I'd come out here tonight and personally make sure you get this check."

Hank lifts off his hat and wipes his hand across his brow before replacing it. He looks at me with a sadness I haven't seen in him before. "She's been giving away a lot of her things. I worry about that girl. Maybe it's just her hormones and it will pass after she has the baby."

He drops his head and scratches the back of this neck. He doesn't see my mouth fall open, or Casey's hand reach out for mine. I feel the squeeze of Casey's fingers and I squeeze back, afraid I will crumple into a heap on the ground if I let go. I close my mouth just as Hank looks back up at me.

"Well, I guess I'll get on outta here. Good luck to you, youngin. And you come see me. Don't be a stranger."

As he walks away, I cover my mouth. I do not think I can fight it back this time. I let go of Casey's hand and run to the edge of the parking lot behind Joe Greene's neon pink Firebird. I drop onto the ground like a dog and puke. Damn it. Tears pour out of my eyes and I hope for rain. Right now. But it doesn't come.

I know now that I have lost her forever. I can't even say for sure if she was ever mine. I think about what Casey said and all the ways she had flirted with boys, obsessed with their approval and attention. She knows what to say and do to make them want her, and maybe I was just like those boys in her

265

eyes. Everyone else thinks of me as a boy, why not Allie, too?

"I guess you aren't okay." It's Casey. He's standing at a respectable distance.

"Yeah, I'm okay." I pull myself up off the ground. "I just need to go home. I have a long drive tomorrow."

"Nashville? I heard you were going. Maybe I'll see you there some time. I start at Vanderbilt in the fall."

"Yeah, look me up," I try to sound nonchalant. Thinking about Casey in Nashville makes me less jealous of him. If Allie was in love with Casey, at least she would be near me every time she visited him. Instead, she is pregnant and planning to marry a monster. I keep my mouth closed tight so I don't get sick again. He gives me a nod and a smile, then turns to walk away. After only a few steps, he glances back as if he just remembered something he wanted to say. But he just waves at me. I watch his back until it disappears into the crowd.

I glance around, trying to find some sign of Tracy. He is supposed to be here to pick me up. There are kids already piling into cars, headlights line up as cars drive out of the parking lot. I walk back to the gates, hoping he will be waiting there. But, when I get close, I see no one. I go there anyway because it's the first place he will look when he arrives.

Almost all of the cars leave. Sadness exhausts me. It has been a long time since I allowed myself to feel this alone. I know every family is not as perfect as they seem, but right now they all seem better than what I have. Momma didn't show up. Even Melinda's parents came to her graduation. They are trying to make amends, agreeing to pay for her tuition, but insisting that she doesn't 'flaunt her lifestlye'. I don't know how long it will last. Melinda is staying in Maryville to be close to her girlfriend, after all. Her lifestyle is going to be flaunted. But, her parents are trying. Compared to my mom, they are the best parents in the world.

The last time I saw Momma was three weeks ago. I happened to be in the laundromat and saw her going into the convenience store next door. She was with a black haired man in a white Toyota pickup. I had stepped outside and waved at her, but she looked like she had no idea who I was. Thinking about it now makes me angry, so I try to think about something else.

As if on cue, Tracy pulls up in the Chevette. I open the door and he starts explaining before I can even get in the seat.

"I am so sorry I'm late. Dawson and I were so close to having everything packed and loaded, we didn't want to quit. We hoped we could go ahead and leave tonight."

The idea of leaving and never spending another night in Maryville feels liberating. But my hands fidget with the envelope from Hank and I have to ask, "Was there a box on the porch?"

"Yes," Tracy gives me a quick look of surprise, "Dawson and I ran out to get some tacos and came back to see it sitting there. It's full of notebooks, it looked like Allie's stuff. How did you know?"

"Hank. He came by and gave me money for my step-dad's land."

"Well, at least that's one more good thing about that bastard being dead."

I slap his arm but my feelings are mixed, "You make us sound awful!"

"Really?" Tracy's mouth tightens. "Well, it's the truth."

When we pull into the driveway, I see that Dawson's truck is gone. He must have already hit the road to Nashville. Tracy puts the car in park and turns off the engine.

"Do you want me to put the box in the car, or do you want to take a minute to look through it?"

I don't want him staring at me while I go through her things. I need to do it in private.

"Just put it in the backseat and I'll go through it when we get to the new place. I want to get out of here and the sooner the better."

Jute,

I hope you know that I don't hate you. You think you love me and love makes us do crazy things. I forgive you.

I guess Dad has told you that I am pregnant. Jim and I feel in our hearts that this pregnancy is a sign from God that we should be together. Our wedding is only eleven days away.

I have worked so hard to transform my life into a life for God. I am doing all I can for Jim and our future family. Jim has been a blessing. I don't know what I would do without him. It is amazing how he always does the right thing. I wish you could see him the way I do.

The hand of God has taken me to this place, and I really want to give all I have to make it work. In order to do that, there are things I have to get rid of. Jim has helped me go through and weed out the things that cause me temptation. I had a bonfire, burning all my old clothing. But, I could not bring myself to burn my notebooks.

Even if I can't burn them, I still can't keep them. Jim found where I had hidden them and he read a few. He was so upset. Maybe I am wrong to do this, but these still mean too much to me not to keep them safe. I hope you will hold on to them, even if I never see them again. I just don't want them destroyed.

These notebooks are filled with my writing, mostly poems. Almost all are about love, sex, and despair. Some of them are about you. I am smiling, thinking of you reading them. But, I am also nervous. Please understand that these pages were filled by the old me. I am a new woman now. I truly want to be a good wife and make Jim a happy husband. It is what I want, Jute. Please respect that and don't contact me. Just the mention of you really upsets Jim. It makes my life very hard.

Good-bye, Jute. Good luck in Nashville. I will always love you.

Love,
Allie

CHAPTER FORTY-ONE

"It isn't hot, Jute! It's the middle of October."

"I may pass out from heat stroke if you close that window. Leave it open! Besides, this room still smells like wet paint."

"You are not going to pass out. I'll be glad when you have this baby and stop being so sensitive."

"I thought you liked my sensitive side."

Tracy smirks at me, then grabs the hammer off the window sill and starts pounding a nail into the blue wall. I chose this shade of blue because it reminds me of Allie's eyes. Tracy agreed it was nice, happy yet soothing. When he finishes hammering in the nail, I hold out the framed John Lennon print for him to hang.

"This was a good find at the thrift store." He says, admiring it, "I think we should decorate the entire room with Beatles memorabilia."

"Only if I find it at the thrift store. We can't exactly afford to go all House Beautiful in this room."

Tracy turns and glares at me. "I was giving you a compliment, Jute. Learn to take it without belittling yourself or me in the process."

He's right. The more my belly grows, the more negative I have become. Everything feels offensive to me. I have twelve weeks until the baby is due and it can't get here fast enough. When I had the ultrasound showing the baby is a boy, I got even more impatient. I am tired of dealing with the fear that overwhelms me from the time I wake up until I go to bed at night. I guess it's hard for Tracy to recognize that I am happy about the baby when all I do is complain about feeling miserable and accusing him of things he isn't doing.

"Is this straight?" He asks, moving the frame slightly to the left.

"A little more to your left. No, wait, go back just a little."

Tracy slides it over as I instructed and lets go. He turns to look at me for my final approval, but his eyes quickly glance over my shoulder. His face lights up. I know Dawson must be behind me. I turn around and see him towering in the doorway.

"This is looking great! We just need some Hendrix hanging up and maybe some Santana cassettes for little Tracy the third." He winks at me because he is messing with Tracy.

Tracy takes the bait. "Shut the hell up! We are not naming the baby Tracy!"

I walk up to him and wrap my arms around him, "He's teasing you, Tracy. Laugh a little."

His voice is steady and a little cold, "You should listen to your own advice."

He pushes by me to walk over to Dawson and stands on his tiptoes to give him a kiss. I see this all the time, but it never stops making me giggle inside. Tracy obviously has a thing for big guys. I don't think he'll ever find one nicer than Dawson.

"How was your day at work?" I hear Tracy ask him as they head out of the nursery. I hear Dawson say something and then Tracy telling him to shut the hell up again. They tease each other all the time. I hear a few creaks on the stairs as they head down to the main floor. The room becomes hauntingly quiet, but this is how I like it.

I'm glad to be alone here.

"What will we name you?" I say, looking into the empty crib. I need to buy sheets for it, but there is still time.

I sit down in the rocking chair, which is refreshingly close to the open window. I keep Allie's notebooks on the bookshelf nearby. When the baby is old enough to reach them, I will move them. But, for now, I like having them close. I come in here and read them often, sometimes aloud. I imagine I will do the same when the baby comes.

I reach down and take a blue notebook from the top, where I had laid it last night. I open it up to the bookmark and see the date: November 7, 1985 9:33 p.m..

"She is a dangling string from my hem. I pull it to break it, but it just gets longer. Trying to fix it makes it worse... worse for my dress, but better for the string. She is free to whip around in the wind, but there is nothing to hold her."

Allie was thirteen when she wrote that.

There are hundreds of little ponderings, metaphors, and poems. Some pages have a single word, which she had studiously timed and dated as if it was equal to all her poems. I miss her. I feel close to her when I read her words, yet I am reminded that I may never see her again.

It isn't healthy to obsess over her like this. Everything I do, I think of her while I do it. The money Hank paid me for the land has been invested in opening a thrift store to benefit the Sexual Assault Center. I think of her every day I go there. Sometimes I pull vintage dresses from the racks and hold them back as if one day she will walk through the door. Sometimes I cry so much I have to have one of the volunteers take over at the cash register. Other times, I am at peace there because it reminds me of the happiest times of my life.

Tracy is right to be annoyed by my constant melancholy. Everything is going perfectly for him. He has put a band together and they have regular weekend gigs. Dawson is a dream come true. They are both excited that we are having a child. I know he feels like he has to hold back a little because I can't seem to catch up with him. I wish it was a choice I could make. I would wake up one morning and decide to be happy again. But, I can't change how I feel.

The baby turns and stretches inside me. My ribs are being tickled from the inside. I put my hand over the movement and let the feeling of joy wash over me. This is one thing that I never have bad thoughts about. I can't wait to have this child. I will make his world what mine should have been. I will make sure he knows that he is loved and he is beautiful, no matter what.

I look through the pages of Allie's notebooks until the streetlights come on outside. The breeze is starting to feel too cool, blowing in stronger bursts through the open window. I stand up and push the window down to close it. I take an orange blanket from the closet and sit in the rocking chair again. I toss the blanket open, watching a wave of tangerine flutter out and settle across my legs. I pull the edge up to my chin and lean back to rock.

My eyes close and I start to daydream my favorite dream. I am unbuttoning Allie's cotton gown and she is apprehensive. I dream of the moment she believes I will not judge her, that I love her. It happened so suddenly, yet it took us years to get there. I play this scene out in my mind again and again. It begins to feel like it has always been in my head and never really happened. Too much time has passed. My mind holds all the images, but my skin struggles to remember her touch.

I hear the door knob turn and open my eyes to see Tracy peering in.

"We ordered Chinese delivery," he says quietly, as if there really is a sleeping baby in the room. He walks over to me and gets on his knees. His hands cup around my protruding belly and he leans his mouth close to my navel, "Do you want sweet and sour pork?" he asks through it.

I laugh and move my fingers through his hair. "Did you have enough Dawson time?"

"Never," Tracy says, kissing my stomach. "But, you know you won't bother us if you come down every now and then and hang out."

"I like it here."

"Well, I guess that's a good thing. We'll both be spending a lot of time in this room soon, like it or not." He flattens his hands on my stomach and waits. I know he is wanting to feel the baby move. I hope it will so I can see the wonder in his eyes.

"I've been thinking about a name," I venture hesitantly. "You know I plan to change my last name to Duren so it will match the baby's. Besides, I want nothing to do with being a Martin anymore. But, I think we need to make a decision about the baby's first name."

I feel the baby move and watch Tracy stare at his hands in amazement. He repositions his hands to feel it better.

"I would love that." He looks up at my eyes, "I do love you, Jute. You are the only family I have."

"I feel the same way," I say, sliding my hand over his. "Do you have any thoughts about a name, other than not wanting him named Tracy?"

"Right, Tracy is out. I want him to have a name he doesn't need to explain."

I laugh, "So, Jute is out as well."

"Yes, that's out. What do you think about John? We could name him after John Lennon because it's the first music we sang together."

"Hmmm. John Duren. I like it quite a lot." I pause, letting the name roll around in my mind. "Do you think we could make his middle name Alvin? It's a combination of Allie's first name and her last name Vining?"

He looks up at the ceiling thoughtfully, "John Alvin Duren. It sounds very rock and roll. I like it."

We both laugh. I say, "Rock and roll, huh? I don't know about that. But, if you are happy with it, I think we should do it."

"I couldn't be happier. Let's go tell Dawson and eat before the wonton soup gets cold."

He stands up and offers me his hand. I take it and let

him pull me up, feeling stiff from sitting in the chair so long.

"I'll be glad when he's here," I say, folding up the blanket and draping it over the rocking chair.

Tracy steps behind me and wraps his arms around me, his hands on my stomach. "Everything is going to be wonderful. Try not to worry so much."

CHAPTER FORTY-TWO

The scream wakes me just in time to realize it came from my mouth. I take a deep breath and look around the darkness. I tell myself none of it was real, but my body shivers.

The door opens and Tracy walks in with Dawson right behind him. They are both wild eyed. Tracy sits beside me on the bed.

"Are you okay?"

I sit up and wrap my arms around him, squeezing him too tightly. Another shiver runs through me.

"The baby was born without any skin." I say, feeling dazed. The dream was so painful that tears come to my eyes. "He was hurting so much. I wanted to comfort him, but my touch just hurt him more. There was nothing I could do to save him."

"It wasn't real," Tracy's voice is steady. His hands on my back pull me closer. "It was just a dream."

His bare chest is becoming wet with tears. "It has been so long since I had a nightmare like that, I thought they were over! I thought everything was better now."

Dawson offers, "Things are better. You are in such a good place, Jute. This isn't about you. It's normal to have bad dreams when you are in your last trimester. The baby's due date is only five days away. It would be unsettling if you weren't worried. Just, try to take some deep breaths."

I feel Dawson sit on the bed behind me. His large hand moves over my lower back, comforting me. His deep voice comes softly, "It's almost 6:00, if you want to get up I'll make us some hot cocoa."

I nod into Tracy's chest and we let go of each other. He stands up and so do I, still shaking. He takes my hand and we walk downstairs together. I see the Christmas tree still in the corner of the living room. We removed the decorations last weekend, but the tree still stands there, drying out.

"That Christmas tree needs to go to the curb. All the needles are going to fall off and then we'll have a big mess to clean up."

Tracy smirks at me, "I see you haven't lost your usual chipper attitude."

His sarcasm is warranted. "Fine, forget I said anything. Leave it there and we'll let the baby play in the pine needles, which will probably still be there by next Christmas if it's up to you."

"You two argue like a couple of old hens," Dawson says, walking away from us and into the kitchen.

Tracy follows, leaving me alone in the living room. I let him go without protest. I stand in front of the tree and imagine how much different next Christmas will be. We are now in a new year, 1991. There is so much to be excited about. But, a feeling of dreariness washes over me. I wonder if Allie has had her baby. I haven't heard from her since the note she left with her notebooks. A dark cloud closes in on my heart. I should be used to it by now. Every happy thought I have precedes inevitable mourning for her. I just wish I knew how she was. Maybe I should call Hank.

I hear someone clinking cups in the cabinet. I walk into the kitchen, squinting in the blinding fluorescent light reflecting off the yellow walls. This color was Tracy's idea. In the mornings, I am seldom prepared for the onslaught of joyful color. I reach the counter where Tracy has set out three mugs. I choose the black one. It will be easier to look at while my eyes adjust.

"Almost ready," Dawson says.

I carry the mug over to the pot on the stove where Dawson performs alchemy on some old fashioned hot chocolate. He pours a final dollop of cream into the chocolaty mix and stirs it with a ladle. The steam rises up from it. I lean forward and take a deep breath. The divine smell of chocolate fills my nose. I exhale, feeling suddenly optimistic. I inhale deeply again, but I stop short when pain shoots through my back. My hand uncontrollably lets go of the mug, sending it crashing into shattered pieces across the floor. I groan with the pain, and reach out for the counter to hold myself up. It is too far away, but Dawson grabs me and steadies me. Tracy is making quick work with the broom so we don't cut our bare feet. Before all the shards are swept up, a second pain pulls my stomach muscles so taut I think they might rip. I bend over with both hands on my stomach. Dawson is holding my arms or I would fall to my knees. I can barely stand. I feel warm, thick wetness in my panties. Panic washes over me.

Dawson's voice emits a calm I do not possess, "It's time. Tracy, get Jute's bag from the nursery. Everybody stay calm, but let's make this quick."

CHAPTER FORTY-THREE

Tracy dashes up the stairs and comes back with my bag, my robe, and a towel. Dawson keeps a hand on my arm and we all walk to Dawson's truck.

"Maybe we should take the Chevette," I say, thinking his truck is too nice for me to ruin.

"Hell no," Dawson says, opening the passenger side door and practically throwing me up onto the seat. "I can't fit in that sardine can. Besides, I have the Emergency Tags."

Tracy climbs in after me and I scoot the towel under me. I see that my water has not broken. The wetness is blood. I don't know what this means, but I am terrified. Dawson climbs in beside me and sees the blood on my gown and the panic on my face. He pulls his door closed, starts the engine, and squeals the tires as he backs out of the driveway and onto the road.

We make it to Nashville General Hospital in five minutes. In that time, I have already had one more contraction with increased intensity. Dawson pulls up to the Emergency doors as the next contraction begins. I try to breathe the way I have practiced, but the pain is crushing. I hold my breath and finally give in to a scream.

Tracy seems frantic and I want to reassure him that I will be fine. But, I can barely breathe enough to speak to him.

When the pain subsides, I slide out of the truck and walk with Tracy quickly through the entrance. A man is standing ready with a wheelchair. I sit and let him wheel me into admissions. We have our paperwork ready, so they move us quickly to a delivery room.

My contractions are now barely separated by reprieve. It seems one barely ends before another begins. Their are two nurses, maybe more, around me. Tracy helps me into the hospital gown while a nurse straps monitors to me.

"My name is Steven and I'm going to be your maternity nurse," he says calmly. I wish I could be so calm. A contraction starts and I groan as I grab the edge of the hospital bed. "I need to check your dilation and report it to Dr. Wallis. He is with another patient, but should be here very soon."

Steven helps me lie back so he can insert his gloved fingers to check my cervix. He pushes against the cervix and I cry out in pain. I am too exhausted from the pain of the contractions to hide it. He pulls his fingers out and removes his gloves. His skin reminds me of caramel, which is more calming than the stark white gloves. His eyes are nearly black and full of gentleness. I focus on them, trying not to anticipate the next pain.

"You are already at 7," he says. "I will call the anesthesiologist and we'll get you some relief," he looks at me and smiles, but I can't smile back. Another pain shoots through me and I nearly black out until it ends.

Another nurse has entered the room and explains that I must have an enema. Now I don't only have pain, but I also get humiliation. I groan a futile protest. Tracy looks at me empathetically and leaves the room. I appreciate that he is trying to give me privacy, but there is really not any to be had. By the time the nurse and I have completed the enema, the anesthesiologist arrives.

"My name is Lena and I'm your anesthesiologist. I want you to sit on the bed with your back to me."

I feel her rubbing alcohol near the bottom of my spine, followed by something wet and rough scratching my skin. "After you finish this next contraction, I will insert the tube. It is very important that you remain completely still. I promise I will be quick."

As my contraction reaches it's peak, my fingers curl tightly around the edge of the bed. Tracy reemerges and puts his hands on my upper arms. I feel a sharp pain of the needle, then pressure on the bones of my spine. Soon I feel the sensation of cool liquid moving into me.

"You can relax now," Lena says as she applies tape to my back. I lean into Tracy and he wraps his arms around me. The next contraction comes and it is no less intense. I moan as I try to suppress a scream. Lena's voice is calm and soothing, "It will take a few minutes, ten or fifteen. You should stop feeling pain from your waist down. If you continue to feel pain, have Steven call me and I will increase your dose."

I lie down on the bed and Steven busily checks my monitors. When I begin feeling numb, he checks my dilation again. A doctor walks in just as he is removing his glove. "She's at eight now, Dr Wallis."

Dr Wallis is a small thin man with gray hair and slight curve to his back. He looks at me and smiles. His hand takes mine and his other hand covers it as he gives it a friendly shake.

"Ms. Martin, I'm here to help you deliver your baby. I have looked over your chart and I think you are going to do just fine. This is your first birth, but you seem to be moving along nicely."

He lets go of my hand and walks over to the wall where he pulls two latex gloves from a box. He slides them on his hands then comes back to my bed.

"I am going to check you for myself because it's good practice, not because Steven is a bad nurse." Dr. Wallis gives Steven a quick smile, then his face transforms with concentration. I can feel slight pressure, but the epidural has kicked in enough that there is no pain.

"You are definitely at eight, maybe eight and a half. We should be able to start pushing within the hour."

A knock comes to the door and it opens to reveal a towering Dawson, smiling widely. Tracy motions with his arm for Dawson to come in the room. Both Steven and Dr. Wallis glance from Dawson to me as if they aren't sure if they should let him in.

"He's a friend of the family," I tell them. "It's okay if he stays."

Dr. Wallis nods and smiles, then turns and leaves the room. Steven stays busy with my monitors and paperwork. No one seems to notice or care what an odd family we are. Tracy gives Dawson an update on everything Dr. Wallis has told us.

Suddenly, I feel strange. Steven looks at my expression and walks over to look under my sheet.

"Your water just broke, it's not the baby yet. But, this is good progress." He walks back to my file and jots notes into it.

I exhale and reach for Tracy's hand.

"Soon," he says, pulling his shoulders up in anticipation. I think it's too bad he can't be the one poked and prodded, ripped and torn to have this baby brought into the world. I look over at Dawson and think how it would be for Dawson to hold Tracy's hand if Tracy gave birth. I giggle a little, but there is sadness inside me. Tracy is holding my hand, but it isn't the same. He loves me, and I never want him not to love me. But, it just isn't the same kind of love as fathers usually have for mothers. I think about my sister and how she had no one at all by her bedside when she went through this. It makes me feel ashamed for thinking Tracy and Dawson aren't enough.

Steven comes back and rechecks my cervix. "Ten and baby!" he says, a bit too excitedly. He steps over to the phone on the wall and pushes some numbers. I hear him say, "Martin is at ten and I feel hair. Do you want me to have her push or wait on you? Okay, will do."

He hangs up the phone and rolls a low round stool to the foot of my bed. He lifts my feet up into stirrups and drops the lower section of the bed. He instructs Tracy to hold one of my legs and tells Dawson he may hold the other if it is okay with me. I nod at Dawson and watch him blink the tears away.

281

He leans down and kisses my forehead before taking his position.

"Okay, Ms. Martin..."

"Please call me Jute," I interrupt.

"Sorry, Jute it is," He smiles in apology. "When you have a contraction, I want you to push. If you aren't feeling them, that's fine. I will tell you when."

His eyes go up to a monitor screen. "Push now," he says.

I hold my breath and push hard, visualizing all of the muscles I am using. I am numb from the waist down, so I am uncertain if I am pushing hard enough.

"You did great, just remember to breathe."

Dr. Wallis walks in the door, smiling and relaxed. Before Steven gets up, he tells me to push again. I remember to breathe this time.

"Okay, relax now. You are doing great."

Dr. Wallis takes Steven's place. He sits down and reaches under the sheet. I feel the pressure, but no pain, "Your baby has a lot of hair," he smiles at me. "He'll be out in no time. Ready? Okay, push again."

A new group of nurses rolls a cart into the room, something for the baby. They stand in wait.

It takes 15 more pushes before I feel the release of pressure and my son is born. Dr. Wallis lifts him up and puts him on my stomach. His skin is bright pink and his hair looks black and matted down. His eyes barely open, squinting and looking pained by all the light and cold.

A nurse walks over and towels him off while Dr. Wallis clamps his umbilical cord. Tracy is asked to cut the cord between the clamps. I still feel nothing they are doing, but I see Tracy's face lit with joy, tears in his eyes. And I see our baby John on my stomach, his toweled off hair looks mousy brown like mine. His beautiful little nose wrinkles up before he lets out a cry.

The nurses take him for tests. They have everything

prepared and it only takes a few minutes, but it feels endless. I crave the feeling of him in my arms where I can protect him.

A nurse named Belinda brings John back to me. She says, "I think he is hungry, mom." She adjusts my gown and helps me hold him so that he is in a good position to nurse. His mouth instinctively latches on to my nipple and he begins to suck for milk.

The nurse is watching him while she speaks to me, "You will feel your milk let down. Don't worry if you don't feel it now, it will happen very soon. There will be a release of oxytocin, which will help you bond with you baby as well as help your uterus shrink back to size. Just keep feeding him regularly and your body will produce as much milk as he needs. Do you have any questions?"

I am crying. My tears are falling on John and I try to wipe them off of him without disturbing him. He is so perfect. I look up at the nurse and try to stop crying. I sniff and say, "My breasts are really small. Do you think I will have enough milk for him?"

"Of course," she says, "Your breasts are just right for your baby. He is going to determine how much milk you produce, not your breast size."

She moves her hand across my short hair and pats my shoulder reassuringly. I stare at John, unable to believe how much I love him already. Tracy and Dawson lean over to look at his beautiful little face. After only a few minutes of nursing, John falls asleep. His mouth relaxes its grip, but quivers as he dreams he is still sucking. We keep staring in silence, afraid our voices might break the spell he has us under.

CHAPTER FORTY-FOUR

Wind pushes through the crack in the window frame, screaming and whistling. All the lights are off in the house, but I have learned to navigate the kitchen in the dark. The microwave light says it is 4:00 a.m.. It feels like it. I just nursed John back to sleep. He had slept four hours straight, which was a luxury for me. But, now our routine is off.

I picture John's sweet little face, the way his brown eyes stare up at me while he nurses. I feel my milk come down and force myself to stop thinking about him. I turn my thoughts to the storm outside. It has been a crazy few days of February weather. Thursday morning we had snow. By Saturday, we were outside in shorts and t-shirts, cleaning up the flower beds. Now it is Monday morning and the sky is lit up with lightning and the rain is beating hard against the window. Another boom of thunder shakes the windows. I hope it doesn't wake John.

I pick up my glass from the counter top and turn on the sink faucet to fill it. I take sips of water while I stare at the rain streaking down the window. It's like a waterfall. It makes me sleepy to look at it. When am I not sleepy?

I consider going back to bed. But, Dawson will be coming home from work soon. If I stay up, I can make him breakfast. Tracy has been passed out asleep for a while. When he has a show the night before, he never gets up until the afternoon. I wish he was awake now.

I down the last drink of water and return my glass to its usual spot beside the sink. Another flash of lightning lights up the side yard and the crash of thunder rattles the windows almost simultaneously. This time I jump a little. I laugh at myself and decide to go check on John.

Just as I take the first step up the stairs, there is a knock at the door. It is so soft that for a moment I think something blew against it in the wind. I look out the small window, but see nothing. Before I think better of it, I open the door. The wind is gusting onto the porch with a slanted downpour of rain. I see a woman in a raincoat walking down the steps of my porch with her hand pulling at her hood, trying to stay dry. She is carrying a covered infant car seat by the handle. She must be a woman from the shelter.

"Hey!" I call out, but I can barely hear myself over the pounding of rain on the porch roof. "Hey!" I scream louder.

The lady turns around and I see her eyes above her scarf. I would recognize them anywhere. It's Allie.

I run to her, the rain instantly soaks my nightgown through to my skin. I wrap my arms around her, but she pushes me aside and runs into the house out of the rain. I follow behind her and watch as she rests the baby carrier on the floor beside the couch. I shut the door and turn on the lamp light. The rain jacket she had draped over her baby carrier matches the dark blue of her own. She leaves it over the carrier and turns to look at me.

I step toward her, but she puts her hand out to stop me. We say nothing. Her eyes stay fixed on mine while her hands pull at her scarf. She slowly removes it to reveal her swollen mouth and bruised jaw. My joy is now tainted with rage. She slides her hood down and I see the blood in her hair. I want to embrace her, but her skittish look holds me in my place.

I keep my voice quiet and say the only thing that feels right, "I have missed you so much, Allie."

I watch her eyes become wet with tears, but she does not move or change her expression. She stands rigid like a nervous patient before surgery. I try to say things to make her feel at ease. "Are you thirsty? I have juice or water. If you would like, I can put your baby upstairs in bed with John so we can talk."

Her eyes look confused and she struggles to speak. Moving her jaw seems to cause her a lot of pain. Through her teeth she asks, "John?"

"My son." Of course she didn't know.

Her hand goes up to cover her mouth and her eyes soften. She walks over and hugs me, pressing my cold and wet nightgown against my skin. But I don't mind. It's her crying through gritted teeth that gives me chills. I push her away so I can look at her face.

"Allie, let me wake up Tracy and he can take you to the Emergency Room while I watch the babies."

She shakes her head in refusal and her eyes beg me to accept it. She speaks from behind her hand, "He will find me."

"You will have to go, Allie. Maybe we can go peek at John and let you calm down a little, then we have to get you to a doctor."

She nods with her hand pressed to her mouth. I know her lip is probably bleeding.

With as much sincerity as I can manage, I smile through my anger. If Jim was here, I would kill him.

Allie bends to pick up her baby carrier. I reach out and take it from her. It feels twice as heavy as when I carry John in his. I want to ask her if her baby is a boy or a girl. I want to ask when her baby was born. Hundreds of questions run through my mind, questions I don't ask because it hurts Allie to speak.

We reach the top of the stairs where a night light shines in the hallway between my room and John's. I point to the right and lead the way. Allie stays close behind me. My heart swells with love as I take each step closer to John. When we reach his crib, I can see him sleeping on his back with his arms up.

I whisper to Allie, "When his face is relaxed with sleep he looks so much like Tracy."

Allie's hand grabs my arm and she pulls me to look at

her. Her eyes are inquisitive and a little shocked. "Tracy?"

"Yes, we were both pretty lonely. But, he could never replace you." When the words leave my mouth, I regret them. The last time I mentioned loving her, she ran away and nearly ran over me. I turn away from her so I won't see her reaction.

I put the baby carrier down and walk over to the wardrobe for a dry nightgown. I change quickly, feeling like we are kids again, nervous about our nakedness. When I turn back to her, I realize she is transfixed on John and not even looking at me. I step beside her and see that John's eyes are open, staring up at her.

Allie's raincoat swishes as she reaches down to touch the hair on John's head. I recognize the expression of love in her eyes. There are experiences we share, despite having been apart for so long. It makes her even more beautiful to me. I want to touch her, make her feel pleasure wherever it will not hurt her. I don't know if she can sense my thoughts. If she can, would she be afraid of me?

I hear a small cry from the baby carrier. Allie looks down at it and then back to me as if she wants to say something. She holds up one finger. Wait. She points to herself and then points out the door. She says, "Wait." She holds up her finger again and nods. She turns and walks away. I wait.

The baby's cries get louder, so I pick up the carrier and take it to my bedroom where the sounds will not disturb John. I turn on the bedside lamp and put the carrier on my bed. I pull off the raincoat and see a bald baby in a blue sleeper with farm animals all over it. He is looking up at me with pale silvery blue eyes. He is squinting against the light of the lamp. His hands reach for me with greater control than John has developed. He must be older.

I reach down to unbuckle him when the rain begins to pick up. Another flash of lightning lights up the sky outside my window and a loud boom rattles the windows. The baby doesn't seem to notice. His eyes are looking at me expectantly. I slide my hands under his waist and lift him. He cries as if I have injured him. I put him down on the bed, worried that I have done something wrong. He is still screaming in agony. I start to panic. Where is Allie?

My hands move against the better judgment of my brain. I don't want to think bad thoughts. The only way not to be haunted with questions is to find the answer. What is hurting him?

I unsnap the square plastic closures of his sleeper, revealing bruises on his ribs. I have to stop when I reach his navel and see gauze soaked through with puss and blood. It reminds me of a lady from the shelter who came in with burns. But, who would burn a baby? Oh, God.

The pain in the baby's cry is all-consuming. My instincts are to hold him, but holding him causes him pain. The only thing I know to do is what I would do for John. I lie beside him and roll him on his side to nurse. Initially, he cries harder, but once he is latched on and swallowing milk I feel him relax. His eyes close and I am glad he can't see the tears running down my face.

Where is Allie?

More lightning and thunder, closer together. The rain slams the window of my bedroom. Again, lightning flickers, seeming farther away. But it is followed by a different kind of loud crack. It was the loud crack of a gun. The scream of a woman makes me shudder. I have never heard Allie scream this way, but I know it is her. I can not leave the baby on the bed alone. I pick him up, cradled in my arms still attached to my breast. He grunts and I feel his gums press hard together, biting me to endure the pain I cause him.

I should not take him downstairs. I run to John's room and place the baby down at the other end of John's bed. He grunts, then cries with heartbreak, but I can not stay. I run downstairs and out the front door, desperate to find Allie.

I freeze where I stand at the bottom of the porch steps, the heavy rain hitting my face. I see her lying on the lawn with her legs contorted unnaturally beneath her. Blood is pooling

288

around her, flowing in the streams of rainwater. My heart stops beating and I am deafened by the sound of my own scream. I run toward her, hearing Jim scream from somewhere in the dark, "You! You, evil filth of Satan! You demon whore!"

I hear the shot before I feel the bullet hit my shoulder. My muscles tighten in shock and I fall to the ground, nearly landing on top of Allie. The rain is so heavy, as heavy as my pain. I look into Allie's eyes and she blinks. She is alive.

Jim lets out a moaning wail of despair and rage before I hear another shot. I flinch and wait for the hit, but it doesn't come. Behind me, I hear a thud and assume Jim's final bullet took his own life.

"Allie," I say through my tears. The rain is falling on her face, her eyes open through it all. I prop myself up on my uninjured arm so that I can look down at her. She blinks again, slowly, her eyes rolling up before moving jerkily in my direction.

"Oh, Allie, please don't die. Stay with me!" But, there is a sick feeling in my stomach as every second that passes leaves her face more pale. All of her blood is leaving her.

"I love you, Allie! I forgive you and I love you and it's okay. You were my savior and I love you. Always." I can barely see through the rain and my tears. I don't know if she is still breathing. But, she can't leave without knowing, "Jim is dead. No one can hurt your baby now. Allie, you did the right thing. Please believe me that you are good, so incredibly good and I'll never stop loving you!"

Bright flashing lights push away the darkness. I can see Allie's blue eyes staring coldly up into the black sky as drop after drop of rain beats against them. Her skin is snow white. I lay my head on her chest, weep, and curse the gods.

By the time hands are on me, lifting me onto a stretcher, I can not discern who is who, what is where, my own body from the hard ground below, or my skin from the hands clutching onto me. The only thing I can discern is the sound of babies crying, screaming out into the night for mothers who have let them down. I promised John I never would, but he is only a few weeks old and I already have. Still, I am alive and Allie is not. What will become of her baby? What will become of me?

I am wheeled into the ambulance. The bright light is painful. I close my eyes and feel hands all over me. A needle effortlessly slides into my vein. I slip down a mountain slope covered in snow, falling, rolling, spinning, swirling, fading into darkness.

John

I hear myself crying, but I am not crying.
The woman with the blue eyes leaves and Mom takes the
Crying out of the room.
The Crying gets louder and flashes make the room light up and
I feel alone.
Loud sounds come out of the far away darkness. Some boom
and some shriek.
Mom brings back the Crying and puts it beside me.
She will give me milk now because the flashes make me afraid.
The Crying says that Mom is gone.
When another light flashes, I look for her.
She is gone.
I hear the low booms and loud claps.
I cry now to tell her I need her.
My crying is louder than the Crying.
My arms and legs punch and kick. I cry for her.
My hand touches the Crying.
The Crying touches my face with an arm.
The Crying has legs to kick and is kicking.
We are close like I get with Mom.
I turn my head and see the Crying has eyes.
The Crying has an open mouth. It smells like milk.
I am sad and scared. We are alone.
A light comes into the room.
Round and small, sometimes big and hurts to see.
It shines on the Crying and goes dark.
I hear the Crying get very loud, loud as the light was bright.
Then the Crying moves up above me and is going away.
The room fills with another flash. I am alone.
I cry for Mom.
I cry and cry until Dad comes.
He smells different, like Mom and something bad.
I want to cry again, but he gives me milk his way.
He is crying and tears fall on me.
His crying is sad and scared and says Mom is gone.
She is gone.

292

CHAPTER FORTY-FIVE

Sometimes I open my eyes when I feel a cool breeze. Sometimes I leave them closed with indifference. When I do open them, I see it is midday and the field is full of clover and butterfly weed. A storm cloud shades all of this, every time I open my eyes. But never is there rain. I have been lying here for years. Always cool breezes. Always butterflies. Always the light filtering through the darkened sky. Never rain.

This time I open my eyes and the light is blinding. I squint my eyes closed again and hear humming. Something warm in my hand. Now I remember. Allie is dead. I try to force my eyes open and lift my head. But the pain in my neck and right shoulder cause me to freeze in agony.

"Jute! Don't move. It's just me. It's Drew. I'll get the nurse."

I hear a chair slide as I let my head fall back the mere centimeters I had lifted it. Flashes of memory enter my mind like the flashes of gunfire on a battlefield. Mostly, I see Allie's eyes staring up into falling rain. I feel tears in my own eyes. I don't want to remember, but I do. Soon I hear feet walking against linoleum.

"Mrs. Duren, are you awake?"

I open my eyes and see dark brown eyes staring into mine, concerned. Too concerned. I close my eyes again.

"I'm your nurse, Delphia. Try not to move, it's very important to relax and rest and don't try to lift your head. We are trying to wean you from Morphine and bring you back to the world of the living so you can go home soon. We switched you to Neurontin. How are you feeling?"

An overwhelming need to get up and walk away from here or die this instant is how I feel. How can I not move, with the world falling apart around me? I don't open my eyes when I ask, "Where is John?"

There is hesitation and then I hear Drew clear her throat and a chair sliding up to my left. "It's three a.m. and John is home with Tracy. I told him I would stay with you. He hasn't wanted to leave your side."

The sounds of beeps and whirs fill in where my words should be. We listen for a long time before I hear the sound of shoes shuffling across the floor. The nurse has left.

Drew's voice is full of forced optimism, "I know I'm probably not the person you wanted to wake up to. But, when I heard what happened, I had to come. You are my sister. We can't do this anymore, Jute."

"Do what?"

"Pretend that the other one deserves blame for what Daddy did."

"He's not our Daddy."

"You know what I mean. You always acted like I had a choice in that. Somehow I was flawed because I didn't stop him from touching me."

I open my eyes and squint at her in the bright light of the hospital room. Her strawberry blond hair has been cut to her shoulders. Her bangs nearly reach her eyelashes, almost touching the deep blue of her eyes. She is still a hundred times prettier than me, even though she has been crying and looks exhausted. I close my eyes again. I don't know what to say. I feel her hand slide into mine and squeeze.

"You had Allie. You had somewhere to go to get away. I had nothing. No one. All I had was the thought that if I went along with what he wanted, he wouldn't hurt me. It was all I had, Jute."

The tears are running from my eyes and I want to turn

my head away, but the intense pain running from my neck to my right hand prevents me from moving. I hear her chair slide and soon she is dabbing a tissue on my face. I don't dare open my eyes to look at her again. It hurts too much.

She sighs and sits down. Her hand goes back into mine. She says, "I'm sorry. What more can I say? I look back on it now and I see things I could have done. I could have killed him. I could have suffocated him in the night. But, I was just a kid and Momma loved him so much. Every time I ever tried to resist, he do something to hurt Momma. Remember the time she cut her hair short? It was because he had cut it in her sleep. And that time he pushed her off the porch and broke her ankle, remember? All of that was because of me. I just stopped resisting because I didn't want him to hurt anybody. I tried to protect you both and then you hated me for it."

"I didn't hate you. It just hurt to see it. I loved you."

"I know you say it hurt you, but it's not the same. Be glad you don't know, Jute. Stop being mad at me."

"I'm not mad at you. I was just a kid, too. And I'm sorry. I should have fucking killed him myself instead of running away."

I hear her give a small laugh through her tears, "Sometimes, when you were gone, I would open your box of notes from Allie and read them. I was so jealous, and worried for her when she went through that thing with Bobby, and I was happy for you to have her... when I wasn't being jealous."

It is nearly too much to hear. My heart is shattering with longing, but knowing that Drew shares a small part of those memories makes me want her to never leave. I squeeze her hand and listen to her sniff. I am afraid to ask the questions that beg to be asked. But have to ask them.

"Where is Allie's baby?"

"I don't know. The papers aren't allowed to say, just that it was taken into protective services until relatives are located."

Immediately, my stomach feels sick. "What about

Hank?"

"Oh, God, Jute! I forgot you had no way of knowing. I mean, it's been all over the news. Allie went there first, to Hank's house. She was already gone when Jim got there. The police suspect he was looking for your address. They're saying on the news that Allie came to you because you work for that abuse shelter and you were friends. They don't know..."

Maybe she is still talking, I can't hear her over my crying. The pain it causes in my body is nearly unbearable.

"Nurse!" Drew is calling from far away.

Very little time passes before I hear her come into the room. Delphia's soft southern voice is steady, "I got you, sweety. Try to breathe regular breaths, in and out, and I'm going to up your dose of pain meds just a little. I know it's hard. I know it hurts. Just try to breathe steady and this will kick in real soon."

"Don't put me out," I plead, instantly recognizing that I now care what happens to me. I would feel better if I was knocked out. But I don't want to leave Drew.

"This won't put you out. It will just ease the pain. But, there is a reason you need not move. If you get sleepy, the best thing for you to do is shut your eyes and let it happen."

I feel Drew's hands gently cupping my face, "I'm so sorry. I will leave you to rest if you want."

"No." I open my eyes and look at her, so close to me that all I see is her face. She still looks like the little girl I played with before we had a step-dad, only her eyes now hold a heavy sadness. "Stay."

The nurse pats my good shoulder, "Rest, Ms. Duren. I mean it." She leaves the room and the door shuts.

"Well," my sister says, "I'll stay. But, I think that's about all the heartache we can stand to talk about for a while. What do you think?"

I can't answer a question like that. We both know the heart never breaks of heartache, no matter how unthinkable the affliction is.

"I brought you something." She digs into her purse and pulls out two bottles of nail polish. "I'm going to paint your nails. You can chose Irresistible Red or Amber Waves. I looked for Amber Kisses, but I guess they don't make it any more."

How I manage to smile and feel a small joy at this moment, I can't say. But, I feel like maybe life will actually move forward. The pain will surely lessen because no one is here to hurt us anymore. Even the loss of Allie is not the loss of love. When the ways of a love end, the love itself does not. None of it was in vain. To John, to my sister, to Tracy and Dawson, that love between Allie and I will ripple out forever ahead of me. It hasn't died.

"Amber Waves."

Winter Suns
(Winter Seedlings book 2)
Now Available

A teenage girl in Eastern Kentucky has been isolated since birth. She experiences abuse from her father as unquestionably the will of God. She obeys his rules in hopes of banishing her demons and finding redemption. But when she breaks a rule in order to teach herself to read the Bible, she discovers something more powerful than God's laws. A hidden letter written sixteen years prior by a woman named Allie to her lover, Jute, reveals both disturbing and electrifying secrets. She feels called to find Jute and deliver the letter to her, even if none of the maps in the Bible show the way to Nashville, Tennessee.

Meanwhile, in Nashville, Jute has decided to let go of Allie's things. She asks her son, John, to take the boxes from the attic to the barn. To him, it's all junk. He was never told about Allie. But, when John discovers an old photograph tucked inside one of the notebooks, he is instantly drawn into the mystery of what happened to the girl. What he discovers is even more horrifying than the secrets his mother is hiding. He wants to forget it all, but he can't.

Other Books by Julie Roberts Towe:

Silencer

Hold This Close: A Winter Seedlings Prequel

Acknowledgments

There are a few people I would like to thank for making this book possible. My family allows me the quiet time and space I need to write. My mother made this path seem normal by writing in her journal every day for decades. My brother, Moose Roberts, set an example by creating whatever the hell he wanted. I gained insight from many people, but would like to mention Charles Robinson, Emily Mensch, Wayne Towe, Shannon Duncan, and Matt Spriggs for sharing their expertise where I was lacking it. Anna Wand created an amazing cover. Lastly, I would like to thank all my friends and family for their encouragement and optimism.

I would appreciate your feedback, too.
Please consider rating, reviewing, and telling friends about Winter Seedlings.

https://twitter.com/aweezazee
https://www.facebook.com/jrt.writer
http://julierobertstowe.wordpress.com/

You can also send feedback the old fashioned way:
Julie Roberts Towe
Stitched Wing Publishing
1719 Angel Parkway Ste 400-116
Allen, TX 75002

www.ingramcontent.com/pod-product-compliance
Lightning Source LLC
Chambersburg PA
CBHW020916200626
46814CB00001BA/364